SLOW
MOTION

SLOW MOTION

WAYNE JORDAN

DEVON VAUGHN ARCHER

BET Publications, LLC
http://www.bet.com
http://www.arabesquebooks.com

ARABESQUE BOOKS are published by

BET Publications, LLC
c/o BET BOOKS
One BET Plaza
1900 W Place NE
Washington, DC 20018-1211

All Kensington Titles, Imprints, and Distributed Lines are available at special quantity discounts for bulk purchases for sales promotions, premiums, fundraising, and educational or institutional use. Special book excerpts or customized printings can also be created to fit specific needs. For details, write or phone the office of the Kensington special sales manager: Kensington Publishing Corp., 850 Third Avenue, New York, NY 10022, attn: Special Sales Department, Phone: 1-800-221-2647.

ISBN: 1-58314-616-4

First Printing: November 2005

10 9 8 7 6 5 4 3 2 1

Printed in the United States of America

CONTENTS

Capture the Sunrise

Wayne Jordan

This story is dedicated to
my family and friends
in Barbados and in the United States

To Kathie Denosky, the epitome of talent

ACKNOWLEDGMENTS

Thank you to my editor, Demetria Lucas, who has taken my unpublished ramblings and helped me to turn them into a story that touches the heart and soul.

To my students at the St. Michael School, who understood when I returned assignments a day or two later.

To Gwynne Forster, Angela Benson, and Felicia Mason, who showed me many years ago that writing does not only take talent, but knowledge of the craft of writing.

To the late Carmel Thomaston (Fay Robinson) of The Painted Rock Writers Colony, who provided a place for me to associate with other writers.

To the incomparable Kathie Denosky, one of the most talented authors I know.

To Debra Ross: this story is as much yours as it is mine.

To my first critique partners, Starla Criser and Julie Skerven.

To my agent, Cheryl Ferguson, who read this story years ago when she was the president of the Multicultural Romance Chapter. You were one of the first to read this story. There are many more to come.

To my current critique partner, Francine Matthews, who's yet to read this story! The next one is yours.

To the BET family of authors, old and new. You have all been a source of inspiration. I promise to continue the tradition of excellence.

To my publisher, Linda Gill, who had the vision to embrace a male romance author. Thanks for allowing me to write under my own name.

And to My Lord and Savior Jesus Christ . . . without You I am nothing.

CHAPTER 1

Taurean watched the storm rage outside. Lightning flashed and thunder rumbled while raindrops drummed against the roof of the tiny beach house. So much for the magnificent tropical nights the attendant had promised him on the flight to Barbados. His first night on the island, he had expected to be lulled to sleep by the gentle lapping of waves on the shoreline. Instead, here he was, haunted by the violence of a storm.

Storms brought all the tortured memories of his brother, Corey, to mind. Throughout his life, Corey had hated storms. Taurean remembered well the nights his youngest brother had crawled into bed with him, his slight body shivering uncontrollably.

Ironically, there had been a terrible storm the night Corey died. It had been a clear reflection of his younger brother's troubled state of mind and a symbol of the pain and suffering he'd endured as an adult.

That night Taurean had realized he loved his brother more than anyone else in the world and for seven long years he had suffered the consequences of his actions. It was the reason he was unable to sleep at night. His brother's pain-filled eyes continued to haunt him.

But he didn't want to think of all that had happened to him. That was the reason he was here—to move on with his life and forget the past.

A brilliant white flash of lightning filled the room, then a loud rumble of thunder. The light on the bedside table blinked, flickered—like his brother's short life—then went out completely.

Drawn from the past, Taurean closed his eyes. A sense of dread gripped him. He shivered, wondering what his buddies would say if they saw that a little thunder and lightning could reduce him to a frightened boy.

Then he heard it—a noise that didn't belong in the midst of the storm. It was the sweet laughter of a child. Had he sunk so low in his desolation that he was actually beginning to hear things? What the hell was happening to him? Who could be banging about downstairs at this time of night? Crazy things were happening to him these days. With his luck, it was probably a burglar.

The tinkle of laughter again reached his ears.

No, he hadn't imagined it.

Taurean jumped out of bed.

Lightning flashed, and he heard the laughter again. This time it was not a child's. It was deeper, older, huskier, a woman's. Why on earth were a woman and child downstairs? He pulled on a T-shirt and track pants.

As he made his way cautiously down the stairs, the voices became clearer. At the bottom step, he realized the laughter came from the kitchen. Taurean carefully advanced to the archway separating the kitchen from the rest of the cottage and watched two dark shadows move away from the door and farther into the room.

There was another flash of lightning and he saw them clearly.

A woman and a little girl stood in the middle of the kitchen, holding each other as they shivered. Rain dripped from their clothes. The child shook her head, showering the pair with water.

Laughter erupted from both of them, but there was a sense of desperation about the scene before him. He felt like an intruder prying into a moment that was not meant for him. He shifted, and the floor creaked.

Simultaneously, they turned in the direction of the noise. On seeing him, the little girl screamed. Stark fear filled her eyes as she grabbed the woman.

"There's no need to be afraid," he said softly.

They both continued to stare, but did not respond.

Did they understand English?

He could tell they were terrified.

The child was the first to speak. "Is he going to hurt us, Mommy?"

"No, I'm not," he answered, careful to keep his voice gentle.

Taurean wondered what could have caused a tiny child to be so distrustful. What had caused the fear in her eyes, and her mother's?

He did not want to think about it. The knowledge saddened him.

The lights suddenly came on. He'd forgotten about them. When the storm had struck, he'd raced upstairs, and jumped under the covers.

They stood staring at each other, unsure of what to do. He noticed the keys in the woman's hand. So she hadn't broken in. She must have a legitimate reason to be there.

She spoke for the first time. A husky, gentle tone, belying the fear he still saw in her eyes. "I'm Alana . . . Alexandra. There must be a mix-up. I didn't expect anyone to be here. I'm taking care of the beach house for the summer. My friend Paula knows I'm here."

"That explains a lot," Taurean answered, nodding. "I'm Taurean. Paula is my brother's wife. Patrick told me no one had rented the beach house for the summer. He probably wasn't aware Paula had given you permission."

He saw the apprehension in her eyes.

"You could give them a call if you don't believe me," he offered.

He could see she was thinking about it as she scrutinized his face, his eyes, then relaxed.

"I believe you. You have the Buchanan eyes. I met Patrick at the wedding." She paused a moment, then said. "You weren't there."

"No, I wasn't." He looked for the disgust in her eyes but saw none. She probably didn't know. His parents must have made sure of it.

Her next words confirmed his suspicions. "I didn't know Patrick had another brother."

"I'm sure you wouldn't have been told," Taurean said, keeping his voice devoid of emotion. He rubbed his head, not sure how to handle the situation. "Well, it doesn't make sense for either of us to leave tonight. The rain's not going to stop any time soon. We can discuss this in the morning."

With that, he turned to leave. He stopped before he reached the doorway.

"There's food in the refrigerator. The bedrooms are upstairs. I'm in the first room on the right. The one next to it is empty. I'll make the bed for you."

As he turned and walked up the stairs, Alana cautiously watched his every move. What a strange individual, she thought. His eyes had been hauntingly vacant, but he was . . .

"Mommy, can I have something to eat? I'm hungry. And some soda?"

Alana gave her a stern look.

"Of course, honey, but no soda. You can have some milk."

"Aw, c'mon, Mom. Milk! Can't I have some soda?"

"Melissa, it's milk or to bed."

"Okay, milk."

"Good, let's see what's in the refrigerator."

Melissa ran to the refrigerator and opened it. Alana followed, surprised by the contents on the shelves. Instead of the junk food and microwave dinners she expected, it was well stocked with "proper" food. She wondered how long the stranger planned on staying.

She took out a large carton of milk, found two glasses and poured for them. After a short search of the cupboards, she found crackers and strawberry jelly, Melissa's favorite. Alana spread the jelly on some crackers and they sat quietly for several minutes, each giving in to the need to satisfy their hunger.

"Mom, is that man going to make us leave? Are we going to have to go back home?" Melissa asked, her timid gaze seeking reassurance. "Is he going to hit us?"

Her daughter's words brought tears to Alana's eyes.

"No, he won't, honey," Alana said around the lump in her throat. "He seems like a nice person."

Her eyes wide, Melissa stared at the archway where the man had stood. "He is so big. Bigger than Daddy."

Alana felt her daughter's pain and mistrust of men. Melissa trusted few men. The image of Melissa as a lively, happy child caused an ache so intense Alana almost cried out.

She hated Blake for what he had done to her daughter. Hated him for taking Melissa's trust. His drinking had almost killed her little girl's spirit, but Alana had vowed he would never hurt her daughter again. That had given her the courage to leave him. Even if she had to kill him. Never again would she allow a man to be so much in control of her that she lived in his shadow.

She hoped they would be safe here on the island, giving them time to heal. They were going to start a new life. One without the presence of a man. But until Patrick's brother was gone, that would be impossible.

Life was so darn ironic. They had wanted to be in a safe place but a man was already in residence—one who disturbed her.

He was tall, and had the palest brown eyes she had ever seen. The shade of his golden brown skin seemed to speak of mixed parentage, black with white. He was muscular, and large, with shoulders that seemed to go on forever.

His head was completely shaved, the style so many black men preferred these days. But it only served to emphasize the haggard face that bore the signs of a hard, cruel life. Despite this, he appeared healthy and fit, but she sensed weariness in him.

It was as if he'd seen far more of the dark side of life.

Physically, he seemed so much like Blake, but bigger. There the similarities ended. She had glimpsed tenderness in his eyes when he looked at Melissa. She wondered why Paula or Patrick had never mentioned him.

She'd seen the look of wariness and sadness in his eyes when he'd realized she didn't know of his existence. What had caused his unhappiness? What had hurt him so deeply? Whatever it was had somehow made him vulnerable and human. Like her, he seemed alone, and she recognized a kindred spirit, but her own inability to trust overrode any thoughts of finding out more about the man.

"Come, Melissa," Alana said as she shook off her disturbing speculation. With her arm around her daughter, she walked up the stairs. "Let's go to bed."

As had become his custom, Taurean could not sleep. This time, however, his mind was filled with the image of a woman with eyes like a doe caught in the headlight of an oncoming car.

Alana Alexandra.

The name was perfect, musical. Despite having arrived in the middle of the night and being drenched by the rain, she looked beautiful. She had that light chocolate complexion he always found appealing. She was not short, but there was a fragility about her that seemed ethereal. Seeing her as she had been tonight stirred him more than some of the scantily clad women he had seen on the beach.

Alana stirred feelings he had thought long buried. She intrigued him. Maybe it was her eyes, so vulnerable, so full of fear. He had instinctively felt like protecting her. He sensed she was running from someone. Her daughter's words had not only served to confirm his suspicions, but had also made him angry at the person from whom they ran.

The fear he sensed in them both made him feel like taking them in his arms and telling them everything would be all right, that no one would hurt them again. What scared him more than anything was that he meant it. And he was in no position to offer anyone his protection.

Disgusted with himself, he shook his head.

Even now, after all he'd been through, he was still trying to right the wrongs of the world.

Would he never learn?

He'd always been like that.

Helping anyone and everyone in need. In high school, he'd been the champion of the underdogs. He'd fought for the geeks and nerds in the class. The one to stand up to the class bully. The one to rescue the damsel in distress.

That was how he'd met his first girlfriend, Carla. The kind of girl to send a teenage boy's raging hormones into overdrive, she'd decided she wanted him and he had no choice in the matter. His hormones hadn't put up a fight, but had given in the first time her lips had touched that private untouched part of him.

He smiled, the memory of that encounter still vivid in his mind after all those years.

An image of Carla came to mind. She'd been so beautiful with that smooth darkness he always found appealing. She always appeared calm and in control. But he discovered that under the cool exterior was a woman who knew what she wanted and did not hesitate to go after it.

She enticed him with her supple body and the skill of a lover far beyond her age. And eventually, she discarded him like the other boys who'd come under her tutelage.

At first he'd been hurt. He had loved her. But then he realized that the experience was all part of growing up and he had experienced some of the best sex available at the time.

He wondered why Carla came to mind after all these years. Though Alana and Carla were physically similar, there the similarity ended. Where Carla radiated strength, confidence, and blatant sexuality, Alana's fragility was evident in everything she said and did.

What he did see, however, was the way she'd protected her daughter, like a lioness. He saw fear in her eyes, but he also saw the promise of defiance.

He walked over to the window and breathed in deeply of the cool tropical air. Even at night the island's beauty beckoned him to the window, time and time again. He'd stood in this same spot several times during the day, and despite the storm, he felt the gentle calmness that the island radiated.

Oh, well, there was nothing more he could do tonight. Maybe he should give Patrick a call.

He reached for the cordless phone, wondering where he'd placed it. He found it and dialed the one number he'd bothered to memorize. The phone rang softly, then was answered.

"Hello." Patrick's voice came over the line, its firmness giving him comfort.

"Patrick, it's Taurean."

"Hey, bro, it's great to hear you. I was a bit worried when I heard the news that a tropical depression had hit the island. Is everything all right there?"

"Yes, it wasn't too bad."

"That's great. I was planning to call you tonight anyway, so I'm glad you called. Paula only informed me today that a friend of hers, Alana, was staying at the beach house. I didn't get the chance to tell her about your staying there since she'd gone to the conference when you left. And she clear forgot to tell me about Alana. Hope this hasn't caused a problem?"

"Ah . . . that's why I'm calling. I've met her and her daughter. What's the deal with them? Something doesn't seem right."

"I'm not too sure since Paula and I haven't had a chance to really talk about Alana, but she's a close friend of Paula so she's fine. Met her once a long time ago at our wedding and she seemed like a really nice person. Paula is still away at the technology conference in Orlando, but I'll ask her about Alana tonight when she calls."

"OK, I just wondered about Alana. She seems a bit strange. She and the daughter. They were afraid of me."

"Of course they were afraid. It's not every day that you meet a huge black man in a house in the middle of the night. Who wouldn't be scared," he said, followed by a laugh. "But as I said, I'll have a chat with Paula. But what about you? How're you enjoying that warm sunshine and those fabulous beaches?"

"Still having a bit of trouble sleeping, but things are getting better. The island's perfect."

"Isn't it? Paula and I spent our honeymoon there. We didn't want to leave at the end of the two weeks."

"Thanks for letting me use the house. I really appreciate it."

"No problem. What are brothers for? Well, bro, have to go. I'm working on a project for the office. Have to give a presentation tomorrow." He laughed and then his voice turned serious. "Love you, bro."

"I know. Love you, too!"

Taurean heard the click of the phone and smiled. Patrick had always been the openly affectionate one. One thing he could say: Patrick had always been there for him. No matter what!

Again, he smiled and then started laughing.

Boy, his brother must have had a wild honeymoon. When Taurean had met Paula, he'd been amazed at the bubbly, friendly woman. She never seemed to stop laughing, finding joy in everything she did. And in the short space of time, he'd grown to love her. She embraced him like she'd known him for years.

One day, she looked at him after he told her about his past and said, "You're a brave, special person. I'd have done the same thing." She held his hands and kissed him on the cheek. "Don't worry, everything will be all right. Give it time."

And for some reason, he'd known everything would be all right. Maybe not that same day, maybe not in a year or two, but someday he knew that things would be all right.

Again, he looked out to the sea, hearing the waves rumbling against the shore.

Yes, he knew everything would be all right.

He only hoped that everything would be all right for Alana and the little girl.

He thought his past had changed him, hardened him. But here at the first opportunity, he felt the need to help the first stray souls that came along. Maybe he hadn't changed so much after all.

Blake Smyth-Connell's roar of rage filled the house and woke the servants. He paced the empty bedroom, looking for something that would give him a hint about where Alana had gone. There was nothing, not a single clue. She'd left everything behind, as if she'd wanted nothing from him; wanted to erase every memory of him. He'd already accepted that she no longer loved him or needed him, but she was his and he had vowed to never let her go.

When she'd divorced him, he had been devastated, but she planned her strategy well. She surprised him. He never thought she'd be so resourceful. She accumulated enough evidence against him that he had no choice but to give her the freedom she demanded, but he still had control of her as long as she was in New York, living in the house that had been theirs.

He knew why she was gone. She had accepted his punishment for years, but when he had struck Melissa for the first time a few nights ago, he'd immediately realized his mistake. He'd seen the burning hatred in Alana's eyes.

And known that he'd gone too far.

He'd left the house before she could call the police. But his men had been watching her. The servants she trusted so much had been easily bought. She was constantly being watched.

He'd already taken care of the guard who'd let her escape. When he had found Alana gone, he'd wanted to kill the man, but had regained control. To think clearly, logically, he needed to be in charge of his emotions. His father had always told him so.

The portrait of her over the fireplace beckoned him. She was the most beautiful woman he had ever met—dark, with eyes that allowed a man to look deep into her soul. He'd known immediately he had to have her, to possess her.

The weeks of courting and waiting had eventually paid off. She had accepted his proposal. He'd felt a sense of accomplishment when she had smiled at him with adoration and told him she loved him, would marry him.

He remembered the day they were married and the pride he'd felt as he'd watched her walk gracefully down the aisle. The picture of innocence and purity she made had aroused him right there in the church and it had taken all his willpower not to take her right there on the sanctuary floor.

But after they married things had changed. He had changed. He'd become stronger, more sure of how a wife should be handled.

His success in the political world had not come easy. As a young

African American, he'd had to work harder, and longer hours than others. Initially, the pressure of the favors he'd had to accept had kept him awake at nights.

Now, the darkness was so much a part of him, he embraced its intensity. He would find her, and when he did, she was going to be sorry.

He walked over to the phone and picked it up. He knew the person who could help. His father would know what to do.

CHAPTER 2

The storm left as suddenly as it arrived, leaving a natural untidiness in its wake. Taurean stood at the window, looking toward the Atlantic Ocean. Despite the storm, the island's beauty amazed him.

While he watched, the sun rose slowly from its sleep, at first peeping cautiously out, changing the sky from a soft, dull gray to pale peach. When it appeared in its full splendor, the color changed to brilliant orange and finally a shimmering blue. On the roof, doves cooed, while the harsh alarm of a rooster could be heard from the tiny chattel house in the distance.

Vivid color flashed at the door of the chattel house and a tiny woman came outside. She looked in the direction of the beach house and, seeing him by the window, waved. He raised his hand in acknowledgment, wondering who she was. She continued to look in his direction, and he stared back. She waved again, turned and walked into the house.

For a while he continued to embrace the tranquility of the tropical morning. Then, like the sweet melody of the island's calypso, he heard them. They were awake. He heard the gentle laughter of the woman and the musical giggle in response. He was going to have to sort that problem out. By midday he hoped they would be gone and leave him to his solitude, and the peace he needed. He felt a sudden sense of emptiness at the thought of their going.

Confused by the emotion, he quickly dressed and hurried downstairs. If he was beginning to feel like this, the sooner they were gone, the better. He needed to be alone. That was the only way he would heal.

When Taurean entered the kitchen, they were sitting at the table. The little girl was eating a bowl of cereal; the mother was peeling an orange. They looked up at him and he realized nothing had changed. That they continued to look at him with fear on their faces annoyed him. Anger simmered inside him at the man who had placed it there.

"Good morning," he said, trying to keep his voice as gentle as possible. He did not want to make them more scared than they already were. "Did you sleep well?"

Neither responded. Instead, they looked at him warily. He smiled, hoping it would put them at ease. It didn't work.

Alana looked at Taurean. Her fear was replaced by caution. He appeared no different in the light of day. The hardness and ruggedness she'd noticed the night before seemed more real now that it was daylight, making him appear larger, more cruel.

He seemed accustomed to being faced with violence and cruelty. His face bore the marks of a man whose beauty had been marred by pain. A stark ragged scar trailed along his left cheek, just below his eye, while the slight twist of his nose suggested it had been broken. She could tell that he was a survivor, one who lived by the strength of his body and the power of his fists.

Her body tingled in response to his stark primitive masculinity, and she knew in that moment he could be dangerous—dangerous to her hard-earned freedom. It was this same quality that had attracted her to Blake. An attraction that ended in abuse, and grief.

"Mommy, you're hurting me!"

Melissa was struggling to move. Alana's unexpected response to Taurean had caused her to grip Melissa's shoulders tightly. She turned to comfort her daughter.

"Sorry, honey, I didn't mean to. Let me kiss it better."

Alana kissed Melissa's shoulder and then hugged her—this little girl who meant the world to her and whom she would die protecting had to be her first thought.

But Taurean seemed different than Blake. Despite his size, he had the saddest, yet gentlest, eyes she'd ever seen. Last night, she had been surprised by his attempt to reassure them that they had no need to be afraid. Then the look in his eyes was gone, and a wall had been erected. Only a blank stare of indifference remained.

He confused her.

At one point she'd noticed the anger and wondered if it had been focused on her. His eyes were so different from Blake's. They reflected his every emotion. Her ex-husband's eyes were cold. It was only after they were married that she'd realized that Blake's smile and his whispers of love never reached the frost in his vacant eyes.

Taurean saw the pain in Alana's eyes and knew that something was wrong.

For a while, he was forgotten as the mother and child consumed their breakfast.

He felt like an outsider. He did not belong here. They needed to be by themselves.

He turned and walked away, knowing it would be a while before they realized he was gone. The thought filled him with sadness. He didn't have anyone to hug and make him feel better. It was troubling to him that he wanted that now. For a long time, he'd wanted to be alone. Now, feelings and wants he'd denied for so long were suddenly beginning to surface.

Taurean walked out the back door and stepped into the sunlight. As he headed toward the beach, the salty freshness of the tropical air tickled his nose, and the sadness started to lift. Maybe this would be the place to help him recover. Maybe he could finally put his guilt to rest and hope that one day God would forgive him.

A glimpse of bright color caught his eyes. The woman from next door was coming his way, carrying a basket.

"Morning to you, young man. I'm Bertha Gooding. Welcome to Barbados!"

Her voice was happy—full of life and energy. He could tell he was going to like her.

"I brought a little something for you to eat. I saw when your wife and little one arrived last night. The taxi woke me. I'm sure they'd love some warm Bajan muffins. I've added a few bananas, golden apples, and mangoes."

He looked at her in amazement. Then he smiled. So this was the Mrs. Gooding Patrick had told him about. He'd forgotten that his brother had told him about the friendly old woman who lived nearby. Somewhere in the back of his mind, he remembered someone telling him that Barbadians were extremely friendly and hospitable. This was clear proof.

"Thank you. I'm sure that Alana and Melissa will be pleased." He felt the need to explain. "However, she's not my wife. She's just a friend of my brother's wife. There has been a mix-up with the rental for the summer so I'm going to have to see about a hotel for them."

"Now I know why you seem familiar. You're Patrick's brother. You look so much like him. Those beautiful golden brown eyes. Oh, I'm so in love with those eyes." She placed a hand delicately on her breast as if about to swoon, but quickly regained her composure and continued.

"But sorry, you're not going to have any luck with the hotels. This is the month of our Crop Over festival and all the hotels and guest houses are sure to be full." She wore a look of satisfaction that he found strange.

"Well, I have to be going. Have a lot of housework to do. Hope you enjoy the meal. And be sure to tell the young lady she can come and visit any time. Since my husband passed away—Lord, rest his soul—I'm always glad for the company." She said this with a sad, whimsical look on her face, which didn't last for long.

She blew him an elegant kiss. With that she turned and strutted away, her voice raised in a funky island ditty.

Taurean turned, his stomach rumbling as he caught the tantalizing aroma of the muffins.

So that was Bertha Gooding!

Alana and Melissa were still in the kitchen when he entered. The little girl looked up at him and he was again made aware of the fear he'd seen the night before. He smiled, hoping that it would put her at ease. She continued to stare at him and slowly her fear abated, replaced by mistrust.

He held out the basket in his hands. "Our next door neighbor brought us breakfast. Do you want to do the honors?"

Alana looked at him with uncertainty. She knew that to refuse would be silly. Melissa was glancing at the meal with hunger in her eyes.

Alana held out her hand and took the basket from him, wondering if the neighbor was the Mrs. Gooding Paula had mentioned.

"I'll get some more plates," he said to her. To the child, he asked, "Do you want to help me while your mommy prepares the breakfast?"

Melissa hesitated and with her mother's prompting went to set the table.

Alana placed the basket on the table and opened it, the smell of hot coffee and warm biscuits filled the air. There were also muffins and a bunch of ripened yellow bananas. Golden fruit she did not recognize rounded off the meal. She placed these on the table, making sure that the man had a large helping of everything.

She placed Melissa on one of the stools by the counter. When they were seated, Taurean joined them, his frame too big for the small stool. Having him here was strange, Alana thought. Blake had rarely eaten with them. He'd either slept late or was gone before she woke up. He had not been a breakfast person. The presence of this stranger was disconcerting.

For a few minutes, they sat in silence. Taurean could feel the little girl's gaze on him, but not wanting to be the cause of the fear in her eyes, he continued to eat. Finally, he looked up and she glanced away.

A few seconds later, she turned her eyes toward him again. This time, he looked her full in the eyes. Then he smiled and an expression of wonder came on her face. It almost made him laugh. It was as if she'd not expect him to be able to smile. As a teenager, he'd been told on many occasions that when he smiled it transformed his face into that of an angel's and could melt the heart of the most stubborn individual. Maybe what the girls had been saying back then was true.

A hint of a smile touched her lips and he felt a tightness in his chest. Her response affected him more than any of the women who had succumbed to his charm. In less than a day, this little girl had begun to touch him in a special way, and he wanted to take away her fear and see her laugh and jump and play like other children. He knew he'd opened up to them because he, too, was a victim.

He'd had his fair share of fear, but his strength had kept him from being hurt. He could protect himself. This child only had her mother to protect her, and she, too, needed protecting.

Sitting with them made him feel uncomfortable. It was like eating with a family. He had fantasized about a loving family—a beautiful wife and three happy children. Now, here he was with a woman and child with the saddest eyes he'd ever seen.

But there was no laughter. No love.

Alana broke the silence when she asked the question he knew must be foremost in her mind.

"What have you decided to do?"

For a moment Taurean hesitated, his thoughts in conflict.

"There's going to be a problem getting a room at any of the hotels on the island. The woman from next door says that this is a festival month and all the hotels are booked full. Would you have any objections to sharing? Patrick and Paula will let you know I'm not dangerous.

"I spoke to Patrick last night and he told me that Paula forgot to tell him about your visit. When I decided to come to the island, she'd already left for a conference in Orlando, so Patrick only found out about your being here yesterday when she called and told him."

He did not believe what he had said. All morning he had been looking forward to their leaving. He acknowledged the surprise on her face and knew that she was weighing the pros and cons.

Her reluctance made him angry. When her response came, he realized that for a moment his heart had stopped. He did not want them to leave.

"We'll stay. We'll try not to get in your way. I could do the cooking if you want me to."

"That's fine. But I'll pull my weight. We can share the cooking." He paused, annoyed by her skeptical expression. "Yes, I can cook. So there's no need for that look."

"I'm sorry, but it's unusual to find a man who can cook and not be ashamed to admit it."

"Well, I actually enjoy cooking. You're in for a pleasant surprise."

"I look forward to it." With that, she turned to her meal.

They continued to eat in silence, and he sat watching them, confused by the unexpected turn of events. He hoped he could handle being around them for the rest of the summer months. He'd planned on being alone.

But he had all intentions of avoiding them as much as possible.

The rest of the day was a pleasant one. Alana and Melissa spent the early hours of the afternoon on the beach. For the first time in months, Alana saw her daughter enjoying herself. As she watched Melissa running on the sand, looking for shells to add to her already large collection, Alana knew she had made the right decision.

Her back propped against one of the many coconut trees that lined the shore, she inhaled the freshness of the afternoon's breeze. The branches' wide canopy provided a welcome shade from the heat of the day. She'd have to get some suntan lotion for Melissa since neither of them was accustomed to the tropical heat.

"Mom, look, there's a bird over here. It's hurt." Melissa's voice was full of despair.

Alana ran over to where her daughter was in tears.

"Is she going to die? I don't want her to die. Can we take care of her until she's better?"

The tiny bird was still a baby. She had fallen from the branches of the tree overhead.

Alana looked around and saw two others close by. At the same time, Melissa saw them, and tears began to flow from her eyes.

"Mommy, why did God let them die?"

Alana did not know how to answer.

"There's no need to worry. The babies have gone somewhere safe." The voice was a strange one, a woman's.

They both spun around and saw Taurean and an elderly woman, who wore a bright, flowered dress, walking toward them.

The woman smiled, her pale gray eyes sparkling. "I'm Bertha Gooding. I live in the chattel house in the distance. Just got a call from Paula, and she asked me to come over and introduce myself. Taurean told me he'd seen you come in the direction of the beach."

"I'm Alana, and this is my daughter, Melissa. Paula did say she would call. And thanks for the breakfast. It was kind of you."

"The pleasure is all mine. It feels good to have someone to take care of. Since my husband died, it gets lonely out here."

She turned to Melissa. "There's no need to worry about the bird. She'll be all right."

As she spoke, Alana noticed Taurean moving toward the baby bird. He stooped to look at it. Carefully lifting it, he cradled it gently in his powerful hands.

"Mommy, Mommy, he's going to kill it. Stop him!"

"No, I won't hurt it." Taurean looked Melissa full in the eyes, as if willing her to believe him. "Come, let me show you she'll be all right."

Melissa hesitated, but curiosity got the better of her. She glanced at Alana for assurance and when her mother nodded, she knelt next to Taurean.

Alana watched as Taurean showed Melissa the bird, all the time whispering words of comfort to it.

Mrs. Gooding drew closer to Taurean and Melissa. "We're going to have to find somewhere safe for her to heal. I have a small cage at home that we can put her in. Come, let me take her. She must be hungry."

She reached out to take the trembling bird from Taurean, and he placed it gently in her hands. "Alana, you and Melissa can come and help me. Maybe you'd both like a cold glass of fresh lemonade?"

"Can we, Mommy?"

"Sure, honey. How can we refuse cold lemonade?"

Mrs. Gooding turned to Taurean. "Would you like to come with us? I'm sure I have a beer or two on the ice."

"Sorry, I'm going to have to pass up the invitation. Maybe another time."

"Well, what about dinner tonight? I was planning to invite all of you."

"That'll be great. What time?" Taurean asked.

"Eight OK?"

"Perfect."

"Well, see you later. I'll bring Alana and Melissa back in a while."

Holding Melissa's hand, Mrs. Gooding walked away. Alana followed close behind them.

Giving in to the urge, Alana looked back. Taurean stood watching them. Despite his size, he appeared fragile, vulnerable—and very lonely.

The next day, Alana walked slowly back to the beach house, the warm sun caressing her back. It was like heaven here. She realized she'd not thought about Blake for hours. She felt safe. She didn't know why, but there was just something about the island.

As she walked toward the house, she wondered what Taurean was doing. She was thinking about him more and more. Some tragedy had caused the pain and sadness in his eyes.

But he scared her, and she knew why. She was attracted to him, but the size of his body terrified her. His strong muscular arms could easily break her neck with one slight twist. But somehow she knew that he would never raise his hands to hurt anyone unless he was protecting someone he cared about. The gentleness in his eyes when he looked at Melissa, though conflicting with his harsh appearance, was proof enough.

Last night, she'd been disappointed he'd not gone with them to dinner. When she and Melissa had left for Mrs. Gooding's house, Alana realized that the rented car he drove was missing. On arrival at their neighbor's house, she'd been told that Taurean had called and informed Mrs. Gooding that he'd got tied up and couldn't make it.

She could not understand her feelings for Taurean. Her initial response to him had been one of caution, but now, she thought of him often and it confused her.

Yesterday had been even more proof of the conflict he represented. His gentleness with the bird still amazed her, though she'd already realized that his size was not a reflection of character and personality. But his care and concern for the bird had not been expected.

Instead of entering the house from the back, she walked around to the patio at the front. It would be a nice place to sit for a while. She'd go upstairs and get the book she was reading.

When she turned the corner, she stopped in her tracks. Taurean was on the verandah.

Naked.

She could not move.

She took a closer look.

Upon inspection, she saw he was not naked. He was wearing a pair of shorts that were almost the color of his skin.

Her heartbeat quickened as her eyes devoured the perfection of his tanned golden body. Its power and sensuality made her every nerve tingle.

His muscles rippled with every movement as he exercised. Sweat glistened and made him shiny and slick. An image of him lying above her flashed in her mind, and she closed her eyes with the rush of heat that worked its way down to the core of her femininity. Her breathing increased and she felt as if she were choking. She shook off the image, reminding herself that she'd sworn off men for a very good reason.

She turned to go back in the direction she had come.

"Leaving so soon?"

It was almost a whisper.

Gentle.

She stopped, not willing to turn around, knowing he would see the desire in the tenseness of her body. She felt the heat of embarrassment. Taking a deep breath, she turned, hoping that she looked in control.

He'd stopped doing his sit-ups and now sat, his eyes focused on her. For a moment her gaze rested on his hairy chest, then downward as she noticed the slight bulge at his crotch, made more noticeable by the soaked shorts that clung to every muscle of his body. She took a step forward, barely unable to suppress the urge to run her hands across his rippling abs.

What the hell had come over her? She forced herself to stop just before she reached where he sat.

His eyes still focused on her.

She realized he was waiting for her reply.

"I was just coming to sit on the verandah. The breeze feels wonderful. I was planning to sit out here for a while and read. Melissa's helping Mrs. Gooding feed the bird. I'm sorry I disturbed you."

"Don't let me stop you," he replied, a bright twinkle in his eyes. "There's plenty of room. I don't mind sharing."

"I'll be back in a while." With that, she walked steadily into the house.

Taurean's eyes followed her through the door. Her body appeared tense, and the making of a smile curved his lips. She felt something for him. Of that, he was sure. The desire he had seen burning in her eyes had instantly sparked a flame of response.

In that moment, he realized something important. He wanted her. He wanted her lying under him so he could bury himself deep inside of her. And he knew he would have her. It was an inevitable truth.

It scared him.

Strangely enough, there was more to his feelings. He also wanted to see her smile. He needed to take her pain away.

The door opened and she came outside holding a paperback novel. He looked at her in wonder as if he were seeing her for the first time; as if the reality of his desire was something he could not believe.

He extended himself on the floor and started the next round of exercises he did every day. Abs first, followed by two hundred push-ups. Yes, two hundred to help restore the control he seemed to need around this woman he'd just met.

He was aware of her closeness when she sat and opened the book, as the subtle hint of flowers wafted through the air. Her scent was so fresh and pure that his mind and body refused to concentrate on the exercises he was doing.

What was he trying to do? Alana couldn't keep her eyes off of Taurean. He kept on doing the push-ups and did not appear to intend to stop. She tried hard to concentrate on the book in her hands but the intense darkness of Katherine Hart's *Night Vision* could not hold her attention. And Hart was her favorite romance writer!

After what seemed like hours, he eased from the floor and slipped into the chair next to her.

"What are you reading?"

She showed him the book.

"*Night Vision.* Excellent book. Read it last year when it came out in hardcover and was on the bestsellers' list. I've also read the sequel, *Future Vision.* Hart's one of my favorite writers."

She looked at him as if he were crazy.

He smiled. "Yes, I know what you are thinking. What's a great big man like me doing reading a book by a romance writer?"

Her face turned red and she did not respond.

"I borrowed the first one when I read the review of it in a magazine," he explained.

Again, she said nothing.

She closed her eyes, and he wondered what was going through her mind. What could he do to make her less afraid?

She opened her eyes, stood abruptly, and looked at him with that intense fear.

"I have to go," she said, and without waiting for a response she headed toward the door.

Taurean watched as she walked away, wanting to follow her and take her in his arms. His fist struck the chair's arm. Her fear angered him. Did she really think that all men were cruel, that he would harm her? Her response had hurt him more that he was willing to admit.

Minutes later, drenched in sweat, he tried in vain to exercise the image of her from his mind.

When Melissa returned from Mrs. Gooding's home, she demanded that they go to the beach. The motherly woman seemed to have had a strange effect on her daughter. Alana felt a surge of hope. Her daughter was beginning to heal.

As Alana strolled on the beach with Melissa, she could not help but respond to the lush beauty surrounding her. The island was absolutely magnificent. Along with the coconut trees, tall palm trees were scattered along the water's edge. The sparkling sea beckoned with a soft whisper as waves lapped gently against the shore. In tidal pools, children laughed and frolicked, their mothers sitting patiently on the sand. The sharp smell of charcoal grills preparing burgers made her mouth water.

"Mom, can we go into the water now?"

Reluctantly, Alana realized that it was time. Since they had arrived on the island, Melissa had been asking about swimming. Unlike her daughter, Alana felt no desire to jump and prance in the water. But there were times when a child's need came first. This was one of those times.

"Yes, honey, we can go in now."

"Yeah, yeah! Let's go!"

"OK, let me just put my bag down first."

"Come, Mommy, hurry!"

Alana quickly dropped the beach bag she carried and the straw hat she wore on a beach chair under one of the many palm trees. She followed Melissa into the gently breaking waves.

She held onto Melissa's outstretched hand and shivered as her daughter said, "There's no need to be afraid, Mom. I'll take care of you."

Alana entered the sea, her heart beating fast. Cool water lapped at her feet. It wasn't as bad as she thought.

Melissa, beaming with excitement, slipped her hand from Alana's and plunged into an incoming wave. She screamed in delight.

"Mommy, this is fun. Come in!"

Alana held her breath, sliding further into the water until it covered her breasts. The cool water felt great, refreshing. For a while, she remained still, allowing her body to adjust to the temperature and movement of the surf. Melissa was jumping and skipping, foaming spray splashing around her. Alana closed her eyes, the silky feel of the tide caressing her skin.

"Mommy, look here!"

When Alana turned, water splashed into her face. Giggling, Melissa tried to escape. Soon, there was a water fight in progress. A group of island children nearby joined in and eventually the sound of laughter filled the air.

Exhausted, Alana stopped playing. Melissa was safe and enjoying herself. She would go on the sand and bask in the warm sun for a while.

She stretched out on one of the beach chairs and looked toward the sea. A surge of joy filled her at the sight of Melissa in the water. She had done the right thing bringing Melissa here. In just a few days, the island had done wonders. This energetic child was the one she remembered.

Melissa and a girl around her age raced out of the water. Tired, they sprawled on the sand. As they talked about "girl things," they dug in the sand and eventually a lopsided castle took shape.

They continued to build the castle until the girl's mother called her, leaving Melissa without a playmate.

Melissa yawned and returned to Alana. Lying on the beach chair beside her mother, she was fast asleep in minutes. The lull of the gentle surf was soothing, and Alana felt her eyes begin to close as well. A rest would be good.

That was how Taurean found them—fast asleep on the beach. The sun had moved toward the west, and the tree under which they lay shaded them from the still-hot sun.

He sat close to where they were and for a while watched them. What was the truth of their story? He had to admit that he was curious. There had to be some reason why they were hiding out in the beach house. When he'd spoken to Patrick, his brother had not said much. Paula had not yet told him the whole story.

His gaze rested on Alana. She was a beautiful woman. Lying like this, she looked relaxed. There was no evidence of the tenseness she carried around like a shield. For the few days they'd been at the house, Alana and Melissa had avoided him like skittish colts—as if at any moment they expected him to pounce on them.

The first time Alana had had any serious contact with him had been yesterday while she read. Even then she'd been cautious. Did they actually think he would just hit them for no reason? Again, he thought of the "Daddy" the girl had mentioned and wondered if Alana were divorced. Was her ex the man that had put that haunted look of fear in their eyes?

Alana stirred on the sand, and her body shifted. Her breasts rose with the movement and pointed firmly toward the sky. Black and beautiful. Just how he'd always loved his women. Nice firm breasts, long smooth legs, a flat stomach, and an abundance of thick black hair that his hands ached to stroke. She didn't look as if she'd given birth to a daughter of that age.

He wondered how old the little girl was. Seven, maybe eight? But she definitely looked like her mother. She was going to break hearts when she grew up.

He sat there looking at them, enjoying the gentle music of the waves breaking gently on the shore. The tide was slowly going out, reflecting the release of his pent-up stress. The slight caress of a late afternoon breeze cooled his heated body and he felt himself slowly relax. He knew that, like them, he would fall asleep.

When he awoke, the sun was low on the horizon. He shifted in their direction and found the little girl staring at him. Their eyes locked and then the fear was instantly there, again. She reached over and shook her mother strongly.

"Mom, wake up. It's the man."

Alana jumped up and looked at him. She grabbed the girl and rose to stand. He felt a sharp pain at her withdrawal.

He needed to say something.

"You're going to have to be careful about falling asleep in the sun. You could get sunstroke. Hope you remembered to put your suntan lotion on," he said.

She looked at him as if she was unsure whether to reply or not. She seemed ready to grab her daughter's hand and run. Then she noticeably relaxed.

"Thanks, I used lotion. Mrs. Gooding warned me about the sun. I didn't realize that I would fall asleep."

"The heat and the rhythm of the waves do that to you. Make you sleepy."

There was silence. He felt uncomfortable, at a loss for words. "Did you enjoy your swim?" he heard himself ask.

She hesitated. "Yes. The water was . . . relaxing. I love everything about the island. The sun, the sea. Melissa loves the sea. She wishes she could swim."

"I could teach her."

"No!" The reply was sudden, harsh, but she had the grace to look embarrassed at her rude response. "I'm not sure that's a good idea. Melissa's not good with strangers."

He turned toward the child, noticing the spark of interest in her eyes, but apprehension and then fear replaced it.

"OK, I understand, but the offer still stands."

He knew he'd intruded enough. "I'm going into the water. See you all later."

He left them standing there as he ran toward the sea, diving in with what he hoped was an impressive glide. It was only when he struck the water that he realized that his body was tensed—and very hot.

CHAPTER 3

Taurean came awake. It was a dream again, but this time it was different. Instead of the walls closing in on him, his dream had been one of passion and fire. Alana had come to him, naked, her long, raven hair flowing all around her. She'd slowly teased him into a state of full arousal and taken him flying off the cliff of passion. He had felt himself falling and falling . . .

He could not get Alana out of his mind. In this short space of time, she was already part of his every thought. What was he to do? Maybe he should leave. The confidence he'd felt early in the week was no longer there. Last night, they'd been to dinner at Mrs. Gooding's. This time he could not refuse and it had been a disaster. And it hadn't been their fault. He was the one to blame. He's been silent and brooding, affected by Alana's closeness. Mrs. Gooding had realized something was wrong and had looked at him often, her eyes questioning. He'd felt like applauding Alana. She'd really tried to enjoy herself. Even getting Melissa to take part in what little conversation there was. And then he'd just stood up and said he had to leave.

Now, he remembered the relieved look on their faces and felt like laughing, but then he'd been so embarrassed, he'd made his exit as quickly as possible. They must think he'd just left the mental asylum.

But there was something in the way Alana affected him that he couldn't understand; that made him feel all crazy inside. He wanted to ask her why she was running, but he knew that the progress he'd made would be a thing of the past. Maybe he should just leave. But the thought of leaving scared him. He knew that to leave would be to see the last of Alana and Melissa. And he knew with his very soul that he could not do that. He wanted to see them happy.

Leaping out of bed, he threw on an undershirt and sweat pants. He was hungry. He walked down the stairs and was surprised to hear the television on. When he entered the living room, he saw Alana and Melissa lying asleep on the couch. He'd heard them come in from Mrs. Gooding's, but had not come downstairs. He had heard their laughter and ached to join them, but knew they didn't want him around.

Now, they lay fast asleep, cuddled into each other. He felt an overwhelming need to touch them, to protect them, but for now, he was satisfied to observe them.

Sprawled in the chair next to them, he looked at them and realized how beautiful they both were.

For a long time, he sat there, confused by his thoughts.

Suddenly, two wide, very awake eyes stared at him. But, unlike this afternoon, there was no hint of fear. Only the bright-eyed innocence of childhood curiosity.

"Hi," he said cautiously.

For a moment, she did not reply and then she spoke.

"Hi," Melissa echoed.

A smile touched his lips, and she responded with a wide grin. It was like sunshine on a rainy day. The sting of tears clouded his vision. Unexpectedly, his stomach growled, and suddenly, they were grinning at each other.

Standing up, he held out his hand to her.

"I'm hungry. Want to go get some milk and cookies?"

He anticipated the look of fear, but never expected what she did.

Tentatively, she held out her hand.

"And strawberry jelly?" she asked.

Again, they grinned at each other. He held her hand gently, and they walked silently to the kitchen.

Switching on the light, he lifted her onto the nearest counter, and she giggled.

He turned to get the snack for them, all the time knowing her eyes followed him.

"Mommy said that you won't hurt us like Daddy." The uncertainty was there.

"No, I won't," he told her. So Alana was running from an abusive husband. "Only bullies take advantage of little girls and I'm not a bully."

"Yes, like Jeremy Batson at my school. He's big, and always picking on the small kids." She paused as if thinking about what she'd said.

"You're big," she reasoned. "Bigger than Daddy."

Her words said a lot. He knew he had to be careful with his answer.

"Yes, I am. Even as a little boy, I was bigger than all the other children in my class. My brothers and father are all big, but that doesn't mean I have to hurt others."

She was silent for a moment as if thinking about what he was saying.

"I like you. You were kind to the baby bird."

Eyes misting, Taurean lifted her from the counter and placed her on a chair. He wanted to hug her but knew the time was not right.

"I like you, too."

And again they were both grinning as they sat eating their milk and cookies and strawberry jelly.

Alana eased her eyes slowly open. For a while she was not sure where she was, but the quiet noise of the television brought her to the present.

Barbados.

She was safe. She reached over for Melissa and immediately panicked. Where was she?

She jumped up.

Blake.

The last thing she remembered was that they had been watching an old rerun of *Bewitched*, one of Melissa's favorite TV shows.

Then she heard voices drifting in the silent night from the direction of the kitchen. The voices were Taurean's and Melissa's.

She hurried down the dim corridor.

When she entered the kitchen, they did not notice her. She could tell they were eating, though all she could see were Taurean's broad back and the top of her daughter's head as it bobbed up and down. She stood at the door, not wanting to disturb them.

They were talking, but she could not hear what they were saying.

Suddenly, Melissa laughed and the sound was as beautiful as the music of a tropical bird at night. Tears filled Alana's eyes and she stepped back, not wanting them to see her. She could not believe what she'd just seen. For so long, her daughter had been too quiet, too reserved. It was only with her that Melissa sometimes opened up and smiled.

Now here she was, smiling and grinning as if she had known this stranger for years. Her response to Mrs. Gooding was no surprise. The motherly islander with the gentle face and voice would soothe the most scared child, but Melissa had opened up to this man who, like her father, radiated power and strength.

Taking a deep breath, she walked cautiously into the room. Simultaneously, they turned and saw her.

"Mommy, Mommy, Taurean made a snack for me. He likes strawberry jelly too. He can make a peanut butter and jelly sandwich for you." She turned to Taurean. "Will you make one for my mommy?"

"I'm not hungry, honey," she said to Melissa. Glancing toward Taurean, she said, "Thanks, but there's no need."

"Well, sit with us until Melissa is finished."

She sat at the table, forced to sit next to Taurean. The closeness of the small table and chairs caused her leg to brush against his and a jolt of hot electricity raced up her leg. Her body tensed, and she looked at him knowing that he had to have felt the spark. Their eyes met, and she found herself lost in the tenderness she saw there.

It scared her.

She looked at Melissa. She was finished.

"Come, honey, it's time for us to go to bed. It's way past your bedtime. Thank Mr. Buchanan for the snack."

"Thanks, Mr. Buchanan," Melissa whispered. "I'll make a snack for you tomorrow."

He smiled at her. "I'll look forward to it. Sweet dreams."

She responded with a shy smile. Turning, she placed a hand in her mother's. When they reached the door, she looked back and waved.

Alana did not look back.

In the distance, Taurean could see the first hint of the morning. Sunrise was his favorite time of the day. Its subtle colors somehow soothed him. It was one of the many things he loved about this beautiful island.

The image of two angels floated in his head, and he smiled. He felt relaxed. He'd fallen asleep easily, one of the first times he'd slept the whole night since coming to the island. Getting Melissa to respond to him in a positive way had moved him. She was a sweet child, and he admired tentative steps of courage as she'd placed her hand in his. He'd enjoyed the childlike innocence of her conversation, but when he looked into her eyes, he saw the knowledge of a child far beyond her years. He hoped she'd be able to recapture her childhood before it was completely gone.

But it was her mother who most intrigued and affected him.

"Alana."

The name slipped like honey from his lips.

Damn, how had he allowed this to happen to him? There was something about that woman that aroused feelings in him that he had thought long buried.

He didn't want this to happen; didn't need the emotional turmoil that came with caring for someone. Look what had happened when he'd involved himself in Corey's life.

His thoughts turned to his brothers. A part of him ached to see them. He missed the warm camaraderie he had with his brothers.

The oldest of his brothers came to mind. Taurean and Patrick looked so much alike that people often thought they were twins. Just a year apart, they'd already been at school when Daniel was born six years later, and at first they'd resented the intruder who insisted he wanted to be a part of their small group. Finally, they'd let him in, but Daniel had other ideas about his path in life, and by his teens had found his own friends, zealous individuals that embraced religion with passion.

Taurean was not surprised when Patrick had informed him that Daniel was now the pastor of a church in New York. He was the dutiful son, and he had always worked hard to please their father. Daniel's fervor for God had scared them at times. Taurean had often wondered if Daniel didn't belong in heaven, and had only been sent to earth to ensure that he and Patrick repented for their many sins.

Taurean always looked up to his oldest brother. Patrick had been there for him, even during the trial, but had made it clear that, though he would support him, he did not condone what Taurean had done.

And then there was Corey. Three years younger than Daniel, he'd been a quiet child and Daniel had been his protector from the day he was born. While the other brothers took after their father, Corey had been a slim, frail child favoring their mother's size and features. It was only in high school, when he'd started track and filled out, that he developed a firm strong body, but he'd never have the mass and bulk of his older brothers.

Taurean felt the familiar twinge of sadness that came each time he thought of his baby brother and what he had done. The sharp stab of guilt he still carried like a weight around his neck shot through his body. He knew that the horror of what he had done would haunt him for the rest of his life.

He still remembered the look of contentment on Corey's face, when he'd said, "Yes, I'll do it."

Despite all their faults, he loved his brothers, and knew they loved him. He remembered the nights when they'd stayed awake chatting about girls and cars and their dreams into the early hours of the morning.

Dreams! Where had they gone? He had always wanted to run his own business, but he now realized that dreams were like castles made of sand. His castle had definitely crumbled.

At least Patrick and Daniel had accomplished what they wanted. Patrick was married with two kids and a beautiful wife, Paula, and was the owner of a successful construction firm in the heart of Chicago. Not only was Daniel the pastor of his own church, he and his wife were six months pregnant with their first child. Like Patrick, he'd moved to the city. That much Taurean had been able to get from Patrick when he'd spoken to him.

Well, they were his family, and he knew that sometime he'd have to go home and face them. The thought scared him, but he wanted to see them. Maybe next month he'd take the trip back to Illinois.

Now, he was not ready.

The man walked confidently into Blake's office. Blake, refusing to look up, continued to read the papers in his hands. He did not acknowledge the man's presence.

The man cleared his throat.

Moments later, Blake looked up, his expression one of indifference. He did not offer the man a seat.

"So what do you have for me? Where's my wife?"

The man's expression faltered.

"I haven't found your wife yet, but I'm getting real close. I received some information about someone who may have seen her. There is evidence of a woman leaving the Philadelphia airport with a child about your daughter's age. I need to check this out."

Blake tried to control his joy. He wanted it to be them. He opened the top drawer of the large mahogany desk and pulled out an envelope.

"I want you on the first plane to Philadelphia. I expect a call." He stood, taking his wallet from his pants pocket and dropped several large bills onto his desk. "That should be enough to keep you for a while. Don't let me down."

The seedy man looked at the money greedily for a moment, then grabbed it, and stuffed it hurriedly into his coat pocket. Without a word, he left.

Blake felt disgust. In this line of work, he met some of the sleaziest of persons, but this man oozed filth. Despite his seedy appearance, Blake could not help but admire his quick work.

His thoughts moved to Alana.

His sweet Alana.

He was going to have to punish her when he found her. Let her know who was in charge. He felt a thick wetness in his hand and looked down. The pen he held had broken in two, its point stuck in his palm. Blood trickled onto the white pad on the desk. He was going to break her damn neck between his hands and slowly watch the breath leave her fragile body. She should have known that no one gets away from him and expects to live.

He opened the bottom drawer of his desk, carefully removing one of the pictures he kept there. He placed it on the desk, his eyes fixed on the face that belonged to him. God, she was beautiful. He'd taken the photo when they were on their honeymoon. Back then, he'd literally worshiped her. Memories of the days they spent in the room stirred his blood, making him angry that she could still arouse him in a way that took complete control of him.

He lifted the picture, and slowly brought it to his lips.

Then he hurled it against the wall directly before him.

The sound of smashing glass broke the silence.

Calmly, he stood, heading in the direction of the private bathroom very few knew was there. Constant thoughts of Alana did this to him and he needed to work. A cold shower would bring relief for a while, but he knew he'd never be totally satisfied until Alana was back where she belonged.

He closed the door behind him, stripping quickly, and entered the shower.

When he turned the faucet on, the sudden jolt of cold water stunned him, causing him to groan. He shivered with pleasure.

Yes, this was exactly what he needed.

CHAPTER 4

The hot sun scorched the city of Bridgetown. It was Saturday morning and Cheapside Market was a kaleidoscope of color and activity. The constant honking of horns and the shouts of the hawkers gave the market a life of its own. Men and women hustled to get the vegetables and fruit they needed for the traditional Bajan Sunday lunch. People shouted at friends, glad to see each other after a hard week at work. Mrs. Gooding had told Alana that Saturday morning in Bridgetown was a social event, a time when friends met and shared their hopes and dreams, and their fears.

Alana, with Melissa, meandered through the thick crowd, amazed at the scene before her. She had never seen anything like it before. Everyone seemed to know each other.

The sweet smell of ripened fruit filled the air, while brilliant flowers bloomed in the baskets of flower vendors. A plump hawker held a shiny red apple out to Melissa as they passed close to her.

"A juicy apple for de pretty lil' pickney?" A toothless smile touched lips cracked with age.

Melissa looked toward Alana for approval. When her mother nodded, she took the apple.

"Thank you," she whispered shyly.

"How much are they?" Alana asked. "I'd like a dozen."

"They fifty cents each. Nothin' for de one for de sweet lil' gal chile." Dark brown eyes twinkled. "Next time ya must buy all ya fruits from Elsie." Her singsong accent was like the tinkle of steel-pan music.

The hawker placed the apples in a brown bag and handed them to Alana. "Thank ya. And don't forget Elsie. I sell de best fruit on de island."

"We'll be sure to. Come, Lissa, let's find Mrs. Gooding. We seem to have lost her."

Taking one of the apples from the bag, Alana bit into it. Juice dripped from her lips. It was sweet, full of the warmth of the tropics.

Alana looked around, searching the area for Mrs. Gooding. As if by magic, she appeared next to them, her straw basket brimming with fresh vegetables and fruit, a harried look on her face.

"Girl, it's fun dealing with the hawkers. I got me some good bargains." A look of satisfaction lit her face. "I bought some mangoes for Melissa. I can see she likes fruit. Come, it's time to go. We'll go into the heart of Bridgetown another day."

Reluctantly, Alana followed her. There was something about the market that fascinated her. As they walked away, she glanced back, trying to capture the image with its vivid, colorful chaos. Yes, she would definitely come back.

They left the bustle of the market behind and headed in the direction of the parking lot. The large building they had passed just a short while earlier loomed before them. As if she had heard her thoughts, Mrs. Gooding answered the question on Alana's mind.

"This is our General Post Office. Just over there is where you can find the minibuses. Next time we come into the city we can take one. It'll be an experience you'll never forget."

The loud honking of horns could be heard in the direction she pointed. White vans with broad purple stripes across the sides were parked in line. As soon as one filled and left, another took its position.

"Melissa, how would you like a snow cone?" Mrs. Gooding asked.

"A snow cone? What's that?"

"Come on, I'll show you." With that, she led them in the direction of the minibuses.

They approached a woman who was surrounded by a small crowd of people all wanting snow cones. The woman, her head covered with a colorful scarf and wearing a bright yellow apron chatted cheerfully with her customers. It was fascinating watching the speed at which she worked. She filled the plastic cups with large scoops of finely crushed ice, then added thick colored syrup.

"You can both try one. They're refreshing. My favorites are the guava, Bajan cherry, and coconut."

With skilled hands, the lady filled two cups with mounds of snowy ice. She squirted the creamy white syrup onto the ice and handed one to Melissa and one to Alana.

Greedily, Melissa took the cup and placed it to her lips. A look of pure delight brightened her face. Alana nibbled on the ice. The mild flavor of coconut cooled her dry lips. It tasted like heaven.

"Oh, it's good."

Mrs. Gooding thanked the lady and lead them out of the minibus terminal.

A few minutes later Mrs. Gooding's red sports car was traveling swiftly along the lush, green countryside. Soon they were singing, and Alana felt the warm rush of happiness. For the first time in months Melissa was laughing. The island seemed to be already working its magic.

Cane fields lay almost bare. Cane stumps and plant debris lay upon the dark soil, while here and there ash mounds of cane trash were home to egrets searching for worms. The harvest was over and this was the time for celebration.

Crop Over, Alana had heard the festival called. After Paula told her about Barbados, she had read as much about the island as possible. The festival, as she remembered from her reading, was rooted in the island's slave history. During slavery, at the end of the harvesting of the crop, most plantation masters would reward their slaves with a period of celebration. The modern version of this was a month of events in July that culminated in a large street party, *Kadooment.* There were many events of the festival and Alana hoped she would be able to go to some of them. From all indications, it was a time of exciting revelry.

They drove eastward toward the beach house. More empty cane fields were evidence of the end of the harvest season. In every village they passed, small children out from school tumbled and frolicked on lush pastures that seemed to be common in each village. Boys of all ages played cricket, the national sport.

While passing through one of the villages, Mrs. Gooding pointed out a church. The old colonial building stood majestic and regal, and seemed out of place in the tiny village.

"There's a strange story surrounding this church. On every occasion that the tomb of the ancestors of the current plantation owners was opened, the coffins had shifted from their original positions."

For some strange reason, Alana felt the need to stop. "Can we stop here for a while? I'd like to see the church."

Mrs. Gooding drove the car into the churchyard.

Walls, dingy with age, hinted at their original color. Despite this, there was something magnificent about the building.

Leaving the sleeping Melissa and Mrs. Gooding in the car, Alana entered through heavy carved doors. Her eyes slowly adjusted to the darkened interior. It was cooler, quieter. She felt a sense of peace. Heaven had been captured for eternity in this sacred place. Tropical sunlight pierced the stained glass windows and created a multitude of colors.

Candles lit the alcove walls of the church, adding to the feeling of sanctity in the interior.

Alana drifted around the building, admiring the framed pictures of saints and the bronze statues that lined the walls. Toward the back of the church, she found a framed document. It was a clipping from an old newspaper. Her eyes scanned the aged document and she realized it listed names of African slaves in the graveyard outside.

She heard a noise and turned to see an elderly priest walking toward her.

"Good morning," he welcomed. His eyes sparkled.

"Hello, you have a beautiful church."

He beamed, pride on his face. "Yes, I do. I try everything in my power to preserve it. It's become difficult over the years, but God has provided." He paused then. "You're a visitor to our island?"

"Yes, I've only been here for a few days. We were passing the church and my friend told me the story about the tomb."

"Yes, we get visitors here year round who are curious about the unexpected."

"I was just reading this document and they mentioned a burial ground for slaves. Is it possible to see it?"

"Come, I'll take you."

He held her elbow and guided her outside. As they walked toward the burial ground, he told her the fascinating history of the church.

"The slave burial ground is over there." He pointed to a small green gate. "I'll leave you on your own. It was a pleasure meeting you. Enjoy the rest of your stay on the island." He walked back to the church.

The burial ground was well-kept, but smaller than the main one she had passed through. The grass was trimmed neatly, while tropical flowers bloomed magnificently. The burial ground felt alive. As if for some reason the souls of the slaves had some intimate story to tell her.

Alana strolled around reading the names on the tombstones. She was struck by an unexpected feeling of oneness with the individuals who had died. This was the first time she was confronted by the reality of slavery and it saddened her. This was her past, her history.

Her adopted parents, the Delaneys, had told her about her real parents. They had met the young married couple while on holiday on the island and had been so impressed with their work they had invited them to work for them. A few weeks after their arrival in New York, a drunk driver had hit the car they were driving, killing them instantly. Attempts to find relatives on the island had been futile and the Delaneys had taken their timid, silent daughter into their home.

Alana always hoped that one day she'd return to the island. So when Paula had told her about the beach house, she'd jumped at the opportunity. Barbados seemed the perfect place to hide. Maybe one day she'd be able to discover a closer connection to the island, a bit more about her past.

As she strolled among the crudely made crosses that marked the graves, the names of slaves jumped out at her and she wondered if any had been her ancestors. Filled with emotion, the long pent-up tears began to flow. She knelt on the ground and thanked God for life and her daughter and most of all for her freedom.

The reality of slavery had always been a source of sadness and anger in her life. Being adopted and raised by a white mother and father had not been easy for her. But her parents had loved her and made sure she had the opportunity to meet people of all races while allowing her to explore her own African American culture and history. She'd loved them without reservation, and the times when prejudice raised its head, she handled it with maturity and the conviction that God had made all people equal.

It'd only seemed natural to marry a man who embraced both cultures. Ironically, he trapped her in his own form of bondage.

When she rose to leave, she felt as if she'd buried a part of her life.

The sun shone down in full splendor. Crystal-clear water splashed gently against the white shore. In the distance, a tiny fishing boat bobbed with the movement of every wave. A warm breeze cooled the burning rays of sunlight.

But Taurean was lonely. In the few days since Melissa and Alana had come into his life he had grown accustomed to the comforting presence Melissa represented and the sweet sound of her laughter. Melissa smiled more and they had become the best of friends. She followed him everywhere. She was still somewhat reserved around him but more and more, she was beginning to open up to him.

He had grown to care for her.

She had begun to trust him.

He saw it in her eyes whenever she looked at him. The fear he'd seen so often on that first night and the days that followed was no longer there.

Only a look of adoration.

When she looked at him like that, he felt his heart lift and then a sharp ache deep down inside that made him dream of what his life would be like if he'd not spent crucial years of his life in prison. While there, he'd dreamt of the perfect wife and two sons, the spitting image of their father.

But never about a daughter. Maybe it came from being one of four sons. Now, a third child completed the family portrait he painted in his mind.

A daughter with soft eyes that sparked with life and curiosity—the spitting image of her mother.

The now familiar sting of tears drew him from his musings. He was beginning to feel something was wrong with him. He had never been one to cry easily. Men didn't cry. Not even after Corey's death had he given in to the grief lodged like a great stone in his chest. But on his first night behind the gray wall of the New York State Penitentiary, he had finally given in to that grief and the tears had flowed. He'd vowed never to cry again.

An image of his family came to mind—Corey, Patrick, Daniel, and his mother and father. Unlike Patrick, who had attempted to visit him, neither Daniel nor his father or mother had come. His father's decision had not surprised him, but he'd hoped his mother and Daniel would visit. He'd learned the extent of his father's control when his mother had not. He wanted their forgiveness.

During his teenage years, he had seen his mother crushed under his father's righteous power and he had been amazed that his father could stand in church every Sunday and preach love and forgiveness. During the trial, his father had sat in silence but his look of condemnation had been enough to show his disapproval of Taurean's act of mercy. His father had not even allowed his mother to speak to him. What had crushed him most was the smile of triumph that had briefly touched his father's lips when the judge had declared him guilty.

His brother Patrick had not understood his choice, but he had been willing to forgive. The thought of his brother's pity had forced him to state clearly that he did not want any visitors, and after the first year, Patrick had given up.

When Taurean had spoken to Patrick just a week ago, his brother's response had not been what he expected. He had invited him to spend some time with him and Paula in Chicago. Taurean had accepted the offer. At the end of their first day together, he'd known he had to get away. While Paula was at work, he'd told his brother he couldn't stay. Patrick had mentioned the beach house on the island of Barbados. It had seemed perfect.

And here he was, feeling alive for the first time in seven years.

He looked out to the sea. The tiny boat was still there. There were times in the past few weeks when he'd felt like that boat. The waves, though, had been rougher. It had been hard admitting to himself that he was scared. But Patrick had seen his discontent and had offered this solution. He wanted his life back. He wanted to be the carefree individual he'd been before. He knew, now, there was hope.

With the wind in his hair and the sun in his eyes, he screamed at the top of his voice, knowing he would be all right. He was finally beginning to heal. He was ready to explore his feelings for Alana.

He ran up the beach not knowing where he was going. He just wanted to run and run. With the wind on his face and the sun on his back he kept on running.

Suddenly, he tripped, landing heavily on the sand, the fall knocking the breath from his body. Shifting on his back, he looked up at the sun, white-hot, and not able to control himself, started to laugh.

The laughter drifted down the beach.

The car turned in to the driveway of the beach house. It had been a great day. On the way home, Mrs. Gooding had taken them to a tiny zoo and Melissa had appeared fascinated by the antics of the green monkey that was native to the island.

Alana had drawn the line at purchasing one for her daughter. It had hurt her to disappoint Melissa but she still needed to be firm. She did not want a spoiled daughter.

As soon as the car came to a stop, Melissa jumped out, eyes darting in the direction of the beach. Alana knew she was looking for Taurean. Since the night she'd found them in the kitchen, the two had become almost inseparable. She was still surprised at Melissa's acceptance of a man who was so much like her father in size. But Melissa no longer showed any fear of Taurean.

For the past few days, he'd been teaching her to swim and they spent every waking hour in the sea. Not liking the water, Alana preferred not to join them. Instead, she had remained on the patio reading, but glancing often in the direction of the beach where Taurean was teaching Melissa.

But it'd reached the stage when even reading did nothing to lessen her discontent. For some reason, she felt this overwhelming desire to paint again. She'd not put brush to canvas for years. When she'd first married Blake, she'd painted in her free time, until Blake had pronounced her "hobby" a thing of the past. She was denying him the honor of her company, he'd argued. And willing fool, she'd given in to his demands.

That situation had thrown out all thoughts of painting full time. He didn't want her to work, but neither did he want her focusing on something he considered trivial and a waste of his and her time. She'd felt the stirring of rebellion but had weakened and given in to Blake's demand.

Now that she controlled her own life, she hoped she could reclaim her gift. Mrs. Gooding had promised to take her to buy art supplies the next time they went to the city. She ached for Saturday to arrive.

"Well, I have to be off," Mrs. Gooding announced. "I have choir practice at the church tonight so I'll give you a call in the morning."

With that she blew the car horn and waved good-bye.

"Come, Melissa, let's go get something to eat," Alana instructed.

"Can I go down to the beach and find Taurean?" Melissa said, eyes turned toward the beach.

"Not now, Melissa. You've been in the water enough for the day. I know you're tired so you're going to have a rest, and then we'll see what'll happen."

Surprisingly, Melissa led the way into the house. She must be really tired, Alana thought. She actually gave up without a fight.

In a short time, Melissa was in bed fast asleep and Alana headed in the direction of the patio. She was going to continue the new book she had started.

For a while she read, the gentle tropical breeze warm against her face. The peacefulness was soothing and her eyes slowly began to close. Her thoughts wandered down the beach where she knew Taurean was. He was like a fish. Always in the water. She loved to see him swim, his lean body darting through the crystal water.

Placing the book on the bench, she headed toward the beach. She was drawn by the thought of seeing him and she could not resist any longer. She wanted to see him, and for once in her life, she wanted to be bold and daring enough to fight the demons haunting her.

When she reached the waters' edge, she searched, her eyes combing the water.

He was not there.

Disappointment washed over her. She was turning back toward the house, when she saw a movement further up the beach.

It was Taurean.

Alana walked slowly to where he lay. She approached the grove of trees expecting him to turn when he heard her, but he didn't.

He was asleep.

For a long time she gazed at him, devouring his hard male perfection. He was one fine *brotha*. She smiled at her use of the word. Pleased with herself. Blake would be shocked at her use of slang.

He lay on his back, his skin darkened and toned by its exposure to the sun. Relaxed, his face had lost the unsmiling visage that she knew hid a gentle smile. The hint of a beard added to the ruggedness he bore with such ease. Her eyes worked their way slowly down his body. She could not help herself. Her body tightened at the sight of his firm nipples buried in a mass of curly hair that tapered down his stomach and disappeared beneath the line of the loose trunks that did nothing to hide the generous bulge of his manhood. She swallowed deeply and started to turn away when she realized that he was awake. His light brown eyes were looking directly at her.

The heat of embarrassment washed over her. God, how was she going to get out of this one? This was the second time she had been caught lusting after him and she hated herself for her weakness.

"There's no need to go. I could do with the company." He smiled. She felt her embarrassment fade. He was deliberately trying to put her at ease and she silently thanked him for it.

"I didn't want to disturb you. You were sleeping so peacefully."

"It's fine. I haven't had a conversation with an adult for a while. Why don't you join Melissa and me on the beach sometimes?"

"Sorry, but I'm not a fan of the water. I'll leave that pleasure for you and Melissa."

He contemplated what she said for a while.

"So how do you like it here in Barbados?"

"The island is as beautiful as Paula promised. I can't believe the sand on the beach is so white and clean. The few beaches I had been to were all dingy gray and the water was a grayish green. The water here is so blue."

He started to laugh, the masculine sound mingled with the gentle pounding of the surf.

"Let me correct that misconception. The seawater is never blue. It's the reflection of the sky on the water."

She looked to the sea in amazement. Then she saw the humor in her blunder and joined him in laughter.

"Boy, I must sound like a real dummy. Blue water!"

He continued to smile, but in a pleasant, humorous way.

"Not a dummy, just lacking in scientific knowledge."

"Well, thanks. That's a perfect way to lessen the blow of my stupidity." She laughed again.

He went silent for a moment and then asked the question, "So how long are you staying here on the island?"

She hesitated, not sure what to say.

"We'll be here for the rest of the summer."

"Then you're back to your husband?"

"No, I'm divorced." She had decided not to lie and say that Blake was dead.

"Sorry to hear about the divorce." Now he was the one who looked embarrassed. "But you and Melissa seem to be enjoying the island. Me, if you were my wife, I would never have let you come on a trip like this without me."

For a moment, there was silence, both of them unsure of where the conversation would go.

"What about you? Have you left your wife behind?"

"Sorry, I'm not married, and I'm just here to relax and recuperate."

"What do you do back in the U.S.?"

For the briefest of moments, he hesitated.

"I'm unemployed. I've been..." Again, he hesitated. "I was just released from prison."

Instinctively, she jerked away. She was looking at him cautiously, the haunted, wary look back in her eyes. He cursed himself for having been stupid enough to tell her. He should have known how she would react.

She continued to stare at him, her initial reaction replaced by embarrassment. He could tell she had questions, but she seemed unable to speak.

"I'm not a rapist, so there is no need to be afraid."

He hoped his voice was gentle, reassuring. He reached for her, but she drew her arm back wildly as if he were a snake ready to sink his fangs into her soft flesh. She looked ready to bolt down the beach as quickly as her feet would take her.

He searched his mind for something to say.

Nothing.

"What for?" Her voice was laced with mistrust. "How long?"

"Seven years. I didn't rape anyone," he reiterated. "There's no need to worry. One of these days when I've buried my demons, I'll let you know the whole sordid story, but I'm not ready for that just yet."

She looked as if she wanted to ask more but instead she mumbled, "I've got to go. Melissa may be awake and looking for me."

With that she turned and hurried toward the house.

He rose from the sand, angry that he'd gone against his own reasoning and told her the truth. He'd had no intentions of telling her about his time in prison.

At least, not yet.

She was too vulnerable at this time. And to suggest that he was capable of violence without an explanation didn't make sense.

Or did it?

Maybe, in some sick way he wanted to let her see the ex-con, the prisoner, the outcast from society; wanted to force her to stay away from him. He felt some strange need to protect them, but maybe he just needed to butt out of what was really not his concern.

He glanced in the direction she'd taken, her scent still wafting in the air. Even now her presence lingered, assaulting his senses and stirring his long-dormant need to touch a woman. His awakening almost dropped him to his knees with its intensity. And with it came the realization that he was very much a man.

He became aware of his growing erection. The familiar throbbing, pounding sensation raced to his head, flashing an image of a naked Alana reaching for him.

He closed his eyes, enjoying the heat that warmed his cool body. Alana had somehow taken control of him, making him as randy as a teenager at the onset of puberty.

Rising from the sand, he headed toward the house. The issues he'd dealt with in prison seem minor in comparison with the emotional turmoil he'd been through since Alana and her daughter had invaded his life.

He needed to take control.

Soon.

But first he needed to take a long, cold shower.

Melissa watched as Taurean strolled toward the house. He reminded her a bit of her dad, but she now knew that it was only because he was big.

He was not like her dad at all.

Her dad would never have taken care of the baby bird like Taurean did. He'd held it exactly as he should, and she knew that he would not hurt it.

She also realized that he always looked sad. At least he wasn't grumpy anymore. She wondered why he was so sad. She wondered if he was married and had kids. But, if he had a wife and kids, he wouldn't be here on the island by himself. Would he?

She was glad she was on the island. She loved it here. She loved the sea, which was so different than the water at the pool when her mom took her to the country club.

She missed her friends, and wished there were kids her age around. Mrs. Gooding had promised that she'd make friends at church, so she was hopeful.

She was glad that her mom and Taurean were friends now. She wanted her mom to be happy. If they stayed on the island maybe they wouldn't have to see her father again.

There was a knock on her door.

"Melissa, are you up? Want to go over to Mrs. Gooding's to see the baby bird?"

"Sure, Mom. I'm coming."

Yes, she loved it here on the island.

CHAPTER 5

Alana allowed her mind to drift, enjoying the now-familiar sounds of the island. Blackbirds chirped, while palm fronds rustled in the constant easterly breeze. In the distance, the gentle surf played a musical soothing balm for her thoughts.

Thoughts of Taurean Buchanan.

His confession had kept her awake during the night, but in the wee hours of the morning she'd come to the realization that she had to trust her instincts. One of the many things she had learned about Taurean since the night she'd arrived in Barbados was that he was an honorable man. But she was disappointed that he'd not trusted her to tell her the whole story.

It was Sunday. In the distance, church bells rang in harmony. Melissa lay next to her on the bed where she had fallen asleep.

She glanced at the clock on the bureau. 7:00 a.m. She had to wake Melissa. Church began at nine.

Earlier in the week, Mrs. Gooding had invited them to the 9:00 a.m. service at her church and Alana had gladly accepted. Church had always been important to her—even after she married Blake. For Blake, it was a way of maintaining the perfect family image.

For her, it was a source of strength and comfort.

What had surprised her was that Taurean had agreed to go. At every turn, he was a source of wonder and she never ceased to be amazed by the conflict he represented. He confused her in more than one way.

Most of all she could not understand her attraction to him. She had never been attracted to the strong silent type before.

There was a knock at the door.

Taurean.

"Alana, are you awake?"

Another knock.

"Yes, I'm up," she replied.

"You're going to have to get up if we're going to be ready on time. We can't keep Mrs. Gooding waiting. Breakfast is almost done. Hurry up and come down."

"Thanks, we'll be there shortly."

Silence.

She was surprised that a man so large moved so quietly. Another one of those paradoxes.

Alana leaned over and shook Melissa. It was going to be difficult to get her daughter up so early.

She shook her again. Melissa stirred, groaning in protest.

"Come, you have to get up. Remember we're going to church. Get up and brush your teeth. Taurean says that breakfast will be done soon."

Racing into the bathroom, Alana quickly brushed her teeth. When Melissa finally stirred from the bed and entered the bathroom, Alana hurried out of the room for the kitchen. Taurean was there at the stove. He moved deftly, cracking the egg he held with one hand.

The table was already set, and the sharp aroma of freshly brewed coffee filled the room.

"Good morning."

His head turned at her voice, and the smile he flashed her was warm and sunny.

"Hi, I'll have this ready in a second. Have a seat."

She sat, enjoying the sight of him by the stove. She tried to imagine Blake preparing breakfast and almost laughed at the picture that flashed in her mind. She felt the familiar stir of longing. This was what she had wanted when she'd married Blake. This sense of sharing and companionship.

How wrong she'd been!

Taurean was so much more than Blake in so many ways. Her eyes locked on the boxer shorts that molded Taurean's firm tight butt, causing her heartbeat to quicken. She forced herself to look away, disturbed by her unexpected reaction.

Taurean placed a plate with scrambled eggs, bacon, and a toasted Bajan salt bread in front of her. He then filled a cup with steaming coffee, its strong aroma reminding her of home.

"Is Melissa going to be down?" he asked. "She'll eat scrambled eggs, too?"

"Yes. There're few things Melissa won't eat."

As if on cue, Melissa tumbled into the kitchen and came to an abrupt stop at Alana's disapproving look.

"Melissa, what have I told you about running in the house?"

"Sorry, Mommy, I didn't want to keep you waiting. Good morning, Taurean."

Melissa sat at the place Taurean indicated, and started to eat. Taurean eased his large frame into the chair next to Alana. His leg brushed Alana's the way it did every time he sat at the table with them, and she felt the familiar jolt of awareness. Their gaze locked and she saw a hot flash of desire in his eyes.

Embarrassed, she looked down. Their unexpected reaction to each other was getting out of hand and could cause all kinds of trouble.

They ate quickly and when Taurean excused himself to go dress, she experienced a feeling of relief. His sitting with them had left her warm and bothered. But somehow it had felt right—as if they belonged together as a loving family.

Leaving Melissa to finish her breakfast, Alana headed upstairs. In the bathroom, she stripped and stepped into the shower, the spray cooling her warm body. She forced all thoughts of Taurean Buchanan from her mind.

On returning to the bedroom, she found Melissa lying on the bed, eyes closed.

"Girl, you had better hurry. I'm not going to speak to you again," Alana scolded.

Melissa opened her eyes and leapt off the bed. Lips pouting, she stood glaring at her mother. "I don't want to go to church. It's going to be so boring."

"Melissa Smyth-Connell, this is the last time I'm going to speak to you. Get in the bathroom, now!"

Tears settled in her daughter's eyes, but Alana continued to glare. Melissa had to understand obedience even though her renewed sass brought joy to her mother's heart.

Melissa turned and walked into the bathroom, closing the door behind her. Alana smiled. Thank heavens, her stubborn daughter was back. Blake hadn't killed her spirit.

Standing in front of the mirror on the wall, the image Alana saw revealed a woman of average height. She was slim; had always been. After Melissa's birth she'd quickly regained her slenderness, all evidence of childbirth gone. Many of Blake's friends and associates did not believe she was the mother of an eight-year-old child. Blake had made sure she kept in shape, hiring a personal trainer to work with her every day.

Skin dried, Alana removed the pale green dress from the hanger and slipped into it. She'd bought it when Mrs. Gooding had taken her into town to buy the art supplies. The dress was made of Sea Island cotton and fitted her loosely without hiding the slight swell of her hips and firm breasts. The person looking back at her bore no resemblance to the dignified formality that she had been expected to symbolize as Blake's wife.

She preferred the woman before her now. She looked alive, human. Nothing like the porcelain ornament she'd become at Blake's hands.

Unwrapping the scarf from around her head, she relished the silky feel of the mass of thick mahogany hair that cascaded well past the curve of her shoulder. She had often wanted to cut it, feeling that it made her look innocent and naive, but had never had the courage. It was one of her few vanities.

She flicked a comb through it, loving the satiny touch against her face. She added a pale red shade to her lips and darkened her lashes. She noted that her eyes, once sad, were now wide and bright, flickering with life, the sadness that had been there for years, gone. And she had to admit that the island and Taurean were responsible for the changes. A slight squirt of Obsession, and she knew she was at her best.

"Mommy, I'm finished. Help me put on my dress," Melissa said, returning from the bathroom.

Alana walked over to her daughter, carrying the red dress with red frills that Melissa had insisted she buy for her.

"I'm sorry, Mommy. I love you." Her daughter hugged her.

"I love you, too, honey."

She put the dress over Melissa's head. Looking at her daughter, she felt pride that only a mother could feel for a child. She'd done well. She wondered how long Melissa would remain her little girl. The thought scared her, but she knew that day would come when Melissa would grow into a woman and have her own life and children.

Slipping on her shoes, Alana took one last glance in the mirror. Yes, she was definitely ready.

"Mommy, you look beautiful."

"Thank you, honey. And so do you."

She held out her hand to Melissa, and they left the bedroom in search of Taurean.

When they reached the sitting room, he was already there, looking out the window toward the sea.

Taurean turned when he heard them, and Alana's heart gave a jolt.

He was stunning in a suit.

She could not help but stare at him.

He'd shaved. The straggly beard and moustache he wore had been trimmed neatly. A white shirt and black jacket contrasted with his golden tan. A silver stud glimmered in his left ear. She hadn't realized his ear was pierced. He'd never worn the earring before. Somehow, it gave him a rugged masculine look.

Their gazes clashed and she saw the flash of awareness. It was as if they were alone. Heat warmed her body.

"You're ready?"

It was a silly question, but one she knew reflected his state of mind. "Yes, we're ready."

"And who's this beautiful lady?" Taurean teased, turning to Melissa. He bowed gracefully.

"It's me, silly. Melissa!" She giggled.

"It is? So, where's all the sand? I didn't even recognize you in your Sunday best. You're so pretty."

"Thank you, sir. You're such a gentleman," Melissa curtsied, a smile on her face.

At her antics, he laughed. The deep masculine sound was unexpected, but stirred something inside Alana.

"Come on," he said, "we have to go. Mrs. Gooding is waiting on us."

They strolled over to Mrs. Gooding's house. Melissa skipped ahead.

Mrs. Gooding came out when she saw them. She was wearing a yellow and white dress with large sunflowers that seemed to blossom in the sunlight. On a woman of lesser confidence, the dress would have been ridiculous, Alana observed. On Mrs. Gooding, it was bold, flamboyant, a reflection of her vibrant personality.

Minutes later, the red Suzuki was speeding along a lonely country road. From her position in the back seat, Alana looked at the middle-aged woman closely. She was a handsome woman and Alana could tell that in her youth she was stunning. What surprised Alana was the beauty of her skin. She seemed almost youthful in appearance, as if she would never grow old. It was difficult to guess her age; she could have been anywhere from her late forties to her late fifties but she looked younger. She'd said her husband had died over fifteen years ago.

Next to Alana, Melissa chatted cheerfully about the shells she'd found on the beach the day before.

Mrs. Gooding turned the car into the church parking lot just as the bells began to ring. She found a lone spot at the far end of the lot. "Quickly, we only have five minutes to get in our seats," she cautioned.

When they entered the building, heads turned in their direction and Alana realized the picture they must present.

A family.

The thought disturbed her. People had always commented on how well she'd looked next to Blake. With Melissa, they'd been the perfect American family. She wasn't sure if she believed in the concept anymore. Families were based on love and trust. She'd trusted Blake and look what he'd become—and done. At this moment, she didn't feel as if she could totally trust another man. She wouldn't even entertain the thought of Taurean Buchanan as a husband. She'd be crazy to. Besides, he was still a stranger. Though there was a part of her that believed he was a man to be trusted, she hardly knew him, and the fact that he had not told her the reason why he'd been in prison only made her caution more justifiable.

As they sat, the sad moan of a flute was heard. The melody was hauntingly simple, but added to the spirit of sacredness.

The church was a modern one, totally different from the one she visited on the way home from Bridgetown. Despite its stark plainness, there was a peacefulness that made her feel relaxed and at home. The only touch of color was several vases filled with pink and white roses, and brilliant red hibiscuses.

A tall man took the pulpit. He greeted everyone and gave each of the visitors a special welcome. His voice filled with sincerity, he said a short prayer and then invited the choir to sing.

The opening bars of a familiar Negro spiritual sounded from a slightly off-key piano. Then, a single voice was heard, a boy's. Soon, Alana was lost in the passion of the child's singing. For one so young, his voice shimmered with the reality of the pain and suffering of his forefathers. But as the song came to an end, a crescendo of angelic voices joined the boy's, rose, and soared toward heaven.

The song was powerful and moving, and Alana felt an unexpected comfort. She knew the song was for her. God was real and would keep her and her daughter safe. For some unknown reason, she looked at Taurean sitting next to her and knew that she would tell him the truth about her past. He returned her look, his warm gaze touching her, holding her captive. But it was not the desire she sometimes felt. It was something more and she saw it reflected in his eyes and was amazed by the beauty of it and the promise it held.

Taurean felt the message of the words of the song. For years he'd hated religion and what it stood for. It was this religion that had made his father reject him, had condemned him to prison for the seven years of his life he would not regain. But he knew now that something was different. God was speaking to him and he felt the burden of years of guilt begin to lift and knew that he only had to ask for forgiveness.

When the pastor took the pulpit, he spoke of guilt and freedom, and again Taurean knew that the words of the sermon were for him. He listened and when the pastor ended in prayer, he quietly whispered the words "Forgive me," knowing that God had heard.

The pastor left the pulpit and the congregation stood to sing a series of lively choruses. Taurean clapped and moved to the music that was now a source of joy and comfort. Next to him, Alana and Melissa were clapping and swaying to the music. Again, Alana's eyes met his and he knew that she had felt the power of the music and the pastor's words. He saw a rush of emotion, but serenity had replaced the haunting sadness in her eyes. He smiled and when she returned it, he knew he would tell her about his brother and about the guilt that had torn him for years. He also knew he wanted to keep her safe from the man who had forced her to run and hide.

Minutes later, when the service ended and he stepped outside, the sun was high above, its rays warming Taurean's once cold heart. For the second time in as many days he felt totally alive.

A few days later, Alana sat on the bench in the garden under a sprawling almond tree, the book she was reading open on her lap. Melissa was down by the beach with Taurean and the Blackman twins, Karen and Kerry.

Alana and Melissa had met the twins' parents, Marc and Anne, on Sunday after church. Alana had liked the bubbly young woman and her equally effervescent husband. The girls had immediately become friends, and had already begun spending hours on the phone chatting. When Melissa had asked if the twins could visit, Alana had been glad to consent. The look of delight on Melissa's face had been confirmation of her daughter's need for friends of her own age.

She looked around her, wanting to paint, the tranquility and beauty stirring her need to create. She'd been able to purchase most of the supplies she'd wanted from an art store in Bridgetown, but she'd not been ready to paint.

Now she was. Despite the need, she was afraid. She hadn't picked up a brush for years. When she'd married Blake, her career as a graphic artist had ended. To an extent, she'd been glad. In the early months of marriage, she had been able to remain at home and paint to her heart's content. Eventually, with Blake's gradual change, she'd not been allowed to paint anything.

Here on the island, she felt the desire to capture the island's beauty on canvas.

She also wanted to paint Taurean.

As expected, thoughts of him came into her mind. She remembered the day at church and how things had changed. The awareness that threatened to consume her had blossomed and grown. During the night, she would awake soaked in the aftermath of a feverish dream in which she'd fully participated, wanton and bold.

The gravel crunched. She did not have to look up to see who it was. Taurean.

She closed the book, knowing that tawny gold eyes would be fixed on her. He came to stand in front of her and she felt the familiar warming of her body as his gaze caressed her. Her body tingled. She wanted to see him look at her with that longing in his eyes.

She stared at him, unable to speak, devouring his big, firm body. He had showered, but still carried the scent of the freshness of the sea. Dampness glistened in his hair.

She wanted him.

The thought shocked her, making it difficult to breathe.

"Is something wrong?" The husky deepness caressed her. A dimple to the left of his mouth appeared. He seemed to be trying not to smile. Was her desire so obvious?

"No, I'm fine," she replied, hoping that she sounded calm.

He sat. He wanted to say something. He lifted a hand and slowly ran it through his hair. Tiny drops of water scattered.

"How would you like to go to dinner tonight? Marc and Anne have invited us out."

A date?

Her heart started to race. She wasn't sure she was ready to date again. "What about Melissa?"

"Mrs. Gooding has already agreed to take care of her and the girls."

Alana hesitated, unsure of what to do. "I'll go," she heard herself say. Was she going crazy? "What time do I have to be ready?"

"Marc said six-thirty. They're taking us to dinner and a calypso show."

"OK, I'll be ready. Where're the kids?"

"They're upstairs, changing out of their swimsuits. Bertha told me about a place just north of here along the beach where I can find lots of Bajan sea grapes. The girls want to go fruit picking, so I promised to take them. With your permission, of course. I know this is the time of day you like to read and relax."

"Thank you, I could do with the break. The three of them, together, can be a handful. But the twins have been good for Melissa."

He nodded in agreement. "Well, later. I'll go get them. I'll bring them back in time for supper."

He turned to leave.

Alana watched him go, her eyes fixed on the loose swagger of his hips. What was she going to do?

Taurean pulled on black slacks and slipped the pale blue shirt he wore inside, buckling the belt.

Well, he was ready for their date. Date? No, they were just going out with friends. Weren't they?

The butterflies in his stomach were causing havoc and his hands were shaking. He breathed slowly, trying to control his racing heart. He felt so inadequate. He'd not been out socially for years and the thought that he would do something to embarrass himself made him nervous.

He exited the bedroom, closing the door quietly behind him. He took his time going downstairs, hoping that it would delay the inevitable.

In the sitting room, he waited patiently for Alana, his eyes darting toward the entrance at every sound he heard. Melissa, Kerry, and Karen were already at Mrs. Gooding's. They had a night of activities planned. He had heard them discussing the night while on one of their never-ending searches for shells.

He smiled. At the rate they were going, they'd soon be able to open a small tourist shop and put most of the shells on sale. But the girls had other plans for the shells. He'd seen the twins with a craft book on how to make shell jewelry, so he was sure they'd all be soon wearing shell chains and bracelets dangling from all parts of their bodies.

Laughter rumbled, ready to erupt from deep inside. He'd never thought he'd enjoy himself so much around kids. Patrick and Paula's kids had been OK, but he'd avoided them unless they had to come near. Often he'd seen them stare at him and then quickly look away as if he were the boogie man.

He felt sorry for Mrs. Gooding. Those girls were not going to sleep in any hurry, especially since the twins were out of school.

But, he'd enjoyed the day on the beach with them, his heart swelling with pride when Melissa had swum for a few feet before she'd sunk. She'd rushed to him and hugged him tightly. Then, she'd pulled away, surprised at her own reaction.

There was a noise at the door, and when he turned around his body tensed.

Alana was a vision of loveliness. Hair cascaded around her. She was wearing a slip of a dress that hugged every curve of her body. Her firm breasts pointed invitingly toward him. He felt the primitive desire to take her up to his room and make love to her.

"You look beautiful!" He'd not meant to say the words out loud, but they'd slipped like warm honey from his lips.

"Thank you," she said. "I wasn't sure what to wear, but I thought this would be all right. You look quite handsome yourself."

"The dress is perfect." He didn't know how to respond to her compliment, so he ignored it. "Well, let's go and wait on the patio. Marc and Anne should soon be here. The dinner reservations are for seven thirty."

As he locked the door behind them, the headlights of Marc's car turned into the driveway.

"Hi, Alana and Taurean," Marc's friendly voice shouted from the blue Toyota. "Sorry we're a bit late. We stopped over by Bertha to see the kids. Let's hope she's still alive in the morning." His blue eyes twinkled.

They laughed.

"Yes," Taurean echoed. "I hope she survives the night. But from what I've seen of Bertha, I'm sure she can stand her ground. Maybe it'll be the kids who get worn down."

Taurean opened the car door for Alana. When she was seated, he circled the car and slipped into the seat next to her. At least he remembered how to be a gentleman. That much had not changed. He grimaced at his paranoia.

"We're going to a restaurant on the south coast. It shouldn't take us too long to get there. The concert center is in walking distance so we shouldn't have any problem getting to the show early. There's sure to be a big crowd tonight."

The car moved off and soon they were driving on the lonely country road.

"How much do you know about calypso?" Marc asked.

"I know some of the Caribbean groups," Taurean replied. "I've seen some of the Caribbean videos on BET but I've never heard any of the groups live."

"Well, you're in for a treat. We're going to one of the most popular calypso tents on the island. Every year, as part of our Crop Over festival, we have a calypso competition and most of our musicians and calypsonians take part. Some of the calypso music you'll hear tonight won't be the party kind of calypso or soca you hear on BET, but a more medium tempo and dealing with social issues."

For the rest of the drive, Marc filled them in on the workings of the calypso competition. In about twenty minutes, they arrived at one of the most popular nightlife areas on the south coast of the island, St. Lawrence Gap. Marc pulled into the parking lot of a restaurant, its neon sign flashing BLAKEY'S.

In a corner of the softly lit interior, a group of men gently played on glittering steel pans. Pulsating reggae music rose from the instruments.

Alana and Taurean tried Bajan cuisine instead of the traditional continental fare also offered on the menu. Alana tried the night's special: flying fish in a thick peanut sauce with rice seasoned with the spices from the nearby island of St. Vincent. Taurean, on Anne's advice, tried a dish of pickled breadfruit and chicken served with a side of grated sweet potatoes, which had been steamed and seasoned.

As they ate, Marc, the untiring calypso enthusiast, continued his commentary on calypso and history of the Crop Over festival, increasing their anticipation for the rest of the night's entertainment.

Alana sat listening intently to Marc. She was fascinated by his knowledge of the festival. With every word he spoke, she saw and felt his passion for calypso music.

Occasionally, her eyes strayed to Taurean. His closeness made her aware of his maleness, his gentle sexuality. She couldn't keep her eyes off him. She loved the way he looked tonight. She'd grown accustomed to seeing him in the colorful shorts he wore each day or the loose trunks he wore when he went into the water. But now, he looked different—debonair.

And damn, didn't he look sexy!

When he shifted in his chair, his leg brushed against her cool skin until it eventually settled comfortably against her leg. Flames sparked, caught, and warmed her body that had been cold for so long. She started to perspire, her breathing increasing.

She reached for her glass of water, and watched in horror when her fumbling hands knocked it over. Liquid sprayed across the table. Instinctively, she jumped up, not wanting her dress to be soaked. Embarrassed by her clumsiness, she grabbed for a napkin, and started to dab frantically at the spreading water, her eyes averted, unable to look any of them in the face. An incident like this would have made Blake angry.

Strong hands covered hers.

"I'll get the waiter to do that."

Alana looked at Taurean, then the others, expecting to see disgust on their faces, but instead saw understanding. Totally overwhelmed, she felt the sting of tears in her eyes.

"Excuse me, I think I need to go to the ladies' room."

She turned and started to walk, realizing she didn't know where the room was. She stopped a passing waiter and headed in the direction he pointed.

Inside, she felt the tears begin to fall. She'd never felt so silly in her life. The incident had reminded her of the many times Blake had subtly ridiculed her in front of family and friends. After a while, she'd ceased to care, indifference her only shield from his verbal abuse. Why had she felt embarrassed now? She didn't know. Maybe it was a delayed reaction after years of abuse.

The click of the door drew her from her thoughts. She glanced in the mirror to see Anne enter the room.

"You all right?" her new friend asked.

"Yes, I'll be fine. Just a bit embarrassed at what happened."

"There was no need to be. It happens to me all the time. I'm always tipping things over." Anne walked closer. "I don't want to be presumptuous, but I know that something more than spilled water is bothering you. If you need a friend, someone to talk to, I'm a good listener."

Alana turned and looked at the smiling woman, noticing the gleam of genuine concern in her eyes. She already liked this woman a lot. She would love a friend. She'd not had a friend in years. Not since Paula at college. Not since marriage to Blake. Someone to talk to, laugh and cry with would be wonderful.

She held out her hand, not sure what she should do. Instead, Anne gripped her in a warm hug. "Thanks for caring but I don't want to ruin the evening by rehashing old wounds."

"Alana, everything will work out fine tonight and we'll talk when you're ready. Let's get you looking presentable, then we can finish dinner. We have to leave for the auditorium soon."

"Thanks, Anne, I promise we'll talk. I definitely need someone to talk to."

"Well, feel free to visit me any time. We'll have a long, girls' chat. Leave the kids with Taurean or Bertha." Anne looked at Alana with understanding, as she took her makeup kit out of her handbag and went to work on Alana's face.

The Blackman's car drove off. Anne, head through the window, was waving wildly at them. "I'll call you tomorrow, Alana. We girls must have a day out soon."

Alana waved in response.

Taurean stood silent, watching Alana.

As he had all through the night.

He'd enjoyed himself. Marc and Anne were crazy. The night had been so much fun. They'd kept both Alana and him in stitches with their anecdotes about their daughters' early years. He hadn't expected to enjoy himself so much, but he'd wanted the night to go on and on.

After the incident with the glass, he'd been unable to keep his eyes off of Alana. When she'd returned from the ladies' room with Anne, she'd changed, regained her composure. Alana had responded to Anne's funny personality and he'd been amazed at the transformation. The too-serious, quiet woman had become animated and witty.

This Alana was even more appealing, and he'd felt like a randy schoolboy every time he'd looked at her. Her eyes had come alive and sparkled with a joy that radiated around them and captured each person they saw in their grasp.

He noticed the habit she had of slowly running her tongue over her lips when she took a sip of the glass of white wine she'd chosen to go with her meal.

And he almost came undone.

Often, during the night, he wanted to take her in his arms and kiss her senseless, and he'd seen the desire reflected in her eyes. She'd been aware of his feelings and avoided looking at him.

The Blackmans' car disappeared round the curb and he became aware that she was looking at him. His eyes locked with hers and he saw his desire mirrored there.

As if in slow motion, he stepped toward her, bending his head. His lips touched hers, tentative, gentle, like a butterfly landing on a fragile bud. Cautiously, he experimented, getting accustomed to the shape and feel of her mouth. But the heat inside took control and he deepened the kiss, wanting to taste the very core of her soul. His tongue plunged inside. Tongues entwined.

A soft moan escaped her lips and the sound seemed to thunder through him.

His pulse raced.

Her sensual reaction made him harden with arousal. He ached to touch her, wanted her to feel what she did to him. He rubbed himself against her.

Suddenly, she pushed him away.

She was breathing hard, a harsh sound coming from her lips and then he saw the stark fear in her eyes. Unexpected tears swelled and threatened to fall from her eyes.

"I'm sorry. I shouldn't have. I'm not ready for this." He heard the despair in her voice. "I'm sorry."

She turned to go and he reached to stop her. His hand rested on her arm, pleading.

"Don't touch me." Her voice was suddenly cold. Condemning. Her cry of anguish nearly tore him apart. She turned and ran into the house as if demons from hell were after her.

For a long time he stood on the patio and looked out to sea. A pain, sharper than any he'd ever felt, pounded in his head and it wasn't just the pain of unrelieved passion. And then suddenly the reality of his state struck him full in the face, causing him to stumble. He was in love. The wonder and despair of it were heavy burdens.

Slowly, he walked toward the beach.

Heart beating fast, he fought to regain control, his focus on the twinkling lights from the fishing boat he'd seen before as it bobbed on the sea's gentle movement.

He felt much like that boat with his emotions bobbing up and down. Desire, need, wonder, and despair all tossed about within him. He stood there staring out at the water, wondering how he'd ever be able to control the storm of emotions building in his soul.

Alana stood at the window watching the lone figure in the distance.

What had she done?

She'd never meant to let something like that happen, but for some reason she'd known it was inevitable. She'd known that her desire to kiss Taurean would lead to this moment.

Why she'd run had nothing to do with her not wanting him, but more with the fact that she did want him.

And that had scared her more that the fact that Blake hovered in the background of her mind like a menacing shadow.

Life was so crazy and unpredictable. She'd given up trying to understand its rhythm and subtleties. She was just an ordinary woman in an ordinary situation . . .

No, definitely not ordinary. What she was going through could not be called ordinary.

She never expected that so soon after she'd vowed that no man would control her heart she was slowly falling again. And to a man with a checkered past and one who was a study in conflict.

Her own conflicting emotions ebbed and flowed within, causing her to lose track of the things she'd hoped to accomplish here on the island.

And falling in love was not one of them.

She didn't want to say it, but she'd felt the first stirring of what she knew was more that just affection.

She had no intentions of allowing it to happen.

Not again.

Never.

CHAPTER 6

The next few days Alana avoided Taurean as much as she could, which turned out to be not very difficult since he seemed very intent on doing the same thing. Every morning when she awoke, he was already gone. The note stuck to the refrigerator stated that he was exploring the island. At nights, when she, Melissa, and the twins were over at Mrs. Gooding's making the girls' costumes for the Kiddies Kadooment, she would hear the rental Jeep pull up. By the time they reached the house, he'd be in his room.

Next morning, he'd be gone.

What had happened on Sunday night still disturbed her. She had allowed herself to be consumed by desire. For the first time in years, she'd been kissed as if she were special. Taurean had awakened feelings she had thought were buried and that scared her. It was like her attraction to Blake all over again. She'd just escaped the entrapment of a relationship and here she was ready to hurdle blindly into another one.

Was she crazy?

Maybe she was. No woman in her right mind would be dreaming the things she dared to dream. Especially after enduring the kind of abuse she had . . . and a failed marriage.

Wasn't she going to learn?

She was worried about Melissa, too. She could tell that her daughter was hurting; that she missed Taurean and did not understand why he didn't go to the beach with her anymore. She no longer smiled as much. Often, Alana would see her searching for him.

But he never appeared.

Fortunately, when the twins, Karen and Kerry, were around, Melissa seemed to forget him.

Alana looked at the unfinished canvas. She'd been sitting on the stool waiting for the past fifteen minutes to capture the perfect moment.

The sky still bore a hint of night. The sun had not risen, but she knew that it would soon begin its steady morning march.

Patiently she sat. Her hands poised.

Then the moment arrived.

Sunrise.

Her hands moved skillfully, swiftly, like a tireless hummingbird. Darting here, then there, until the colors took shape and form and the brilliance of the sunrise emerged on the canvas. Alana knew it would be one of her best pieces.

Golden sunshine was captured for eternity on the canvas.

For a while, she sat silent.

Motionless.

Exhausted by the emotional draining of the creative process, but feeling a joy and excitement that she was finally able to paint again. She knew that before her was the best thing she'd painted in years. What had been missing in the past few years was back. The painting breathed life and the warmth of the sunshine was back.

The darkness and gloom were gone.

She pulled the next canvas from her portfolio, squeezed additional colors onto the palette, and waited, knowing that they, too, would come.

Minutes later, in the distance, she heard a steady flutter of wings.

They were here. The flock of seagulls.

They flew overhead and she trembled with excitement, anticipating their daily dance. Moving gracefully, like the chorus in a tropical ballet, they twisted and swirled. The birds knew they were on stage and gave their finest performance.

Again, Alana's skilled hands worked fervently to capture them for eternity on the canvas. When she finally looked at the painting, she saw that it was another masterpiece. A symbol of what she was seeking to achieve—freedom.

Placing the brush on the palette, she looked out to sea and saw the sun of the new day. This was the day she would start to live again, she thought. Yes, she could paint. The talented woman who'd been full of passion and life had resurfaced. She was tired of running, tired of the pain and unhappiness. She had to make a start, had to make peace with Taurean.

She folded the easel, gathered her equipment, and walked toward the house. Melissa would still be asleep. The island air had been good for her. She was forever eating and was no longer the pale, fragile, frightened child she had been a few weeks ago. She smiled more, was more relaxed.

There was a flicker of blue at Taurean's window. He stood there focused on her. Uncertain, she waved at him and he nodded in acknowledgment, his face expressionless. She felt a deep sadness as the threat of tears moistened her eyes. She was glad he was above her. She did not want him to see her crying.

Slowly, she walked into the house, her heart heavy.

The sweet smell of baking tantalized Alana's nostrils when she knocked on the door of Mrs. Gooding's house. She wondered what delicious pastries Mrs. Gooding was creating today. She'd promised that she would help the older woman with the costumes for the children.

As she stepped onto the patio, three laughing children tumbled out of the house, plaits flying in all directions, and screaming at the top of their lungs. The three came to an immediate halt when they saw her. Melissa raced toward her with a squeal of delight. Karen and Kerry followed quietly, nothing like the picture she had just witnessed.

"Hello, Mrs. Alexander, how are you?" they said in harmony. Their eyes twinkled with mischief. They were good for Melissa, she thought.

"Hi, girls. So you've been working hard on your costumes? Where's Mrs. Gooding?"

"Alana, I'm here." The elderly woman came outside. "The girls have been helping me. I've just given them a little break. They wanted to check on the baby bird. Come, let's go inside, I could do with a break too."

When the girls disappeared in the direction of the shed behind the house, Mrs. Gooding led her into the house through the hallway and into the quaint sitting room where she entertained.

The room was a mass of confusion. Crepe paper, feathers, and glitter lay scattered about the room. The girls were going to be in a band in the Kiddies Kadooment. The Saturday before the final weekend of reveling there was a small street parade for children. They paraded in bands with a specific theme and costumes were made to depict aspects of the theme.

The twins and Melissa were in a band called Tropical Wildlife and were to be egrets, the slender white birds found on the island. The girls were so excited.

"Would you like something to drink? Some iced tea? Mauby?" Mrs. Gooding asked when Alana was seated.

"Some mauby would be nice." She seemed to have acquired a taste for the local drink made from the bark of the carob tree. Despite its slightly bitter taste, Alana found the beverage to be tasty and quite refreshing.

"Yes, it gets like this during the summer. Soon, there will be a lot of rain and the occasional storm or hurricane."

"Hurricane?"

"Yes, hurricane. It's the hurricane season, so anything is possible. Though we haven't had a serious one in years," Mrs. Gooding said. "They always seem to skirt the island.

"I remember, as a young girl, hearing of a hurricane named Jeanette that struck the island. I'm sure it was sometime in September of 1955."

The shrill ring of the phone broke her conversation.

"I'll be right back. I'm expecting a call from one of my church sisters."

She soon returned, balancing a silver tea tray. She filled two glasses and sat in the chair next to Alana.

"So how's Taurean? I haven't seen him for a few days." The question was unexpected and Alana felt her face flush with embarrassment.

"He's rented a Jeep and has been busy exploring the island. He's gone from early in the morning until late at night. We only catch a glimpse of him sometimes."

Mrs. Gooding stared at her, a thoughtful look on her face. "What's wrong, Alana? Has something happened?"

Alana was not sure what to say. She decided that she'd be honest. She needed someone to talk to and Mrs. Gooding's natural friendliness gave her the confidence to speak.

"Yes, something happened . . . um . . . he kissed me the other night. The night we went out with Anne and Marc."

"So what's the problem? A handsome man kisses you and it affects the two of you in this way?"

"There's more to it than that." She hesitated. "I'm not free."

"You aren't?"

"My ex-husband is a powerful man, and . . . "

Before Alana knew it, tears were flowing from her eyes and she was telling Mrs. Gooding all that had happened. She wanted the other woman to understand.

Instinctively, Mrs. Gooding placed her arms around her and the tears slowly subsided.

"I'm not sure what to do," Alana finished.

"Be honest with Taurean. I'm sure he has his own secrets to share."

Alana thought about it for a while. Mrs. Gooding was right. Taurean did have his secrets. There were so many questions she'd wanted to ask, but she had respected his privacy.

"You're right. I'm going to tell him. He needs to understand."

"Yes, I think that would be best."

At that moment the children raced into the room. They were ready to help again. Alana was glad for the diversion. The reality of Blake was still a very dark shadow hovering on the horizon and she knew that he would be searching for her, if he wasn't already.

But she needed to make things right with Taurean. If not for her sake, she had to do it for Melissa. Taurean deserved better than the way she'd treated him. He'd been the perfect gentleman from the night they'd arrived on the island, and all she'd given him in return was mistrust and rejection.

Maybe it was time to get over her paranoia, and treat the man with the respect he'd always shown her.

Yes, before the night was over she would make things right.

Afternoon had come and Alana sat in a beach chair watching the girls splash and swim in the water. She could tell they were having a good time. She had been surprised how easily Melissa had accepted the twins as her friends. Fortunately, they had come at the right time. Her daughter missed Taurean, but now Melissa was so focused on the girls and the upcoming Kiddies Kadooment, she had not had the time to think about him.

Alana had been surprised when she'd seen the Jeep still parked outside the beach house this morning. She'd grown accustomed to Taurean's disappearing act each day.

In a chair next to her, Mrs. Gooding—no, Bertha, her new friend had insisted—was fast asleep. As soon as she had placed her head on the reclining beach chair, she'd closed her eyes. Occasionally a gentle snore was emitted. Alana laughed softly. She had grown to care for the vibrant, youthful woman.

A fearful scream pierced the air.

"Help, help! Mrs. Alexandra, it's Melissa, she's gone."

Alana jumped up, the cold hand of fear gripping her. Her mouth opened to scream, but the sound stuck in her throat. Instinctively, her feet carried her toward the sea, her eyes searching frantically. She scanned the water, but could not see anything. Then, Melissa's tiny head surged up, a foaming mass of water around her.

Her daughter screamed and then disappeared.

Alana raced toward the sea and plunged in. She couldn't swim, but she refused to let her daughter perish. Beside her, she heard a splash and a dark shadow flashed past her. She wasn't sure what or who it was, but she had to keep going. Her hands started to tire and she felt herself sinking. Her feet touched the seabed. Lifting her head from the water, she realized she'd only gone a short distance. She could easily stand.

Gasping for air, she jumped up and saw Taurean's lithe body swimming in the direction of a body floating on the water. *Please don't let her die. Please God, help her!*

Taurean had grabbed hold of Melissa and was swimming back toward Alana. When he could stand she saw him take her daughter and start to blow into her mouth.

Her arms were tired but she continued to struggle toward them, the water an unnecessary burden, her heart pounding until she could hear every beat in her head. But she kept going. She had to be sure that her daughter was alive.

When she reached them, she watched as Taurean turned Melissa's head to the side and water drained from her mouth and nose. Melissa gasped and her eyes opened. Alana did not know what to do, but she followed Taurean as he walked swiftly out of the water.

Bertha was rushing from the direction of her home when they reached the shore, her eyes wide and startled. She was crying.

"Is she all right?" she asked.

Taurean responded, his voice strained, "I think we should get her to the hospital."

"I have the car ready. I called Marc to get the children. He should be . . . "

Before she could finish, Marc's car was turning into the drive. The car screeched to a stop, pebbles scattering.

Walking swiftly, Taurean carried Melissa to the car. Alana followed, her eyes focused on her daughter, who'd started shivering.

"Mommy, where's my mommy?" The fear in her daughter's voice nearly broke her.

"I'm here, honey," she reassured. She reached out to touch her daughter.

At the car, Alana opened the door. Taurean slipped inside, holding Melissa firmly.

"Let Marc take you to the hospital," Bertha shouted. "I'll stay with the children."

In no time, the car was speeding toward The Queen Elizabeth Hospital. Alana, sitting next to Taurean, watched her daughter quietly, stroking her forehead to comfort her. Melissa was no longer crying. Her eyes were closed, but she was breathing steadily.

Taurean held Melissa tightly, as if he didn't want to let her go. The hands that held her trembled. He was whispering to her softly. Alana could not understand what he was saying, but she was reminded of the incident with the baby bird.

He turned in her direction and she saw the dampness in his eyes. He was crying. This giant of a man was crying for her daughter. She reached over to him and covered his trembling hands with hers. His gaze returned to Melissa and he continued to talk soothingly to the sleeping child.

* * *

When they arrived at the hospital, Melissa was asleep. A nurse rushed toward them, directing Taurean into an examining room, where a doctor quickly began to examine her. Reassured that the doctor would do his best, Taurean led Alana back to the waiting room where Marc sat waiting. He jumped up when he saw them.

"How's she doing?" he asked.

"She's going to be all right," Taurean reassured him.

"Thank God, she's in good hands."

He hesitated for a moment. "I need to get back for the girls. They'll be worried . . . And Mrs. Gooding. Here are my car keys, I'll take the bus back so you won't have to worry about getting home later."

He hugged them both. "She's in good hands," Marc said. Reluctantly, he turned and slowly walked away.

As soon as Marc was out of sight, Alana turned to Taurean. The tears started to fall. "I don't know what I'll do if she dies."

Immediately, Alana felt strong arms fold around her and she took comfort from them. Burying her head in the warmth of his chest, she allowed herself to give in to the grief and worry that threatened to overpower her.

For what seemed like hours, Taurean held her, stroking her hair tenderly. The constant rhythm was soothing and comforting.

"Mr. and Mrs. Alexander?"

Alana slipped from Taurean's arms as they both rose.

"Yes." Alana was the first to reply. In the back of her mind, she'd heard the doctor's mistake, but, focused on finding out her daughter's condition, she didn't correct him.

"Is Melissa all right?" she asked.

"Yes, she's going to be fine. She's awake and wants to see you. Follow me." His voice was gentle and reassuring.

"Come with me, Taurean."

He took the hand she held out and together they followed the doctor, both aware of the sense of dread that filled the silent corridor. She'd never liked hospitals, associating them with the death of her parents and the few times she'd "fallen" and had her so-called "accidents."

At the end of the corridor, the doctor entered a room. A nurse was sitting talking to Melissa. When Melissa saw them, she smiled weakly.

"I'm sorry, Mommy."

Alana rushed to her and took her in her arms.

"Mommy, I'm sorry I didn't obey you. I wanted to prove to Karen and Kelly that I'm a good swimmer. They told me not to go so far out. I just wanted them to like me more."

"But, sweetheart, they like you." She drew her daughter closer.

"I know but I wanted to impress them." Tears pooled in Melissa's eyes.

"Oh, honey, you don't need to impress people when they already like you," Alana said gently. "You just have to be yourself."

Alana turned to the doctor. "Is she going to be all right? When can she go home?"

"I'm going to keep her in for observation overnight. In the morning, I'll make a decision. You can both stay with her overnight. I'll get a nurse to take you to one of the rooms we provide for parents. We prefer you to be nearby."

"Thank you, Doctor." Alana heard herself reply.

As the doctor walked away, the reality of what he'd said sunk in.

He'd said a "room." Was she going to have to spend a night sleeping in the same room with Taurean?

How on earth was she going to handle it?

Taurean stepped into the room and closed the door behind them. The nurse had taken them directly there when Melissa finally fell asleep.

He surveyed the room. Good, there were twin beds, so they didn't have to sleep next to each other. Relief washed over him and he realized that Alana, too, had noticeably relaxed. He watched as she headed to the bed closer to a window.

"I'll take the bed over here," he said, pointing to the bed farthest from the room's single window. A stupid comment since she already stood by the other, but the silence made him uncomfortable and he could think of nothing else to say.

"Do you want me to get you something to eat? he asked. "You only ate the salad from the cafeteria this afternoon."

"Thank you, but I'm fine," Alana replied. "I'm really not hungry. I just feel a bit tired and have a slight headache. I'm going to get some sleep."

With that she slipped off her shoes and headed toward a door to the left of her bed which must have been the bathroom.

She entered, closed the door.

By habit, he walked to the window, needing to see the outside. Even here in the hospital, the familiar desire to move beyond the confines of the four walls overwhelmed him.

Traffic moved along the road just beyond the hospital's gardens. He could not see much but the jagged line of dimmed headlights moving swiftly along. In the late evening, the cars were probably transporting city workers eager to reach the comfort of their homes.

The bathroom door opened, and Alana reappeared. She'd taken her hair down, and the flowery scent of soap tickled his nose.

"Fortunately, there're disposable toothbrushes in the bathroom, so you can freshen up," she informed him.

He nodded and moved toward the bathroom. He took his time brushing his teeth, giving her time to settle down.

When he returned to the room, Alana had already slipped between the covers, her eyes closed.

Turning the lights off, he crawled between the covers, hoping that he too could get some rest. He knew sleep wouldn't come easily. Hospitals were definitely on his list of "Least Favorite Places To Be" and the association with Corey and prison did not help. He hated the overpowering scent of illness and death that permeated the air.

And then he heard it.

A sniffle.

A sob.

Alana was crying.

Unsure of what to do, he continued to listen. Should he say something? Would she be embarrassed if she knew he could hear her?

"Alana, what's wrong?"

At first she didn't answer and then her voice came to him, sad and in despair.

"I don't know what I'd have done if she'd died. She's the only thing I have. The only constant in my life."

"But she's all right now, Alana. Don't dwell on what could have happened. She's alive."

"I remember when she was born." Her voice was heavy, loaded with emotion. "Blake wasn't even there. He was at a conference. But when I held Melissa in my arms for the first time, I felt as if God had given me a most precious gift."

She paused. More sniffles.

"She was the most beautiful baby I've ever seen. She just stared at me with those big brown eyes and I fell in love. I knew I'd do anything in my power to protect her from all that was bad in my life."

"I can tell she was a beautiful baby."

"I remember her first step, her first word, the first time she said 'Mama.' She took a long time to talk, but when she got started, there was no stopping her. Boy, could she talk! And the questions. She just wanted to know about everything."

"Yes, I've definitely experienced the talking part. You should be proud. You've done a good job of raising her. She's a lovely child."

"I wonder what she's doing now. She's not accustomed to being by herself."

"I'm sure she is fine, Alana. You shouldn't be worried. The doctor promised someone would call if she needed you. You need to get some sleep."

"I know. Can you come here next to me? Just until I go to sleep?"

For the second time that night, he didn't know what to say, but she needed him.

He couldn't refuse.

Rising from the bed, he wondered if he was about to make a stupid mistake.

He slipped onto the bed, remaining on the covers. He moved closer, wrapping his arms around her. Sparks charged, and immediately, an awareness of her proximity tensed his body.

Time ticked by and his body slowly hardened, the inevitability of arousal.

Alana shifted, her body moving closer, her lips almost touching his. And then he felt it. The softest of kisses, a whisper, a warm breeze. His body responded, his breathing quickened and he captured her willing lips between his teeth before placing his mouth on hers.

For what seemed like hours, he enjoyed the taste of her. But the simple pleasure built up to an intense wildness inside, and he felt that he could not get enough of her.

And then he was pushing her away.

Damn, I must be sick. The woman had almost lost her daughter and here he was taking advantage of her.

"I'm sorry, I didn't mean that to happen," she said, her voice filled with regret.

"I'm the one who should be sorry. I'm going to leave the room for a while. I need to get some fresh air. You get some sleep. I'll be back."

Quickly, he rose from the bed. He needed to get away. To cool the smoldering fire that had again heated his body until he was delirious with his wanting for Alana.

He could feel her eyes on him, but he had no intention of looking back. He just wanted to get away.

He slipped from the room, closed the door behind him, and moved slowly down the empty corridors. Hospitals were too much like morgues during the night.

A few minutes later, he stood outside Melissa's room. Maybe spending the rest of the night here was the best thing. He'd been glad the nurse allowed him to enter after he promised not to wake the child.

Melissa lay asleep.

He lowered himself into the chair next to her bed. Looking at her, no one would ever think she'd almost lost her life. Her face broke into a smile. Yes, she was traveling somewhere in dreamland.

He'd understood exactly what Alana meant when she said she'd have lost it all if he'd not rescued Melissa. This little girl now played an integral part in his life. He loved her as if she were his own. Now, he thanked God that he'd stayed at home and not gone on one of his island safaris.

He closed his eyes, willing the drowsiness before sleep to come. His mind wanted to go a place where he preferred not to at this time.

To dwell on Alana and that kiss would surely take him to that place of sweet torment he visited regularly whenever an image of her flashed in his mind's eye.

No, he needed to get some sleep.

His final thought before he succumbed to the tiredness in his body an hour later had everything to do with the woman who'd somehow stolen his heart and mind.

Melissa opened her eyes and for a moment she panicked. Where was she?

She glanced around, coming to rest on the man who sat in there.

Taurean.

He was asleep.

All that had happened during the day came back to her. Now, she remembered what had taken place. She'd nearly drowned and Taurean had saved her. She'd been so scared when she swallowed all that water and couldn't breathe. She was never, ever going into the water again.

OK, she was never, ever going back into the water unless Taurean was there.

She'd known that he'd come and save her. When she was under the water she'd asked God to help her and then she'd heard Taurean's voice and knew everything would be all right.

She wondered where her mother was. Maybe she'd gone back to the house. But, no, she knew her mother would never leave her.

She glanced at Taurean where he lay asleep. He looked kind of funny with his mouth wide open.

She smiled.

Taurean made her smile and she loved him. He didn't treat her like a stupid kid. He always listened to whatever she had to say without making her feel like a baby as most people she knew. And Karen and Kerry liked him too. He made them laugh all the time.

She wished he were her daddy. When she told her two best friends she wanted Taurean to be her new daddy, they'd agreed to help her. They'd taught her so many things about the island and suggested they go on the Internet to find out a bit about obeah magic. Then they'd work a spell on Taurean and her mommy.

But she did not agree. She wanted Taurean to love her mommy for just being who she was. If she worked a spell maybe it could wear off, and that would be trouble.

No, she was going to tell Karen and Kerry about her real plan.

She was just going to be a matchmaker.

Then maybe they'd learn to love each other.

She already knew she loved Taurean and she hadn't needed any of the obeah thing. Sometimes her friends were just too crazy.

Well, she'd just stay awake for a little while and imagine that Taurean was her daddy and just sitting there to protect her because she was ill.

Yes, he'd make a perfect daddy.

The drive home the next evening was quiet. Marc had left the car as he'd promised and for that Taurean was grateful. Melissa had immediately fallen asleep.

The silence in the car was stifling, the tension crackling like static energy. For some reason, Taurean didn't know what to say. The memory of what had happened the night before flashed in his mind, and he knew the image of Alana lying on the bed, her lips full from his kisses, would be forever in his mind.

He glanced at Alana, noticing the rigid line of her back while her hands gripped the side of her seat.

She turned her head toward him.

Their eyes met, sparked, lingered.

She turned away, her skin flushed.

He wanted to say something, wanted to reassure her, but she spoke first.

"I'm sorry about what happened last night," she whispered.

"There's nothing to be sorry about, Alana." He wanted to ease the embarrassment she felt. "You needed someone to comfort you. I was glad to be there for you. Why should you apologize for a kiss both of us wanted?"

Alana didn't respond and when he glanced at her again, her eyes were closed, her brow lined, her thoughts private. He wished he could get inside her head in order to understand how she felt. Sometimes her emotions lay exposed and bare for all to see, while at other times, a thin veil hid each subtle change.

He knew she experienced the same jolt of electricity, that same spark of fire that burned deep inside the core of his soul and refused to be put out. He wanted to know if it was more than just a physical thing and if she was slowly falling in love too.

He wanted to ask her, but it would only be a mistake to ask at this time.

When the car pulled up outside the house, Taurean took Melissa from Alana.

Leading the way into the house, he carried Melissa up the stairs and entered her bedroom. He placed her on the bed, gazing at her as she slept.

He turned to Alana and saw the depth of gratitude reflected in her eyes. Overcome by emotion, he opened his arms and she slipped into them. For a long time they stood there, gazing at the sleeping child.

Awareness of her softness came, her gentle curves stirring feelings he'd tried to put under control for the past week. Her closeness and the soft apple scent of her hair tickled his nostrils, and he felt the stirring of arousal. He inhaled deeply, wanting to savor the moment.

Gently, he stepped away. "I'll go down and call Mrs. Gooding. Let her know that we're back home." He turned to leave.

When he entered the kitchen, he headed straight for the phone. He quickly called Mrs. Gooding and informed her that everything was fine.

Next, he prepared supper, glad for the activity. They'd eaten at the hospital cafeteria during the day. Now he wanted some palatable food.

She'd surprised him. Despite their brief discussion in the car, she'd come willingly to his arms just now. It had been difficult to leave her. All he'd wanted to do was keep her in his arms, feeling her softness, comforting her.

He forced her image from his mind.

Methodically, he started the meal. He chopped vegetables, peeled potatoes and dropped them into the saucepan. He added spices and sprinkled salt. Soon, the soup was simmering.

Switching the small television on, he sat staring at it, troubled by what had transpired over the past few weeks.

Without warning, he started to tremble. Unexpected tears flowed from his eyes and it was then that he realized how much Melissa meant to him. He had grown to love the little girl and his trips around the island had left him with a sense of emptiness. He enjoyed their days on the beach and he wondered what would have happened if he had gone on one of his expeditions that day. He was glad that the Jeep had broken down. It had baffled him, when he could not find anything wrong with the vehicle.

The thought that Melissa could have drowned weighed heavy on his heart. He would not have been there to save her. He had been acting like a child, allowing his feelings to push Melissa and Alana away.

The hours that he'd spent with Alana while Melissa slept had made him realize how much he cared for her. He'd enjoyed knowing she'd needed him, was depending on him. When Alana had come to Melissa's hospital room the next morning, she'd awakened him. Her face bore no evidence of what had transpired in the room. But he'd seen the spark of heat in her eyes. The kiss had affected her.

He'd sat nearby while Alana talked to Melissa, occasionally glancing in his direction, her face expressionless.

Of course, their encounter in the hospital bed may have affected him more than he wanted. Each time he saw her, he ached to kiss her again, wanted to take her in his arms and feel her arch against him.

When the doctor had finally examined Melissa and said she could be taken home, a wave of disappointment had washed over him. Alana no longer needed his shoulders, his comfort.

The reality was that he loved Alana.

Loved her more than he loved himself.

He wanted to protect her and take her fears away. He wanted to hear her laugh and share in her joys. He wanted to hold her at night and make long, deep, passionate love to her.

He wanted to see her swollen with his child.

Taurean leapt from the chair, amazed at the wonder of his discovery.

He walked over to the window and looked out. In the distance, he saw the light from Mrs. Gooding's house and saw the figure at the window. He could not see her clearly, but could tell she had seen him and waved. He waved back, experiencing that sense of familiarity again.

Like life, the island held its mysteries. So many things intrigued him about the island and the current path of his life. He had no idea where he would be tomorrow or two years from now.

But now was more important.

Somehow, he'd been given a second chance to live.

And he knew life was going to be all right.

CHAPTER 7

No one and nothing stirred in the house. Taurean had expected that Alana and Melissa would be asleep. He'd slept all day and into the early hours of the evening. The stress of spending two days at the hospital in close proximity to Alana was taking its toll.

He glanced at the clock next to his bed. It was about ten o'clock and all the lights were off. He crept downstairs and turned them on.

He needed to get out of the house. He needed air. He felt stifled, trapped. Memories of prison slammed into him.

The moon shone bright. In a few nights, it would be at its fullest. He strolled along the beach, absorbing the velvet tranquillity. The thought came to him. The water would soothe him. He felt daring, adventurous. Why not? There was no one around. Alana and Melissa were asleep and the lights in Mrs. Gooding's house were off, so he could take his swim.

He slipped off his clothes and let them drop to the sand. The night breeze blew soft, cooling his heated body. He stepped into the water, slowly lowering himself into its chilly silkiness.

Floating on his back, he gazed at the starlit sky. Millions of tiny diamonds twinkled. A star, tired of its stationary position, shot toward earth. What could he wish for? Alana popped into his mind. He was not surprised. She was in his every waking thought. He sighed in frustration. He needed to put her out of his mind completely and permanently.

For a while he floated, absorbing the music of the tropical paradise. Deliberately, he blocked everything from his mind and soon all he saw in his mind's eye was a black, endless void.

                                    * * *

Alana glanced at the clock on the bureau. It was just after ten o'clock. They'd slept since returning from the hospital. She looked into Melissa's room and found her still sleeping. Maybe now was the time she should talk to Taurean. He had saved her daughter's life and she owed him an explanation for her actions.

She knocked on his door. No one answered. The door was ajar. She pushed it and looked inside. He wasn't there. He was probably watching television.

She walked downstairs, calling his name.

No answer. She strolled outside.

The moon was bright, but tall palm trees lining the beach blocked her view, so she could not tell whether he was there or not. Instinct told her not to go any farther, but she kept on walking anyway. As she neared the trees, she heard the consistent splash of movement in the water. Someone was swimming.

She knew it was Taurean.

Concealed behind a tree, she watched him swim leisurely around in a circle, his long arms not seeming to tire. Finally, he stopped and stood, walking in her direction. She was about to call his name when she saw him clearly.

Taurean was naked.

And magnificent.

Moonlight caressed his massive frame from his broad shoulders to his well-toned legs. Her eyes feasted on him, unable to look away. Her body shivered, reacting to its rapid build of desire. Her gaze trailed down his hairy chest to the flat ridges of his stomach, and down lower to his manhood. Her breathing quickened, and she forced herself to look away. An image of him lying on top of her flashed in her mind. Unable to control her need to see him, she looked toward the sea.

Taurean had reached the sand, and bent to pick up something from the ground. He did not put it on but turned toward the sea, his tight, round behind exposed to her devouring gaze. She had to go. The white-hot desire that the sight of his naked body had awakened erupted, and the heat within threatened to consume her. Sweat trickled down her face. If Taurean asked her to make love, she could not refuse him. She wanted him. The guilt that she had felt the day before no longer bothered her. She knew that by making love to Taurean, she'd be under his spell, could easily want to give herself to him. A tropical bird screeched and Taurean turned in her direction. Alana lay against the tree, hoping he wouldn't see her.

He finally pulled his pants on and slowly walked toward the house, but not before she heard his words echo on the wind.

"What am I going to do?"

* * *

She slipped quietly into the house, and started up the stairs. Halfway up, she heard footsteps on the landing above her, and then the quiet closing of a door. She knew it was Taurean.

As she passed the bathroom, she heard the shower running. An image of Taurean's masculinity flashed in her mind, vivid and real. His nakedness had affected her more than she wanted it to. She stifled the overwhelming urge to join him. Placing her forehead against the door, she closed her eyes, feeling the heat surge within, needing the coolness of the water she knew would be trickling down his . . .

She pushed away from the door when she heard the water stop. Moving quickly, she entered her room, closing the door behind her, placing her back against it. She was breathing quickly, the heat spreading all over. What was she doing to herself? She was behaving like a sex-starved teenager.

She glanced toward the bed. Melissa was still sleeping but Alana was too keyed up to rest. Not sleepy, she decided to return downstairs and watch television. A good movie was one of her weaknesses. She needed to do something to take her mind off what she'd seen tonight. For a while, she listened, waiting for the sound of his bedroom door closing. She didn't want to make things worse by meeting him with a skimpy towel wrapped around him. The sound came and she moved quickly.

In the family room, she flopped on the couch, and flicked through *TV Guide*. *Ghost* was on Channel 8. She switched on the television. This movie would be perfect to purge *his* raw image from her mind. The movie was almost halfway over but she had seen it many times before and knew the story by heart. Soon, she was caught up in the beauty of the story.

There was a noise and she turned and saw Taurean standing under the archway. He had changed into a white shirt and black shorts that reached down to his knees. Water glistened in his hair. Damn, what was he trying to do to her?

"Hi, what are you watching?"

"*Ghost*," she replied. It was almost a strain to speak. Sexy was the word that came to mind.

"*Ghost?*" he asked, a single brow lifting.

"Yes, *Ghost*. A picture with Demi Moore, Patrick Swayze, and Whoopie Goldberg. It was nominated for an Academy Award."

"Don't think I've ever seen it."

"I'm sorry," she said. She felt sad for him. So much of the world must have passed him by in prison.

He slid onto the couch next to her and asked, "Mind if I join you?"

"I'm not sure if you'd like the movie. It's maybe a bit too romantic for you."

He laughed, eyes flashing with humor. "I can enjoy a little romance like anyone else." He drew closer, eyes focused on the television.

For the next hour, she sat quietly, occasionally responding to his questions about the plot or joining his deep laughter at the antics of the delightful Goldberg.

But she was totally aware of his presence; the image of his naked body was locked in her mind. Despite this, for the first time in weeks, she felt relaxed in his company. She was no longer afraid of him.

When the credits scrolled up the screen, she felt his gaze on her. Embarrassed by the tears she knew were pooled in her eyes, she refused to turn toward him. A deep chuckle forced her to turn.

"What are you laughing at? The movie was touching."

"OK, it was! I should have expected you to cry. Don't all females cry at movies like this?"

She continued to look at him, an unexpected joy bubbling inside. When she burst into laughter, the stunned expression on his face was indication enough that he thought she was going crazy. His deep, husky laugh blended with hers.

Finally under control, she decided the time was right. She had to tell him before she lost her courage.

"Taurean, there are some things I need to tell you. Maybe they will explain my reaction and behavior. I didn't want to hurt you the other night."

He said nothing, so she continued.

"It's my ex-husband. I left the U.S. because he's been stalking me, still trying to control my life. I couldn't handle it any more. For a while, I didn't have the strength to fight back. He's big, like you, strong." She paused, the familiar stab of pain in her chest.

"A few nights before we left, he broke into the house, and when I asked him to leave and attempted to call the police, he beat me. Melissa woke up and heard what was going on, and came downstairs. She jumped on him and he struck her. It was the first time he'd ever hit her. It was then that I knew I had to get us away. I'd blamed myself for what had happened to our marriage. Eventually I stopped blaming myself and told him he needed to get help, and that I wanted a divorce. It took me two years to accumulate enough information on him to force him to give me what I wanted, but those years were hell."

She paused again. Telling Taurean was not as easy as she thought. The pain of Blake's abuse was like a festering wound, raw and exposed. Tears stung her eyes. She did not want to cry, but the trickle of dampness seemed to have a mind of its own.

"Paula gave me a solution and I decided it was the best thing to do. I realize now that I can't live like this. I'm going to have to confront Blake sometime, but I needed this summer to be strong. I'm scared of what he can do, but I'm no longer afraid of him. I don't want to run for the rest of my life."

Taurean was silent, thoughtful, his face devoid of expression.

But when he spoke, his voice was strained, angry. "I think I realized what was happening. I knew there was a man involved, but I thought maybe he'd died and you were recovering. Why didn't you get help from the police?"

"Blake is a powerful man, a U.S. senator. He's also from one of the oldest, most powerful families in Reading, Pennsylvania. His father has a lot of friends in high places. I had to do it myself."

"So he's probably searching for you right now?"

She trembled at the thought, but knew it was a reality.

"Yes, I'm sure he is. But I made sure that our tracks were well covered. We changed our names and didn't come directly here but went to Jamaica first."

"If he's as powerful as you say he is, he'll find you."

The truth of what he said sunk in, but surprisingly Alana felt no fear. For some reason, she knew that with Taurean's support and friendship, she could stand up to Blake.

"I'm no longer afraid of him, but I'm not sure I'm ready to face him yet. I'm afraid for Melissa. I can't let him take her away."

"Alana, there's no need for either of you to be afraid. I'm here." She saw the determination in his strong jaw, in the cold steeliness of his eyes.

She heard the sincerity in his voice. He meant every word he said. The implication of his comment was not lost, but she preferred not to dwell on it for the moment.

For a while, she sat quietly, allowing him to internalize what she had said. He was quiet, contemplative.

"I killed my brother." She almost didn't hear his whispered statement.

"I killed my brother," he repeated his words, this time louder, a cry of intense anguish. "Corey."

She wanted to reach out and touch him, comfort him, but all she did was look at him, unsure of what to say. For the briefest of moments, an image of Blake came to mind, brutal, murder in his eyes. But immediately, she erased it. Taurean was nothing like Blake. The man before her was grieving. She did not know what had happened with his brother, but somehow she knew Taurean was not a murderer. Knew it as well as she knew the sun would rise in the morning. She looked at him, feeling his pain.

"He had AIDS and was dying. He asked me to pull the life support, to help him. He couldn't bear the suffering anymore."

Taurean's voice cracked. "You should have seen him. He was in so much pain. So frail. He'd been a track and field athlete. Strong. Tall. He looked at me with those sunken eyes and said, 'Taurean, help me please.'

I couldn't bear to see him in pain. I gave him his wish, and spent the last seven years in prison because of it."

As he spoke, he started to cry. Throwing caution to the wind, she pulled him gently to her, laying his head next to her breasts. Her arms wrapped around him while his body shook. An anguished cry tore from deep within him, and she realized that he must have suffered while in prison. She held him while the guilt he had lived with for years poured from his tormented soul. She whispered soft words of comfort, wanting to take away his pain and purge his tortured mind.

She cared for him. And if she allowed herself to, she could learn to love this big, gentle creature with the harsh exterior.

For a long time, he lay there, not saying a word. She felt his breathing quicken and realized that he was affected by the closeness of their bodies. She wanted to kiss him and she boldly did. Lifting his head, she pulled him toward her, tenderly placing her lips on his. Like a hungry butterfly, she sipped softly from him.

She pulled him closer and heard his sharp intake of breath. Their gazes met, and she saw the shock in his eyes.

"I'll be gentle with you," she said with a smile. "I just want to kiss you without feeling guilty and without any lies between us. Last night you wanted to comfort me. Now, it's my turn."

He didn't need another invitation before he placed his lips on hers. His gentleness surprised her. The yearning inside her was wild, intense. The kiss deepened, a hint of desperation blazed between them. Alana reveled in his onslaught, knowing he wanted her. Her confidence in his need made her bold. When his tongue parted her lips, she blossomed willingly, wanting to taste more of him. Their tongues touched and he suckled on hers.

Liquid fire surged through her, its heat intense, igniting the most delicious flame inside. She rubbed her body wantonly against him.

He pushed her away.

She looked up at him dazed, feeling empty, disappointed by his sudden absence.

When he spoke, she heard the regret. "Alana, neither of us is ready for this. There are too many unresolved issues that we need to take care of. I want you. More than I've wanted any other woman. But not like this; not when we need to take care of the things that continue to haunt us."

And then he put his arms around her, kissing her on the top of her head.

She felt safe. Snuggling up to him, she closed her eyes.

Taurean watched her as her breathing slowed. She looked relaxed, as if there was not a care in the world, but he knew that so much had to happen between them before she learned to trust again, and he wanted— no, needed—her to trust him.

* * *

The phone rang. Blake continued to let it ring. Who the hell was calling at this time of night? He tossed the picture of Alana he'd been holding across the bedroom. When it struck the wall and the glass shattered, he felt the hot rush of pleasure.

"Yes," he snapped. He was in no mood to be polite.

"Senator, it's me. I've found her."

Another rush of pleasure.

"Where is she?"

"She's staying on the island of Barbados. In a beach house on the south coast of the island."

"Where are you now?"

"I'm staying in a beach house close by."

"I want you to watch her for a few days and then call me back. I'm not ready to get her yet."

He put the phone down, glancing around the room where just weeks ago he'd beaten her violently.

It felt empty.

Anger boiled inside him as his gaze rested on the prim white robe Alana wore at night still draped over a chair. She would sit in front of the mirror, the brush slowly taking long strokes through the hair that reached to just past her shoulders. Often, while they were still married, he'd watch her, the nightly ritual having the most sensual effect on him.

He trembled, imagining her lying beneath him, the room suddenly growing warm. He missed the soft silky feel of her skin. He remembered how he would bury his face in her hair and cry out with the intensity of his release, inhaling the fresh apple scent of the shampoo she used.

Blake closed his eyes, quelling the desire to get on the first plane and fly to Barbados. He had to plan. He just couldn't rush it. Yes, he had to be cautious. On the island, he wouldn't be able to call in any favors. In a few days he'd go to Barbados and bring Alana back with him. The key was Melissa. He would get her first and everything else would fall into place.

He laughed loudly. He was enjoying the game. And it would be a game. He needed a vacation, and why not enjoy some tropical sunshine while he was there. Maybe a voluptuous tropical maiden, too.

He moved to pick up the phone, but decided against it. His father could wait. He would go to the island first and when he returned with Alana, his father would be proud of him.

He stripped off his clothes and slipped into bed, his body hard in anticipation of what he would do to her.

CHAPTER 8

Taurean felt the softness of the pillow next to him and snuggled closer. The pillow felt strange, softer, and smelled of warm raspberries on a winter night. He reluctantly opened his eyes, not wanting to emerge from the laziness of sleep. It was not a pillow on which his head rested but the gentle mounds of a woman's breasts.

Alana's breasts.

Images of the night before flashed in his mind and he realized they had fallen asleep on the couch in front of the television. He snuggled closer, reluctant to move. It was perfect waking next to her. The woman who'd somehow chipped away at the ice around his heart. And she hadn't even set out to do that.

What they had talked about last night came to mind and he felt a hot anger at the man who had been her husband. There was no need for her to be afraid anymore. He would protect her and Melissa. He would help them to be rid of Blake Smyth-Connell and then he was going to marry her. How was he going to do that? He didn't have a job, didn't have any money, and society would always see him as a murderer.

But he intended to do it. He was going to find a job. He was an experienced accountant. Maybe he could settle on the island and find a job. He knew it would be difficult, but he could try.

If not on the island, perhaps another place. Patrick would help him. He would prefer to do this on his own, but reality demanded that he forget his stubborn pride and take the help Patrick had offered.

Alana stirred and he looked at her. Asleep, she was lovelier, her face relaxed, void of the emotional stress that was evident when she was awake and which she carried like a heavy burden. The lines of worry he often saw on her forehead were not there. Her lips were soft and succulent. He hardened with the memory of the passion that had flared between them.

He watched as she slowly emerged from slumber. Her first expression, when her eyes flickered open, was one of disorientation, then surprise, and finally embarrassment.

"Good morning," she said, a hand flicking bangs from before her eyes.

She began to noticeably relax. He wanted to put her at ease. "Don't worry, I'm feeling a bit embarrassed, too. Did you sleep well?"

He knew that he sounded silly, but he could think of nothing else to say.

"No, I didn't. You snored all night," she teased. Her response surprised him. She seemed different, playful.

At the expression on his face, she smiled. "Just kidding. I slept like a log. It's time I got up and checked on Melissa. I don't think either of us would want her to see us like this."

With that she uncurled herself from around him, eyes averted. She slipped off the couch and turned to leave. Before she reached the archway, she stopped.

"Thanks for sharing what you did with me," she said. "It must have been difficult."

"No, it wasn't as difficult as I thought. You're a good listener—the first woman to see me cry."

"I'm honored," she responded, but the glint in her eyes showed her concern.

"I'll be just fine. I'm a big boy now." He felt an unexpected pleasure at the sadness in her eyes.

"Well, I definitely must go and check on Melissa. Today is the parade rehearsal and she needs to get up early. I'm going to have to call Mrs. Gooding to ask her what time we need to be ready."

"Take your time. I'll prepare breakfast. Pancakes."

She nodded and walked out of the living room, the soft sway of her hips sending his hormones racing like a randy teenager. What was he going to do?

When Alana entered the bedroom, she found Melissa propped up in bed and engrossed in the latest installment of the American Girl series, featuring the delightful heroine Addy.

"Hi, sweetheart. Reading already? How're you feeling?"

"I'm feeling better, Mommy. My head's not hurting anymore."

"So does that mean you can go to the rehearsal for the Kiddies' Kadooment? If you're not feeling well enough we can stay at home."

"No, we have to go. If we don't I won't know what to do on Saturday at the parade. Didn't the doctor say I'm all right now?"

"Yes, he did. Well, you've got to get up soon. Bertha is picking up Anne and the girls first."

She reached for the phone on the bureau and punched in Bertha's number. Alana felt strange calling her Bertha, after weeks of "Mrs. Gooding," but their neighbor had insisted.

While it rang, she watched Melissa leave the bed and enter the bathroom. She smiled to herself. Just a few days ago she couldn't get the child up to go to church.

Bertha's cheerful voice came over the line.

"Hi, Bertha, it's Alana. Just called to ask you what time I need to be ready?"

"Oh, I'll be there in about two hours. I'll call Anne and let her know I'll pick her and the girls up first. Marc's gone to Trinidad on business."

"Believe it or not, Melissa is already awake, so we'll be ready."

Bertha laughed. "Melissa's up? She must be really excited about Kiddies' Kadooment."

"Yes, it's all she's been talking about for the past week."

"Well, I'm sure she's going to enjoy herself. I'll see you in about two hours."

Alana replaced the receiver and turned to Melissa.

"Melissa, we're going to have to start getting ready. Breakfast first. Taurean says he's making pancakes. We have two hours to get ready. You don't want to be late, do you?"

Alana left the room and headed downstairs for the kitchen, when the phone rang again. She picked it up and a male voice asked for Taurean. She shouted for him and he came running, a frilly white apron flapping around his hips.

Damn, what was he trying to do to her? A man wasn't supposed to look sexy in an apron. But he did.

She placed the phone in his hands and walked quickly toward the kitchen. Breakfast was already on the table. Maybe eating would take her mind off him.

She was finishing her meal when he returned. He looked at her, his eyes dull, sad. She could tell that something was wrong. Before she could ask, strained words tumbled from his quivering lips.

"My father had a heart attack last night. Patrick and my mother want me to come home. He doesn't have much longer."

"Oh, Taurean, I'm sorry." She moved toward him, wanting to comfort, but unsure of his reaction.

"It's all right. Patrick has already made reservations on a flight that leaves at one. I need to leave as soon as possible. I was lucky he could get a flight. Few people leave the island around this time. No one likes to miss Crop Over."

He turned to walk away, but stopped when he reached the archway. "I'll take the Jeep I rented to the airport. The rental company has a pick-up at the airport so I won't have to worry about that. I'll go pack what I need."

She nodded and he quickly left.

She watched as he walked away, knowing the pain he must feel. She'd seen it in his eyes from the moment he'd entered the room.

Strangely enough, she'd learned to read him, his changing mood, despite the often cool exterior. Under the surface, the heart of a strong but sensitive man beat to the rhythm of life.

Just as Taurean departed, Melissa raced into the room.

"What's for breakfast? I'm hungry." She looked around. "Where's Taurean, Mom?"

"He's upstairs packing. His dad has taken ill and he has to go home."

"He can't go. Mom, don't let him go." She heard the anguish in her daughter's voice, echoing her own inner feelings. Melissa started to cry.

"Melissa, he needs to be with his dad right now."

"Why? Dads only hurt you."

A sharp pain tore through Alana's stomach. She walked over to Melissa, slipping her arms around her. "Melissa, all dads aren't like yours. Do you think that if Taurean was your dad he would hurt you?"

For a moment Melissa was silent. "No," she finally replied.

Taurean walked into the room just then. Melissa rushed to him, flinging her arms around him tightly. Taurean held her close.

"Lissa, I have to go."

Reluctantly, she released him. "Are you coming back?"

"Of course, I'm coming back. Who's going to teach you to swim and help you collect thousands of shells?"

"You promise?" She stared at him intently.

"I promise." He bent to her, placing a kiss on her forehead. "I promise," he repeated.

He turned to Alana and mouthed the same words.

Holding Melissa's hand, he walked to the door. Bending he kissed her again and said, "I'll be back."

Alana watched as the car pulled away, her daughter waving until it disappeared.

For the briefest moment, Alana questioned his promise, but immediately, she rejected the doubt. The calm steady look in his eyes had glistened with honesty. He would be back.

* * *

The jet touched down at O'Hare on a wet Illinois evening. Taurean looked out his window, seeing the familiar white structure, but not feeling the satisfaction that he knew came from coming home. He unbuckled his seatbelt and picked up the only bag he carried. He did not intend to stay long. He knew that his visit would not be a happy one. He was an outsider.

In a daze, he went through the usual routine. Cleared immigration, then Customs and soon he stood outside waiting for whoever would pick him up.

"Taurean!"

A woman's voice. A petite woman was waving at him. Paula. He walked slowly over to her, a smile on his lips. He liked Paula. Who wouldn't? She was a cheerful, generous soul. He was glad to see her. She'd been kind to him when he'd stayed with her and his brother after being released from prison.

When he reached Paula, her arms locked around him. By this simple action, he knew she wanted him to know she cared. Despite the chilly air, her concern warmed him, and he felt disappointed when she moved away.

"It's nice to have you back in the U.S. Patrick is in the car. He's parked illegally. Didn't want to pay to go to the parking lot. You know your brother. Always in a hurry."

For a moment, she stopped and turned to look at him. "We really missed you, Taurean. Patrick was worried about you. But you look better. More relaxed."

He heard the sincerity. Felt her love.

"I'm better. Healing." He wanted to be honest with her. "The guilt is no longer there. I just need my family to forgive me."

She gazed at him with the glimmer of tears in her eyes.

"Come, let's go. Patrick is waiting," she said, holding his free hand. "He's anxious to get back to the house. I'm glad Oak Park is only a few miles from Chicago. Your mother called us early this morning, so we rushed right over. Your father has refused to go to the hospital. He says he wants to die at home."

They strolled to the white convertible purring in the no parking zone. Patrick sat in the car, his body tense and ready for departure. His eyes flicked from left to right, anticipating a policeman's arrival. On seeing his brother and wife, he revved the car engine, poised for escape.

"Come, there's a cop coming. I don't want to have to circle again." Laughter erupted from him.

A warm feeling filled Taurean. This was definitely Patrick. Fun-loving, crazy. Just like Paula. He never ceased to be amazed at how perfect they were for each other.

Taurean quickly slipped into the front seat, almost falling as Patrick pulled into the moving traffic. He heard Paula squeal in protest. Soon, the car sped swiftly along the highway.

"So how's my little brother? Met any beautiful island women?"

"Yes, I've met two of the most beautiful women in the world."

Paula touched him on the shoulder. "Sorry about that, Taurean. Patrick forgot to tell me where you were going, and when Alana needed my help, I just told her to go. I was away on business."

"It was no problem. Everything worked out just fine. Paula, I need to talk to you about her later," he said over his shoulder. Then turned to his brother. "How's Dad?"

"He's not doing too well. The doctor says it's just a matter of time. Dad's been sick for a while, but never told anyone. Not even Mother." He paused. "He keeps asking for you."

"For me? I wonder why?" Taurean heard the bitterness in his voice and felt ashamed. His father lay dying and he thought only of himself.

For a moment, silence filled the car's interior.

"How's Mom holding up?"

"Oh, she's trying to be brave, but I know she's having a hard time. She seems to be in control as usual, but she's hurting. She misses you."

Again, Taurean felt the rush of resentment. How could she miss him, when she had not been there for him when he'd needed her most?

The words of the pastor at Bertha's church came to mind. *In order to be forgiven, one must be willing to forgive.* The words had haunted him for weeks and now the reality of them struck him. He needed to forgive his parents.

The car turned into the familiar driveway. The stark white house was devoid of any frills. Practical, but it had been home. There had once been a cozy warmth inside. Despite his father's strictness, Taurean had never doubted that their father loved them. Their mother had created a home of love and laughter.

A fear as consuming as fire flared inside him. This was the first time he'd been home since his arrest for murder. The memories of Corey flashed in his mind and he saw his brothers, all four of them, running in the garden, kicking a soccer ball, and tumbling and stumbling with each other. Those had been happy days.

And he had destroyed them.

Patrick drove the car into the garage. A door that led into the house burst open and a tall, graceful woman stood in the opening.

"Mom," he heard himself cry out. The memories began to tumble in on him and he needed to have her arms around him, but knew it wouldn't happen.

He slipped out of the car, wondering what to do. Slowly he walked up to her and saw the uncertainty reflected in eyes golden like his. Her arms went around him, and he knew that he was home.

For what seemed like hours, she held him, then reluctantly withdrew her arms. His cheeks were wet with her tears.

When she spoke, her voice trembled with emotion. "Forgive me, son."

And he felt the heaviness of the burden that had gripped his heart for years, lift. He felt like the little boy who'd always found comfort in the knowledge of her love. Holding his hand, she led him inside the house.

"Come, your father wants to see you. I promised that I'd bring you up as soon as you arrived."

She led the way, her hand holding his, a firm pressure applied as if she wanted and needed the contact. They walked up the stairs, and she left him at the door of the master bedroom.

For a moment he stood still. As a child, this room had been forbidden. He felt like a little boy going for his punishment.

He pushed the door open cautiously. His brother Daniel sat by the bed, holding their father's hands. His lips moved fervently. He was praying.

When Daniel saw him, he sprang up and wrapped his arms around him. Again Taurean felt that overwhelming happiness inside. Daniel had been one of those who condemned his act of mercy.

"Taurean." The voice was weak, feeble. Taurean turned to his father. And the reality of the circumstance hit him. His father was dying.

A shadow of his former self, the tall, burly man's sunken cheeks emphasized sharp, firm bones. His eyes, once bright and filled with fire, were now dull. His father tried to raise his hands.

Taurean slipped from the arms that held him. He looked at his brother closely, not certain what he was looking for.

"We'll talk later," Daniel said. "Dad's been asking for you. He wanted to speak to you alone."

Quickly, Taurean went over to the bed. When his father held out his bony, gnarled hands, he took them tenderly, disturbed by the frail man who lay before him.

One fragile hand squeezed his, and Taurean slipped to the floor, his knees bent in humility.

His father tried to speak, but a harsh cough racked his body. Taurean held him, feeling helpless. "I'll call Mom," he said.

"No, you . . . stay with . . . me. Need to . . . say something." His father spoke slowly, the words forced from lips distorted with pain.

Lifting his hands, he cupped Taurean's face. "Taurean, I'm sorry. I love you. Need you to . . . forgive me."

The words, laced with pain, echoed in the room. For the umpteenth time in weeks, Taurean felt the slow flow of tears fill his eyes, then spill down his cheeks.

"It's all right, Dad. I love you. There's no need for forgiveness."

His father closed his eyes. Taurean continued to hold his hands, the time slipping slowly by, the old grandfather clock's ticking a dreary monotonous comfort.

He watched as his father slept. He was breathing softly, not with the harsh sound that Taurean had heard when he'd first entered the bedroom.

He heard a noise at the door and he turned to see his mother standing there. She smiled at him.

"He's sleeping, breathing easier. He's at peace with himself." She placed her hand on Taurean's head, her hand gently stroking it. She always did that when she was talking to one of them.

"Mom, I came here expecting to ask him for forgiveness and he's asked me to forgive him. Why?"

"Because he knew that he was wrong; that for years he was living a lie. Preaching to others about forgiveness and not being able to forgive his own son."

She stopped. He could hear the anger in her tone.

"I, too, was wrong. I allowed your father to keep me away from my child and that was weak, but I felt that it was my duty to obey my husband. I should have realized that I could have been the one to heal his coldness.

"When Corey died, he felt that you had taken away one of his precious gifts. He is a strict father, but he loves every one of you. When you were in prison, I would hear him pray to God to take care of you. But he was so stubborn that he was not willing to forgive." Her head was bowed. He could hear the tears in the huskiness of her voice.

"Why didn't you come to see me?"

"I let him convince me that we were doing the right thing. And my grief at Corey's death blinded my reason. When I did eventually try to reach you, we were told that you'd refused to accept visitors or letters. You didn't even let Patrick tell us that you were out until you'd gone to Barbados. He refused to give me the number; he felt that we had hurt you enough."

With that she took Taurean in her arms and they held each other.

Taurean knocked on Daniel's room.

"Come in, Taurean."

His brother had this uncanny knack of knowing whoever stood by his door. *Seems that after all these years things haven't changed.*

Taurean pushed the door open and entered.

A single candle flickered in a corner of the room, its dull light casting shadows that danced across the walls. Curtains drawn, a trickle of sunlight fought to enter, but was unable to penetrate the room's gloom.

Daniel knelt on the floor.

His mouth moved fervently in prayer.

A few minutes passed before he stopped and rose slowly, turning to look at Taurean.

Time passed as they appraised each other, both wondering what would be the best way to handle the situation.

Daniel spoke first.

"It's good to see you, Taurean. You look well. The island seems to agree with you." He moved forward with firm, measured steps.

He stopped directly in front of Taurean.

"I could say I'm sorry, but I'd be a hypocrite to do that." He hesitated as if unsure of what to say.

"I missed you. I love you. You're my brother and even if in my self-righteousness I hurt you, you know I still love you. I'll be the first to admit I was wrong to treat you as I did. I don't condone what you did but you're my brother, and I love you. Always did."

Taurean fought for words. Never in his life had he expected this, but he realized that his brother was asking for forgiveness.

Without warning, strong arms wrapped themselves around him. He held on tight, savoring the moment.

They stood holding each other, unable to break apart. Needing to hold each other, drawing strength from each other in this time of need, knowing that both needed to bury the past.

"So, I heard you got married." Taurean broke the silence.

"Yes, Lorraine. She's six months pregnant. We live in New York—Brooklyn—so she couldn't be here. She's been ordered to bed rest. We've tried to get pregnant before and each time she lost the baby. This is the longest she's been, so we don't want to take any risks."

"I'd love to meet her," Taurean said genuinely. "So I'm going to be an uncle?"

"Yes, you'll have a nephew. We did the ultrasound a few days ago. We didn't want to wait."

"Well, bro, I'm proud of you. Patrick told me about your church in New York. Never thought you'd leave Oak Park."

"I didn't either, but when God wants you somewhere you really don't have a choice."

"I know what you mean."

For some reason they stopped, looked at each other, and broke out laughing.

Yes, things with his brother were going to be all right.

* * *

During the night, Reverend Robert Buchanan passed away. Taurean became a source of strength, like old times. He'd always been the strong one, the one to whom everyone turned. At last, he knew he'd really come home.

His father's death had left him with sadness. He would never be able to recapture the seven years he'd lost touch with his family. But comfort came in the knowledge that his father had asked for his forgiveness.

He also found comfort in the fact that he'd made peace with Daniel.

The day of his father's burial shone sunny and bright, reminding Taurean of the island and Alana and Melissa. He missed them like crazy but knew that for these few days his mother, his family, needed him.

That evening as he sat on the swing that had hung from the tall oak for as far back as he could remember, his mother came to him.

"What's wrong, Taurean? Something is bothering you. You're sad. I feel a restlessness in you."

"I'm leaving for Barbados tomorrow."

"Why? Do you have to leave already?" He heard the disappointment in her voice.

"Yes." He hesitated, wondering if he should tell her. "There's a woman. I love her. She needs me. I have to go back to them."

"Them?"

"Yes, she has a daughter, Melissa. She's divorced."

"By all means you have to go back to her. You've been through so much pain. You deserve some happiness." He heard the joy in her voice. "She must be special?"

"Yes, she's definitely special. She's been through so much and I don't know how to help her."

He told her about Alana and Melissa; about Blake and the fact that they were hiding. And while he spoke, the need for them grew heavy around his heart.

As the pale orange sun slipped slowly behind the trees, he poured his heart out. His mother listened, holding his hand while he spoke. She possessed a calmness that he didn't quite feel. He knew that the task ahead of him would not be easy, and hoped he was up to the challenge.

The day had been a great one and the kids were fast asleep. Karen and Kerry were staying overnight with Melissa. They had planned to stay up all night, but as soon as their heads hit the pillows they had fallen asleep.

Alana had not had so much fun in a long time. Marc and Anne had planned a picnic in the north end of the island. They'd invited most of their friends and the day had been one of leisure and fun. Alana was sorry that Taurean had not been there. He would have enjoyed himself. Marc and Anne's friends were like them—fun loving and friendly.

As she sat on the patio, she remembered the last time she and Taurean had stood on that same beach and he had kissed her and awakened buried desires.

She missed him, wondered when he would return. He'd promised her, but she knew what promises were. Blake had made so many promises.

But she wasn't being fair to Taurean. He'd revealed so much about himself to her. The pain of losing his brother. The guilt of having assisted in taking a life. She had seen and heard his pain. He was a special individual. Caring, sensitive, and gentle. She knew that he had started to heal as she had. She wondered what he was doing, hoped that his father was all right. That his reunion with them had not been as devastating as he'd expected it to be.

The sharp shrill ring of the telephone jarred her from her deep thoughts and she rushed into the house to answer it.

"Hello."

"Hi, Alana. It's me, Taurean." His deep baritone was clear, tender.

Her heart quickened. "Taurean, how's your father?"

"He died a few days ago. The funeral was yesterday. I'm sorry I didn't call before."

"I understand. I'm sorry to hear about your father. Are you all right?"

"Yeah, I'm holding up."

"And your mother and brothers?"

"Mom's hurting, but she's strong. Patrick and Daniel are taking it a lot harder—especially Daniel."

For a moment there was a pause.

"Do you miss me?" he asked, his voice light, playful.

She didn't know what to say but her happiness loosened her tongue.

"Of course not," she teased. She heard his deep laughter.

"Sure," was his knowing reply. "I miss you, too, and Melissa. How's she doing?'

"She's upstairs asleep. Kerry and Karen are over for the night. We went on a picnic today. They're exhausted."

"It's tomorrow that's the Kiddies' Kadooment, isn't it? I'm sorry that I'm going to miss it."

"She wants me to take pictures for you to see. She's sure you're coming back."

"What about you? Didn't you think I'd be back?"

She didn't answer.

He was silent. She knew she'd disappointed him with her silence.

"Alana, we'll talk when I return. I have to go. I have to be up early to get on the first flight to LaGuardia. I have to meet with my father's lawyer in New York later this week, so I'm not sure how long I'll be there. Give everyone my love."

"Bye, Taurean." She didn't want him to go.

"Bye," he responded.

When Alana heard the final click, she placed the phone to her heart and felt its steady beat. Happiness filled her and she smiled in contentment. Taurean was coming home.

CHAPTER 9

Kadooment Day dawned in a blaze of color. The perfect day for the kind of revelry that would take place on the streets of the island. The weatherman on the news the night before had promised a rain-free day, and for the Bajans preparing to enjoy the day, the promise of perfect sunshine was welcomed.

Alana quickly warmed milk and scrambled eggs for breakfast, knowing that Bertha would soon arrive to take them to the National Stadium. Marc and Anne and their daughters, Karen and Kerry, would be joining them there. Alana was not only looking forward to spending the day with her new friends, but all she'd been told about the Crop Over festival had sparked her curiosity to learn more about the island's culture and its people.

This was the perfect opportunity to experience all that she had heard. The Kiddies Kadooment the Saturday before had been exciting, and the girls had totally enjoyed themselves. They were already talking about next year's event.

Today, however, Grand Kadooment was for the adults, a much larger version of the children's event.

Alana had hardy slept during the night, each time waking to the darkness and willing the morning to come quickly. Before the clock could strike six, Melissa had crept into the room, her infectious excitement reflecting Alana's own anticipation. Her daughter had enjoyed the Kiddies Kadooment so much she couldn't wait for the final street party.

Alana wished Taurean were here, but she knew that he was dealing with his father's business in New York. She'd thought of him frequently at night when sleep refused to come. Having to face another death in his family was something that he should not have to deal with at this time, but life was so unpredictable.

Yes, unpredictable.

Just like hers . . .

Before she could complete the thought, footsteps thundered down the stairs, drawing her back to the task at hand.

Melissa ran into the room, coming to a sudden and ungainly stop before her.

"Melissa!"

"Oops!" For a moment her daughter's face stilled with genuine repentance, and then in a flash, she gushed.

"Is breakfast done? I'm hungry. We have to eat quickly. Auntie Bertha will soon be here. Aren't we meeting Karen and Kerry by the stadium? We can't keep them waiting."

Alana laughed. "Melissa, will you please slow down. We have a whole hour before Mrs. Gooding arrives. Eat some cereal. I've warmed some milk and the eggs will soon be done."

She watched as Melissa sat, poured cereal into the bowl, added milk, and tried to wolf everything down in one mouthful. Her daughter never ceased to amaze her.

"Melissa, don't let me have to speak to you again. I know you're excited, but take your time."

Alana spooned scrambled eggs onto two plates, placed one for Melissa and the other for herself. She poured two glasses of milk, and then she sat.

For a while they ate in silence, both lost in their secret thoughts.

Melissa stopped eating, concern on her face.

"Mommy, I wished Taurean was here. I miss him. The carnival today would cheer him up. He must be sad because of his father's death," she rambled.

"I wish he were here too, honey, but he needs to be with his family right now."

"I hope he knows we're his family too."

"Yes, I'm sure he does. Mrs. Gooding will be here soon. You still have to go and dress when you're done eating."

Melissa finished her meal and rushed upstairs, returning in record time dressed in her special Crop Over T-shirt, shorts, and a broad straw hat. The honking of Bertha's car horn sounded her arrival. She was early.

"Mom, it's Auntie Bertha. Let's go! Let's go!"

"OK, OK, put the things in the sink. I'll get the stuff we're taking from upstairs."

Alana rushed up the stairs, excited at the promise of another day of revelry. Yeah, Kadooment Day may be signaling the end of the sugar cane harvest, but to her it was the beginning of things to come.

Golden sunshine poured down like rain onto the thousands of people dancing and gyrating in the streets. The pulsating beat of the festival's most popular calypsos accompanied the bands creeping slowly along the street.

Today was the day when most Bajans forgot their worries and cares, and for twenty-four hours, it was just "bump and wine" and "jump and wave" to the sweet hypnotic music.

For more times than she could count, Alana watched in amazement as a too-scantily clad woman grabbed the closest male to her and proceeded to move suggestively against him. Willingly, the equally scantily dressed male joined in the dance, as bodies pressed against each other, touching, sliding, slipping onto each other.

Alana was a bit shocked at the sensual nature of some of the dancing, and forced herself not to place her hands over Melissa's eyes several times during the day.

Her gaze met Anne and Bertha's, a knowing look between them, but they realized that Melissa, Karen, and Kerry were more interested in the costumes and antics of the revelers than the nature of the dancing.

Laughter and cheers of appreciation flowed from the crowd as an amorous couple sauntered down the street, their movements increasing as they played to the onlookers.

At midday, Alana could not believe the energy that the revelers possessed. Didn't they tire? she wondered.

Some stopped along the way to buy snow cones. Others grabbed the cups of water provided along the way.

But they never seemed to get tired!

Earlier, in the National Stadium, she'd watched the parade of costume bands before the judges and had been awed at the beauty and creativity of the designers. The colors of the rainbow had been captured by their skilled hands, creating costumes that moved in oneness with the vibrant energy of the partyers.

Now, with Bertha and the kids, she stood on the side of one of the streets where locals and tourists watched the bands as they traveled like snails along the route on their way to the Spring Garden Highway where the final "jump up" would take place.

A feeling of oneness with the Bajans filled her. She did not want to leave this beautiful island. She hoped that whatever happened she'd be able to stay.

"Look, Mommy, look," Melissa screamed. She and the twins were laughing at the antics of a young man who was dressed as one of the island's green monkeys. Alana joined in their laughter, intent on erasing thoughts of Taurean from her mind.

At least for one day!

For the next few hours, they walked along the streets, enjoying the movement of vibrant colors around them. With the occasional stops to eat from one of the many food stalls that lined the streets, Alana and the other adults welcomed the chance to rest. Somehow, the girls didn't seem to tire. Instead, they ate quickly, determined not to miss any of the action.

As late afternoon approached, Alana, still amazed at the unwavering energy of the revelers, knew that they could not be human, that they possessed some super strength that kept them going and going and going.

Maybe responsibility lay with the local rum that poured from half-filled bottles into the plastic cups provided in abundance, which now littered the streets.

As the sun sat on the horizon, casting shades of red and orange on the multitudes overflowing the Spring Garden Highway, they came to a halt, tired and hungry. Like the girls, Alana watched, with childlike wonder, the firework display that signaled the end of another Crop Over festival.

After five weeks of celebration, the island would return to its peaceful state.

Alana watched when, finally, tired Bajans of all ages struggled home, all happy and contented. Despite not having been in a band of revelers, she, too, felt contented.

The phone was ringing when Alana and Melissa entered the house.

Taurean again.

Her heart leapt!

Before Alana could, Melissa rushed and picked the phone up.

Almost immediately she dropped it, and screamed, her tiny frame shaking with fear. Alana moved quickly, picking the phone up from where it had fallen.

Placing it to her ears, she asked.

"Who is it?"

Blake's voice came over the line, controlled, commanding.

"It's me, honey. I'm coming to take you home."

Trembling, she put the phone down and grabbed Melissa, who by now was crying and still screaming at the top of her lungs. Whatever Alana tried to do, her daughter would not stop.

Lifting Melissa, she carried her into the living room, and reaching the couch, bent to lay her on it. Melissa refused to let go, her arms gripped around Alana's neck.

Moving with her daughter's body, Alana lay next to her, her arms holding her gently.

The soothing refrain of an old Negro spiritual, dormant in the place where childhood memories remain forever, rose to the surface, and she sang to her daughter.

After what seemed like hours, the tears slowly subsided and Melissa fell into a restless sleep cradled in Alana's arms.

There was a knock at the door and the cold hand of fear touched her heart.

"Alana, Alana, it's Bertha. What's wrong? I heard Melissa screaming."

Alana put Melissa on the couch and hurried to the door. When she opened it, Bertha wrapped her arms around her, offering the comfort she needed. Trembling, she held on for dear life, not wanting to let go.

Bertha unwound her arms and led her into the house.

"What's wrong? You put the fear of the Lord in my heart, girl."

"It's my ex-husband. He called. I'm not sure if he's on the island. He told me he was coming to take us back home. I won't go with him. I won't."

"There's no need to be afraid. He can't harm you. Tomorrow morning, we'll go to the police and make an official complaint."

"No, I can't do that. Blake will not stop until this is over. I'm going to have to take Melissa and leave."

With those words she told Bertha the story of her marriage, the abuse she suffered, and their daring escape.

"Don't worry, child." Bertha's voice soothed with its sweet Bajan rhythm. "I had an idea what was wrong. Everything is going to be all right. Taurean will be back soon. He'll take care of you. Didn't you say he was only going to be in New York for a week? I'm sure he'll be here any day now."

"I know, but I don't want to burden him with my problems. He has his own to take care of. You don't know Blake. He could come tonight."

"Taurean will be fine. He's strong and brave. He'll know what to do," Bertha reassured her. "Where's Melissa?"

"She's in the living room. I finally got her to sleep."

"OK, but I don't think it's safe to stay here tonight. You go get a blanket to wrap around Melissa, and you're going to stay the night at my home. When we get there, I'll make us a hot pot of tea, and we'll talk."

She carried out Bertha's instructions quickly.

When she'd heard Blake's voice, all she'd wanted to do was pack their bags and run. Bertha had provided a calm that she needed at this moment.

She would go to Bertha's house, but she hoped she wasn't placing the woman's life in danger. If she left the island it would be because she didn't want those she'd grown to care for to come to any harm. She knew what Blake was capable of, and the reality of his power made her wary.

Yes, the desire to run was overwhelming, but where could she go? Who would help her? Would she have to run for the rest of her life or until Blake finally found her?

No, she would not let Blake destroy the peace she'd found here on the island.

She was going to fight.

Morning dawned and Alana awakened to the smell of hot coffee, and with a pounding headache. She'd remained awake until the early hours of the morning. Finally, tired, she'd fallen into a fitful sleep. Bertha's presence had been a comfort, but against a man like Blake, the elderly woman would be as helpless as she was.

Slipping out of bed, she found her toothbrush in the overnight bag she'd brought with her. She walked into the bathroom. The face looking back at her was haggard, evidence of the long night she'd spent.

Blake had found her. Where was he?

In Reading? On the island?

She didn't know but she knew they would have to leave. She had to run again. Going to the police was out of the question. Blake was a powerful man. He had friends in high places and she knew he would have no problem taking Melissa from her to get her back. He knew she would never let him take Melissa.

She finished brushing her teeth. Before turning off the tap, she splashed cool water on her face. She looked at herself in the mirror. Had she really expected that her splashing water on her face would have made some miraculous change? A fear greater than any she experienced before churned deep in her stomach until she felt as if she would throw up. Bending over the sink, she breathed deeply, the nausea slowly subsiding. Washing her face again, she left the bathroom and went to wake Melissa.

In the bedroom, Melissa stirred and slowly opened her eyes. She looked around, at first uncertain of where she was. When she saw her mother, she smiled, but a look of fear shadowed her eyes as she, too, remembered what had happened the night before.

"Is he here, Mommy? Is Daddy here?"

"I don't know, Melissa, but I'm not going to let your father hurt you."

"If Taurean were here he wouldn't let Daddy take us. I wish he were here. He promised he would come back."

"He's coming back, honey. We'll stay here by Bertha until he returns." Alana held her daughter tightly, wanting to reassure her.

Her eyes brimming with tears, Melissa looked at her mother. "I'm scared, Mommy. I miss Taurean. I think he'd make a good daddy."

"Taurean will be back. He promised you. Your dad is never going to take you away from me." *He'd have to kill me first,* she thought.

As she held her daughter, Melissa's words lingered, echoing her own private opinion. Taurean would make a good dad. She knew that as much as she knew the sun would rise each morning.

She said the words to Melissa with confidence, but hoped that Blake didn't do just that—take her away, and kill her.

White fluffy clouds hung low above the island in the distance. The husky voice of the flight attendant came over the intercom announcing that it was time to fasten seat belts. Taurean complied.

He was home.

Home. In a few short weeks, Barbados had become home. He'd fallen in love with the island and he wondered if he would eventually decide to live here. He'd inherited a lot of money from his father. Much more than he'd expected. He'd not expected anything. That plus the trust fund that had been left for him by his grandfather was enough to keep him for years to come. He had enough security to make it possible to propose to Alana and take care of her when the problem of her ex-husband was resolved.

Despite the fact that they had lived a modest life, his father had been from one of the town's oldest and most affluent families. His father had given up joining his own father's multimillion-dollar company to become a minister. He'd not wanted any of his father's wealth.

There was a screech at his side and he groaned. It was that damn woman again. From the time she'd gotten on the plane, she had practically shoved her ample breasts in his face. At first, he'd been flattered, but a quick conversation revealed she didn't have a smart bone in any part of her body. Talk about dumb blondes. She was the epitome of that stereotype.

"Oh, you haven't fastened your seat belt. Let me help you. Before he could stop her, her hands fumbled with the belt, lingering at the bulge at his crotch.

"Oops, sorry, but you're a big boy," she said with no embarrassment, her tongue moistening her lips in what he assumed was an attempt to be seductive. "Are you going to be on the island for a long time? We could get together for some excitement."

"I'm really sorry, but my wife and daughter are on the island."

"Oh, shucks. Well, next time."

Her mouth puckered in a delicate pout, she turned and stared out the window.

I can't wait to get out of here, he thought.

She shifted in the seat and her elbow accidentally jabbed him in the side. "Opps, shucks, I'm sorry. Did I hurt you? Let me kiss it better," she offered with a playful wink.

"It's all right. No harm done." He firmly moved her hand away.

Finally, the plane touched down and slowly taxied along the runway, coming to an eventual stop. Without waiting to say good-bye to the woman, he quickly unbuckled his seatbelt, retrieved his bag from the overhead compartment, and slipped out of the seat. The blonde's eyes were still closed. He was going to make sure that by the time she reached the arrival hall, he would be gone.

With only the shoulder bag, he quickly cleared Immigration and Customs.

When he stepped out into the sunshine, he immediately felt the warmth. He stood quietly, inhaling the sweet tropical air.

Damn, it was good to be back.

"Taurean, Taurean, over here."

Taurean turned to see Bertha waving frantically at him. He had hoped she received the message he'd left on her voice mail just before he boarded the plane that morning. He'd told Alana he'd be back this weekend, but she hadn't known exactly which flight he would be on. He'd boarded this flight at the last minute as a standby passenger.

When he reached her, Bertha hugged him.

"It's good to have you back," she said. "We missed you."

He felt a strange warmth inside. He hadn't expected them to miss him.

"Let's go. The car is over there." She pointed in the direction of her car, under the shade of one of the many almond trees in the parking lot.

He followed her, answering her questions about his father. Bertha pulled out of the parking lot and swiftly drove north on the highway.

"I wanted to meet you because I wanted to say something important. Alana told me she told you about her ex-husband. She's feeling a bit scared right now. He called last night. Told her he was coming for her and Melissa. She doesn't know what to do. They're staying at my home."

Taurean felt a surge of anger. "Are they all right? Where is he? On the island?" His hands clenched. "I'll kill him if he hurts Alana or Melissa again." When he spoke, he had to try to control the rage.

"I'll take care of them," he growled. He didn't need to say more, but with his words, he'd told her he'd claimed them as his own. "I'll take care of that bastard."

"Be careful, Taurean. Alana's ex-husband is a sick man. He's not being rational. He's lost it. He's not going to leave without them." He heard the anxiety in her voice.

"The only way he's going to take her is over my dead body. Is he on the island? Have you called the police? Where are they?"

"They're at my house. Melissa insisted I take you straight there. Alana called Blake's office this morning and the secretary told her he was at a meeting. He's playing a game with her. She's afraid, but she's not the same person she was when she came here. She's stronger. She'll fight him when the time comes."

He recognized the inevitability in her statement. Yes, Blake would come. He knew that as much as he knew the sun would rise tomorrow. And that he would take a life again if it meant protecting someone he loved.

The thought of loving her never ceased to shock him. He loved her. He internalized the feeling, basking in the inner glow that surged inside. She had given him a reason to live and had brought joy like golden sunshine into his life.

For the rest of the drive, he was quiet, reflective. Blake's intrusion placed a dark cloud over the feelings that bubbled inside him. His heart pounded in anticipation of seeing them again. Melissa was just as important as her mother. He'd always love her. From that first night, when he'd seen the stark pain in her eyes, he wanted more than anything to protect her. He hoped that he could be the hero they expected him to be. He would try to be, even if it meant risking his own life.

Alana stood watching the road. She'd been watching for the bright red car for the last half hour. Taurean had called Bertha early that morning and asked her to pick him up at the airport.

In the distance, she heard Melissa's and the Blackman twins' squeals of laughter. Marc had built a tree house in the old mahogany tree in the back. When she'd told Bertha about her ex-husband, and Melissa's reaction to her father's call, Bertha suggested letting Karen and Kerry come and stay over the weekend. It would help to keep Melissa's mind off her father.

Though she'd called Blake's office a few days ago and his secretary had informed her that he was in a meeting, she decided to stay at Bertha's until Taurean's return.

Melissa had noticeably relaxed when Alana had told her that her father was not on the island.

A flash of red crept between the trees along the road and Bertha's car appeared. It sped down the driveway and spun to a stop by the patio. Taurean stepped from the car and stood looking at the window. He knew that she was there. Their gazes locked and he smiled. She moved swiftly from the window. She needed to get downstairs.

Needed to feel his arms around her.

When she reached the door, he was standing on the patio.

He dropped his bag and she hurled herself into his arms. She nested in the comfort they offered and knew that she was safe, that everything would be all right. He'd come back to her. Feelings she did not want to voice hovered on her lips.

"I missed you," were the only words he said before she felt his lips on hers and she tasted the musky manliness of him. He was breathing hard. She opened to him, her need obstructing all the dark uncertainty in her mind. She became aware of his arousal. Felt the hard length of him pressed against her stomach, setting her on fire. Opening her eyes, she pulled her lips reluctantly from his.

"I didn't think you'd come back."

"Didn't I tell you I would?" She heard the disappointment in his voice.

"Yes, but . . . "

"No buts. I said I'd be back. I need you to trust me. I'm not Blake."

With his arms around her, he led her into the house.

"Come, you have to tell me what has been happening."

He rested his bag on one of the couches and sat on the other, pulling her to him.

"Blake called. He said we were going home with him." Her voice trembled. "He's not on the island yet. He's toying with me. When he comes, I won't be able to stop him."

He took her hands in his, looking into her eyes. "Alana, you need to trust me. He's not taking you or Melissa anywhere."

For a long time they sat like that. Then, there was the sound of a stampede. Melissa and the twins were coming. Reluctantly, Alana left the strength of his arms as he stood to await the onslaught.

Three bundles of energy flew into the room, hair flying in all directions.

"Taurean, Auntie Bertha said you were back." Despite her friends' presence, Melissa ran into Taurean's arms and held onto him for dear life.

"I missed you," Alana heard her say. "I'm glad you're back. I haven't been able to swim since you were gone."

"We'll teach your mother to swim yet."

"We can go today?"

"Yes, later. Just let me get something to nibble on and talk to your mother, and I'll be there." He turned to Karen and Kerry. "Do you have your swimsuits?"

"Yes, we do," they said in unison, delight on their faces.

"OK, girls, let's be ready in an hour." Melissa was a trooper. She didn't sound like a girl who'd almost drowned a few weeks ago.

The girls rushed out of the room, and he heard them tromping up the stairs.

"How on earth do you handle the three of them?" he asked. "They have so much energy."

"Sometimes I wonder," she replied, shrugging. "Maybe it's because I love them."

Two hours later they were splashing and screaming in the sea. Like a little boy, Taurean was splashing and jumping with them. Alana had decided to put her swimsuit on, but was cautious about getting in the water. Despite her own near tragedy, Melissa had quickly overcome her reservations about getting into the water. It was not so easy for Alana.

Slowly, she crept closer and closer, until she tested the water with her toes. She smiled. It was perfect.

She walked in until the water reached her breasts. It felt cool and refreshing. She moved through the water, her body growing accustomed to the gentle lull of the surf.

"Enjoying yourself?"

She turned to smile at Taurean.

"Yes, I love the water, but what happened with Melissa is more that just a memory."

"You're doing fine. Melissa may seem all brave about getting in the water, but she's definitely not going far out again. It'll take time, but you'll soon put that niggling of apprehension behind you. Bad experiences always make us a bit fearful."

"It's hard to imagine you afraid of anything. You're so big, confident."

"Don't be fooled by my size. There are things I'm definitely afraid of. Death, closed spaces, and . . . storms. I've never liked storms. Neither did my brother Corey. The night he died there was a really bad storm. Maybe that's why I have a strong aversion to them. It reminds me too much of him and what I had to do for him. The night you arrived here I was upstairs in my room trembling to death."

She looked at him, feeling as if she were seeing him for the first time.

"Alana, we need to talk. Maybe dinner or a drive around the island. Just the two of us."

"That'll be fine. I'd like that."

"Taurean, Taurean, there's a crab on the beach. Come and help us catch it." Melissa's voice floated in the wind.

"Well, duty calls." He raced over to where the girls were squealing, leaving Alana to steady the pounding of her heart.

Alana and the girls had gone up to bed more than an hour ago. One of Taurean's favorite movies, *Glory*, with Denzel Washington was on Channel Eight. He'd stayed up to watch it. As the credits scrolled up the screen, he heard the pitter-patter of tiny feet and turned to see Melissa standing by the door.

"Hi," he said, memories of a night not too long ago coming to mind.

"Hi," she replied. She smiled. He loved to see her smile.

"You hungry?" he asked.

"Yes."

"Want some milk...and strawberry jam and crackers?"

Her face lit up. "Yeah, and soda."

"Soda? Where did that come from? Thought you were a milk girl."

"Not any more. I'm not a baby any more. I'm getting big. Kerry and Karen drink soda all the time."

He lifted her up. "Sure you are but you're not too big to drink your milk. Keeps you healthy. I'm going to drink milk."

They'd reached the kitchen and he plopped her down on one of the counter stools.

"Taurean, can I ask you something? If you were my daddy, would you hit me and Mommy?"

Taurean almost dropped the glasses he held in his hands. What the hell was he going to say to her?

He turned around, saw the hopefulness in her eyes, and walked over to her.

"Honey, no father should ever hurt a child or his wife. No, I would never, ever, hit my wife or children. When you love someone you don't hurt them."

"Does that mean that my daddy doesn't love me?" Melissa asked.

The question tore at his heart.

He wasn't sure how to answer, but he could try. "No, Melissa, I'm sure your dad loves you, but he was probably having some problems and not thinking too clearly."

"I wish you were my daddy."

The words were said with sincerity and he felt an ache in his chest. Eyes filled with adoration gazed at him.

"If I had a daughter, I would want her to be just like you."

She looked up at him with the broadest smile he'd ever seen on her face. "Let's get that snack," he told her.

With her help they got the snack ready and returned to the TV room. He flicked to the Disney Channel and they sprawled on the floor eating the jam and crackers, and drinking milk.

Melissa eased close to him, resting her head on his lap. For a while they watched the picture, engrossed in the adventure tale.

"Taurean, I love you," she said, her voice filled with drowsiness.

He kissed her forehead, smelling the freshness of childhood.

"I love you, too," he replied, hugging her tightly, as her eyes flickered and closed, the hint of a smile on her lips. Drawing her close, he gave into the comfort of holding her.

He now knew the pride and love a father felt for his child. Melissa did not carry his blood, but he loved her as if she were his own.

He felt happy and sad at the same time. The presence of Melissa's father still lingered in the background. He wanted that situation to be over. There would be no real future with Alana if Blake remained obsessed with her.

But there would be no thought of that tonight.

No, he was going to sit and enjoy the antics of the characters from *The Lion King*.

Later, he'd have to deal with Blake Smyth-Connell.

CHAPTER 10

Alana came to him in a dream that night, naked, her hair cascading around her shoulders. Moonlight from the opened window caressed her dark mahogany skin.

As she flowed gracefully toward him, he felt the painful pleasure of arousal and wondered what to do. He'd not been with a woman since long before prison and the thought that he would not satisfy her flashed in his mind for the briefest of moments. He watched as she came slowly closer. Light from the moon trickled into the room casting dark shadows that tenderly caressed her slender shape, making her even more beautiful. A hint of raspberry wafted toward him, stimulating his already heightened senses.

When she reached him she stopped. Her eyes, flaming with desire, focused on him.

"Stand," she commanded. The firmness and power in her tone was so unlike the Alana he'd come to know that his heart quickened with excitement. This Alana was different but yet the familiar qualities remained. Her face was serious, intent on the task she was about to perform.

He stood, and she drew closer to him, her body barely touching his. She reached out to him, sliding her palms up his chest as she slipped the shirt over his head and tossed it on the floor. His boxers were next. She bent, sliding her fingers slowly under the elastic, pulling them down, her hands grazing the curve of his hips. He groaned in pleasure, her hot touch branding his warm flesh.

She placed her hands on his chest and pushed him gently onto the bed, straddling him. Her head moved toward him, her lips gently resting on his. A shiver of excitement coursed through his body as his lips parted to receive her invasion, but she surprised him. Instead, she began to nibble on his lips, raining soft kisses on his nose, then his eyes. She had taken control and he felt weak, vulnerable. He tensed, the unfamiliar helplessness giving way to the mounting excitement. He struggled, not wanting to abandon himself to the feelings she stirred inside.

A cold dampness touched his ears and he tried to contain the cry that threatened to erupt. When she nipped on the sensitive lobes of his ears, he gripped the sheets, aching for release, knowing he'd lost the battle.

Slowly, her head moved southward, her mouth burning his chest, his nipples, leaving no part of his body untouched. Each kiss added fuel to the mounting passion. When she reached his stomach, she moved skillfully, instinctively finding the sensitive spots on his body. The butterfly touch, sending tingling shivers along his spine, caused him to twist and turn beneath her.

She moved lower still. She gazed at him, hard, firm, in all his male glory. When she held him in her hand, she looked up, eyes wild with passion. A flash of pure lightning surged through his body, burning him. He moaned when her lips surrounded him, the sound echoing in the silence of the room.

He breathed in slowly, trying to return from the peak of release. She continued to gaze into his eyes, the shimmering desire intensifying. Uninhibited, lips parted, face flushed, she was even more beautiful. He wanted her; couldn't wait any longer. He felt a need to take control, to give her the same enjoyment she'd given him. He flipped her over, glorying in the feel of her silky nakedness beneath him.

At first, he kissed her gently, his passion increasing as he was swept along by his need. He ran his hands over her small and fragile body. He hoped that his largeness would not overwhelm her. When her legs widened giving him greater access to the hot core of her being, he knew they would be the perfect fit. Desire burned like a flame inside him. He wanted to take her, wanted to feel himself buried deep inside her, but he needed to pleasure her first. He wanted her to know that he loved her; that making love was not what she'd come to expect; that it was more important to him to focus on her need, her want.

His lips found the sensitive spot at her neck where her pulse beat rapidly. She moaned his name and he felt pride that he was the one whose name she used.

His gaze moved to her breasts, firm and aroused, rising provocatively toward him. He took one dark nub in his mouth and suckled deeply, enjoying the taste of her. Beneath him, she groaned, eyes closed. Her fingers reached his head, drawing him closer. He fastened on one nipple and then the other, the hotness of her burning body filling his mouth.

He moved his mouth over her, slowly settling between her legs and enjoying the sweet flowery smell of her. He feasted on her, tasting her very essence. She writhed in bliss, her grip on him tightened, and he knew that she was near that moment of ultimate ecstasy. Seconds after the thought, he heard her cry out, her body trembling with the intensity of her release.

He felt touched, moved by the gift she'd given him. He'd reached her most intimate depths and he'd felt connected to her in a special way.

Slowly he raised himself above her, entering the moist warmth of her body. She held him tight, drawing him deep inside and he almost lost control. Her eyes were opened wide, pleasure-filled. Gripping his buttocks, she drew him closer, until he was buried deep inside her. Then she pulled him toward her, locking her legs around his waist, moving her hips at a slow leisurely pace. He joined her, reveling in her boldness. With every measured thrust he discovered a new sensation, a new high of awareness, a deeper meaning to the art of lovemaking.

Gradually, he increased his movement, plunging smoothly into her again and again, feeling the knowing tingle of release. The hard thrusting of her body moved him toward the edge, and when she screamed in pleasure for the second time that night, he joined her in his own cry of fulfillment.

Taurean's eyes snapped open. His breathing was irregular, and sweat popped out on his face. He blinked and quickly looked around. He was alone. It was all a dream. But it had been so real.

His body still tingled all over from the intensity of the passion between them. He lay for a long time, the images from the dream still playing in his mind.

Suddenly, Alana came awake, her body aching all over, wishing for release from the passion she'd just experienced. Her body bathed in sweat, she trembled in the aftermath. She looked at the pillow beside her, expecting Taurean to be lying there, and was surprised when he wasn't. The dream had been so real. She remembered how she'd gone to him and they'd made the most glorious love. She'd never been like that with Blake. He'd be unable to touch the core of her soul and Taurean had done it in a dream. Blake had never been concerned with pleasuring her, only gratifying his need, grunting and sweating profusely, as he lay heavy on her, his weight compressing her like a vise.

Rising from the bed, she walked over to the open window. The sea lay calm, and she reached her hands out to embrace its tranquility. Love was the strangest thing. She didn't know what to do about this attraction to Taurean. Maybe she needed some hero to charge into her life and save Melissa and her from the evil dragon. Maybe she needed someone to help her forget the years of pain and suffering Blake had inflicted on her.

She laughed. She felt silly and fanciful. A man such as that didn't exist. Only men who fooled you with their gentleness and kindness, and then when the time was right they pounced and devoured you without mercy.

That had been her way of thinking, but Taurean had taught her differently. He'd come gently into her life and made her dream of happily-ever-after again.

She returned to the bed, slipping between the silky covers, a breeze blowing cool through the window. Closing her eyes, the image of a tall, gentle man fixed in her mind, she fell asleep.

Blake placed the suitcase on the bed, lifted the phone, and dialed the number he'd already stored in memory.

Palms sweating in anticipation, he waited for the receiver to be picked up. On the tenth ring, he heard it lift. The game would continue. A man's voice answered. For a moment Blake was at a loss of words. He listened to the deep voice repeat a greeting, then heard the sharp click of disconnection.

There was a pounding in his head. Red-hot rage consumed him and he slammed the phone down. The bitch had a man staying in the house with her? Alana was already sleeping with another man? *Doesn't she have any respect for me?* He would show her. She had to be punished. He was no longer her husband, but he owned her.

He started to shake, his body racked by the rage boiling inside. Another man had defiled her, had her, and tasted what was his. The thought sickened him. He tried to block the image of another man taking her and felt the pain in his head pounding, knocking.

Blake looked around him in search of something to destroy, but then realized the folly of that action. He closed his eyes, breathing deeply. Slowly, he regained the control that was so much a part of him. He fell on the bed. The game was not over. Yes, it would take a different direction, but it was definitely not over. Alana would rue the day she walked out of his house.

Taurean replaced the phone. He knew who it was. The silence had spoken volumes. Blake Smyth-Connell—a name so aristocratic in sound, but one camouflaging the mind of a sick bastard. Taurean would be lying to himself if he were to say that he was not afraid. He knew what men like Blake could do to a woman as vulnerable as Alana. Yes, she was gentle, but he had seen sparks of defiance in her eyes and stance when she'd spoken of protecting Melissa. He knew she would do anything to protect her daughter, but her fragility was no match against a man with her husband's kind of power.

Passing through the kitchen, Taurean exited the back door. He needed to think. Down by the sea was the one place where he felt at peace, where he felt that nature was listening to every word he said, comforting him with its serenity.

The morning was beautiful. Birds singing, the sun already out in its full glory. In the distance, some island boys played cricket. A few others were diving off a low cliff into the water.

How carefree being a child could be. No worries, no real problems. He wished he were a boy again. But the reality of life was that he was a man. A man with responsibilities, and a new life to begin. One he wanted to have with Alana and Melissa.

Then he saw her. She was painting. She stood, her focus on the boys.

He walked toward her, needing to be with her, wanting to see what she was painting. He approached quietly, not wanting to disturb her.

She turned toward him and smiled. Despite the smile, he saw the turmoil in her eyes. She returned to her painting abruptly, as if she knew he'd seen too much of her pain and vulnerability.

She was using watercolors. The softness of the tones was perfect for this tropical paradise.

He watched, mesmerized. The paintbrush moved with the expertise of one who had studied and perfected her craft. It was the skill of the gifted. She was not just painting, but creating a feeling, a mood, a glimpse of the human soul. She had captured the essence of the scene before her. There was a wild freedom in what she'd painted. One boy was captured forever leaping from the cliff, poised on a journey reaching for the sky.

When Alana finished, she lay the brush down. She stood before him, drained. What she had created had affected her intensely, emotionally.

"You're good. I realized that you purchased paint and brushes, but thought it was just a hobby. I didn't know that you were an artist. I can see you've had training."

"Before I married Blake, I worked at an advertising firm. But I've always loved painting, especially watercolors. That's how I met Blake."

Alana paused. Talking about Blake wasn't easy.

"I had a showing at a local gallery and, as senator, he was the specially invited guest. I fell in love with him that night." There was a whimsical sound to her voice.

"He was so different back then. At first he was tender, so gentle. He treated me like a princess, and for the first time in my life I felt like one. But then he changed. The late nights . . . and the women. And then I became just a possession. Just one of the many treasures he'd collected to put on display for his friends. He wanted the perfect political wife. That was all he wanted."

"He's a crazy individual. How could he not love you, Alana? Any man would be lucky to have your love."

He hesitated, wanting to tell her how he felt.

She turned to look at him, her eyes pooled with tears.

"I am in love with you, Alana."

He needed to say more. "I know that this is not the right time and place. There's too much going on in our lives, but I had to tell you. *Needed* to tell you that."

She opened her mouth to say something. He placed a finger to her lips. "No, not yet. Let's get over this hurdle looming before us, before you say anything." He paused for a moment and then reached for her hand. "Come walk with me on the beach. We'll still be able to see everything."

For a while they walked in silence. Taurean embraced the sweet smell of the morning. The soft scent of Alana's perfume mingled with the tropical smell and it took all his self-control not to take her in his arms and kiss her deeply. Her hand in his trembled and he knew she was as aware of him as he was of her.

"We're going to work this out together, Alana."

Blake stood on the cliff looking down on the scene before him. He'd seen them holding hands and the anger had grown until intense fury threatened to consume him. He wondered what Alana would think if she knew that he was watching her. He'd moved into a beach house about a mile from the one where she was staying.

The wind blew and he was certain the scent of her wafted in the air. His manhood hardened and he closed his eyes, savoring the powerful stir of arousal. She had always been able to arouse him without any effort. She was the most beautiful woman he'd ever seen. He'd loved the silky feel of her legs wrapped around him when he made love to her.

The thought of her tightness increased his arousal until the need for release resulted in a steady throbbing pain.

He saw a flash of color from the beach house and Melissa raced toward her mother. The noisy snit. He'd hated her from the time she was born. Alana spent all her time with the whining, crying child, refusing to let the nanny do what she'd been hired for.

She'd stopped going to important functions because of Melissa's frequent crankiness. He'd married Alana because she was important to the image he wanted, and that image did not include a child at the time. It'd been too early. Four years earlier than he'd planned.

He looked down at the woman he still considered his wife, his possession. He didn't care what any court judge had said. She was still his. *'Til death do us part.*

Words from one of his father's many lectures on manhood came to mind. Always make sure that you're in control. Always make sure that your wife knows who's the boss.

He sat on the cliff watching Alana and planning what he would do next.

Alana shivered.

She'd been standing looking out to sea for what seemed like hours. She should call Melissa, who was walking the beach looking as if the world was on her shoulders. She'd not been in the mood for chatting when her daughter had come flying from the direction of Bertha's house with a bag of the cookies she'd made.

A cloud passed overhead, darkening the area where she stood.

She shivered again.

She wondered if Blake were near, wondered whether he'd come to the island to get her himself or got one of his cronies to do his dirty work. But wondering made no sense. She knew Blake. Knew that he'd come after her. She had to be mentally prepared to face him.

He was close by. He may not be on the island, but she could feel the darkness coming.

"Melissa," she shouted.

Melissa turned, hesitated for a moment, and then raced toward her.

Alana opened her arms and held her daughter close.

"Mommy, you angry with me?" Melissa's questions pained her.

"I'm sorry, Melissa. I didn't mean to make you sad."

"Where you thinking about Daddy?"

About to say no, she decided against it.

"Yes," she confirmed. "I was thinking about your dad."

"Don't be afraid, Mom. Taurean says he'll take care of us. He's bigger that Daddy. He won't dare come to Barbados."

Alana heard her daughter's words and wished that she could say them with such conviction.

She knew Blake better, and knew it was just a matter of time before he arrived.

Later that night, Taurean switched on the television in his room and flicked through the channels. Blake's call had left him unable to sleep. He focused on the TV, trying to calm the rage that boiled inside.

The word *Barbados* perked his interest, and he listened attentively to the words of the weatherman. A tropical depression had created storm conditions far out in the Atlantic Ocean and was making its way westward directly toward Barbados. If it kept on its current path and speed, it would reach the island in a few days. He tried unsuccessfully to control his trembling body, his fear of storms surfacing.

He whispered a silent prayer, hoping that it would remain a storm. But somehow, he knew that it would become a hurricane.

Jumping out of bed, he moved unsteadily to the window, looking out to the sea, his mouth dry, his ears ringing.

Somewhere out there, a storm was coming.

CHAPTER 11

With her head back against the passenger's seat, Alana raised her hands to the sky. They'd been driving for almost an hour, the only sound the soothing rhythm of the reggae from a Bob Marley CD.

Just after seven this morning, Taurean had knocked on her bedroom door, reminding her that he wanted to leave early so they could drive around the whole island.

Alana wondered if she'd ever grow accustomed to the beauty of Barbados. She was glad she'd agreed to the drive around the island instead of dinner.

With the showers of August came the island's most vibrant colors. A skilled artist had somehow captured the many shades of green on his palette and liberally sprinkled the island's foliage, giving the island a lush, fertile look.

Unlike the U.S., there was no summer, winter, spring, or fall, just the days of glorious sunshine and days of rain that beat against the rooftops.

She sneaked a glance at Taurean, the latest of many she'd taken during the past hour. They'd not spoken much, preferring to enjoy the silence, but her awareness of him drew her eyes in his direction, each time accompanied by a quickening of her heartbeat. In the silence, she could hear and feel the steady flow of blood as it pulsed in her veins.

She was scared, but the bubbling inside signaled the excitement and happiness she felt. She wanted to break out in song, as often happened in those old black and white musicals she loved to watch. But Taurean would think she was going crazy.

She was glad Taurean had decided to still come on the drive despite the tropical storm nearing the island, since it was several days away. She remembered Bertha's words when she'd told her about the trek Taurean had planned.

"You ain't got nuttin' to worry 'bout," she reassured. "You ain't hear that God is a Bajan?" she'd asked in the island's dialect, emphasizing her point. Bertha didn't often use dialect, but when she did, she was a sight to behold. The language variety of the locals was meant for the drama.

A presumptuous boast, but a sentiment shared by the locals. Bertha's explanation, however, had seemed a valid one. No major hurricane had struck the island in years, always missing or bypassing the island after some miraculous change in direction.

Alana smiled. Yes, it seemed like the Bajans were a praying people.

"What's so funny?" Taurean's voice broke the silence.

"I just remembered something that Bertha told me last night when I called her. It's a bit strange, but there seems to be some truth in what she said."

Alana quickly related the essence of the conversation.

Taurean laughed. "Well, we'll find out in a few days if what the Bajans believe has merit."

They both laughed again, the infectious sound echoing around them.

"We're going to reach the Park soon. I discovered it on one of my trips around the island. It has one of the most spectacular views of the East Coast," Taurean injected.

Five minutes later, a colorful sign welcomed them to one of the island's national parks. Farley Hill, the former home of Sir Graham Briggs, the famous British liberal planter, had once been one of the island's most beautiful homes. Its beauty was forever captured on screen in the Harry Belafonte movie *Island in the Sun*. The Georgian mansion, however, was destroyed by fire in 1965, but its ruins still remained as one of the park's attractions.

At the ticket booth, Taurean paid the entry fee and followed the sign that took them to the parking lot.

When the Jeep came to a stop, he jumped out and Alana followed. Taurean took the picnic basket out of the back seat. Alana's stomach growled. She didn't realize how hungry she was.

"So where do we go from here?" she asked, adjusting the floral sarong she wore.

"Come follow me. We don't have far to walk, just a few minutes and I'll take care of that hunger with the feast I've prepared."

"You should have let me help."

"No, this is your day. After all you've had to deal with, you need some time to relax and enjoy life a bit. You've been here for most of the summer and haven't seen much of the island. We'll stay here for an hour and then I'll take you along the East Cost until we reach the parish of St. John and then back into Christ Church."

As they exited the parking lot, Alana became aware of the abundance of trees that inhabited the park. Scattered under the canopied shade, picnic tables provided a place to sit and enjoy the park's beauty.

They climbed a gentle incline before Taurean indicated the place they would sit. A man and woman walked toward them, unaware of their presence. The two stopped suddenly, and soon lips locked. They remained oblivious to their audience.

A bit embarrassed, Alana looked away, cheeks flushed at the thoughts running through her head.

An image of her kiss with Taurean flashed in her mind. She glanced at him, realizing that he too had gone silent and she wondered if he was thinking the same thing.

When they reached the table Taurean had indicated, he placed the basket on the table, and proceeded to take out the eats he'd prepared.

The spicy aroma of succulent fried chicken and the tang of macaroni and cheese wafted through the air, causing her stomach to growl again, this time louder.

Taurean laughed. "I'm sure you're going to do justice to the meal. The pleasure is entirely the chef's. Come, let's sit and dig in."

Alana complied as he filled each of the plates with hefty portions. Too hungry to care how much he'd given her, she waited patiently while he added potato salad and vegetables, and then placed a plate before her.

She did not hesitate, taking the fork, filling it, and raising it to her mouth. The first bite assaulted her taste buds. His macaroni and cheese tasted better that hers!

She'd perfected the dish because it was a favorite of Melissa's, but the way the cheese melted in her mouth almost made her groan with pleasure.

A tingle ran up her spine and settled in the back of her neck.

She looked up.

Taurean was staring at her with this look of amazement in his eyes.

"What's wrong?" she mumbled, pausing before she could place another brimming fork full in her mouth.

He hesitated for a moment.

"You're one of the most beautiful women I know."

She did not know how to respond.

She'd not expected this.

"You haven't seen many women in the past few years, have you?"

The words left her lips and somehow she wished she could catch them in her hands and take them back.

Taurean's eyes darkened, veiling the hurt he felt at her words.

"I'm sorry. I wasn't making fun of your being in prison. I didn't mean it the way it came out."

"It's OK. I'm still a bit sensitive about this prison thing. Prison doesn't hold good memories for me."

"I know, and I'm really sorry."

"Apology accepted. But let's not spoil the day being sorry. Tell me a bit about yourself. Your childhood. Your dreams. Your future."

"Remember, I told you I was born here, but the island looks so different from how I remember it. I can't even remember who my friends at school were."

At that moment, a black bird flashed by, startling both of them. Landing on a branch above them, it eyed them intently, and then as suddenly as it had appeared, flew away.

Taurean laughed at the bird's antics before he asked her, "Do you remember your parents?"

"I don't remember a lot about them. Only what the Delaneys told me. I still have a few pictures of them, but that's all. I take a look at them on their birthdays and mine. Just to keep their faces in my mind. While I'm here I'll try to find out where they are buried."

"So your adopted parents treated you well?"

"Yes, they did. Like I was their own. But it wasn't easy growing up with white parents. Yes, they sent me to the best schools, but for a while I lost touch with who I was and where I'd come from.

"When my adopted dad died and then my mom, it wasn't easy. Suddenly all the people I called friends weren't there any more. I no longer belonged in their circle."

"Is that when you met Blake?"

"Yes, that's when I met him and fell hopelessly in love. Everything seemed so perfect. I was no longer by myself. Maybe I thought I was in love because he represented all that I'd become, and I wanted to continue living like that. My work wasn't enough. I wanted to paint but the money left after their deaths went to other members of the family."

She paused for a moment, the memories too vivid, too painful.

"So do I get to hear a bit about your family now?" she asked. "I've revealed enough about my past."

"OK. I lead a pretty insignificant life. Just my three brothers, Patrick, Daniel, and Corey."

His voice softened at the mention of his younger brother, and she saw the telltale flash of pain in his eyes.

"People used to call the three of us 'The Buchanan Brothers.' We were pretty close, despite our differences. Patrick and I were always together. Daniel with his church friends and Corey . . . always on his own. We were so different in many ways, but we loved each other with a passion. Everyone knew you didn't touch one of the Buchanan Brothers without inviting the wrath of the others.

"Maybe we were close because of our father. We knew Dad loved us, but he was obsessed with his religion and perfection, and because of that we were punished a lot. He'd always say, 'Spare the rod and spoil the child'.

"Mom, she was different. Sometimes I'd wonder how she could let our dad do the things he did to us. Sometimes prison felt like heaven when I remember some of the things about home."

"Seems that we've both had lives laced with some form of abuse," Alana observed.

"Yes, seems that way."

For a while they sat in silence.

Toward the east lay the lands of the Scotland District. Gently rolling hills punctuated by the occasional valley. In the distance Alana could see one or two small villages nestled between the winding roads that lead to the coast. Toward the horizon, she caught a glimpse of the Atlantic Ocean beating its waves against the rugged beaches that lined the east of the island.

The horizon itself was clear. White fluffy clouds filled the sky, unaware of the hurricane. In a day or two, depending on its speed, the east coast would feel the full fury of Ivan's anger.

Alana sighed, breathing in the freshness of the clear sea breeze.

A butterfly floated by and she stifled the urge to get up and run after it as she had done as a child.

She sat in amazement when Taurean jumped up and shouted.

"Let's catch that butterfly."

Without hesitation, she joined him and they leapt, twisted, and jumped until the butterfly landed on a bright red hibiscus. Taurean placed his finger to his month, silencing her.

He reached out and gently held the beautiful insect.

"Isn't it beautiful?" he said, his voice filled with boyish wonder.

"Yes, it's lovely. I haven't seen a butterfly in ages. I remember as a child one of my friends and I catching them and keeping them in a jar."

Suddenly, Taurean let it go and it flew away swiftly. Soon, it was a small dot in the distance.

"I feel like that butterfly sometimes, don't you? In a strange sense we've been through so much that is similar yet different. Both of us trapped by circumstance. Now, we are free we're not even sure what to do about it.

"When I first arrived on the island and started to explore, it was to get out of the house, but then I started to enjoy it. There's nothing like driving with the wind in my face, and the sense of utter freedom I get while stand-ing here looking down on the coastline, or standing on the top of a cliff and seeing the endless expanse of water that seems to go on and on."

He reached out and took her hand, wanting to feel her warmth.

They sat there, neither saying anything. No words were necessary for the moment of oneness they felt. Comfort came from being next to each other.

As the day's light gave way to the oncoming darkness, Alana wondered how this episode in their lives would end. For now, the promise of a new beginning, of things wondrous, kept them dreaming of a future filled with happiness and love.

It was not just circumstance. There was something more going on here. Somehow destiny had drawn them together.

The mood changed and then it happened. That strange, exciting, scary moment when all senses are heightened and something profound and mind-blowing happens.

Alana felt the warmth of Taurean's hand slide slowly up her arms, felt a deep probing desire that she'd known was there but had not taken her totally in its grasp before.

She was coming alive.

She turned her head away from the hills and glanced in his direction.

And it slammed her immediately. If she'd not been sitting she would have been knocked over by the intensity of his gaze.

Unadulterated lust poured from his eyes or was it her eyes reflecting her own emotion? She could not tell. All she knew was that she wanted this man more that anyone she'd ever met.

There was just something about Taurean Buchanan that made her world turn upside down until she felt the kind of excitement she always experienced on a roller coaster.

Without thinking, she leaned forward. She had to taste his lips on hers.

She wanted to touch him as he'd touched her.

And Taurean obliged.

And then he was touching her, his firmness gripping her as if he wouldn't let go.

She closed her eyes, wanting to taste the essence of who he was. She didn't want to be distracted by a flying bird or a fluttering butterfly. She just wanted to experience him.

She groaned when he parted her lips, his tongue flickering in to tan-gle with hers like two kids at play.

But nothing like this could be child's play. This was man and woman drawing from each other in a serious dance of passion.

And then it was over as suddenly as it had begun, and he was gasping for air like she was.

He looked at her intently as if seeing deep inside her soul.

"I hope you don't expect me to apologize for that."

"I was about to say the same thing," she replied.

"Come here, closer."

She obliged.

She shifted, placed herself between his legs and her head on his chest, and he wrapped his arms around her.

"There's more to come, but now is not the right time. Let's just relax for a while before we leave for Christ Church."

So she did what he said, savoring his hardness against her.

As the streetlights all over the island flickered on, Taurean focused on the road ahead. One hand was on the steering wheel, the other on Alana's leg. Her hand lay on his.

Damn! What had he done? Even now his arousal strained painfully against the zipper of his pants, and he shifted uncomfortably in the seat.

He'd kissed her again before they'd left the park. It was different the second time.

A desperate, clinging, deep assault that had left him feeling hungry for more of Alana.

Over the radio, the lovely voice of a local artist crooned a ballad that spoke of being heroic. Taurean listened and knew he was nothing like that.

They all wanted him to be their hero, but he wasn't. He was just an ordinary man, in somewhat unordinary circumstances.

He was no hero, but he would do all in his power to make sure nothing happened to Alana and Melissa.

His attention returned to Alana, who lay asleep in the seat next to him. She was tired and slept like a baby, her steady breath causing her breasts to rise gently.

He needed to purge all thoughts of sex from his mind. He'd probably go crazy and resort to the method of release he'd used in prison, but he didn't want to go there.

He'd taught himself how to be in control. *He* was the master of self control. Or so he'd thought, until this woman had barreled her way into his life and heart, changing his cynical view of life. She'd taught him how to look beyond the pain and see the sunrise.

She'd suffered too, but she'd been a fighter in her own quiet, simple way, and despite her initial fragility and fear, she'd grown strong. He could see the new strength in the way she walked and the ways she spoke of her past and her future.

Yes, she was afraid of what her ex-husband represented, more so because of the danger to her daughter.

He turned into the driveway to the little house he now called home and slowly came to a stop.

He shook Alana awake.

"Alana, we're here. I'll get Melissa from Bertha."

She slipped slowly from her sleep. She looked like a kid coming awake. "Thank you. I'll go start dinner."

"No, let's just order some pizza. I'm sure Melissa has eaten already. I'll ask Bertha the best place to order from."

She exited the car, and he followed.

"I'll be back soon."

She smiled and turned toward the house.

Watching the sway of her hips as she walked away, he thought, damn, didn't she still look as fine as she had this morning.

CHAPTER 12

The local meteorological office upgraded tropical storm Ivan to Hurricane Ivan two days later. Taurean listened as the weatherman announced the latest advisory. On its current path, Ivan was expected to pass slightly south of the island, bringing heavy rain, high winds, and flooding, especially in the south of the island.

Less than twenty-four hours away from Barbados, Ivan presented a rare threat to the island. With each passing hour, the burning lump of anxiety in the pit of his stomach increased. He'd never experienced a hurricane before, but, as expected, its impending visit brought memories of Corey to mind. Despite having come to terms with the guilt that had haunted him while in prison, he still remembered his brother's last day vividly.

Since the early morning, he'd thought of Alana and all that had happened on their drive. At first, he had been disappointed. He'd wanted so much to hear her say she loved him. Then anger at Blake had replaced that emotion. Blake, who had destroyed her ability to trust and love. But Taurean was angry with himself for falling in love with her.

The trip around the island had convinced him of the extent of his love for her. Spending the whole day with her had drawn him closer to her, allowing him to see the woman she could be. Only the dark shadow of her ex-husband hovered in the background, keeping her from the joy of being totally free.

The phone rang, jolting him from the depths of his despair.

"Hello," he said, picking up the receiver.

Silence, then the usual click.

Since their trip around the island two days ago, so much had happened. Every few hours the phone would ring and there would be a long, ominous silence. He'd told Alana and Melissa not to answer the phone, as if he had no doubt that Blake was the caller.

He put the phone down and immediately it rang again.

He picked it up, about to say something not too polite, when Marc's voice came over the wire.

"Taurean, Marc here. I know that you're not too sure what needs to be done about the hurricane, so I'm on my way over there to give you a hand."

"Things to be done?"

Marc laughed. "Yes, there're a lot of things. I'll help you. You need to secure the windows with shutters. I'm not sure if some are already there but I can check when I get there. I'll be there in fifteen. Can't let anything happen to my new friends!"

"Thanks, Marc, I'll go to the basement and see if I find any shutters down there."

Taurean switched the television off and hurried downstairs. When he reached the sitting room, no one was there. He wondered where Alana and Melissa were. He checked the kitchen and was passing the den when he heard someone humming. Easing the door open, he saw Alana sitting at her easel. Her head was bent, her focus on what she was painting.

As if instinctively aware of his presence, she looked up.

"Hi." She smiled.

"Hi," he replied. "I just came to let you know that Marc is coming over to help me get the house secured in case the hurricane reaches the island."

"Oh, I heard it on the television too. The last report told us to expect rain in the late evening. Some of the businesses in town are closing early." He noticed a spot of red paint on her nose.

"Just wanted you to know in case you hear a lot of hammering, it's just the two of us working. When we're finished here, I'm going over to help Marc with their home."

"Can I help?"

"That's OK, Marc and I can handle it. Where's Melissa? Haven't heard her this morning."

"I left her upstairs reading. She was angry. She wanted to go to the beach to search for shells, but I told her that she had to wait until the hurricane passed."

A horn honked.

"It's Marc."

As Taurean walked away, he turned and looked back at Alana. Already she'd forgotten him, her focus on her easel.

For the next hour or so, he helped Marc prepare the house for the inevitable. Despite the threat of Ivan, he enjoyed the easy camaraderie of working side by side with his new friend.

It felt strange.

His brothers had always been his only close friends. In prison, he'd made no attempt to be friendly, preferring to be on his own with his guilt and pain. Loving and caring for others only hurt. He'd even refused to see Patrick, who had always been there for him. Now, feelings and wants he'd denied for so long were suddenly beginning to surface.

When the task was finally completed, Marc made a call on his cell phone, then turned to him.

"Taurean, we're going to have to stop at the hardware store on the way to my house. I've used a bit more of the wood than I expected to. We have to go now. The hardware store I'm going to closes in fifteen minutes."

Taurean contemplated telling Alana they were leaving, but she was so focused on her work that he didn't think she'd realize he was gone. He opened the car door and slipped inside. He wouldn't be gone long. Nothing could happen in such a short period of time.

Blake watched as the car drove off. A warm rush of excitement surged through his body, causing every pulsating nerve to tingle. The anticipation of holding his wife again aroused him. Soon, he'd be buried deep inside her. Then, he'd kill her.

As he glanced in the direction of the house, he wondered what she was doing. Probably reading to the little snot. They were always reading.

The sudden opening of the door forced him from his musings. She was coming out. Maybe he'd get his chance.

It was Melissa.

Disappointment was quickly replaced by delight. She would be just as good. Alana would be next.

He watched as Melissa skipped from the house toward the beach. Where was she going? Rage threatened to consume him. She may not be his favorite person in the world but she was his daughter. Why was Alana letting her traipse about on the beach alone when a hurricane was on its way?

In the distance, dark clouds billowed on the horizon, increasing his anger. He was definitely going to have to punish his wife.

Melissa stooped to pick something off the sand. He heard a squeal of delight and knew she'd found what she was looking for. Strangely, it made him happy. He wondered why he'd never been happy, wondered what had gone wrong that he'd not accepted the love his wife had offered. They could have been the perfect couple, the perfect family.

But his father had always said never let a woman control you; that if you fell in love with her, you'd lose not only your heart and soul, but also your logic. So he'd set out to possess Alana and whenever he felt the strange warmth that he associated with love, he found the willing arms of a woman who was guided by the color of the money he left on the bedside table.

At that moment, Blake realized he had to make his move. He noticed a trail of trees that Melissa would have to pass to get back to the house. He'd wait for her there.

As he moved slowly along the cliff's pathway and slipped into the dense undergrowth of trees, he started to tremble with anticipation.

Soon, she would be coming toward him. He sat there, hidden from view. She searched for a while and then headed in his direction, her feet hardly touching the ground. She was like an angel.

He dug into his pants pocket quickly, taking a rag and tiny bottle out. He soaked the rag with liquid from the bottle, flinching at the sharp scent that stung his nostrils.

When Melissa was close enough that he could almost touch her, Blake slipped from behind the tree.

At first, she did not see him, but she must have glimpsed the shadow from the corner of her eyes. When she turned, he saw the look of recognition, then stark fear replaced it. She opened her mouth to scream, but his quick hands stifled the noise. He pressed the moist cloth he held in his hand over her nose and watched with excitement as she slowly slipped into darkness.

Alana placed the brush down and stretched her neck. She looked at her watch. Time had slipped away. There was something she wanted to sketch. By now, evidence of the storm should be visible. She did not have time to paint but she could sketch the rising violence before the hurricane arrived. She picked up her pad and a pen. She wanted to capture this moment on paper.

Passing through the kitchen, she heard the sound of the television in the family room. Good, she observed, Melissa was watching TV. No need to disturb her. She'd only be gone for a few minutes.

Outside the wind had increased in strength. The sun had disappeared and in its place gray clouds hung low in the sky. In contrast, black ominous clouds swirled and twisted on the horizon, evidence of the chaos to come.

A cliff in the distance seemed a perfect vantage point and Alana quickened her pace. She knew she was being crazy to leave the house, but a few minutes were all she needed to sketch what she wanted.

She found a small trail that lead up the cliff's face and found a spot to sit. The wind, increasing in strength caused her to stumble, impeding her climb. Again, she wondered at the folly of her action. But she was already here.

When she reached the top, she stood looking out to sea, fascinated by the awesome scene before her. Waves crashed against the cliff on which she stood. She tasted fear, but she swallowed the feeling, and sat on the ground, the pencil in her hands moving swiftly across the paper.

When she was finished, Alana stood, intending to leave, and noticed the shadow of someone from the corner of her eyes. She gasped, startled that someone was there. Then, all she felt was a blinding pain in her head and the terrifying darkness of oblivion. The name she whispered before she crumbled floated along with the howling wind.

"Taurean."

Melissa stared at the man who was her father and wondered why he'd changed so much. She remembered watching a movie on television with a man who'd gone crazy and he looked just like her dad did now.

Her father's eyes were just like the man's. They seemed blank—not the look of dislike she'd seen there previously, but a wild, crazy look that made her scared.

He glanced in her direction, his eyes probing.

"So how's my sweet daughter?"

She did not answer.

"Cat got your tongue?" He laughed, a high-pitched cackle that caused her to tremble.

Melissa was afraid, but she wasn't worried. Taurean would come get them. She glanced toward the bed where her mother lay still asleep. Maybe he'd placed some of the smelly stuff over her mom's nose too.

She'd been surprised when she'd awakened in a strange bed, but as soon as she saw her father sitting in a chair next to the bed, she remembered what had happened.

She had to wake her mom if they were to be ready when Taurean came. She wondered how long they'd been here.

"I'm hungry," she told her dad.

"You're not getting anything to eat. Just keep quiet. I'm thinking."

"Please, daddy," she whined.

He frowned, trying to decide what to do.

"OK, but I won't be cooking anything. I'll see what's in the cupboard."

With that he slipped from the room.

Melissa immediately reached for her mother, shaking her.

But her mother just continued to sleep.

* * *

Dark, ominous clouds hung low over the island. The rain, a steady drizzle, tapped against the moving car. Trees, accustomed to swaying happily in the warm tropical breeze, bent under the strengthening wind. As the car pulled into the driveway, Taurean experienced an uneasy feeling.

Something was wrong.

He shrugged the feeling off. Maybe it was just the coming of the storm. Maybe it was the current chain of events he called his life.

He stepped out of the car, momentarily loosing his balance as a sudden gust of the wind belted him. Raindrops stung his face and arms, quickly drenching his shirt. Then he heard a voice. Alana's, calling him.

He looked toward the house, then at Marc, wondering if he, too, had heard the sound, but Marc remained unmoved.

Again, Taurean glanced at the house.

"Taurean, what's the matter with you? Seen a ghost?" Marc shouted over the raindrops.

Taurean wiped the rain from his face. "Nothing, probably just the storm. Thanks for the help. Get home to Anne. She's probably wondering what's wrong."

"Yes, didn't expect the car to break down. We got back just in time. This baby's going to get serious. Let's get your supplies out of the car. I'll be back to see how you're doing as soon as it's all over. The phones will most likely be out of order."

Holding the bags in his hands, Taurean watched the car drive away. Drenched, he turned and walked quickly into the house.

Something was wrong. The sound of the television led him to the living room, but no one was there. He switched the TV off.

It was quiet, too quiet.

The apprehension increased, now a knot coiled tight in the pit of his stomach.

He shouted for Alana, but no one answered. Where were they?

He called again.

Maybe they were at Bertha's?

He entered the den, dropped the bags on the floor, picked up the phone.

No dial tone.

He slammed the receiver down and headed toward the stairs.

Taking two steps at a time, he quickly reached Alana's room. He knocked. No one answered. He pushed the door open.

Empty.

One of Melissa's books lay open on the bed.

He looked out the window, but all he saw was the darkened sky and the swirling wind.

* * *

Hours passed and still the rain kept falling. Taurean's only thought was for Alana and Melissa. He'd gone over to their neighbor's house and had found no one, only remembering later that Bertha had told them she'd be helping a sister from the church who couldn't take care of herself and needed someone there if the hurricane did strike the island.

He'd searched the surrounding area, hoping that some clue, something, would give him an idea of where Blake had taken them. Only when the winds had grown too strong and flying debris had almost struck him did he return to the house.

He didn't have any evidence, but he was convinced that Blake had taken Alana and Melissa. He blamed himself for not taking them with him to Marc's house.

Taurean could hear the harsh, cruel howling of the winds. The house began to shake, trembling under the weight of the hurricane's strength.

Awareness of its power caused him to shiver. His concern for Alana and Melissa had made him forget his fear of storms. Now, the raging chaos outside brought him back to reality.

The wind continued to roar, its deafening sound echoing in his head. Again the house shook, the walls creaking as they shifted in the wind. He could hear the sound of trees cracking and crashing to the ground.

Suddenly, the lights dimmed, flickered, and went out. As winds of over seventy-five miles an hour battered the island, Taurean paced in the darkness of the sitting room, his anger increasing at his need to find Alana and Melissa.

A smiling Alana came to mind. Here he was, just a few short months after release from prison and he was already in love. He could see her clearly: her lovely hair, sparkling eyes, and the soft swell of her lips. Alana had made life worth living again. For years, he'd been tortured by the guilt of Corey's death, and now he was finally at peace with himself. He thought of the Sunday at church and the inner serenity he'd felt afterward.

He loved Alana.

She was more than just the sunshine in his life. She was life itself.

He wanted more than anything else in the world to see her happy, totally happy. He'd seen a glimpse of the woman she could be.

A vibrant, witty individual.

But there was another side of her he loved: the quiet, serious individual who found pleasure in the colors of nature; the Alana who sat waiting quietly for the right moment to capture the sunrise. Just like he now had to wait patiently for the eye of the storm. He'd seen her leave the house early each morning to go and paint. He'd even seen the finished products and knew she was a brilliant, talented artist.

He'd caught a glimpse of a passionate woman, and he wanted that woman in his arms at night, wanted to wake up next to her in the morning, wanted to see her swollen with his child.

And as suddenly as it had begun, the wind stopped. He raced outside. What greeted him was beyond his imagination. Trees that must have taken years to reach maturity now lay broken on the ground. He walked along the beach, his eyes appraising the few houses beyond Bertha's.

Nothing.

When he returned to the house several minutes later, he searched for Alana's cell phone, wondering if the signal would work, but his search proved futile.

Then he heard a noise in the silence. Someone knocking on the door. Relief washed over him.

They were back.

He rushed downstairs and flung the door open. A strong gust of wind pushed Bertha into the house, causing him to step back. He caught her, noticing the worried look on her face.

He moved her aside, putting his body against the door and forcing it shut.

"Where's Alana and Melissa?" he demanded.

"It's Blake. He has them." The words gushed from her lips, emphasizing her fear.

His heart dropped. "That bastard! Do you know where they are? If that son of a bitch lays a hand on either of them, I'm going to give him the beating he deserves."

"He's holding them in a beach house beyond the cliff. I tried to call the police, but the lines are down. While I was at Sister Clark's making sure she was all right, her grandson came home and told her that he'd seen a man take the little girl from America. I tried to get my car started but it wouldn't start. Even the cell phone wouldn't work. Sister Clark's son just drove me over when the winds died down. You need to go as soon as possible. Though we're only getting the occasional strong gusts, the eye of the hurricane will soon pass and the winds will get strong again."

"I'm going to go and get them." He reached for the door.

"Taurean, you can't leave now. It's not safe. I've asked Mrs. Clark's son to find Marc. He'll be here soon. You have to wait."

"I don't care. I have to go. They'll be expecting me to come for them. I don't want to let them down. I love them. They need me."

Taurean placed his arms briefly around her. "I'll be fine," he reassured. He turned and stepped into the already strengthening winds.

Alana slowly drifted from unconsciousness. She attempted to open her eyes and a blinding pain pounded in her head. She tried again and felt the tears flow, but this time she endured the discomfort. As her eyes adjusted to the bright light, she recognized her ex-husband. She tried to speak, but realized a gag covered her mouth.

"You're awake. Back from the land of the dead." He laughed, a sick, wild sound. "I should have killed you, but I wanted to see you suffer first."

Alana tried to sit up. Another bolt of lightning flashed in her head. She glanced at Blake and knew fear that went beyond any she'd ever experienced. There was a strange look in his eyes. Before, they'd always been cold, controlled. Now, she saw the wildness of a man who had reached the edge. She saw death, darkness, and evil.

Where was Melissa? Her gaze flicked around the room, then back to Blake.

He smiled evilly at the expression on her face. She knew then that he would kill her.

As if he could read her mind, he spoke. "Yes, I'm going to kill you. You deserve to die. You left my home with my daughter and took refuge in another man's bed." He paused, tightening her gag.

"You're mine," he continued, his voice steady, calm. "How easily you have forgotten your wedding vows. It's going to give me the ultimate pleasure to kill you and Melissa."

Melissa was still alive, Alana thought. *Thank God.*

She shook her head, opening her mouth to speak, but the cloth hampered her. She wanted to tell him that she'd go back to him, if he didn't hurt Melissa, but he only smiled.

"You want to say something. I don't want to hear it. If you had something to tell me, why did you leave me? We could have worked it out, but instead you ran away to another man." His voice was loud, angry.

She shook her head again, trying desperately to hold back her panic, her tears.

"No, don't lie to me! I know you. I know how your body responds to a man's touch." He glared at her intently, condemning. "Remember this. Until you die, you are mine. No other man will ever touch you again."

Untying the rag from around her mouth, he drew closer, his lips hovering over hers. She twisted her head, but he gripped her hair, causing tears to spring to her eyes. With the other hand he stroked her cheek, then along her neck.

"So sweet. Like fresh roses on a summer day," he murmured.

Then he seemed to fade away to another place in his memories. He leaned his head back, his eyes closed, his face contorted with passion.

"I remember the day we got married. You were so lovely. All in virgin white. Like a maiden to be sacrificed, to me. I was so proud of what I had acquired. That first night, I enjoyed taking your virginity. That was the pleasant surprise. A virgin over twenty-five. I was lucky."

He lowered his head further, an evil gleam in his eyes. Harshly, he pried her lips apart, laughing when she twisted her face away.

"You know what I remember most? The cry of pain you made when I rammed into you and took your innocence. When you screamed, I knew you were mine."

His loud ranting hurt Alana's head and she groaned, attempting to put her hands to her ears and block out his vulgarity, but they were tied.

The ropes dug into her wrists. Sharp pain coursed through her body.

Outside she could hear the hurricane raging. Was Melissa safe? she wondered. This was dangerous weather, but she knew Taurean would come. She whispered his name. He'd be here as soon as he could. She just needed to keep Blake occupied until then.

Lightning flashed through the loud scream of the wind and Alana felt the sky begin to fall, and then for the second time, she fainted.

When she awoke again, it was to the voice of her daughter.

"Mommy, Mommy, wake up."

Alana slowly opened her eyes. Melissa lay on the bed next to hers, her hands also tied. She was crying.

"Mommy, I'm scared."

"It's all right, honey. There's no need to be afraid. Just try not to get Daddy angry. We'll pretend that we are going to go back home with him. We have to keep him happy." She struggled to sound calm, not wanting to scare Melissa.

Melissa nodded.

Good, she understood what they were to do. Alana hoped that she could keep Blake calm. If he felt she would remain with him, maybe he'd let them live. She was more concerned about her daughter.

"Mommy, Taurean is going to come for us," Melissa said with the un-wavering innocence of a child.

Before Alana could respond, the door creaked open.

"Oh, both of my sweethearts are awake. Aren't we a happy family?" Blake mocked.

"Blake, I was wrong to leave you. It was a stupid mistake. I didn't really want the divorce," she pleaded. "I want to forget all this and go back home. I want to try again."

He looked at her, the expression on his face one of uncertainty.

He bent toward her, his lips hovering above hers. He was going to kiss her. She felt the slow rise of bile in her stomach and tried not to show her disgust.

His eyes flamed, then turned to ice, and he laughed, a harsh, hollow sound. When he finally spoke, his voice was chilly, like winter frost.

"Do you think I'm an idiot, Alana? Do you really think I believe your words? As if I'd want you back after you slept with that man. That ex-con. You give me up and then sleep with a criminal? You deserve to die!"

His eyes reflected the madness of his mind, and Alana expected him to hit her. Instead, he smiled at her, turned abruptly, and walked out of the room. His laughter echoed and mingled with the harsh sound of the howling wind.

CHAPTER 13

Outside was dark, oppressive, but Taurean needed to reach the beach house on top of the cliff before the winds reached full strength again.

He had no time to waste.

Like magic, he ran quicker than he had ever done before. Perhaps his mind was playing tricks on him in his anxiety. Maybe it was his fear and desperation or just pure raw energy flowing through his veins, that made him run like the wind.

The climb up the cliff was another surprise, but he was able to make his way up the steep, slippery path. After running for more than five minutes, he'd expected the ascent to be difficult, but he felt light, agile, energetic.

Maybe it was God helping him.

He reached the top of the cliff and looked in the direction of the house that he'd passed on a few occasions. The house no longer stood. Its large stones lay crumbled and in heaps where the walls had once been. Taurean circled the house, wondering where he should start looking. In one corner, he saw a bed trapped under a wooden beam, in another a stove crushed under the weight of a wall. Could they be under this massive destruction?

No, they have to be alive. *Oh, God, please!*

"Alana, Alana!" he shouted again, then listened.

Not a sound.

Then he heard a distant scream.

He turned, his senses alert, but could see no one. Trees blocked the path to the cliff on the other side of the rubble.

He raced in the direction of the scream, his heart beating so fast he could hear its pounding rhythm in his ears.

When he cleared the undergrowth of the trees he saw Alana. Blake held her, a glistening blade at her neck. She was quiet, silent as if she'd accepted the inevitable. To the left, Melissa sat on a boulder, her hands tied.

Taurean called her name and her eyes flicked in his direction.

"Taurean, don't let him hurt my mommy!" Melissa pleaded.

He approached cautiously, helpless, not knowing what to do. He had to be careful.

The man who held Alana's neck was a handsome man. But Taurean could see why they'd been so afraid of him. Blake was a large man—like him. The only difference was that Blake was lighter in complexion. But he could see that the man had lost control. Eyes red as blood stared at Taurean with hatred and disgust. The hand that held the knife trembled with rage.

Taurean was moving nearer when the man, his voice laced with venom, spoke.

"So here's the mysterious lover," Blake hissed. "The man who stole my wife. You're the reason she's going to die. I would have been willing to take her back, but she's no longer pure. You defiled her. She has to be sacrificed if she is to be pure again."

Taurean took a step forward.

Blake stepped back, taking Alana closer to the cliff's edge.

"Stay where you are," he demanded. "I'm going to kill her right now. I'll take a flying leap and take her with me."

Taurean remained still, unsure what to do. He couldn't take the risk of moving closer. The wild look in Blake's eyes indicated he would have no problem with doing as he'd just said.

But time was running out. The hurricane would resume soon. On the distant horizon, he could see the dark storm clouds approaching.

Cautiously, Taurean took another step forward.

"Don't do it, Blake," he said, trying to sound calm and reasonable. "Who's going to take care of Melissa if Alana goes?"

"I don't care. I hate her." He looked in his daughter's direction, an evil, condemning look on his face. "She took Alana from me, with her whining and crying. I told Alana I didn't want a child, and she dared to disobey me."

As the words fell from his mouth, he stumbled and Taurean saw his chance. He leapt toward them, his hands grasping Alana as they stumbled backwards.

The cliff crumbled beneath them and he felt himself falling as he pushed Alana back to the safety of the solid plateau.

Hands gripped Taurean's legs and his body hit against the cliff face as he fell downward. There was excruciating pain, and all he remembered before the darkness was that Alana was safe.

Alana crawled from where she'd fallen to the ground, looked over the edge, and expected to see Taurean and Blake's battered bodies at the bottom. Instead, she saw them on a ledge halfway down the cliff's face. She had to get help. She hoped Taurean wasn't dead.

She shouted to them, but there was no response.

"Mommy, Mommy? Is Taurean all right?"

Alana rose from the ground and rushed to her daughter. Untying her quickly, she held Melissa tight.

"Honey, we have to go and get help." She tried to remain calm, not wanting to scare her daughter. "Come, we have to go."

She gripped Melissa's hand and headed in the direction of the pathway that led down to the beach. As she moved, she felt the first touch of rain. When they reached the start of the trail, she heard Bertha's voice.

"Alana, over here."

She almost fainted in relief at Marc's familiar voice. Marc was with Bertha. Behind him was a tall man Alana recognized from church.

"Are you all right?" Bertha asked.

"Where is Taurean?" Marc interrupted. "Dave and I came to make sure everything was all right and Bertha told me that Blake had taken Melissa and Alana."

"Marc, you have to help him. Taurean and Blake struggled and they fell over the cliff. They're trapped on a ledge."

Marc moved toward the cliff. "Alana, you and Bertha take Melissa back to the house. We'll get Taurean," Marc shouted over his shoulder.

"No, I'm not going. I don't want Taurean to die," Melissa bellowed.

"Melissa, you have to go," Alana said, pressing her daughter to her. "Marc and Dave can work faster if they don't have to worry about you."

Her daughter's face wore a stubborn look, but she nodded. "OK, Mommy," she replied. She turned to Marc. "Don't let him die."

Bertha took the little girl's hand and led her toward the path down the cliff. Alana turned to Marc, noticing the tension in his stance, and that he hadn't responded to Melissa's request.

Alana watched anxiously as Dave, the man from church, set up a safety line between two trees at the top of the cliff. Marc looped a second rope around his waist and over his shoulder, tying it with an antislip knot.

Next, he slipped the rope around the safety line, then tied it around Dave's waist.

Dave took up the slack, playing it out as Marc went over the slippery cliff.

Alana could see the strain on Dave's face. She heard the instructions they shouted. What would have happened if they had not been able to come? Or did not have the skill with the ropes to help save Taurean?

She felt the first fall of raindrops on her arms. The winds, too, had increased their strength, and the raindrops like darts stung her already bruised skin.

There was a tug on the rope and Dave started to pull Marc back up. Marc soon struggled over the edge of the cliff. Deep furrows lined his forehead. "Taurean was conscious for a while, but he's out again. He has a broken hand and a few bruises, but he'll live. I've tied the rope around him, so we're going to have to pull him up," Marc informed them, his voice calm, reassuring.

Relief washed over her. Taurean was all right. She tried to control the tears that threatened to fall.

Dave moved quickly to Marc's side, grabbing the end of the rope Marc held out to him. Slowly the rope began to move. Inch by inch, it shortened, until they were helping a muddy, wet Taurean to his feet, his blood-stained shirt torn to shreds by the sharp rocks.

Alana rushed to him. "Thank God you're all right."

She wanted to hold him, but she made an effort not to, knowing she could hurt him. Lifting a shaky hand, she caressed his bruised face, needing to determine for herself that he was OK.

He tried to smile, but it was more of a grimace, and she felt his pain as though it were her own. He held his twisted arm carefully.

"Yes, I'll live," Taurean responded, his voice echoing strongly in the wind, but his eyes told her he knew how close he'd come to dying. He reached out with his good hand and touched her face, wiping the tears that slowly trailed down her cheeks.

"Where's Melissa? Did he hurt her?" he asked.

"No, he didn't. Bertha took her back to the house," Alana replied.

She turned to look at Marc. He nodded, and she knew that Blake was dead. With the rain beating against her, a wave of sadness washed over her, surprising her. She bit her lips and glanced at the crumbled spot where Taurean and Blake had fallen. She shuddered, feeling a mixture of relief at his demise and regret for what could have been.

"Alana, we're going to have to leave the body. There's nothing we can do for him now. This hurricane is soon going to be back at full blast and we can't be out in it."

She felt a twinge of guilt. Marc was right. There was nothing they could do. If they didn't get out of the increasingly dangerous winds, they could all end up dead. The wind howled around her, echoing the turmoil she felt inside. The branch of a tree flew by, causing her to duck. She stood for the briefest of moments, watching the sea, its waves high and powerful, lashing against the cliff. Yes, they had to go.

Blake was gone.

Deep inside, she felt intense pain. Life was so profound. She'd expected relief when she achieved her freedom. Instead, a heavy sadness gripped her heart. She'd wanted her freedom, but never at the price of a human's life. Fate had decided that Blake should die and Taurean live. Justice and retribution had been taken from her hands. For this she was glad.

She felt a hand on her shoulder.

"Alana, we have to go. He doesn't deserve your tears."

She turned to Taurean, the feel of his hand a comfort. It amazed her how in tune he was with her thoughts and emotions.

As she walked cautiously down the cliff's face, memories of a time long gone flashed in her mind.

Now, Blake was gone. She was free.

Hours later, and after Ivan had finally moved on, Alana pushed the door open, slipping quietly into Taurean's room. Taurean lay there, his eyes closed. Deep lines furrowed his brow and she could tell that even in sleep he was in pain. There was not much they could do right now, but wait the storm out. She was glad that he'd fallen asleep, because she knew that despite the painkiller he must still be feeling the discomfort of his broken hand. Bertha had tried to bandage it as carefully as she could, but Alana had seen the whitening of his lips and the pain in his eyes.

She sat in the chair next to the bed, the light from the oil lamp creating shadows and giving an illusion of comfortable sleep.

She reached out to touch his head, feeling the prick of fine hair. She was startled when a fist reached up and gripped her lifted hand.

For a moment she looked into his eyes.

"How's your hand?" she asked, unsure of what to say.

"It's not hurting as much as it was earlier. The painkillers have helped." He released her hand.

"I wanted to thank you for saving my life. I don't know what would have happened if you hadn't come along. I'd probably be dead, and Melissa too. Blake had lost all control."

"I'm sorry about Blake," Taurean said, his voice quiet, sympathetic. "No one deserves to die like that. It was his body that broke the impact of my fall. But for him, I could be dead, too."

She looked at him, feeling the tears in her eyes.

"He doesn't deserve your tears, Alana. He hurt you and your daughter." She heard the anger in his voice.

"I know. I wasn't crying for him. I was thinking that I could have lost you and you would never have known how I feel."

"How do you feel?" he asked quietly.

"That I love you; that I want you. When you fell off the cliff, I knew that living without you would be unbearable; that you'd broken down the walls of mistrust and unhappiness and showed me what it is to be loved.

"I wish I could give you everything you want, Taurean. But I can't right now." She watched his face sober, felt his hand tighten on hers.

"I need time. I'm going to ask Paula if I can stay with her and Patrick for a while. She's the only person I have now. She's the only person who'll understand. I need to get my life together, before I make any serious decisions about my future or commit myself to another relationship."

She paused, waiting for his reaction. He remained silent, as if overwhelmed by what she'd said.

Finally, he reached out, and when his hand touched her, she felt a fullness inside.

"I want nothing more than to marry you and make you my wife, but I understand what you're saying," he said.

Her heart soared. He wanted to marry her. But she did not respond; could not respond.

She saw the disappointment in his eyes, but his hands stroked her arm, gently, like a parent comforting a child.

"We can't do anything until the immediacy of Blake's death has passed. I agree with you. You need to explore who you are and your independence.

"I've decided to remain here on the island. When all this is over and you're ready to explore what we have, you can come back. I'll be waiting."

He closed his eyes, a smile on his face. She saw the tiredness in the slump of his body.

As he drifted off to sleep, Alana's gaze rested on the man who was her hero, and smiled, inhaling the fresh, rainy scent that still clung to him.

In sleep, he was beautiful, the harsh lines around his lips relaxed. She remembered when she'd first seen him she'd been overwhelmed by his size, wary of his serious demeanor. Now, she realized that it was the armor he'd worn while in prison. In order to survive, he'd had to be strong, distant. These characteristics had become so much a part of him that he'd continued to wear them as if they were an integral part of his personality, hiding the gentle creature inside.

He stirred and the blanket around him slipped to the floor.

Alana looked at him, enjoying the sight of his half-naked body. She had to leave. If she remained, she would only lose control. She wanted to touch him, feel his hands on her.

For the next few months, she needed to be away from him if she was to become the woman she wanted to be. She loved this gentle giant and wanted to marry him, but he deserved a whole woman, one who knew who she was. When she was sure that she'd accomplished that, only then would she return to claim the love that had been given so freely and unconditionally.

She rose from the chair. She needed to check on Melissa again. The day had not been easy for either of them. Her daughter had been fast asleep when she'd arrived back. She fought to remain awake, Bertha said, but the effects of the drug Blake had used still lingered. She'd cried herself to sleep.

Alana walked along the corridor, the quietness a soothing balm after the chaos of the past few hours.

Gently pushing the door to Melissa's bedroom open, she slipped quietly inside. Melissa was still asleep. As usual, she lay sprawled across the bed. Alana sat next to her, her hands reaching out to her daughter. She stroked the child's smooth skin.

This was the second time in less than a month that she'd almost lost her little girl, Alana thought. She remembered the night not so long ago when she'd awakened her daughter from a troubled sleep. Now, there would be no more fear of this kind in her daughter's life. She intended to let her daughter grow in a loving, nurturing environment—with Taurean. But as she'd told him minutes ago, she needed time.

Melissa needed time.

Her daughter had been through a traumatic experience. She'd heard her father say that he hated her. And she'd seen him fall to his death. For any child of eight, there would be some emotional scarring. Alana hoped she'd be able to help her daughter through it.

Alana walked over to the window. The view before her was so different from the one to which she'd grown accustomed.

Trees, once tall and majestic, lay broken on the ground. Flowers, bright and colorful, had been scattered afar.

The hurricane reminded her of her life. For the past few years, she suffered the abuse of a sick man. Yes, she'd come through the experience battered, but she'd proven herself to be strong, proven that she could take control of her own life. Now, she had to pick up the pieces, rebuild. She had to show herself that she could take care of herself and her daughter.

She watched as the island came alive again. A flock of seagulls flew over the sea, creating their familiar dance. In the midst of the drifting clouds, a glimmer of light was forcing its way through their denseness.

And as she stood by the window, golden sunshine burst forth, bringing the promise of another warm sunny day.

A wave of hope washed over her. She was free. But she wondered if she would ever truly be; if she could dream of a life of happiness with Taurean. She hoped somehow she would be able to bury the past, with all its darkness, and embrace the sunshine that Taurean was willingly offering.

But she knew she would face more challenges.

Alana moved toward the bed and slipped onto it next to her daughter. Melissa was the most important person in her life, and she couldn't repay Taurean for all he'd done for them.

She had to leave the island. Needed to make herself whole before she could commit herself to love and marriage again. Only when this happened would she return to the island.

It would only be a matter of time.

Taurean was drifting off to sleep when Bertha entered the room. She smiled. "So how's my hero feeling?" she asked, her voice soft and gentle.

"Just a bit sore, and tired. I've been trying to fall asleep, but can't get these images of Alana's crazy ex-husband from my mind."

"I'll just sit here while you rest. Do you mind if I sing? I used to sing this song for my husband when he was ill. It always made him feel better."

When he nodded, she reached out and took his hand in hers, and she started to sing a haunting Negro spiritual, her husky voice soothing.

She squeezed his hand and he looked toward her.

Something suddenly clicked. She reminded him of someone. Those eyes, those unforgettably kind eyes.

A long-buried memory hurtled into the present, bringing with it images of the night he'd pulled the life support from Corey's frail body.

The night he'd helped ease his brother of the pain.

He'd run from the room where Corey had suffered for months and wandered aimlessly all night, guilt consuming him.

He'd walked and walked for hours, until he found himself outside a tiny chapel. A single, flickering candle had beckoned him inside. He'd needed to ask God's forgiveness, needed God to understand.

Inside he'd found no one and had knelt with relief before the altar. Tears of pain and regret had poured from his soul, and when he'd turned to leave, he'd found a tiny woman kneeling in prayer next to him. Her eyes had opened and she looked at him.

"There's no need to despair. God understands your guilt and pain. Just believe he forgives."

She'd smiled at him with lively, caring eyes, and he'd bowed his head in shame. When he opened his eyes she was gone.

Now, he turned to look at the woman next to him. She reminded him of that woman. Not the total physical appearance, but the eyes were the same.

Full of love and compassion.

Maybe God provided comfort when needed.

The summer had been a strange one. The events punctuated by things he couldn't explain, feelings he couldn't understand.

But at each change in tide, he'd known that somewhere out there, some greater being watched over him.

When he eventually drifted into the world of dreams and of angels, two of the angels he saw were the spitting image of a woman and child who'd captured his heart.

Alana could not believe that a week had passed since the tragic events that had taken place on the island. Returning to the U.S. was not something she really wanted to do, but she had to do this, not only for herself, but for her daughter.

She'd already called Paula and made arrangements to be picked up at the airport when they arrived.

Now, she stood looking out to sea for the final time. She'd miss the place she now called home. The island had provided some of the healing she desired.

There were so many places on the island she wanted to paint. Already she had several paintings that were her best work. Somehow, the place of her birth had captured not only her heart, but her soul.

She inhaled deeply as if it were the last time she would, but she wanted to carry back the spirit of the island inside her so her memories would be vivid and real.

The crunch of sand behind her forced her to turn.

She knew it was Taurean approaching.

She'd hoped he'd come, wanted to see him one more time before she left. This would be her one chance to say good-bye without Melissa glaring at her.

Melissa's mood ranged from angry to sad. She kept complaining that she'd miss Taurean and her friends. Alana had tried to reason with her daughter, but to no avail. Melissa had hardly spoken to her in the past few days.

Taurean placed his arms around her.

She'd not expected it, but she found comfort in his warmth.

"I don't want to go," she told him.

"I know, but you need to."

"Yes, I need to." She sighed. "Melissa's not happy. She's not saying much."

"She'll come around. I'm sure she understands but she's going to miss Kerry and Karen. I think she wants to be sure she's coming back to the island."

"Of course, we'll be back. I told her that."

"Yes, but she's a child. She's been forced to grow up so quickly in the past few months, but she's still a child."

Alana paused for a moment. What Taurean said was so true. Melissa's life in the past year or two was more than a child of that age should have to endure. Visiting Paula and Patrick in Chicago would be good for her. The recent events remained ingrained in her mind, and Melissa had been traumatized by them as well.

Taurean glanced at his watch and said, "It's almost midday. We have to go. Marc should soon be here. I've already brought the suitcases downstairs. Melissa was on the phone."

"OK, I'm coming soon. Just let me stay here for another minute."

The weight of his arms left her, and she heard his retreating footsteps. She looked out to the sea one last minute.

Yes, she was leaving, but she would be back.

Taurean knocked on the door of Melissa's room.

At first there was no answer, then he heard the sniffle of cries.

He knocked again.

"Melissa, may I come in? It's Taurean. I want to talk to you."

He heard soft footsteps and the door slowly opened.

She stood there, tears in her eyes. It nearly broke his heart. How could he make his little angel better?

Suddenly, she flung herself in his arms.

"I don't want to go! I want to stay with you," she cried.

"I know how you feel, sweetheart, but your mommy needs you with her right now. You have to be a big girl for her."

"But suppose we don't come back?" she asked.

"Didn't your mommy tell you she was bringing you back?"

"Yes."

"So you need to trust her. Has she ever lied to you before."

"No."

"So you see there is nothing to worry about."

Melissa was quiet for a moment, as if internalizing what he'd just said.

"I know, but I'm going to miss you and Auntie Bertha, and Kerry and Karen, and the beach and . . . "

"OK, you're going to miss us all, but you're going to be back."

"Are you going to marry my mommy?"

"I hope so . . . but you and your mommy have to think about it first."

"But I've already thought about it, and I want you to be my daddy."

Taurean's chest tightened and he felt a wash of pleasure. Her words touched him and he wrapped his arms around her and kissed her on the top of her head. Damn, he loved this little girl.

"Yes, and I love you too. Don't worry, one day you are going to be my daughter."

He heard footsteps on the stairs.

Alana.

"Come, it's your mother. We have to be going. Dry those eyes, and be a brave girl for your mom."

He felt Alana's heat behind him and turned to her.

"Marc is here," he heard her say.

"On time as usual. Come, Melissa, we have to go. I'll stop by Bertha's on our way out. I'm sure she's going to want to say good-bye."

"I've already spoken to her," Alana said. "She came over last night and wished us good-bye. She's going to a meeting at the church, so she won't be at home."

Five minutes later, Alana looked back at the beach house that had been her home for the past weeks. She sat next to Melissa and her daughter's two best friends. Taurean sat with Marc in the front seat. Anne was at work. She was going to miss her friend.

A wave of sadness swept over her. She wondered when she'd be back. She had to admit she was excited about her plans when she reached the U.S.

In the distance, she saw the Grantley Adams Airport, its scaffolding hinting at the changes taking place to its physical structure.

Yes, she too had changed while she was on the island.

She was excited about returning to the U.S. There were things she wanted to do before she returned to the island. A showing of her art, of course, topped the list. She couldn't wait to continue work on some of the painting she'd done.

A few months of work!

But she was definitely going to be back.

CHAPTER 14

Gray clouds hung low in the sky, bringing with them a thick, damp op-
pression. Elm trees raised their branches to the sky, as if mocking the
solemn mourners who stood around the gravesite.

Alana stood alone, away from the gathering. Blake's father had made
it clear that she would not be welcome at his son's funeral. As far as he
was concerned, she had killed his son.

But Alana needed to be there; needed to let his parents see that she'd
not been broken by the years of abuse. She had also done it for herself.
In some symbolic way she needed to prove that she could face her demons.
Only when she had done this would she be able to move to the next level
of her inner growth.

Alana watched as Mr. Smyth-Connell glanced in her direction. With
the look of recognition came one of intense hatred. He turned away and
whispered harshly to his wife.

The fragile woman placed the final wreath on the gray casket and
turned to the pretty young woman standing next to her, Blake's sister,
Whitney.

Blake's father turned and again stared in Alana's direction. He started
toward her, his steps firm, purposeful.

Alana trembled. She felt like a rabbit cowering from a swooping eagle,
its sharp claws ready to rip her apart. She wished she could sink into the
ground. But she had to do this, had to face him.

He stopped before her, so close she could smell the sharpness of his
cologne. "What are you doing here?" he snarled.

Alana didn't answer. She didn't know herself. Maybe it was the guilt she felt. Or the need to see that Blake was really gone; buried, never to abuse her again.

"I'll never forgive you for killing my son. I'm going to ruin you."

Surprisingly, she no longer felt afraid. All she saw before her was an angry, bitter man who did not know how to love but whose power came from the money he had and the size of his body.

"I'm sorry," she heard herself say. She raised her chin, looking him straight in the eyes. "He tried to kill Melissa and me. It was an accident."

"*Accident?* If you had never left my son, he'd still be alive. Your leaving made him crazy. He loved you." Cold venom from his eyes spit at her, almost making her shiver.

"Love? Your son knew nothing about love. He beat me. He hit his daughter. Neither of you know what love is. You are a cruel, bitter man, and you made the same thing of your son."

"A man only beats a woman when she's disobedient. But that doesn't mean he doesn't love his woman."

Alana felt disgusted. She looked at the massive man who was trying so hard to be remain in control, to exert his power, and what she saw was a puny, pathetic creature.

"Like you love your wife? I look at her, and I feel sorry for her. To think that I could have become just like her. Thank God I had the courage to run away."

She looked him full in the eyes, feeling only pity for this man who tainted and hurt everyone he encountered.

"I feel sorry for you. You're a cruel, evil man. One day you're going to die a very lonely and unhappy man."

She saw a flicker of something in his eyes; surprise, wariness, but then it was gone replaced by the coldness that threatened to freeze her into a lump of ice.

Alana turned and walked away.

Yes, Blake's burial was a step closer to her desire for peace of mind.

Taurean replaced the receiver. Patrick had just called and told him that he and Paula were worried about Alana. She had been staying with them at their Chicago home for the past few weeks, but according to Patrick, she'd become quiet and withdrawn.

In the weeks since Alana and Melissa had left the island, images of them dwelled constantly in his mind. On the few occasions they'd spoken, he'd noticed a change. She was different: distant, and quieter.

He wondered what was worrying her; wondered if what they'd shared was already over. A dark sadness overcame him and he forced himself to embrace the beauty around him. He missed her so much there were times he didn't know how to handle the feelings of despair that threatened to consume him. He regretted not asking her what was wrong. When he'd shared his concern with Marc, his best friend had told him to give her time.

Melissa, too, came to mind. The last time he'd seen her, she'd been crying. The events surrounding her father's death had affected her emotionally and she'd wanted to stay on the island with him. He'd wanted so badly to go with them, wanted them to be a family. He wondered what she was doing. Probably watching television, or reading one of those girls' books that she devoured with such fervor.

He was going to return to Illinois. He needed to see that they were all right.

Patrick had also told him that she'd made contact with one of her former teachers who now ran a gallery in New York and wanted to do a show of her work. A plan that had been in the works before she left the island.

She'd never told him her plans.

Taurean wanted to hear her say that she loved him, missed him, but she never did. And the pain of her withdrawal had hurt him until he no longer slept nights, waking from nightmares he didn't wish to remember.

An image of her came to mind, and his body responded immediately. He could almost taste the sweet honey of her lips; feel the soft silkiness of her delicate body. His need for her was like a raging fire.

Maybe if she saw him she'd realize how much she loved him.

He was definitely going to book a flight for the weekend.

As he limped along the beach, the pain in his leg and the throbbing in his arm were reminders of his escape from near death. He didn't want to think about what had happened, didn't want to think about the fact that he'd almost lost Alana and Melissa.

There was a scurrying by his feet and he glanced down. A crab had crawled from its hole and was looking at him intently. It seemed to cock its head to one side and then swiftly slip back into its hole.

Taurean lowered himself onto the sand, his gaze on the spot where the crab had disappeared. Was the crab afraid, and alone? Did it have a family somewhere beneath the sand?

Strangely enough, he'd never seen a pair of crabs. They always seemed to be alone—thick-shelled, grouchy individuals. That was no way to live.

He felt the tears begin to fall, and he cried. He cried for his brother, Corey, for his father, and for the love of a woman who, for the briefest of moments, had turned him into a hero.

When he was spent, he made up his mind to fight for the woman he loved.

*   *   *

Twinkling stars appeared. The sky was clear, no clouds hid the brilliant glow of the moon. Footsteps crunched on the sand.

"Taurean." It was Bertha.

He looked up reluctantly, hoping she wouldn't see the evidence of tears in his eyes.

Bertha's face bore a look of concern.

"How are you doing?"

"Oh, I'm fine. The pain is still a bit trying, but I'll live."

"How're Alana and Melissa? Have you heard from them recently?"

"I spoke to both of them on Sunday night. I spoke to Patrick a few minutes ago. He and Paula are worried about Alana. They say that she's become withdrawn, too quiet. I'm going to see if I can get a flight tomorrow. I have to find out what's wrong. But I'm not sure if she wants to see me."

"Oh, Taurean, you know that's not true. You know she loves you. She just needs time. I think she needs you right now."

"I wish I could be as certain as you are, but I'll definitely go. I *need* to see them."

A gentle wind wafted from the north, bringing with it the warm scent of drying leaves. There was sharp crispness in the air with it. Reds, oranges, and shimmering gold colors everywhere. Autumn was at its most lovely. But already the breeze bore the chilly promise of winter.

The vibrant warmth of the island came to Alana's mind.

"Barbados," she whispered softly.

Memories of a time gone. Memories of a man whom she loved. She'd spoken to him just a few days ago—Sunday to be exact. Since then, she'd wanted to call him, but she was afraid.

Afraid of her love for Taurean.

And she did love him. Knew it with every day that passed, but she was afraid of what that meant. She'd thought that Blake's death would have buried all the pain, all the memories, but it had not. At night she would wake up, Blake's harsh face before her.

She realized that she would never make Taurean happy. Blake had killed that part of her. He'd killed the woman inside. Yes, she'd found her art, but the thought of loving, making love, terrified her. She did not want that feeling again, that vulnerability that made her helpless.

When she walked away from Blake's father at the funeral, she'd not been afraid of him. He could not hurt her emotionally. She didn't care for the man. It was the loving that made a person vulnerable, gullible.

But Taurean was not like that.

Was he?

She wasn't sure. He could change. Yes, he'd shown that he was capable of being gentle, but a good man could change. She'd seen it with Blake.

Damn, at times she was so confused, while at others she knew she was doing the right thing by not seeing him.

She was going to concentrate on her art as she had been doing for the past few weeks.

Her former teacher at the gallery, Nicholas LaClair, had committed her to a show. She had most of the paintings ready. Only the final painting was not completed.

She was not sure about the eyes. Eyes were the image of a man's soul. She wanted to see Taurean's soul. Only then would she know what to do.

The leaves crackled and she turned around, a smile on her lips.

She felt the blood drain from her face.

Taurean.

What was he doing here?

The returning smile on his face wavered. He'd seen her reaction.

"Hi."

Alana could not find her voice to reply. She still did not believe he was here.

She closed her eyes wondering if she were hallucinating.

She slowly opened her eyes. He still stood there, a look of concern on his face.

"Is something wrong? I hope I didn't scare you?" His voice was strained, forced, as if he were overcome with emotion.

"No, I'm all right. You're the last person I expected to see."

When she saw the flicker of pain in his eyes, Alana realized that her words had hurt him.

"I'm sorry. I didn't mean it that way."

"Alana, I had to come. I need to know what is wrong? We have to talk." The words tumbled from his lips. He was nervous, his hands twisting unconsciously.

She wasn't ready for this yet, but she owed him that much.

"I need to finish up here. Is after dinner OK?"

She saw his disappointment, but he smiled boyishly.

"Yes, that's fine with me. I'll go inside. Are Patrick and Paula at home? I'm not sure if they know I'm here. I dropped my bags on the porch when I saw you sitting over here."

He moved to go.

He stopped.

"I missed you, Alana." It was almost a whisper.

Then he turned and walked away.

She watched him leave, his tall frame somehow seemed smaller, frail. She could tell that he was unhappy, knew that he'd been hoping she'd embrace him.

But she couldn't.

When she'd looked up and seen him, her heart had stopped beating for the briefest of moments, but most of all she'd felt an intense fear.

Alana continued to watch him as he walked away from her. She wanted to run after him, but she knew she couldn't.

She was angry with herself. What had caused her to be so afraid of him? Now, she was convinced that seeing him and being with him would be a bad decision. She'd thought that in the past few weeks she'd grown strong. She'd been proud of herself when she confronted Mr. Smyth-Connell at the funeral.

Yes, she was stronger.

She'd actually let the man she loved more than life itself walk away.

Was she being strong?

Or did she just lose the man she loved?

The overwhelming sadness that Taurean had felt hung heavy on his heart. The warm moisture of tears threatened to spill. Damn, what was happening to him? This emotional stuff was taking a toll on him. He should have stayed in Barbados. He'd only made things worse by coming here. To say he was disappointed with what she'd said to him yesterday was an understatement.

He wished his mother were here. Maybe she'd use some of her wisdom to help him decide what to do. As a child he'd always been able to draw on her strength. Maybe that was why he'd been so disappointed when she'd not be there for him during the time after Corey's death. He'd been devastated.

His troubled thoughts returned to Alana. What was he going to do?

Did she still love him?

"Taurean!" It was Patrick. He turned in the direction of his brother's voice.

Patrick sprinted toward him, coming to an abrupt stop before him. His face was drenched in perspiration.

"Man, you should have come with me on the run. Damn, I feel great." He paused, realizing that something was wrong.

"What's up, bro?" Taurean saw and felt the concern. "Is it Alana?"

Patrick had always been so perceptive. It would be silly to deny what was wrong.

"Yes. She doesn't want me here."

His brother placed his arm around his shoulder and started to walk toward the house.

"Taurean, I want you to listen to me carefully. Life is not as straightforward as you expect it to be. Since you were young, you've always felt that you had to solve everyone's problems.

"Alana has just been through the worst experience of her life. You feel that you have to be the one to help her through this. She's confused and uncertain about her future, and now trying to find out who she is and if she's capable of taking care of herself and Melissa."

"But I can take care of them. I want to take care of them," he said.

Patrick could hear the despair in his brother's voice. "But that's not what she wants right now, Taurean. She needs space."

Taurean looked closely at Patrick, who had years of wisdom on his face. He loved his brother, and despite Patrick's fun-loving personality, he'd always been the level-headed one, the one to think before he leaped.

So unlike himself.

"Talk to her and then go back to the island. Give her the space she needs. Think about it. If you ask too much of her too soon, you may lose her forever."

His brother turned and walked away, leaving Taurean with thoughts he didn't want, thoughts that only served to increase his sense of dread.

Taurean knocked on the door of Alana's room. He heard the shuffling of feet, and then she stood before him.

She looked at him questioningly, as if wondering what he was doing there.

"I came to tell you good-bye. I've decided to go back to the island."

She did not respond. The look of relief in her eyes was enough to dash all his hopes of a future with her.

What did he expect? That she would jump into his arms and beg him not to go?

"Why?" When she finally spoke her voice was cold, distant. She was the picture of control.

The question, however, surprised him.

"Because of you."

"Me?" she questioned. He saw something flicker in her eyes, but the chill returned quickly as if what he had seen was a figment of his imagination.

"I realize that you don't need me; that you need to be by yourself. I came rushing in as usual, thinking that I could solve every problem.

"That's what Patrick told me. And I know he's right. When he called and told me that something was wrong and that you were unusually quiet, I felt I had to come to take care of you.

"I've done the same thing I promised I wouldn't do. Stopped you from being strong, taking care of yourself.

"I'm sorry, Alana. I just love you so much that I feel helpless, like I've lost control and I can't do anything to help you." He felt the wetness of tears in his eyes. He didn't want to cry. Didn't want her to see him weak. He wanted to be strong for her.

"Taurean, listen to me, and I want you to really listen this time." She placed her hands on his chest, as if wanting to give him comfort.

"Taurean, I love you." She paused as if she needed to think about what she had to say.

"I'm scared," she continued, "because I've learned that love can be just a word. But it must be manifested in action too. My heart tells me I do, but my body is saying something else: that it's scared.

"When I look at you, I see a man that I want to make love to, but don't know if I can respond. I dream about making love to you, and sometimes I wake up crying with pleasure; other times I wake up trembling and screaming.

"You deserve more than that. You deserve a whole woman, one who's warm and totally willing. Right now I'm not that woman. Maybe Blake's death is too near."

She reached out her hands and wiped a trickling teardrop from his left cheek. "When do you leave?"

"I'm just going to pack and leave as soon as possible. I have to stop in New York to meet with my grandfather's lawyer. My grandfather left money for me that I was to collect on my 30th birthday, but I was in prison. There's a plantation house on the island that I'm thinking about buying. I've been thinking of opening a bed-and-breakfast. I'm not sure I want to come back here to live. I miss the island."

"I do, too. Your idea sounds fantastic."

She paused for a moment.

"Taurean, I promise you that everything is going to be all right. I'm already feeling better, much better. I need to spend the next few months painting. The show is planned for November. I want to have as many paintings ready as possible."

She stopped speaking, and looked at him strangely.

"Can I ask you to do something for me?" she asked.

"Of course."

"I want you to kiss me."

Her request surprised him. He hesitated.

But then he saw the flame in her eyes. Despite her confusion, the conflict tearing her up inside, she still wanted him. He felt his chest tighten in anticipation, knowing that he had to take control, knowing that he had to take his time and not scare her. He wanted her to trust him and know that he would never hurt her.

Gently, he lowered his head, his lips taking hers cautiously. She moaned and his body tensed. He couldn't lose it.

Her lips opened at his probing and with it he tasted the tang of the orange she must have eaten for breakfast.

Taurean kissed her firmly but gently, savoring the firmness of her breasts against his chest, her nipples against him.

Unexpectedly, her arms twined around him, drawing him closer, bringing his hardness close to that secret garden he so wanted to enter.

Moving involuntarily against her, a wave of red-hot fire coursed through his body. He was losing control. He had to stop. But she felt so damn good. So perfect.

His hands found the zip at the back of her dress and slid it down, the dress falling around her.

She wore no bra and her breasts rose firm and eager toward him. He lowered his head, enjoying their loveliness, his lips moving tentatively against one nipple, drawing it between his lips. He suckled, nibbled, her groans exciting him, releasing the years of sexual frustration that had been trapped inside him.

As he suckled, his hand found the core of her being. He pressed his hands against the moist flower. Again, she moaned, a strained, frustrated sound that tore from deep inside.

Taurean gently lowered her to the bed, his eyes on her face, seeing the love she felt for him. He lifted her skirt, his hands sliding her panties down. Gently he parted her legs, his fingers finding and kneading her nub of desire.

She was wet, ready for him, but he knew he couldn't take her. He had to give her pleasure, not think of his own desires.

He looked at her, her eyes closed, her face filled with the pleasure he was giving her. He felt her tense, her body close to release.

Capturing her lips again, he stifled the cry that tore from deep inside her, a primal anguished cry. Then he felt the wetness on her cheeks, on his own cheeks.

For what seemed like hours, she buried herself in his arms, her breathing rapid, erratic. She was crying.

"I'm sorry," he whispered softly.

She looked up, and it was then that he saw the embarrassment on her face, in her eyes. She was ashamed of what had happened. She did not know that what had happened to her had been beautiful and oh so wonderful.

"Alana, what's wrong? Talk to me?"

"I feel—I don't know." She stifled a sob. "Exposed. Nothing like that has ever happened to me before."

"Oh, Alana, what just happened to you was made to happen. It's something beautiful that God made for man and woman to enjoy. Are you trying to say that that never happened with Blake?"

"No, it never did."

"He was a selfish bastard. A man who loves his woman always makes sure that she gets her pleasure first. In fact, his pleasure comes from knowing that he's giving her pleasure."

She looked up at him.

"Thank you."

"Alana, I want you to stay with me tonight. Just lie next to me. I'll leave in the morning. When you're ready, just come to me on the island. I'll be waiting."

She smiled as if what he'd said gave her the ultimate joy. She pulled his head down, placing it next to her on the pillow. She drew closer to him, her head on his chest, closed her eyes, and was soon fast asleep.

Taurean held the woman he loved, looking at her as she slept. He wanted to give her so much pleasure. The fact that he was the first to take her to the stars and back gave him a sense of pride. Yes, she was his. She'd come to him on the island. It was just a matter of time.

As his eyes grew heavy, he smiled to himself. Yes, she was going to be his.

But how could he stand the wait?

CHAPTER 15

Alana sat at her easel. She wanted to begin the last painting that day. But she was trembling. Her usual steady hands shook.

She'd spent the early morning mixing the paints to achieve the perfect color for his skin.

Dark bronze.

That's what came to mind. Now that she was finally ready to begin, her hands were unsure.

Was she doing the wrong thing?

No, she needed to do this. She needed to put his image on canvas, and forever capture her impression of him. But that was what worried her. She thought of him in so many ways, but she also saw him as a man, capable of base animal qualities.

She chided herself. She was so sure she'd resolved her conflicted feelings for him. But now she realized she hadn't.

His visit to Chicago had left her shaken. He'd touched her in a way that had given rise to a fear so intense that she'd been glad when she'd awakened the next morning and he was gone.

Two weeks later, she could not get him out of her mind.

Two weeks in which she'd ached to feel his arms around her and the hard touch of his lips on hers.

She wondered if she should call him. Paula had told her he'd be arriving back on the island today after spending time with his family.

She'd realized how easy it could be for a man to control her again. She'd fought so hard and long for her freedom that she did not want to lose it. With Taurean, she knew that she would. He only had to look at her with those whiskey-colored eyes and her body grew hot and moist.

Alana stared at the canvas, the cool cream color conflicting with her dark troubled emotions.

How should she paint him?

The tender Taurean, his gentle hands holding a tiny bird. Or should she draw him diving into the water to save Melissa?

Yes, she would do those, but those would just be used to practice. The image she wanted still eluded her.

"Mommy, Mommy." She turned at her daughter's voice.

Melissa raced toward Alana, her face covered with a big smile.

Alana was glad to see this Melissa. The last two months had not been easy for her daughter. For weeks after Blake's death, she'd awakened screaming at night.

The usual anger rose inside. Even in death, Blake still haunted her daughter. Now that Melissa was seeing a psychologist, the dreams were fewer and fewer.

Putting the palette down, Alana opened her arms to her daughter, and was not surprised when Melissa hurled herself into them.

"So how was the visit to the mall?"

"I had a great time. Aunt Paula is so much fun. Do you like my new sneakers? Aunt Paula bought them for me." The words tumbled from Melissa.

"They're pretty. Did you remember to thank her?"

"Sure, Mommy." She moved to look at the painting Alana had sketched.

"That's Taurean." Melissa went silent for a moment. "I miss him. When are we going back to Barbados? I miss Kerry and Karen, too."

"I'm not sure, honey. We can't go until after my show. Remember it's going to be in a few weeks. We have to go to New York first."

"Are we ever going to go back? Are you going to marry Taurean?"

Alana felt the heat wash her face. She didn't know how to answer.

"I'm not sure, Melissa. There so many things we have to do."

"But Taurean can help us. He loves us. He told me so." She stopped suddenly.

"He told you that?"

"Yes, he told me he loved us and wanted to take care of us. I love him too."

Alana continued to stroke her daughter's hair. To Melissa everything was so simple. She wished that she could be like her daughter, wished she could throw caution to the wind, get on a plane and fly to Barbados. But she couldn't.

She just wasn't ready.

"I know you do, Melissa. And one day we're going to go back, but now's not the time. You go on back to the house. I want to get this painting started. Tell Aunt Paula I've fixed lunch and it's in the oven. I'll eat later."

"OK, Mommy. Can I call Taurean to make sure he's reached the island safely?" She paused. "Please?"

"Yes, but ask Aunt Paula first."

"Thanks, Mom."

Alana watched as Melissa ran off—as usual, as fast as her feet could carry her.

She turned to the canvas. She finally knew how she'd paint him. She remembered that night not too long ago.

The beach.

The moonlight.

Yes, she knew exactly how she wanted him to be.

Two hundred, two hundred and one, two hundred and . . .

The shrill of the phone broke the rhythm of his sit-ups. He placed his hand on the floor of the verandah, and pushed himself up, moving quickly to answer the cordless phone lying on the couch.

Before he could say hello, Melissa's voice rushed at him. He smiled.

"Taurean, it's Melissa. Aunt Paula gave me permission to call. I just wanted to see if you'd reached Barbados safely."

He smiled again. She sounded so mature and grown up.

"Yes, I arrived this morning. I made sure I passed on your letters to Bertha, Kerry, and Karen."

"Oh, good. I chat with them every night on the Internet. They told me Uncle Marc got them a dog. I can't wait to see her. I've never had any pets. When you and Mommy get married, I want a dog and a cat and a bird."

He pretended he'd not heard what she said, preferring not to comment or give her false hope of the possibilities.

Melissa went quiet, and when she spoke again, he heard the disappointment in her voice.

"So, you're going to come to Mommy's show?"

"I can't, Melissa. I'm going to be very busy in the next few weeks. I'm building a small hotel."

"A hotel? Where?"

"On the island, close to where the beach house is."

"Oh, cool, and I can come and stay there when we come back to Barbados?"

For a moment, her voice was interrupted by the beep of call waiting.

"Melissa, I'm going to have to go. I'm expecting an important call. I love you, sweetheart."

"I love you too, Taurean."

He listened for the click when she put down the phone before he connected to the other caller.

It was Marc.

Good, he wanted to talk to Marc about his plans.

He intended to make the island his home.

With or without Alana.

Taurean heard the slamming of a car door and turned away from the sea. Marc was strolling toward him. His friend reached him, easing himself onto the boulder on which Taurean sat.

For a moment, Marc sat quietly, his gaze on the gentle pounding surf, as if he too needed to be soothed by the gentle sound.

"What's up, buddy? I know our meeting is not until tomorrow, but I was passing by, and thought I'd drop by and see how things are going."

Taurean looked at his friend. In the past few weeks, they'd become closer. He'd grown to care for the tall, sensitive man like a brother. While in prison, he'd not had any close friends, and it felt a bit strange when he sometimes missed Marc. The man was the only one he felt comfortable talking to about Alana. He'd still not told him about his past, his prison life. He needed to let his friend know.

"You look pretty down?"

"It's strange, isn't it? I've just started building my future, and I'm not totally happy about it."

"It's Alana, isn't it? How is she? Anne told me she's having her show next week. They seem to talk fairly often."

"Yes, lucky Anne."

"You and Alana don't talk often?"

"We did at first, but things have changed, are different. I can feel her drifting away. My going to Chicago to see her was a mistake. Things only got worse."

"I'm sure everything will be all right."

"I'm not sure I can agree with you, but I'm going to focus on getting the hotel up and running. I'm hoping we can be ready to open in a year's time."

"That's sounds great. That means everything went well at the bank today."

"Yes, everything went great. There are still a few minor details to work out but everything is as good as it can get."

"That's wonderful. Wish I were in your position right now."

"Well, since you feel that way this may be the perfect time to make you a proposal. I need a partner. Someone who knows a lot about finance and management and is willing to work hard. Interested?"

Marc looked surprised. "I'd like to say yes right now, but I need to talk to Anne first. But I'm sure she'll say yes. She knows I haven't been too happy with my job. I want a challenge. Something new. I have some money saved, so I'd be able to inject some capital."

"Don't worry about the finances right now. But I want you to think about it carefully, Marc. There's no guarantee that we'll succeed."

"I know that, but we can give it our best shot. If things don't work out, I'm sure I won't have a problem finding another job."

"You're going to have to work long hours."

"What are you trying to do? I thought you wanted me in."

"I do, but I don't want you to make a mistake that you'll regret without thinking about the consequences."

Taurean released a ragged breath. "I've been trying to tell you something since I returned to the island but the time never seemed to be right. You should know that when I came here I'd just been released from prison."

Strangely, he felt no shame, no guilt while he told Marc his entire history. He knew that Marc would understand.

Minutes later, when he'd finished his story he realized he'd told his friend everything. About prison, and the years of guilt, about his alienation from his family, and most of all, his love for Alana.

"That's quite a story. You've been through so much in the past few years, it's time you reached out for some happiness. You can't let your happiness be determined by someone else. In order to make someone happy, you need to find that same happiness in yourself."

Taurean listened to what his friend said.

"This may sound clichéd, but if you love someone you can't stifle that person. There are times when you have to let that person fly free. If Alana is to be a part of your future, she'll come back to you."

"What you say is true. So many people have told me that in the past few months. It's strange, but I've been told that I'm as stubborn as a mule. Patience is definitely not one of my strongest virtues."

He started to laugh and Marc's quiet voice joined his.

CHAPTER 16

Taurean folded his cell phone and slipped from the car. He slammed the door. Anything to vent the anger raging inside.

Patrick had just called about Alana's show. He'd told Taurean about the rave she had stirred with her painting of him the night before—the private showing of her work. Tonight, however, her work would be on display for the public, and he was not sure how he felt about the nude painting of him.

He turned to the building before him. Marc had heard the old plantation house was for sale and had called him immediately.

As he stood looking at the massive structure, he was amazed at the transformation that the workmen had performed. At first he'd not been sure whether to buy the old building, but when he'd stepped inside, he'd known that he had to purchase it. The house was alive with its past. He could almost see the occupants of the house as they went about their daily tasks. He'd known it would be perfect for a bed-and-breakfast guesthouse.

With the help of one of the island's best architects, Taurean had created the look and feel that he wanted. Now, he could see the plans being put into reality. The building had retained most of its colonial structure.

He gazed around the grounds, admiring what he saw. The landscaper had already performed a miracle. Immaculate lawns had replaced the jungle of bushes and trees that had greeted him when he'd seen the house for the first time. A kaleidoscope of vivid flowers had been the final touch, turning the disorder into a garden of tropical perfection. Majestic mahogany trees remained, but now blended perfectly with the vibrant setting.

He walked toward the beach. Even now he still found solace and comfort in the gentle lull of the surf, in the sea's quiet serenity.

He heard a scurrying by his feet and looked down. A crab had crawled from its hole and was looking at him intently. Again, it seemed to cock its head to one side and then swiftly slip back into its hole. He wondered if it were the crab he'd seen before. It had focused on him with that same bold curiosity. Somehow seeing it gave him comfort.

But he still felt used. He could not believe Alana had done what she did without asking him. Patrick had told him the painting was brilliant and being hailed as a masterpiece, but he didn't care about that. All he knew was that she had exposed him to the whole world. And she'd never even seen him naked.

An image of him swimming in the buff flashed before him. He wondered if she'd seen him having one of his nightly swims.

Damn, he was going to sue the ass off of her.

Before the thought left his mind he regretted it. He knew that he couldn't do anything to hurt Alana.

Then he saw the humor of the situation, and laughter erupted from deep inside.

He was definitely the "butt" of the joke.

On the opening night of her show to the public, Alana stood in the gallery, the soft light from the numerous candles creating a mood of tranquility. Tropical plants and brightly colored flowers gave an island feel to the room. In the background pulsating reggae music stimulated the senses. A wave of nostalgia washed over her. She missed the island. Missed . . .

On the walls, paintings of all aspects of the Barbadian life had been mounted. She felt a surge of pride in her work. She knew it was good, the best work she'd ever done. Somehow she knew the reviews in the next day's papers would be good. She was that confident about her talent.

In the months since Blake's death, she'd painted almost nonstop. She'd spent two months at Paula's and had created pictures of the island. Barbados remained so fixed in her mind, that when she'd put the brush to canvas, she'd had no problem transferring her vivid memories into stunning works of art.

The manager of the gallery who had purchased her work years before had welcomed her with open arms. They'd loved her new work—the brilliance, the colors, the sunshine. When they'd expressed an interest in having a showing of her work, she'd been thrilled, agreeing to complete the required paintings as quickly as possible.

The intensity of the project had helped her to survive in the initial months. But she'd proven that she could do it. That she had her own identity and did not have to live in the shadow of a man. At first she'd been scared, but as the days went by, she had grown stronger and more confident. Even when she spoke to Taurean she'd been able to maintain her distance.

She circled the room, stopping every so often to acknowledge the compliments of the well-wishers. Last night's private reception had been a success, but the true success of her work would only be known in tomorrow's newspapers when the critics either praised or destroyed her.

Eventually, she stood before the painting in the center of the room. She'd wanted to avoid looking at the particular piece, but had been drawn by its magnetic pull.

Taurean looked out at her, walking out of the water, moonlight caressing his body. He was a god, emerging from his home, the sea. The painting was bold, but subtle. There was a hint of the erotic, but the viewer was left to wonder if he was naked under the water. Only the upper half of his body rose from the swirling tide. There was the hint of promise; it tantalized, but maintained an air of mystery.

She felt the familiar quickening of her heart and the sharp tingle of heated blood rushing along her veins. She looked at him, noticing his eyes, golden pools of pulsating emotion. She'd been able to capture the very essence of his soul. She called the painting *The Birth of a Hero*. The name many wondered about, but few knew and understood.

Suddenly, she wanted to leave. She glanced at her watch, relieved when she realized the show would end in fifteen minutes.

She wanted to get home to Melissa. She'd made a decision and she needed to talk to her daughter about her plans. She had proven that she was independent and confident.

Now, it was time to keep her promise, to go after what she wanted most in life.

The babysitter opened the door, and Alana entered the apartment that had been home since she'd returned to New York for the show. Melissa, lying on the couch, waved briefly at her and returned to the world of Disney's *Beauty and the Beast*.

Alana had been sure to get professional help for her daughter. And Melissa was slowly recovering. She was finally able to sleep through the night without waking up in tears. Her talks with Taurean helped too, and for that much Alana was grateful. Melissa was confident about Taurean's love. Alana had grown accustomed to the squeal of delight whenever Taurean called.

She paid the babysitter and joined Melissa on the couch. She pulled her daughter to her and sat to watch the rest of the DVD.

As the credits scrolled up the screen, Melissa turned to her. "How was the show, Mommy?"

"It was great. There were a lot of people there. Most of the paintings were sold."

"I'm glad, Mommy. It's good to see you happy. You look so sad at times. Do you still miss Taurean like I do?"

Alana looked at her daughter, amazed at her perception and maturity.

"Honey, I'd like to go to Barbados and see Taurean. Would you have a problem with that?"

"Can I go, too? Are you going to marry him now? Please, Mommy!"

Alana laughed at her daughter's words.

"Yes, I'd like to, but I'll need to go by myself. There are some things that I have to talk to him about."

For a moment Melissa was silent. "OK, you mean grown-up stuff." Her voice brimmed with excitement. "I'm going to make a card for you to take for him. And one for Kerry and Karen. May I use the computer?

"Yes, you can use the computer."

A wide grin spread across Melissa's face.

"When do you leave, Mommy?"

"I'd like to go tomorrow. As soon as I've talked to Taurean, we'll come and get you."

Melissa squealed in delight. "I've missed Taurean, and Karen and Kerry, Auntie Bertha—the sea, too."

"You're going to have to stay with Auntie Paula for a while."

"It's all right, Mommy. I like Auntie Paula, and Uncle Patrick is so much fun."

"I'll go and call Paula now and let her know that you're coming."

The plane landed as the sun set on the horizon. The cool tropical breeze hinting of flowers brought back memories of the summer weeks on the island.

Alana hailed a taxi and gave him directions to the beach house where Taurean was still staying. She knew that he was refurbishing a plantation house he'd purchased, but he'd not moved in yet.

As the car drew closer to the tiny fishing village that led to the beach house, her stomach tightened. She wondered how he'd react to *her* intrusion. For some reason, she had been distant with him during the past few months. She couldn't explain it, but whenever he'd called, she'd clammed up inside. She was sure that he still loved her. Had heard it in his voice every time they'd spoken on the telephone. But she was no

longer sure he would want to see her. She knew she'd hurt him with her
distance. She had to make things right.

When the car came to a stop in the driveway of the beach house, the
lights in the house were on. He was at home. Her heart started to pound.

She expected him to rush outside but he didn't. She paid the taxi driver,
lifted her bags and walked onto the patio. Resting her luggage and portfolio on the floor, she knocked on the door. It swung open.

"Taurean," she shouted, but there was no answer. He wasn't in the
house, but, instinctively, she knew where he was.

She headed for the back door.

Slipping off her shoes, she dropped them and ran toward the beach.
When she reached the palm trees that lined the beach, she heard the
faint splash of someone swimming. The slow heat of arousal stirred within
her. She didn't have to see Taurean to know he was naked.

She watched as he treaded the water with his usual firm strokes. He
stopped, rising out of the water. As he stood looking out to sea, the
moonlight gently caressed his body reminding her of the picture she'd
painted of him, *The Birth of a Hero.*

Alana slipped out of her clothes and lay them on the sand. She walked
slowly toward him.

At first he did not hear her, but he turned as if aware of her presence.

She almost laughed at the expression on his face.

"Care for some company?" she asked.

He did not respond, but as she drew nearer she saw the burning desire
reflected in his eyes. She glanced down, seeing his arousal. A mixture of
pride and relief washed over her.

She continued toward him, enjoying the power she had over him. He
wanted her, but most of all she saw the love in his eyes. She'd made the
right decision.

When she reached him, she moved into his embrace, loving the feel of
his hard body against her. She felt safe, warm, but was stunned by the jolt
of pure lightning that flashed through her body, setting her on fire. She
trembled in anticipation, knowing somehow that this would be an experience she would never forget.

When his head descended, she welcomed his mouth with lips apart,
wanting to taste his maleness. Tongues entwined, she not only tasted the
saltiness of the sea, but the very core of his soul.

She pushed him gently from her. "I love you, Taurean Buchanan."

His immediate response was the most beautiful of smiles. One that
spread from his lips to twinkle with happiness in his golden eyes.

"I love you, too," he responded, his voice husky with desire. The emotion in his eyes ignited with a spark of passion, and she saw the raw desire
smoldering, burning.

He bent to lift her, and when her feet left the seabed, she placed her arms around his shoulders, as he strolled out of the water. For the briefest of moments, she experienced a flicker of fear, but quickly removed the thought from her mind. She trusted him, knew he wouldn't hurt her. He was so large, but she remembered his gentleness with the tiny bird.

When he reached the line of trees, he placed her tenderly on the mossy sand. She lay on her back gazing at him. He hesitated as if waiting for her approval.

Touched by his consideration, she stretched her hands out toward him. He did not need any more reassurance before his body was pressed firmly against hers. The strong, firm feel of him was enough to send her crazy with wanting, and she shivered as the flame spread, settling hot between her legs. A moan escaped her lips and she looked at him, deep into the pool of his eyes, and she saw the passion reflected there.

"Taurean, I can't wait. I want to feel you inside me now."

"No, I want this to be special. We have to do this right. I have to protect you."

She sighed, but remembered that she'd come prepared for the inevitable. "In my jeans over there, the back pocket."

Taurean moved quickly, and returned before she could miss the warmth of his body. Alana reached for the condom, unwrapped it, and rolled it slowly onto his length, feeling the intensity as his body reacted to her touch.

She wanted him so badly.

When his warm lips tugged on one sensitive nipple, her hands gripped his head, holding it closer. A rush of heat surged up her body. She twisted her head from side to side, the painful build of pleasure almost too much to bear. As he suckled on first one nipple, then the other, she ran her hands on his smooth back, wanting to give pleasure.

His lips touched her all over, finding the most sensitive spots that stoked the burning heat inside her.

He suckled on the throbbing pulse on her neck, causing flickering flames to bring every nerve ending in her body alive. When his warm mouth moved slowly down to the flat of her stomach, her body tightened. His mouth moved tenderly to the delicate flower, already blossoming from his gentle ministrations. He was skilled, taking her to the edge, then bringing her back again, until she was wet and ready to feel him deep inside her.

"Taurean, please. I'm empty inside. I can't wait any longer," she pleaded.

He raised his head, and moved cautiously over her. Her legs instinctively moved apart, eager to welcome him.

When he slipped inside her, she felt the purest pleasure, and was amazed when a cry of utter delight rushed from her lips.

"I love how you feel around me," he moaned. "So tight and warm. I've been thinking and dreaming about this for so long."

He remained still for a while, as she grew accustomed to the size and feel of him. But she could not wait any longer. She raised her hips toward him and was rewarded with a strong silken thrust, causing her to grip his firm buttocks.

Slowly, he stroked her, igniting the heat inside. She moved with him, reveling in the perfection of their movement, her hands roaming, teasing, across his broad back.

Alana felt the tension build inside her and heard the roar of release racing from a distance. Taurean increased his pace, thrusting into her with deep fluid movements. He filled her completely, and she gloried in the fullness of each steady stroke.

"Yes," he groaned. "You are pure magic."

She felt his body tighten, knowing his release was near. The thought took her flying skyward, and when he tensed and groaned again, she joined him as the power of his release forced him to leap with her into that glorious place where sunshine poured like liquid gold over them.

She held him close as he trembled and shivered above her, hearing his words of love. She held him tight, not wanting to let him go, wanting to savor this moment of oneness. He tried to move, but she tightened her arms around him.

"Don't, I need to feel you on me." She stroked his back, causing him to shiver.

"But, I'm heavy."

"No, it's fine, I'm going to have to get accustomed to your size." She laughed, a happy satisfied sound.

He kissed her gently, and she felt the stirring of arousal.

"Make love to me again, Mr. Buchanan," she cooed.

His mouth found an eager nipple and he set about giving her another glimpse of heaven.

Taurean drifted slowly awake. Alana lay next to him, her hair spread around her. Her breasts rose invitingly toward him. He hardened immediately. Making love to her had been more than he'd imagined. Already he wanted her again. He remembered how she'd moaned and responded to him.

Alana opened her eyes, seeming disoriented for a moment. When she saw him, she smiled, stretching lazily.

"Thank you," she whispered.

He grinned. "I should be the one doing the thanking."

"I'm not only talking about tonight. Yes, tonight you taught me the meaning of love. But you've also taught me about trust and gentleness.

When I was in Chicago and New York, I missed you so much. So many times I wanted to drop everything and run back to the island. But I had to stay for Melissa and myself. I did it for you. You deserve a woman who's strong. When I left here after Blake's death, I wasn't that woman." Alana paused for a moment. "There's something I left in the house that I need you to see. Come with me."

She rose, stretching a hand out to him. He held it, pulling himself up, careful not to topple her over with his strength. He slipped on his pants, watching as she dressed, enjoying the sight of her slender frame, unable to believe she was actually his.

When she was finished dressing, he slipped a hand in hers and they walked toward the house. Alana led him into the sitting room where her bag lay on the floor. He noticed a rolled canvas next to it. She picked it up and handed it to him.

"I want you to have this," she said when he held it.

He unrolled the canvas and gazed at the picture before him. An intense emotion rose inside him, and he felt the tears pooled in his eyes.

He could not find the words to speak.

"So what do you think?" she asked.

"I don't know what to say. No one has ever given me something so special." He heard the emotion in his voice, and hoped he wouldn't burst into tears.

"Thank you," he added. "This means a lot to me. But I'm no hero."

"To me you are. That's exactly how I see you. How Melissa sees you. You're our hero."

"At least this is not the naked one. I'm hoping you're not selling that one."

"Definitely not."

She sat next to him.

"Taurean Buchanan, will you marry me?"

He looked up, his heart full of happiness. He drew close to her, his lips poised above her.

"Just say when," he said, as he captured her already-well-kissed lips.

Bertha Gooding switched the television on, prepared to enjoy an hour of her favorite local program. She could finally relax. She'd been sitting in her verandah when Alana had joined Taurean on the beach. She'd quickly moved inside when she realized she'd seen things getting a bit too heated. Everything had worked out as she wanted. She'd never met two people who more deserved to be with each other.

She'd grown to love each of them like the children she'd never had.

Memories of her husband came gently, like a whisper on the wind. She'd experienced a love like that once. When her husband had passed away, she'd thought she could not go on. Now, ten years later, she was enjoying life to the fullest. Some nights she would wake, aching for his arms around her for one more time. She'd loved him so much.

It pleased her to see that same kind of love between Alana and Taurean.

Alana was like a daughter. She'd seen the pain Alana had suffered at the hands of her crazy ex-husband. She'd also seen the hint of a strong, confident woman. And Alana had fulfilled that promise.

Taurean.

What could she say?

She'd grown to love the tortured man with the heart of gold. She remembered when he'd first arrived on this island. Silent and distant. He'd changed from that wary, cautious man to one whose face carried each nuance of emotion.

Taurean's strength lay rooted in the nobility that was so much a part of his personality.

And he was one that any woman should be proud to marry.

If she were thirty years younger she'd have given Alana some stiff competition.

Well, she was glad to see that all was over. She couldn't wait to see Melissa again. She more than enjoyed the conversations they'd had the time Alana had called and Melissa insisted she speak to her "Auntie."

Oh, well. That was all over. She did love her happy-ever-after. She just hoped they'd hurry and give her some more children to call her "Auntie."

EPILOGUE

Taurean stepped out of the shower, dried his skin, and slipped the sweatpants and tank shirt on. His wife lay asleep on the bed and he stood looking at her. He loved her so much that sometimes he felt the intensity of it deep within him.

Her hair spread around her face. She looked so peaceful, almost as if she were smiling in her sleep. He hardened as he looked at her. Damn, what was wrong with him? They'd made love all day while Melissa was at the Blackman's. He'd lost count of the number of times they'd made love, but the stiffness in his back and the pleasant fatigue that he now felt was evidence of the energy he'd exerted.

He looked at her for the last time and slipped out of the room, and headed down the corridor to Melissa's room. He knocked.

"Melissa?" He wondered if she were still awake.

"Yes, Taurean, come in; I'm still up."

He entered the room and she was sitting on the bed reading.

"Hi," he said.

She smiled.

"Lissa, there is something important I need to talk to you about. I've asked your mother and she thinks that you should be the person I ask."

"What?"

"I've been wondering what you'd think if I adopted you, became your father legally."

She was quiet for a while, the expression on her face one of serious contemplation.

"Would that mean I'd get to call you Dad?"

"Yes, but only if you want to."

The expression on her face turned to one of utter delight. She squealed and launched into his arms.

He held her tightly, enjoying the childish smell of her shower gel.

"Feeling hungry, Angel?" he asked. "Want to go get something to eat?"

"Chocolate cake from the wedding?" she asked hopefully.

"Yes," he replied. Alana would get him in the morning, but for now he wanted to give Melissa the world.

He stood, holding his hands out to her, memories of another night like this vivid in his mind.

As they walked down the stairs, he felt a happiness that he could not describe.

A few hours later, Taurean slipped under the covers next to his wife. He placed his arms around her, basking in her warmth.

She stirred, drawing closer to him.

Immediately, he felt the familiar slamming in his stomach that he experienced whenever he was near her. He couldn't get enough of this woman.

Her eyes flickered open and she smiled.

"I woke up and realized you were gone."

"I went in to check on Melissa. I wanted to tell her the good news."

"I thought we planned to tell her together. You couldn't wait," she chided. Her fingers trailed lightly along his arm.

His body tingled.

"Not that good news. I told her about the change of name, and that I'll be her legal dad if she wanted me to be."

"So what did she say?"

"Oh, she agreed but she did ask me to promise her something."

"And what was that?"

"That she'd have a brother or sister soon."

Alana laughed.

"That means she'll be happy with the other good news."

"Yes, she'll be delighted with our news."

He lifted the blanket and pressed his hands gently against the slight mound of Alana's stomach.

"Yes, she'll be more than delighted."

He reached over and switched the bedside lamp off.

"Come, let's go to sleep. I have a busy day ahead of me."

Long after Alana fell asleep, Taurean lay awake. A year ago, he'd have never imagined he'd be married with a wonderful wife, daughter, and, hopefully, a son on the way.

God was good.

He'd not only found love.

He'd somehow captured the sunrise.

Dear Reader:

Thank you for taking the time out to read *Capture the Sunrise*, Taurean and Alana's story.

Years ago, I took up the challenge from a student who dared me to write a romance novel. It's maybe fifteen years since I told her that I'd do it, but I finally have.

Capture the Sunrise is the first in a quartet of stories featuring the Buchanan brothers. I not only wanted to write a story of love, but one of healing and forgiveness. By the time I'd written "The End," Taurean and Alana, both wounded souls, had grown into the people I wanted them to be.

I'll be telling Daniel and Patrick's story later, but next year's story, *Embrace the Moonlight*, will introduce Mason Sinclair, who only discovers he's a Buchanan brother when his mother tells him that his biological father has passed away. By the time you read this letter, that story will be complete, and I'll be hard at work on Daniel's story.

Many years ago, a favorite author of mine said that she wanted her novels to make readers laugh and cry and laugh again. I'm no way as talented as she is, but I've always used her words to guide my own writing. If I've taken you through a range of emotions and left you feeling content, then I've accomplished my goal.

Feel free to visit my Web site at www.waynejordan.com, or e-mail me at author@waynejordan.com.

May God continue to bless you.

Until . . .
Wayne Jordan

Dark and Dashing

Devon Vaughn Archer

To H. Loraine, Marjah Aljean, Jacquelyn V., and those sweet and wonderful nieces of mine who continue to amaze me.

ACKNOWLEDGMENTS

I am thrilled to be one of the first male authors to write for Arabesque and look forward to writing many page-turning romance and romantic suspense novels for years to come.

To that end, I would like to thank my editor, Demetria Lucas, for recognizing my artistic abilities and expanding the Arabesque line to include talented male contemporary romance authors.

Also instrumental in the publication of *Dark and Dashing* in this anthology is my agent, Michelle Grajkowski; who believed in me from the start and has worked diligently on behalf of her clients in helping them to make dreams come true.

I owe a particular debt of gratitude to H. Loraine, the most important person in my life and someone I know I can always count on through thick and thin, for her continual support, unending faith in me, and excellent critiques and editorial assistance.

Finally, I must thank the Man upstairs for His love, guidance, and blessings, which have always carried me through the journey of life and all it embodies.

CHAPTER 1

The celebrity auction had been held at the Shoreline Hotel and Casino for the past five years. Luminaries had come from around the country to the resort town of Oak Cliffs on Oregon's central coast to participate in this year's autumn charity event to promote literacy. The money raised would be divided among various foundations and nonprofit organizations specifically aimed at eliminating illiteracy, as well as supporting local and national programs that encouraged reading among youth.

Conneca Sheridan, local owner of the Sheridan Seaside Inn and a member of the Oak Cliffs Business Association, was participating in her third auction. She sat amidst what seemed to be a sea of mostly women, distinguished by her brilliant butterscotch complexion and unusually attractive midnight-colored hairstyle, which included Senegalese twist rolls up front and layers of long individual braids in the back, cascading across her narrow shoulders. Conneca's tall, model-slender frame further separated her from the pack. She wore a black Ann Taylor squareneck sheath dress, complemented by a beige jacket with padded shoulders and high-heeled mules. A simple pearl necklace and matching earrings completed her look.

Though quite busy with her life, Conneca gladly volunteered her time and was prepared to donate a bit of her hard-earned money for an evening with a celebrity, even if she generally had a disdain for the egotism and arrogance that seemed to go with the territory for most who wore that banner. After all, she reminded herself, it was for a most worthy cause.

Conneca had been particularly concerned with child illiteracy. When she was in college, she voluntarily taught inner-city kids, who had dropped out of school, to read. It was part of a project between the University of San Francisco and the city to rescue children from illiteracy and its devastating implications for both their individual lives and society as a whole. Since that time—or for the last nine years—Conneca had tried to be involved in some form of volunteer work that helped people with one of the most basic necessities and joys of life: the ability to read and write.

Now thirty, still single, childless, and seemingly eons away from her dream of being someone who could truly make a difference in life, Conneca brushed aside past reflections and future yearnings and concentrated on the moment at hand. Beneath thin, slightly arched brows, she focused her big, bold café-au-lait eyes on the next celebrity to be bid on.

Almost immediately, Conneca felt a shiver sweep through her as if she were hit with a gust of wind. An air of familiarity took center stage. She watched as the tall and elegant-looking, handsome brother—built like he never missed a workout a day in his life—walked down the runway with the poise of a person running for office. He was in his early thirties, she guessed, and was a rich fudge chocolate in color. The man abruptly came to a complete halt in front of her as if to flaunt himself in her face.

Conneca batted her lashes at first in annoyance, then in abashment, sure that all eyes were on her—and him—at the moment. But while she may have wished she could shrink into nothingness, that would probably be playing right into his hands, so to speak. *Just be cool, girl,* she told herself determinedly.

Following her own advice, Conneca managed to gather herself, feeling there was no other choice in the spirit of things but to appraise *him*. At well over six feet, he was resplendent in a double-breasted black tuxedo, white shirt, and black bow tie. His head was clean-shaven with only a hint of the raven hair he could have had, which would have been the perfect match for deep, dark, soulful eyes. She noted that on his right earlobe was a small ruby earring. On a taut, square-jawed face was a cute little nose that expanded as a toothy grin spread across a sensual full mouth, as if he were immensely enjoying having every woman in there bidding to be at his beck and call for the rest of the day.

Or maybe me, in particular. Conneca shuddered. *Who was he?* she wondered, piqued. She was sure she had seen him before. How could one *ever* forget such a man machine of a human being, if there ever was one?

Conneca suddenly became aware that he was looking directly at her, seemingly amused by her almost hypnotic stare. She hastily averted her eyes, refusing to give him the privilege of thinking that she might actually be interested in paying for his company in specific, charity or not. She would let some other sister or sister wannabe feed his ego. *I'll set my sights elsewhere, thank you.*

But that didn't stop Conneca's mind from working overtime as to who he might be as a celebrity figure. Perhaps the man was an actor? She scanned her brain. Or maybe a musician. An athlete? A journalist. Or even a politician, heaven forbid! Admittedly, Conneca didn't make a habit of watching many movies or TV programs that he might have been in. And she was more into older music like classical jazz and Motown sounds. She could imagine him being more into hip-hop, if anything. If he was into politics, forget it, she thought. She knew the faces, but at times lost the message in an atmosphere where it was all about *me, me, me,* and often you couldn't really distinguish one person from the next who ran for, or were already in, office.

The reality was that Conneca was far too busy with the inn and everyday life to keep track of who was who in the world of celebrities. Yet that didn't quell her curiosity about the drop-dead-gorgeous brother before her or, for that matter, stop the frustration over her inability to place his face.

Over the loudspeaker, a woman announced in a voice filled with giddy admiration: "All the way from Denver, Colorado, is the dashing, cool-as-he-wants-to-be Maurice Templeton. He's the *very male* half of the wildly successful romantic suspense novel collaboration team known by most of us readers as Alexis Maurice. Won't you please make Maurice feel welcome to Oak Cliffs?"

A rousing round of applause followed, and shortly thereafter the bidding began for the right to temporary custody of the clearly-more-than-willing author.

So that's who the mystery man is, Conneca mused, wondering how she had missed the connection. She knew now where she had seen Maurice Templeton. Or at least his face. It had been on the back of one of his books. A friend had lent her a copy of Alexis Maurice's latest bestselling novel last year called *Danger At Sea.* Conneca had found it a fascinating, suspenseful read with just the right amount of romance and mystery to keep her thoroughly satisfied. She'd completed the book in only two days, though it was over three hundred pages long. She remembered thinking, in seeing the glossy color photograph on back of the book of the attractive authors cheek to cheek, that they seemed like the perfect couple and madly in love or, perhaps, lust.

In fact, she recalled her friend, Nadine, telling her that the two were once married, but far from perfect. Divorced now, they remained connected as writing partners for their novels. Conneca had fixed Nadine with a look of disbelief, and said, rolling her eyes: "They must be using smoke *and* mirrors, or something. If they couldn't make the *marriage* work, it seems like anything else would be asking way too much."

Nadine had hunched her shoulders, chuckling. "Money makes for strange bedfellows, girl! They may hate each other's guts in private. But so long as the books are selling like hotcakes with plenty of butter and syrup, they're keeping the dirty laundry where it belongs and making like they are still lovebirds for public consumption."

Conneca thought the whole thing sounded more like the fiction they wrote than real life, where love obviously didn't always conquer all. But, she thought, hey, whatever worked for them, if not for her.

Conneca had to admit she still found herself curious about the two authors as ex-husband and wife. *Or more like the one,* she realized now in considering Maurice Templeton, who had already moved smoothly to the other end of the runway and seemed to really be enjoying this king- for-a-day scenario. As did virtually all those in attendance, judging by the cat-calls and whistling for this handsome king.

The bidding had gone up to nearly five thousand dollars, by far the most that had been pledged during the auction for any celebrity. Conneca gasped at the notion and wondered who would be crazy enough to donate such an outrageous amount to spend time with this one man, who was probably already spoken for, very conceited, and dullsville behind the brilliant mask—even if it was for a good cause.

Her answer came quite shockingly as Conneca inadvertently raised a hand to scratch her cheek. The auctioneer, a rotund man in his fifties, who looked as if he were wearing a grayish toupee, saw this as her bid of five thousand dollars, and pounced on it like a leopard.

"The pretty lady with the beautifully braided hair has brought the bid to five thousand dollars," the auctioneer bellowed gleefully. "Does anyone care to top that for the privilege of Mr. Templeton's enchanting company, and a most charitable contribution to help remedy one of society's hidden ills?"

Realizing that no other bids were forthcoming, Conneca tried to right her wrong. She muttered some undecipherable words of mistake and protest to no avail.

It was too late.

"Going once . . . Going twice . . ." The auctioneer strained his voice, while peering at his audience, as if trying to will the ante to be upped by some wealthy soul, perhaps an elderly woman who thrilled at the prospect of being rejuvenated on the arm of the famous, handsome author.

It was not to be.

"Gone!" the voice bellowed with finality.

Conneca had just bought the temporary rights to Maurice Templeton for far more than she had been prepared to contribute to promoting literacy. It suddenly left a sick feeling in her stomach. She was barely breaking even with the inn and was hardly in a position to donate five grand for the company of a man who didn't appear as if he needed such expensive companionship to take pity on.

"Damn," muttered Conneca under her breath. *Smile for the folks.*

She flashed pearly white, straight teeth for all to see. Inside, Conneca felt as if she had been sucker punched. She would just have to make the best of it, she decided.

And him.

She looked up at the stage, expecting to see Maurice Templeton's broad grin as he sized her up and considered the possibilities the evening might entail. Instead, Conneca found that the man she had unwittingly won the bid on had suddenly vanished like a thief in the night.

The breathing that raised the hairs at the nape of Conneca's neck was warm and gentle, almost soothing. Before she could turn around backstage, the deep, velvety voice practically sang Stevie Wonder's *Signed, Sealed, Delivered I'm Yours,* baby . . . for the rest of the day.

Conneca met the intriguing, dominating eyes of the author that bore down on her at an angle attesting to his height of at least six feet four inches, compared to her five foot seven inches. His features were even more arresting and virile up close, as was his natural scent mixed with Intuition. Conneca found it intoxicating.

He favored her with a steady, amused grin, as though reading her mind and feeling his potent affect on her body. It made Conneca all the more determined to resist being overwhelmed by the man. Or his celebrity status.

"Maurice Templeton," he said routinely, as if she didn't already know. "And you are . . . ?"

"Conneca Sheridan." She willed herself to keep from shaking on the outside like she was on the inside.

He nodded. "Nice to meet you, Conneca. I like your name . . . it's very intriguing."

I'll bet you do. Conneca was skeptical. *Don't read anything into it that's not there, buddy.*

Maurice stuck out a hand, the long fingers spread like a turkey's feathers. Conneca shook his hand, which was as soft to the touch as it was hard. His skin was smooth as silk, and she noted a half-moon-shaped scar on the back of his hand.

"Happened when I was just a boy," Maurice explained perceptively. "Was fishing with my old man—or trying to—when I ended up being hooked myself instead of the fish. It was really more embarrassing than painful." He gave an uneasy chuckle and pulled his hand from hers, burying it self-consciously in the pocket of his trousers. "Are you always so generous with your money? Or are you one of those 'can't put 'em down' fans of Alexis Maurice novels?"

Part of Conneca wanted to tell him that she had not intended to write a one thousand dollar check to chaperone him for the evening, much less five times that amount! And though she had very much enjoyed the one Alexis Maurice book she'd read, she would hardly call herself a diehard fan of theirs—or his. Or some sort of crazed groupie.

But what was the point in that, Conneca asked herself. She didn't want to come off sounding cheap or irresponsible in bidding much more than she could afford. *Why not feed this brother's obviously inflated ego and try to just get through it?* After all, she'd probably never see him again once they said their good-byes in a few short hours.

Pasting a smile across her thin lips, Conneca said in a self-compromise, "Let's just say that I'm a big supporter of ending illiteracy in this country."

Maurice touched the tip of his shiny nose and said without making waves, "Fair enough. That is, of course, what brought us to this point— even if it is a lofty goal by any standard. Wouldn't you say?"

She fluttered her curled lashes. "Isn't that true for any worthwhile aim? That doesn't mean we shouldn't try."

"I couldn't agree more," he seconded.

Conneca didn't doubt that the task would require a considerable amount of cooperation and education across the spectrum. But in this case, it was worth each grain of hope for every child who could improve upon his or her reading skills.

"Every little bit counts," she told him, as if to justify her involvement and five thousand dollar investment in the effort.

Maurice favored her with one brow raised. "True enough. It's always the little things that grow into big things."

Conneca turned away from his gaze, feeling its warmth as though basking in sunlight. Or perhaps like being in an oven with the temperature continuing to rise to the point of broiling.

A moment of awkwardness stood between them like a brick wall. It seemed to signify the mutual attraction that neither was ready to acknowledge to themselves, much less to each other.

Maurice finally broke the deadlock by saying, "So, are you going to the literacy conference in Denver next month?"

Are you inviting me? Conneca's question was sardonic, knowing full well he was doing no such thing.

"I'm thinking about it," she told him. In fact, she had received information in the mail about the conference, but had not committed one way or the other, knowing that the inn had to take precedence over anything else—including leaving town. But she didn't need to tell him about her business. "Will you be there?" Conneca decided to ask.

Maurice seemed to ponder the question as if he hadn't previously considered it. "Not if I can help it," he said honestly. "I try to stay away from these high-profile events so close to home. You agree to one and the vultures are banging down the door trying to lock you in for every charitable event known to man, woman, and child."

Conneca was only mildly surprised. She imagined that, realistically, successful writers could only give themselves to so many causes before they ended up spending more time on the social and charity circuit than writing. The same was true as well, she thought, of innkeepers. Still, the notion of visiting the Mile High City next month had its own appeal all of a sudden, if only in her mind.

Maurice leaned forward slightly. "Look, I don't know about you, but I'm starved. What do you say we go get something to eat?"

That was always a safe bet, Conneca thought, remembering the previous times she had won the rights to a celebrity guest for a charitable cause. One had been a seventy-nine-year-old world famous concert pianist. The other was a thirteen-year-old boy genius. Everyone had to eat, regardless of his or her claim to fame.

Conneca had a feeling that anything she did with Maurice Templeton would be a different story altogether. And this both excited and scared her like never before. Whether that was a good or bad thing remained to be seen. *I'll just go with the flow,* she thought.

"Sounds like a wonderful idea," Conneca told him in a thick voice.

CHAPTER 2

The woman who sat across from him at the Shoreline Hotel restaurant enchanted Maurice Templeton. He glanced at her small hands resting on the table. Long, perfectly manicured nails were painted a dark and dangerous shade of red. He could only imagine what those thin, supple fingers were capable of. And imagine Maurice did, even when the better part of him warned: *Don't even go there, man.*

Now he appraised the rest of Conneca Sheridan. The fine sister had remarkable sable Senegalese twists and box braids that just wouldn't quit. The latter rested sexily across her shoulders like slightly ruffled feathers. Her facial features were even more appealing. Oval, burnt almond eyes—or maybe milk chocolate, he decided—considered him unsteadily beneath thin, arched brows. Caramel-colored skin stretched tautly over high cheekbones, a narrow nose, and a slightly jutting chin. Her mouth was generous and sparkled with rose-colored lipstick. From what he could see, she had been blessed with a perfect figure of small, high breasts, narrow waist, and long lean legs. Being tall was a definite plus, he thought, imagining her coming up to his shoulders. Perfect for kissing, were it ever to come to that.

Even in the auction room Conneca had stood out like a bright light in darkness, though she had clearly tried to remain as inconspicuous as possible. Up until that point, Maurice had fully expected it to be just another appearance for a worthy cause where all the faces were more or less the same: average and totally forgettable. How could he have anticipated that she would be the one who would rescue him from an evening usually spent blowing his own horn—and Alexis's—to someone hanging onto every word as if authors were somehow literary gods?

Maybe this trip that he had reluctantly agreed to, mainly as a publicity gimmick, would not be so bad and boring after all. Maurice felt encouraged. Or at least the time he spent in Ms. Conneca Sheridan's company.

Maurice guiltily cut into the T-bone steak, forking a hearty piece, while watching his date nibble at a spinach salad with no dressing and only a few bacon bits tossed on almost for effect. "Obviously you've cornered the secret for staying trim," he said with envy.

Conneca's eyes danced with discomfiture, as she looked him up and down, settling on watching Maurice chew the steak as if it were his last meal on earth. She responded with bold admiration, "Maybe we both have."

It was Maurice's turn to feel embarrassed, while accepting what he took as a compliment. It was true, he acknowledged, that he was in great physical shape. He had worked hard enough at it, aside from his passion for well-cooked steaks, jogging and working out regularly.

"So, do you do these celebrity auctions often?" Conneca asked conversationally.

"Maybe four or five times a year," Maurice responded. "Alexis insists that we do them as a means to give something back." He twisted his mouth into a sly grin. "And it's always nice to meet fans—and even non-fans whose benevolence manages to rise above all else."

"I am a fan," she surprised him by confessing.

He had the feeling that Conneca Sheridan liked to keep her true feelings inside for most things, building like steam in a runaway locomotive till ready to explode.

"I really enjoyed *Danger At Sea*."

"Oh, yeah?" Maurice smiled, feeling good in hearing her admit it, when he usually just took it all in stride.

"Of course," Conneca said, batting her eyes. "It was a good story."

I'll bet yours is better, Maurice mused, but he said in reflection, "We had fun working on that one. Even took a cruise ship to the Bahamas for some research."

"That must have been interesting," Conneca said, appearing intrigued.

"It wasn't exactly *The Love Boat*," Maurice laughed, "or, thankfully, the *Titanic*. But we did get to mingle with passengers and the crew, and get great feedback from some brothers and sisters to help with the plotting and characterization."

Over the rim of her glass of Pinot Noir, Conneca asked as if she had given it some thought, "Is it hard to write books with your ex-wife? Or does that somehow work to your advantage in writing romantic suspense novels?"

Maurice lifted a thick brow whimsically, sipping his wine. It was public knowledge that he and Alexis had married in what was supposed to be a fairy-tale wedding of authors. Then they divorced in what was generally seen as a nightmare of epic proportions. Neither pretended they even had much of a friendship left at this point. But both knew that they made one hell of a writing team. It seemed foolish to change the one part of their relationship that worked so well.

So they decided to maintain the collaboration, even if their personal lives had gone to hell and back and were no longer part of the picture, at least as far Maurice was concerned. At times he had admittedly struggled in coming to terms with his failed marriage. What had he done wrong? he'd asked himself. What could he have done differently?

Maurice often wondered if the relationship between him and Alexis as lovers and spouses had been doomed from the very start. Only they just hadn't seen it coming until it was too late.

It had been over a year since the divorce and there had been no one else in his life, aside from the perfunctory blind date set up by well-meaning, but often way-off-base, friends. Casting an eye on the beautiful sister before him, Maurice couldn't help but wonder if it were even possible that there might be something there . . . Could Conneca Sheridan represent the change in the air he breathed?

He turned his thoughts back to her questions, and after a moment, said truthfully, "I'd be lying if I didn't say there are times when writing with Alexis seems almost impossible. The bitchiness and bad blood can make things difficult, to say the least." He gave an uncomfortable chuckle. "But, overall, we've pretty much accepted that we weren't a match made in heaven as man and wife. Fortunately, we're both professionals and don't allow that to be an obstacle in our more successful working relationship."

There, I said it. Maurice somehow felt glad that he had.

Conneca seemed to be favorably impressed with what he had to say and how he said it. Flashing brave eyes at him, she said, "That's really wonderful. If only all ex-spouses or lovers could find a way to get along when they had to, there might be hope for us all yet."

Maurice looked at her engagingly. "Sounds like the voice of experience?"

She pursed her lips thoughtfully. "Who hasn't gotten caught in that web of regrets and wisdom at one time or another?"

Tell me about it. Maurice found himself wondering about the web the sister was spinning around him—capturing his attention like no one had in some time. *Who hurt you?* he asked himself. *Why would any brother in his right mind ever want to hurt you?*

The more questions that popped into his head, the more Maurice seemed to want satisfying answers. He would ask for clarification and details later, believing there would be a later and, thus, more time to explore the life and times of Conneca Sheridan. For now, it seemed more important to satisfy her own curiosity and face some of his insecurities.

Wiping his mouth with a napkin and feeling the heat of the moment, Maurice said slowly, "With Alexis and me, it's been a work-in-progress for quite a while now, which may explain how we've managed to keep the literary fires burning, so to speak. We started out as the best of friends in college and have drawn on that in even the toughest of times. The writing team seemed to come naturally, if not without a lot of damned hard work. I guess when all else failed that old adage always seemed to come into focus for us: 'If it ain't broke, why fix it?' "

Maurice didn't count a broken heart in that equation. That was something Alexis could not repair with all the skill in the world. That war of love and romance was over. In his mind there was no looking back—only ahead to all the possibilities.

He somehow imagined that Conneca Sheridan could possibly fill the void in his life quite nicely. The mere thought lifted Maurice's spirits in ways he could not have conjured up.

Conneca colored in that moment. "Sorry, I-I really didn't mean to pry," she stammered. "I guess I just drew some silly conclusions . . . Well, actually, a friend suggested—" She appeared flustered. "Oh, I don't know what I'm saying—"

"It's all right," Maurice assured her with a friendly smile, already feeling as if they'd known each other for some time, and happy with that. "Speculation about those in the spotlight, good or bad, often comes with the territory."

That said, Maurice found he preferred to move away from the subject of him and Alexis and concentrate instead on Conneca, whom he believed was every bit as interesting in her own right.

"And I'm sure authors and other celebrities bask in that 'territory', for the most part." Conneca turned her head cynically.

Maurice concentrated less on what came out of Conneca's mouth than the mouth itself. He wanted nothing more at this moment than to kiss those lovely, no doubt soft-as-cotton lips. *Damn.* The thought itself threatened to rule him like an African chief, breaking his will with the type of overpowering desire he thought was gone forever but would welcome back with open arms in a hot second.

Maurice refocused his attention on Conneca's enchanting eyes, already planted on his, as if by design. He forced himself to keep his more carnal thoughts in check.

"I'll admit," he told her, "rumor and innuendo, true or false, does make for good copy. It's almost essential these days in promoting authors and their books. As long as the public can be kept interested, writers stand a fairly good chance of being able to make a decent living at what they do."

Conneca dug a fork into her salad. "Leaving the public constantly coming back for more," she sputtered teasingly. "At the risk of sometimes making complete jackasses of themselves."

Maurice let out a small laugh. "Some more than others." He surveyed Conneca intriguingly. *The sister was definitely nobody's fool,* he thought.

But am I being foolish where it concerns her? He fully intended to find that out, and anything else he could learn about the woman who had forked over five thousand big ones to have him at her mercy. *Or was it the other way around?* He decided that the day was still young. Too damn young to want to see it come to an end anytime soon and, along with it, his date with the African-American princess of Oak Cliffs.

Conneca Sheridan had somehow managed, perhaps without even realizing it, to tap into something that made Maurice begin to question all he stood for and wanted out of life. Yet he wasn't sure he was ready to open up a can of worms left sealed for so long for a woman he barely knew. He wondered if this urgent, unspoken desire to have and hold this beautiful sister, which had suddenly stirred within him like poison, had cast aside his common sense. His professionalism. His promise to himself to never again mix business with pleasure.

This is a business arrangement, is it not? Maurice questioned himself. *Meet, eat, smile a lot, sign a book, and say good-bye?* That was the way it had always been. No harm, no foul. Right?

The reality was he didn't know a damned thing about the lady across the table, other than her name, charitable contribution, and obvious beauty. *And the fact that something tells me that she's just as curious about me as I am about her.*

So what was her story? he contemplated. Why was she *stuck* in Oak Cliffs of all places? Perhaps to escape something, Maurice considered. *Or someone.*

But perhaps most curious to Maurice was: why in the hell was a sister with her stunning good looks, who could probably have any brother in the world, much less in this out-of-the-way Oregon coastal town, hanging around ladies seemingly twice her age to bid on male celebrities like him? What cause, commendable or not, could possibly be worth having to put up with egotistical assholes for hours on end at the expense of real quality time with someone who worshipped the ground she walked on?

Unless, of course, he allowed, no such person existed in her life.

Was that even possible? Maurice wondered in disbelief. Even if it were the case, that still wouldn't tell him why or who she spent her time with, if anyone. And he found himself wanting to know.

He was used to working on mysteries, but rarely had Maurice come across one that really captured his fancy like the mystery of Conneca Sheridan. He intended to probe into this further, though against his better judgment, uncertain what the results might be.

Noting that both their glasses were empty, Maurice lifted the bottle and with a devilish smile, said, "More wine?"

Before Conneca could respond, he was already filling her glass, while hoping he was not biting off more than he could chew. It was something Maurice was definitely willing to delve into.

CHAPTER 3

Conneca tried to resist being drawn to Maurice Templeton, even though she was pleasantly surprised to see that he seemed like a pretty down-to-earth brother who was easy to talk to. Their eyes played with each other from across the table between sips of wine. She was insightful enough to know that he was attracted to her. Just as she was to him. It was hard not to be attracted to such a man of his good looks, poise, and obvious talent. But that was where it had to end, she felt determined.

I will not allow myself to fall into a meaningless trap, Conneca thought. *A quickie for Mr. Author just passing through, with no plans to look back. Thanks, but no thanks.*

The way she saw it, getting involved with Maurice Templeton, even briefly, was a losing proposition. She was definitely not interested in a one-night stand, although, Conneca felt she had certainly paid enough for his company to entitle her to as much. And since Maurice was probably in Oak Cliffs just for the evening before departing for Denver or wherever his writing career and whatever other preoccupations he had took him, there obviously could be no future between them.

Not that she was looking for a future right now with him or any man. She had been down that road a time or two. In each case things had ended badly.

The first time was when Conneca was still in college. She had thought she loved Benjamin "Big B" Jenkins, a pre-med student. And she thought he loved her. Trouble was he loved or lusted after her roommate, Fran, more. Conneca caught the two in bed, doing everything but sleeping, and decided they were meant for each other in hell, as they were the two people she had trusted most.

It was nearly five years later, while teaching special education in Los Angeles, that Conneca's heart was crushed again. This time by a slick, city attorney named Donald Brown. Her handsome, single lover had turned out to be very married, with three kids and twins on the way.

After that disappointment or final straw, Conneca retreated from all relationships, fearing that she was cursed where it concerned men. Or certainly in finding one who wouldn't end up betraying and hurting her as if spotting Conneca as a live one a mile away.

Now, three years later, Conneca had run away to her hometown of Oak Cliffs, absolved herself of men and the pain and heartache they seemed to bring, and put her resources and energy into running her family's inn.

That had been enough for her. Only now, in the company of *this man,* Maurice Templeton, with *that body,* Conneca felt her heart racing wildly, like a Greyhound bus out of control. Was the attraction really that powerful? she had to ask herself through clenched teeth. Or was her body actually warning her that it was dangerous to let him get close?

By the time they finished eating, it was after eight. When Maurice suggested they go out for a stroll along the beach, Conneca agreed. It seemed harmless enough, and was another means of making use of the evening with her winning bid. Besides, it had gotten rather stuffy in the hotel/casino, where two busloads of tourists had arrived, ready to win the $250,000 jackpot and enjoy the many interesting things Oak Cliffs had to offer.

"It's gorgeous out here," Maurice said, marveling at the vast ocean as the sun nearly set upon it and them. He was still wearing his tux, but had removed socks and shoes, seemingly anxious to feel the sand between his toes.

"Yes, it is," Conneca responded dreamily. She too had gone barefoot and could feel the evening chill of late September.

"Have you always lived here?" Maurice peered down inquiringly at her. "Or did you just 'inherit' paradise as one thing of beauty to another?"

Conneca chuckled. "I can definitely tell you're a writer with that line!"

"Hey, I just tell it like I see it," he said with a perfectly straight face.

"I grew up here," Conneca told him and could see the surprised look on his face. Sometimes she had a hard time believing it herself.

Maurice raised his thick brows. "So you've never lived anywhere else?"

There was a twinkle in Conneca's eyes. "This will always be home sweet home," she said, "but I think I would've gone stir crazy for sure if I'd never ventured out into the *real* world, so to speak." She paused. "I've lived in San Francisco and L.A. Also spent a few months in Nigeria as an exchange student, if that counts."

"Oh yeah, it counts in my book," Maurice offered, his voice indicating a favorable impression. "I spent some time in Zimbabwe while in college myself. Stayed with friends in Harare. It was a wild and crazy experience, getting in touch with my roots and all that. I'd like to go back someday. Only this time I intend to do it right."

"Meaning?" Conneca interpreted that as suggesting he wanted to go back, now that he had the big bucks, to show off.

Maurice gazed at her. "Meaning in the company of someone special who can appreciate the adventure, culture, and romance of the country as it was meant to be."

"I see." *And what exactly do I see?* Conneca asked herself. He seemed to be saying that Alexis hadn't accompanied him there. Had he gone to Africa before they became serious, then not so serious? Or had he not considered Alexis special enough for the journey, even though they were involved? Maybe she had gone, but did not enjoy the trip, as he would have liked. Or had Maurice expected the grass to somehow be *browner* on the other side of the world than it turned out to be?

For an instant Conneca could imagine herself being transported to Zimbabwe or even Nigeria again with Maurice, where nothing—and no one—existed before them, with the sky the limit on the possibilities afterward. Just as quickly, she snuffed out such foolish reverie, even as Conneca felt the palpable sexual attraction between them, thick as molasses.

Did he feel it too? she asked herself. Or was it only her own imagination playing tricks on her?

"I'm sure it'll happen for you sooner or later," was all she could think to say.

"Yeah, I agree," Maurice muttered thoughtfully.

They walked in silence as waves rolled gently to the shore, falling just short of their feet.

"So what brought you back to Oak Cliffs?" Maurice asked with seemingly more than a passing interest.

Conneca stared at him. "It's a long story," she replied elusively. "And *personal.*" She hoped he wouldn't press it and he didn't.

"That's cool," he said with a shrug. "We're all entitled to our little secrets."

"Thank you," Conneca uttered, feeling foolish. It was just that she hardly knew him enough to start sharing her dirty laundry with him, especially when he seemed in no hurry to divulge his own.

"How does one make a living around here, aside from the Shoreline Hotel and Casino that looks as if they employ half the town?" Maurice fixed his eyes on her curiously. "Or is that a secret too?"

Conneca shuddered self-consciously, knowing he was merely fishing for basic information at the expense of Oak Cliffs itself. "I own and operate a small inn just down the road," she told him proudly.

"Is that right?" he said shocked, his voice trailing off as if disappearing into a thick fog. "I would never have pictured *you* as the proprietor of a lodging establishment."

Her eyes upturned sharply on him. "Why?" she asked, hands on her small hips. "Because I'm a *woman*—or a *black* woman?"

A defensive chuckle escaped Maurice. "No, it's not either of those, Conneca," he said apologetically. "Whatever you may think of male writers—or men in general—I'm definitely *not* a chauvinist brother who thinks that sisters need to be kept in their place, wherever that might be. The fact that I share an *equal* writing partnership with a *sista* who happens to be my ex-wife should testify to that." He regarded Conneca with eyes as tender as they were unblinking.

Conneca chided herself for jumping to the wrong conclusions. Again. He was clearly *not* the typical man in any respect, she thought approvingly.

"So what did you think I did for a living?" she asked him bluntly, wondering if she really wanted to know.

"I really wasn't sure . . . I guess I pictured you more as a fashion-model type, or maybe a tour guide," Maurice said smoothly. "All right, so maybe I considered that you could be doubling as the town mayor . . . and maybe the police chief." He laughed, clearly amused with himself.

Conneca found herself laughing as well. She knew he was not making fun of her, as much as of stereotypes of folks in small towns. "Right, and sometimes you can add gardener, postal worker, judge, and even *inn owner* to the pot also. In most instances, versatility becomes almost mandatory in Oak Cliffs!"

"And we think we've got it bad in Denver!" Maurice made a face.

They continued to laugh like children, walking till Conneca and Maurice found their path impeded. Blocking it was a huge black rock that looked as if it had just fallen from the sky.

"Damn, looks like we've reached the end of the line," Maurice expressed sadly. "Either that, or this is actually where life begins."

Beginnings? Conneca thought fancifully. Yes, maybe this was where the road to happiness began. Where the past ended and the future started to take shape. Was it truly possible to start life over? she wondered seriously. As if the past had never existed. And the future could be written as they lived it . . .

Maurice put his hands on her shoulders, causing Conneca to jump at his touch. Eye-to-eye contact told her he wanted to kiss her at that moment. And she wanted to feel his lips upon hers, as though they belonged together. There seemed to be no middle ground here. No way to deny what seemed inevitable.

Conneca was barely aware of it when they gave in to this mutual need, this yearning to satisfy curiosity. Or was it simply pure unbridled lust? Their mouths connected in an electrifying, lingering kiss that literally had Conneca on her tiptoes, though she felt as if she were floating on air.

Maurice embraced Conneca, their bodies pressed so tightly that they were almost molded together. She could feel every contour of him; the thick bulge in his pants pulsating, desperate to be released and satisfied, as if they were naked and in bed. Conneca's own body ached against his muscled mass, wanting what she hadn't wanted for so long, but fearing it just as much.

If the moment could have lasted forever, Conneca would have gladly welcomed it, savoring the sweet taste of Maurice's mouth on hers. But such only happened in fairy tales, she knew. And her Prince Charming would be a brother frog by morning and halfway across the country, with her but a distant memory to him.

With all the willpower she could muster, Conneca managed to pull herself away from Maurice Templeton. Her bruised lips still stung from his kiss. She turned away from him.

"I'm sorry," Conneca uttered shamefully, in disbelief that she had let him kiss her. Or was it the other way around?

"I'm not," Maurice said without pretense.

Conneca made herself face him, determination on her face. "Look, I'm not interested in some quickie in the sand, Maurice Templeton. You know what I'm saying? It was a mistake to let you kiss me."

He flashed her a look of disappointment. "Me kiss you? That's not exactly the way I saw it. Who really kissed who here?" he challenged her. "I think it was more like we kissed each other."

Conneca flushed. "I don't suppose it matters at this point."

"Oh you don't, do you?" Maurice reached out to her, a wry grin painting his face. "I think we both know it does matter. This was no damned mistake, Conneca. Why fight it, baby?"

Conneca felt as if she had been slapped with the sting of his arrogance. *And I'm not your baby,* she told herself. She backed away just beyond Maurice's grasp, sensing that they definitely weren't on the same page.

"Because there is no future here," she told him, simply put.

Maurice batted his eyes. "Why does there have to be?" His breathing was labored, as if having just completed a sprint. "Why can't we just enjoy the moment for what it is?"

Easy for you to say, Conneca thought. Or any man who lived his life and times in a moment here and a moment there.

"Because I want *more* than *moments* with someone," she snarled. "Actually,

I just want to be free of any more romantic disappointments. So you can take your moment with you back to Denver." She swallowed, willing herself to remain steady on gimpy knees. "I think I'd better be going."

Maurice's nostrils flared. "At least let me walk you back."

"Don't," Conneca said tersely, raising her hands at him, as though to stop dead in his tracks. "I think it's better that we say our good-byes and so-longs here and now."

"I don't!" Maurice insisted, appearing flustered. "Look, you paid five grand to be with me—why not get your money's worth?"

Conneca turned her angry eyes at him. "I think I already have," she snorted, suddenly feeling cheap and used. *But at least I'm still on my feet, unlike how he may have hoped.* "I never wanted a male prostitute. But it looks like that's exactly what I got! Good-bye, Maurice!"

She stormed away and stumbled up the beach, sand flying this way and that, eager to get away from him as soon as possible. Conneca half expected Maurice to come after her, but he did not, apparently getting the message loud and clear: *If you thought it was going to be slam, bam, thank you, ma'am, you ended up with the wrong sister!*

How could she have misjudged him so? Conneca wondered, feeling irate. How could she have felt that Maurice Templeton was different from other men she'd known? Someone she could actually learn to like. Trust. Maybe even *love,* heaven forbid. He had merely validated that her decision to abstain from relationships had been a wise one, and something she would not make the mistake of forgetting again anytime soon.

Maurice watched miserably as Conneca raced away like she had come face to face with a sea monster—*him!* Never before had he reacted with such callousness and lustful desire to have a woman. He had made a damned fool out of himself, frightening her into thinking he was a selfish, salacious bastard.

And hadn't he been just that? *At least through her eyes?*

The truth was Maurice had never wanted someone as badly as he had wanted Conneca this evening. The kiss of her lips had turned him upside down. Inside out. It had broken down the barriers between yearning and having, dreaming and experiencing, and fire and ice. As had the taut feel of her nipples pressed against his jacket and the slenderness of the sister's soft body, so perfectly aligned with the hardness of his own.

Even the smell of her braided hair—natural, wholesome, and sweet as could be—had worked its magic on Maurice, making him want Conneca all the more. It had caused him to react with the rejection he felt, by lashing back even harder. Much more cruelly than he had ever intended.

Now Maurice feared he may have lost Conneca Sheridan before ever finding the sister. Before allowing them an adequate chance to see if what they had between them in the space of a few hours was real or some cruel trick of the imagination. In seconds, it had gone from perfect harmony between them to possibly pushing Conneca so far away as to make closing the gap again virtually impossible.

Maurice shook his head in disgruntlement and self-blame, before beginning to walk slowly back to the hotel, feeling like a defeated man. Or at least a brother who had fallen short of the grand prize: *Conneca Sheridan.*

Maybe I should just quit while I'm ahead? he considered. After all, he hadn't come to the Northwest with romance on his mind. Far from it. Women often threw themselves at him, but he rarely went after the bait.

It was different with Conneca. Yes, she had a healthy share of respect for what he did, but she wasn't a slave to this author celebrity nonsense. At least where it concerned going overboard in giving an author his or her props. But did that mean she wasn't interested in him as a man, in spite of her indication to the contrary? Should he simply ignore the feelings this woman had inadvertently incited in him—feelings that had been absent in his life for too damned long now?

Maurice conceded that in reality he was *not* ahead of the game where it concerned Conneca Sheridan. Not by a long shot. Why, he could no more reject his instincts that there was something powerful between them than he could the collaboration with Alexis that had made them one of the most—if not the top—successful African-American writing tandems, in spite of themselves.

Maurice considered that there was still too much he didn't know about Conneca that he wanted to. As if it were his right to or, perhaps, his destiny. *I damned sure will follow my instincts on this one and let the chips fall where they may,* he thought. *Hopefully on my lap . . . and hers.*

Back at the hotel, Maurice signed a few books for fans who had discovered his presence and noted that he had come back alone. He made some small talk, pretending to be attentive when the truth was that his mind was elsewhere. Like back on the beach where a kiss had sent shivers up and down his spine and caused him to rethink what he really wanted out of life.

And possibly with whom.

A half hour later, Maurice was in his luxury suite, barely noticing the extra amenities fame and fortune had brought him. His American Tourister garment bag lay open on the bed. He hadn't even bothered to unpack. These trips were usually nothing more than overnights, giving him no time to get too comfortable with his surroundings. He would be glad to rid himself of the tux, take a shower, and maybe get some shuteye.

Maurice's cell phone rang, giving him a start. He lifted the phone from his pocket and answered it.

It was Alexis. "Hey, baby," she said routinely. "Just called to check on you."

You mean snoop, he thought. "Hello, Alexis."

"So how did it go today?"

"Pretty good," Maurice answered, sitting on the bed. *Better and worse than I'd expected.* "Got a bid of five grand for charity."

"And your body, hon," Alexis said, as if to remind him. "That's what the ladies really want when they shell out the *big bucks!*"

Not this time, he was confident. And not *that* lady. "I came here to help fight illiteracy, Alexis, and get our name out there—not play the meat market stud!"

"Well, *excuuuse* me," she snorted. "Touchy, touchy. Did someone get on your wrong side today, or what?"

Quite the opposite, Maurice told himself. That was the problem. It couldn't have felt more right.

"Just tired." He yawned, as though for effect. "Barely walked into the room before you called."

"Forget it," Alexis muttered, as if she already had. "Anyway, It's good to hear that *we* charmed the folks out there in Oregon and promoted Alexis Maurice at the same time!"

"Yeah, I'm glad *we* did," Maurice said sarcastically.

"So what time are you getting in tomorrow?" The question was said with a certain amount of expectation.

Maurice had a scheduled flight out of Portland at 10 a.m. meaning he would need at least another two hours to get there from Oak Cliffs, along with up to a two hour wait once he got to the airport. He was just about to share this information with his ex-wife and cowriter, when suddenly Maurice decided he wasn't ready to leave just yet. The thought of having things end as they did with Conneca Sheridan was killing him. He wanted to see this fine and fastidious sister again, see if the sparks that threatened to ignite between them into an all-consuming blaze might not still have flames to be fanned. If he didn't explore the notion now, in all likelihood neither of them would ever know one way or the other.

He, for one, wasn't about to let that happen—not without a fight anyway.

Switching the phone to his other ear, Maurice considered his words, then said to Alexis, "Actually, I've decided to stay in town for a few days of R & R."

"Oh really." Alexis gave an exaggerated sigh. "You know we've got some signings coming up . . . conferences . . . more charity work . . . a book that's due soon . . ."

"Yeah, I know all about that," he groaned. *But thanks for reminding me.* "I also know that the calendar is clear for the next couple of weeks. So I've decided to give my brain and body some rest for a little while. This seems like the perfect place to do it. Or do I need my *ex*-wife's permission?"

The moment he said ex-wife, Maurice regretted it, for this implied that his staying on the coast involved something other than R & R. Which was true.

Of course Alexis picked right up on it. "You do what you need to do, Maurice, all right," she said curtly. "And with *whomever*. Just remember that you and I are still in *business* together. Someone's got to try and keep things running smoothly. And since you've never volunteered, that leaves it up to me."

"I understand, Alexis," Maurice told her contritely, *but only up to a point.* "Believe me, I appreciate your level-headedness when it comes to the writing business." Again, he knew it implied that this didn't extend to *personal* business. But they both knew that neither of them could seem to get it together quite right in their relationship. That didn't mean they still had to be at each other's throats beyond that.

At least not this night.

Maurice sucked in a deep breath and said evenly, "It's been a long day, Alexis. I'm going to get out of this monkey suit and take a shower." He paused. "I'll let you know when I get back to Denver."

"Whatever," Alexis retorted, and hung up.

Maurice thought for a moment that she didn't seem to want to let him go, even though he was already gone, and she damned well knew it. Women, he mused, shaking his head. They could be a trip and a half at times.

But they could also be something truly special, worthwhile, and *head* turning.

Conneca Sheridan immediately came to mind and suddenly Maurice found himself smiling, though uncertain if he had any right to expect anything from her but a snub. *No one ever said this was going to be easy,* he thought. *I sure would never presume that to be the case—not with the likes of this lady.*

All the more reason to jump in headfirst and hope he didn't end up hitting rock bottom in the pursuit.

CHAPTER 4

The Sheridan Seaside Inn had been in Conneca's family for two generations now. It had seen numerous renovations aimed at keeping ahead of the curve in modernization and customer comforts. The beach-front property of twenty-five units on two floors had been passed on to Conneca, an only child, when her father, Bernard Sheridan, died three years ago. Her mother had died when Conneca was only nineteen.

All her life Conneca had resisted the call to take over one of the few entirely African American–owned businesses on this prime stretch of coastal real estate. She'd wanted only to branch out on her own, work with inner-city youth, and escape the at-times-suffocating resort town she felt in some ways a prisoner of.

But that had all changed after her father's death, coupled with a disastrous love life. Suddenly Conneca longed for a return to Oak Cliffs and the safety from the pain of heartbreak she found there. Though she had known virtually nothing about running an inn, having spent much of her earlier years on the beach and at the family quarters before going off to college, Conneca took on the challenge of keeping the family business afloat as the lone remaining member of the Sheridans.

Determined to succeed in her endeavor, Conneca had poured her small inheritance into yet more inn renovations, mindful of the demands the modern traveler had for clean, attractive rooms, access to the Internet, fax machines, copiers, and, of course, the beach. The result had been more repeat business and greater visibility in what was rapidly becoming a crowded beachfront of inns, motels, hotels, and restaurants vying for customer dollars.

But even with a steady flow of guests, the costs of upkeep, renovations, and remaining competitive had kept Conneca from realizing any real profit up to this point. She was still living largely on what little remained of her inheritance. Nevertheless, she expected the situation to improve by the end of the year or early the following year. More importantly, putting all her energies into the inn made it easier to forget the disappointments that had turned Conneca's dreams of having a family of her own someday into a nightmare of losers, being unattached, and solitude.

To Conneca the events of this evening with Maurice Templeton had more or less been warning bells to her that seemed to say what they had with other men: *Me and male companionship simply do not mix very well.* This in spite of the fact that she had been paired with Maurice Templeton for a cause very dear to her. No matter how hard Conneca tried to fight that simple truth, she had more or less come to terms with the fact that she was far better off being married to her business. At least it kept her out of trouble, away from unrealistic expectations and disappointments, and was the one stabilizing force in her life.

Conneca retreated to her tower room, a modest-sized suite consisting of two bedrooms, living room, kitchen with a breakfast nook, den, and a bathroom. In wanting to put her own stamp on what had once been her parents' quarters, Conneca had completely revamped the place, including putting in new hickory and log furniture, modern appliances, and stereo equipment, while turning the den into a combination office and exercise room. She had decorated the cerulean blue walls with scenic landscapes painted by local artists, and removed gray carpeting in favor of cypress hardwood flooring. A circular Oriental rug with jeweltone accents and a crimson border lay near the stone fireplace in the living room.

After freshening up, Conneca changed into a Brooks Brothers double-breasted navy suit with a lilac ruffled blouse and low-heeled dark blue pumps. She ran her fingers across the long braids, tossing them a bit and allowing them to settle over her shoulders. Never feeling comfortable with too much gunk on her face, Conneca took off a bit of the makeup she had worn for the auction, applied a touch of Chanel No. 5 to her neckline, and headed back downstairs, where she suspected her services might be needed.

She would worry later about where to cut corners to make up for the five thousand dollars from the inn's checking account that she had inadvertently donated to literacy programs.

* * *

"How was the auction?" Lee Azikewe asked casually from the front desk, greeting Conneca.

Lee gave a lighthearted chuckle, making Conneca smile back at him. The fifty-six-year-old Nigerian had worked for the family for as long as Conneca could remember. About five feet, six inches in height and portly, he had a cocoa skin tone and a short salt and pepper Afro. Lee had only recently been widowed. He had met his wife, Sonja, in Lagos, Nigeria before both sought a better life in the U.S., going from Detroit to Oakland to Portland before settling in Oak Cliffs. They had no children, though they had more or less adopted Conneca, acting as her second parents, which she fully accepted. Both had inspired her to travel to Nigeria as an exchange student to experience their culture firsthand. Now that Sonja was dead, thought Conneca, all she and Lee had left in this world were each other.

Lee was the day-to-day manager of the inn, while Conneca did all the little things necessary to keep everything running smoothly and efficiently. These included making certain the staff always put the guests first, something her father had insisted upon and Lee seconded. Conneca considered theirs a partnership in running the place. Lee's help and guidance had been invaluable in both learning the business and dealing with the loss of her father.

"Speak up, girl," Lee said anxiously, batting his large ash-brown eyes at her. "Did you meet a rich and lonely celebrity brother who wants to take you away from all this?"

"Not a chance," responded Conneca with a smirk, even as she still felt the potent effects of Maurice's lips upon hers, as if the kiss had somehow possessed her soul and body.

"Oh," Lee frowned sorrowfully. "Maybe next year, huh?"

"Maybe. But I wouldn't count on it," she said flatly. "Most rich celebrity brothers are not lonely—and usually not alone. Besides, I seriously doubt that there are any that I would *want* to take me away from all this."

Especially one man in particular, Conneca thought peevishly. She looked around and suddenly felt good to know it was all hers to focus on.

"That's because you haven't met Mr. Right yet, Conneca." Lee favored her with a serious look. "You're much too young, girl, to settle for being an inn owner for the rest of your life. Not to say that this isn't the finest accommodation in the whole town! But there's more to living than serving others. Your time will come, Conneca. Trust Lee on this."

I wish I could, she thought with misgivings and an eye on the real world.

Conneca knew he meant well—though at thirty she didn't consider herself so young—and would always be there to look after her best interests. Admittedly, she wasn't always sure what those were. Or, frankly, what the future held, not to mention the present. But for the time being, the only thing she found comfort in was the place that bore her family's name.

"Ah, looks like a new guest has arrived," Lee remarked enthusiastically.

In her reverie Conneca had failed to notice the inn door swing open. Much less the familiar and imposing figure standing there, an amused grin curling a corner of his mouth, as if on permanent display.

"I think Ms. Sheridan and I have already met," Maurice Templeton said in a comical voice, causing Lee to raise a thick brow.

"Really?" Lee widened his eyes and looked at Conneca.

Maurice rubbed his bald head smoothly. "Yeah. Name's Maurice Ray Templeton. You see, Conneca here paid good money to spend time with me this evening—before quite literally disappearing before my very eyes like a ghostly apparition." He directed those intense coal-gray eyes at Conneca. "Now I'm hoping I can return the favor."

Conneca narrowed her gaze and stilled her heart. *What the hell is he doing here?* she asked herself furiously. *At my inn? And why?*

"What do you want?" she asked him coldly, though a part of Conneca was admittedly curious. She noted that he had changed into some navy pleated slacks and a maroon Polo shirt. Both fit snugly on his sinewy, lithe frame. A matching black garment and duffle bag sat beside his slightly scuffed ebony boots.

Maurice stood erect like a mythical male monument. "I should think it would be obvious. I want—need—a room. Or," he feigned disappointment, "is my money unwelcome at this nice establishment?"

"Everyone's money is welcome here, Mr. Templeton," Lee responded brightly. "Isn't that right, Conneca?"

Oh hell, Conneca mused, miffed. She knew they were ganging up on her, and winning the battle. But she had to be practical about this. She could scarcely afford to pass on a paying customer. Even when Maurice Ray Templeton was probably the last person on earth she expected to see walk through that door, much less seek accommodations at the Sheridan Seaside Inn.

Had Maurice followed her there? Conneca wondered. *Just what type of game is this brother playing?* Did he actually think that if she couldn't, or wouldn't, buy him sexually that *he* could buy *her?*

If so, he had wasted his time in coming there, she thought firmly. And definitely hers.

"I'll get *Mr.* Templeton checked in," Conneca told Lee, gritting her teeth.

A smile flickered on Maurice's face. "Now that's the type of hospitality I'm sure one comes to expect from the Sheridan Seaside Inn. Am I right?" He winked at Lee, who nodded in forced agreement.

Conneca walked down to the check-in counter and waited until Maurice stood on the other side. Even with the counter separating them, she knew the embers that had burned on the beach between them had yet to be fully extinguished. They seemed to be lying in wait to strike again at any time.

But Conneca fought back the flames determinedly. "Look, if this is some type of attempt to carry on where we left off on the beach," she warned, "then I'm afraid you've made one big mistake in coming here."

"Yes," Maurice said calmly, "a mistake has been made. That entire episode on the beach was one *big* misunderstanding, Conneca. I never meant to imply that you had paid for anything other than some friendly conversation, a nice dinner, and a walk on the sand." He drew his brows together entreatingly. "Since I obviously misled you, I want to apologize for what was quite obviously the *wrong* choice of words . . . though the *right* intentions."

Had it really been just a simple misunderstanding? Conneca asked herself, having second thoughts. *Maybe I overreacted to the moment . . . the man.* Or used him as a backlash against past relationships gone sour.

So did he want a truce? Conneca wondered. To let bygones be bygones? Or did he want something more?

Why is he still affecting me so? She wasn't sure she really wanted to go there.

Conneca met his eyes. "Let's just forget it," she said, striving to keep her voice calm.

"That's cool." Maurice flashed her a prizewinning smile. "Consider it forgotten. But I still need a room."

"Oh you do, do you?" Conneca rolled her eyes skeptically, glancing at his bags. "And I'm supposed to believe you just picked *this* little old inn out of the blue?" Or *black*, she thought wittily.

"Not exactly," Maurice confessed. "I looked it up in the Yellow Pages," he said matter-of-factly. "You know, that fat, yellow book they like to keep in some bottom drawer in the room just in case someone actually needs it, heaven forbid. From that point on, it wasn't too hard to put two and two together when I saw the advertisement on the bottom quarter of a page for the *Sheridan* Seaside Inn. Since I needed a quiet place to put the finishing touches on a novel, and also didn't want to leave things the way they ended between us, it seemed like the perfect convergence." He met her unsteady gaze. "So there you have it, *Miss* Conneca Sheridan."

Conneca felt her knees grow weak. But her mind remained strong, as well as her intent not to fall in the same trap again. Certainly not with the same man *twice* in one night. She wasn't sure she bought into the "finishing touches on the novel" bit, considering that his was a collaborative work. Wasn't it?

Had his cowriter and ex agreed to Maurice working on their novel without her? Or was this how they always collaborated—separate but equal?

Conneca couldn't help but wonder if there really was nothing romantic between them anymore. Even though Alexis Maurice still seemed so perfectly matched, appearance-wise?

Is it any of your business, girl? she scolded herself. *You are not interested in Maurice Templeton, his ex-wife, or their business!*

Or so Conneca tried to convince herself. In a nonchalant tone she asked Maurice, "So how long will you be staying?"

He considered the question. "To tell you the truth, I'm not sure, really. Maybe a week . . . maybe two . . . As long as it takes to get the job done."

And exactly what job was that? Conneca felt more than a little suspicious.

"You'll have to be more specific than that," she advised him sharply. "We can't give you an open-ended room. We have other guests to consider down the line." Even if that were not the case, the vanity in Conneca didn't want to give him the impression that the place was never filled to capacity. As it was, at this time of the year it was rarely a full house. More somewhere in between the two extremes.

Maurice glanced out at the parking lot that was only maybe half full and seemed to be reading Conneca's thoughts. "I see," he said amusingly. "Well, how about if you book me for a month in advance, in your best room available—prepaid, of course?"

Conneca was admittedly impressed, though she tried not to show it. On another level she was a little irritated with the ease of his request, as if money were no object for him. But who was she to resent it if this brother could fork out the cash based on his own honest success? He was living the American dream to be a successful author and more power to him—and his writing partner.

She gave him a professional look. "That would be the eastside tower suite," she said as if it were no big deal. It was on the far end of the inn and an exact duplicate of her suite. There was only one other suite on the premises and it was booked solid well into the winter months, though by different guests.

"Fine." Maurice sniffed indifferently.

He whipped a platinum American Express card out of his wallet, handing it to Conneca. For an instant, as they each held an end of the card, a surge of sexual energy seemed to pass through it, nearly knocking Conneca off her feet. She had to hold onto the counter for support.

She ran the card through the machine. It was processed almost instantly. Conneca could see that the card bearing his full name—Maurice Ray Templeton—appeared well used. Just how many inns had he stayed in? Suddenly she could imagine him with young, nubile, pretty groupies, anxious to share his bed for an autographed book and a friendly smile.

Celebrity authors did have their own groupies, didn't they? Conneca slid the card across the counter toward him.

"Thanks," Maurice said with a full and devilish smile, scooping the card up and putting it into his wallet in one motion.

With his signed receipt for a month's charges, Conneca handed Maurice his key. "That's Room 337. Would you like someone to help you with your bags?" She glanced at them and quickly realized she had set herself up with that leading question.

He hit her with a suggestive look. "Like *you*, for instance?"

She pursed her lips to keep from smiling. "I don't think so. We have *staff* for that."

Maurice feigned disappointment. "That's too bad." He lifted up the garment and duffle bag. "I think I can manage this time around."

This time? Did that mean he'd already made plans to come back again? Conneca pondered. Or did that depend on the outcome of this visit? The thought left her in a state of emotional imbalance as well as uncertainty regarding exactly what to expect out of Maurice Templeton's stay in her inn.

Or of the man himself . . .

CHAPTER 5

Maurice wondered if he had lost all of his damned marbles. What on earth had possessed him to cancel his flight back to Denver, where he and Alexis had made plans to spend time working together on their next novel? He had always prided himself on acting rationally and calmly. Yet now he felt his actions were totally irrational. And he was anything but calm, cool, *or* collected in spite of what his outer appearance might have suggested.

Conneca Sheridan had made his blood boil like never before. Certainly not in *this* lifetime! When the sister literally left him flat-footed on the beach, he knew he had to see her again. But first he had to find her. She was not exactly a needle in a haystack. Still Maurice had been prepared to phone every damned inn in Oak Cliffs if he had to. And, in fact, there were more inns than he imagined in this small hideaway resort paradise. Then he had spied the ad that read: "Romance, Sea, and Tranquillity—All At Your Doorstep." Underneath was: "Sheridan Seaside Inn."

The moment Maurice had entered the place and saw that unforgettable image of long, luminous braided hair, and the lean, sexy, soulful, good-looking sister behind it, he knew he was at the right inn, with the right woman. He had approached the front desk, wondering if it was smart to chase after Conneca like a puppy dog, but decided she was worth the effort. In any event, he told himself, there was no turning back now. Especially when the brother beside Conneca had spotted him and seemed eager to welcome with open arms.

Conneca had shown no such inclination, reacting coldly to him, and rightfully so, he believed, all things considered. Yet Maurice also felt that the sexual and physical chemistry between them was so palpably powerful and *real*, he imagined it could explode at any second. And heaven help anyone who stood in their way. He was certain Conneca had experienced the same intense, almost dangerous sense of wanting, even if she seemed reluctant to admit it for the moment.

What Maurice didn't know was where the hell to go from here now that he had intruded upon this woman's life and disrupted his own. His life was already full of complexities, uncertainties, and regrets. Did he really need others?

He unlocked the door to Room 337. It opened onto a spacious, peach-colored living room. An olive log sofa and chair matched the plush carpeting. Fresh flowers sat in a vase on a wooden table alongside a copy of *USA Today* newspaper. A TV, DVD, and CD players were tucked into a corner, next to the fireplace. Sounds of the ocean, restless at night, whispered eerily through the wood blinds, as if speaking to Maurice in a foreign, haunting tongue.

Not bad, he thought, impressed with his accommodations. Not bad at all.

Maurice put his bags down and took a quick glance at the other rooms. Similarly, they were large, clean, nicely filled with rustic and log furnishings, and very homelike. He decided he would use the smaller of the two bedrooms as his temporary office. His intention had been to finish the last chapters of the latest novel at home, and then hand it over to Alexis to hone, chisel, and shape as she did so brilliantly. But he could just as easily do his part here. Perhaps even more effectively than at home, where there were always distractions of one sort or another to take him away from writing. Here, the only distraction Maurice could see, next to the lure of the beach, was Conneca Sheridan.

Which, he thought honestly, could be the biggest distraction of them all, and clearly the main attraction Oak Cliffs had to offer him.

Maurice noted the phone jack and several electrical outlets in his office, as well as a small, square oak table that could serve as a desk for his notebook computer and printer. Perfect, he nodded agreeably. He could e-mail Alexis the chapters for her editing as he went along.

He went back to the master bedroom. The king-sized bed had a rustic cedar log base, orange-red quilt, and big fluffy pillows. It would be good to sleep in, Maurice told himself, yawning. *But even better to make love in.* He found himself thinking about that very thing with Conneca, and his imagination nearly ran wild with passion and excitement, the likes of which he hadn't felt in longer than he could remember.

Maurice flopped onto the bed and stretched out his six feet, four inches of hard body. He did some of his best thinking in bed. It also happened to be a good place for daydreaming and fantasizing . . . along with lamenting.

I'm thirty-three-years-old and divorced, he thought miserably. His parents had kept the fires burning for more than forty years of matrimony. What did they do that was so right? What had he done that was so wrong?

Maurice recognized that he'd made it as a big-time author with all the perks of the trade, including the dream house he had always wanted. Only it was never in his game plan to live there *alone.* He had his boys to hang out with sometimes and some nice sisters as friends.

Then there was Alexis. The romantic relationship was history, but the connection would always be there—especially since they had to work together. They had a natural chemistry that had produced six international bestselling novels to date . . . and more money than either of them knew what to do with. In spite of everything else, deep down they shared a mutual respect that had made them strong business partners and close confidants.

Maurice wondered if that was enough. Did he owe Alexis any more than she owed him? Could his friends or ex-wife ever take the place of a stable, dependable, loving woman who was his soul mate and kindred spirit?

Didn't he deserve to have a life and love outside the writing? Maurice stared thoughtfully at the stucco ceiling.

"Who the hell am I fooling?" he muttered aloud. *Certainly not myself. Hell yes, I deserve more—much more!* He wanted what any mature, respectable, successful brother wanted at the end of the day: *a woman to love and be loved by.*

Was that really asking too much? Maybe not, he granted.

But there was an even bigger question that entered Maurice's mind: *Can I find it more than twelve hundred miles from home?*

Maybe he was being irresponsible in allowing what amounted to a schoolboy crush to keep him in Oak Cliffs. Or maybe it the best damned move he'd made in some time.

What Maurice was certain of was that he felt something for Conneca Sheridan that he had never known before. He owed it to himself to find out exactly what that was—even if it meant living with the consequences for better or worse.

CHAPTER 6

Conneca jogged along the beach before sunrise, as she did every morning. It was the one time of the day that she could be totally by herself, away from her obligations, fears, frustrations, and the problems the world presented. Certainly the world in which she lived. To Conneca it was like a spiritual awakening breathing in the salty smell of the sea, watching the dawn break, working her heart and legs in perfect symmetry. She wore a green and blue velour warm-up suit and white Reebok running shoes, and felt almost as if she could be out there forever. Such was the terrific shape Conneca was in, and the lure of the smooth golden sand that seemed to stretch without end. Why, she almost felt as though she were floating on air, her braided hair in a ponytail bouncing against her back, while she glided effortlessly across the sand.

"Good morning." The husky voice behind her almost seemed to reverberate with the sound of the ocean.

Glancing over her shoulder Conneca saw that Maurice was right on her footsteps and barely out of breath, as if standing still.

Was there no escape from this brother? Conneca asked herself, only half jokingly, but half serious as well.

"Good morning," she responded, exhaling through her nostrils.

Maurice pulled up beside her, dressed in a maroon jogging suit and black running shoes. His bald head gleamed in the early light as if freshly buffed.

"I thought I was the only one slick enough to beat the sun—and crowds—up and keep in tip-top shape at the same time," he bragged.

"Think again," Conneca quipped, batting her lashes. She could plainly see that keeping fit was as important to him as it was to her. Men who took good care of themselves had always attracted her. Which may have been part of the problem. Too many of them cared only about number one and the hell with everyone else.

Still, Conneca couldn't help but be impressed by the well-defined, taut body of the author running beside her. She wondered what else they had in common, aside from promoting literacy and maybe a stubborn streak a mile long. Then she remembered—still feeling a slight twinge on her lips—*kissing* each other.

Maurice gave her an uneasy grin. "Yeah, well, I have to admit, I've underestimated you perhaps one time too many to my detriment, Conneca."

"Oh?" She risked a glance at him, not sure where this was leading?

"I think so."

"And why is that?" Conneca dared to ask. "Or are you in the habit of making poor judgments on all Northwest sisters compared to Rocky Mountain ones?" She doubted that was the case, but wanted to put him on the defensive anyhow.

"Not at all." Maurice blushed. "Nothing to do with *poor* in my judgments. I think all sistas have a lot going for them. At least most of them." He studied her as they moved gracefully side by side. "Guess I just never figured you to be a runner."

"Right," Conneca muttered, feeling slightly offended. "Just like you never figured me to be an inn owner? Next thing I know, you'll be telling me it never occurred to you that I just might be able to beat your black ass in a race."

Maurice laughed and bent over as if punched in the stomach. "Now, I wouldn't doubt that for one moment," he said. "You certainly look in good enough shape to give any brother a run for his money, no pun intended. From this point forward, I promise to reserve judgment until *after* the fact."

Conneca couldn't help but laugh out loud herself, even as she tried to keep her breathing even and pace herself. "Don't worry, I promise not to hold it against you if you manage to put your foot in your mouth again," she told him humorously.

"All right, I deserved that," Maurice said humbly. "Getting on your bad side once was enough. I'm not sure I could take such rejection again."

Better get used to it. Conneca picked up the pace, thinking: *Let's see what you're really made of, Mr. Big-Time Author.*

Not too surprising to Conneca, Maurice kept up with her without missing a beat.

All of a sudden, as if possessed, she eyed him thoughtfully. "We're not back to our little 'misunderstanding' from last night, are we?"

"Water under the bridge," Maurice assured her, though it was quite obvious to Conneca that it was exactly what was on his mind.

Just as it was on hers.

Wisely, she decided to change the subject, staring out at the ocean, its crystal blue beginning to surface in small waves as the light of day emerged. Sucking in a breath, Conneca asked: "So what's your new novel about?"

Pausing for a second or two, as if creating the plot at that very moment, Maurice responded enthrallingly: "A beautiful woman at the center of a murder mystery with more than a little romance to keep things interesting. Is she the victim of circumstances? Or a cold-blooded killer? It's up to the detective hero to sort things out." He grinned mischievously. "Afraid you'll have to read the published book to find out the answer."

Already Conneca found herself piqued. She had never personally known an author. Did she truly know this one—or even want to? Or was he a cruel caricature?

"Is there a title?" she asked dryly. "Or is that also tightly under wraps?"

Maurice looked at her askance. "Right now it's called *A Woman To Die For*," he said. "But it's subject to change . . . depending on how the story goes."

Is any woman—or man, for that matter—worth dying for? Conneca asked herself both on an intellectual and intimate level. Aside from that consideration, she said to him boldly: "I think you should keep the title. Most readers will probably find it enticing."

"That's exactly what Alex, er, Alexis said," Maurice noted, sweat beginning to run down his forehead. "And, since most of our readers are women, perhaps the title will be a winner—assuming that the tale can carry its own weight as well."

Conneca blinked at him. "Sounds like you have doubts?"

He wiped his brow with a sleeve. "All writers have doubts, Conneca, if the truth be told. There are no guarantees that the readers will fall in love with the story, no matter what the title, plot, or characters. To take them for granted would be a writer's biggest mistake."

Conneca was taken with his seemingly serious concern about staying on the same wavelength with the readers and buying public who made Maurice and Alexis what they were—a success story and famous authors. She wondered if Alexis was of the same mind?

Or *Alex*, to him, Conneca thought, amused that Maurice had found the need to change her name in mid-sentence. *Did he believe I'd be uncomfortable if he used the shortened, more intimate name for his ex-wife?* Or was he the one who was really uncomfortable using it in Conneca's presence?

Just what exactly was the nature of Maurice's nonwriting relationship with his ex-wife these days? Conneca found herself pondering. Did he still have feelings for her? If so, how strong?

For some reason Conneca felt a spasm of jealousy toward the woman she knew only as Alexis or Alex—the other half of a celebrity African-American writing team. The fact that Alexis was very beautiful, if her book jacket photo was any indication, did not help matters any. *Not that I'm competing with her,* Conneca scolded herself. Or maybe she was in some small, silly way that sisters found themselves in competition with one another whether they wanted to or not?

So where is Alexis right now? Conneca couldn't help but wonder why she wasn't there with her writing partner making sure he did not stray too far from their agenda? *Why should I care?* a voice in Conneca's head responded snappily and nearly aloud.

Curiosity finally got the better of her. "Does Alexis plan to join you here in Oak Cliffs to finish your novel?" Conneca tried to make her voice sound as casual as possible.

Maurice glanced at the ocean before facing her. "No," he said succinctly. "Our collaboration actually involves *me* writing the text and Alexis trimming the fat and calories, so to speak. We both know our roles and try to keep from stepping on each other's toes. Though that's not always possible."

Conneca sensed there was some friction between them and who ultimately controlled the finished product, but she didn't want to try to read into something that was none of her business. *And I have no intention of making it my business,* she promised herself.

"Sounds like you have an ideal arrangement," Conneca said, sucking in a deep breath, her legs starting to feel like lead weights.

"You could say that," Maurice seconded, now beginning to breathe out of his mouth. "What's that old saying, 'don't tinker with success'?"

But at what cost? Conneca asked herself, playing Monday morning quarterback. Wasn't success relative? Was it worth losing a marriage over? Making more money at the expense of spiritual, mental, and intimate happiness seemed like a bad tradeoff to Conneca.

They were nearing the inn. Others had begun to creep out onto the sand like ants.

Maurice brushed against Conneca, and for an instant they seemed to be swaying in slow motion like the ocean itself. She felt the heat from his body absorb into her own. It left Conneca lightheaded for a moment or two and she tried to make herself believe it must be due to exhaustion.

But she knew, in fact, that the real cause was none other than Maurice Templeton.

* * *

That afternoon Conneca lent a hand in the kitchen. A group of foreign tourists had come in, taxing the small inn's restaurant staff to the limit. Nadine Waverly was the head chef, kitchen director, and Conneca's best friend. The two were the same age, had grown up together, left the nest, and returned when the pastures no longer seemed greener elsewhere. Nadine had gone to culinary school in Jamaica, married and divorced a Jamaican. She'd worked at several world-class restaurants abroad and in the U.S., before returning to Oak Cliffs to help Conneca revitalize the Sheridan Seaside Inn.

Nadine, who had sworn off men after her divorce and several flings that went absolutely nowhere, had changed her tune when she met a nice businessman in town. Soon they were living together happily and taking things one day at a time.

Nadine was petite at five foot three with an even, brown-tea complexion. She had blond highlights in her curly, bobbed jet-black hair. Behind wire-rimmed maroon glasses were big hazel eyes that never seemed to stop moving. She held a menu on a clipboard in front of her stained white apron and let out a theatrical sigh. "This place is like a madhouse!" she exclaimed.

"What can I do to help?" Conneca asked her friend, who had come to work for her on the condition that she be able to run the kitchen without interference. Conneca had been only too happy to relinquish such authority, especially to someone whom she highly respected as a great cook and a close friend.

"You can start slicing and dicing those sweet potatoes," Nadine directed, indicating a pile on the long wooden table in the center of the room, along with a large knife. "We're having sweet-as-can-be potato soup as the entree today."

"Yummy," Conneca cooed, running her tongue across her teeth. "Will do." She washed her hands, put on gloves, and began to go to work on the potatoes while watching Nadine direct the rest of the staff like a maestro.

Nadine put a hand up to her brow exaggeratedly and said, "Aren't you glad this *isn't* the busy season, Conneca?"

"Ecstatic," she laughed. "The more guests, girl, the merrier!"

"I couldn't agree more," said Nadine, popping a piece of celery in her mouth. "How else would I practice my skills without a bunch of hungry guests?"

"You'll get no argument from me there." Conneca slid the diced potatoes into a pot of boiling water.

Nadine favored her as if a thought had only now entered her head. "You're not going to believe who I saw in the lobby this morning. He probably got lost on his way from the casino, I imagine."

Conneca raised a whimsical brow. "Don't tell me—the president of the United States decided to take a *gamble* and pay our little establishment a visit?"

"You wish," Nadine laughed. "Or maybe not. That Secret Service stuff would be a nightmare! Actually, it was Maurice Templeton, the *insanely* handsome writer. You remember the book I gave you to read by Alexis Maurice, the once-married, now-divorced writing duo?"

"*Danger At Sea*," Conneca acknowledged, smiling. "I know all about Mr. Templeton's presence in town. In fact, he's staying right here at the inn." She felt the color flood her cheeks.

Nadine looked flabbergasted. "Oh, really?"

Conneca twisted her mouth sheepishly. "He ended up—quite by accident, I can assure you—being the man I 'won' the highest bid on at the celebrity auction last night."

"And you're just telling me this?" Nadine voiced in utter disbelief. "Maurice Templeton . . . in the flesh! Staying here . . . Hmm."

Conneca wrinkled her nose. "Get your mind out of the gutter, girl," she teased. "Didn't think it was all that important. Far as I'm concerned he's just another paying customer, nothing more." *Well, maybe a little bit more*, she acknowledged to herself.

Nadine widened her eyes. "Well, did you happen to find out when *this* paying customer's next book is due out? I can't read enough Alexis Maurice novels!"

"Calm down, Nadine." Conneca cut more potatoes and looked up. "I understand he's working on the final chapters of a new book during his stay here," she informed her proudly. "Stay tuned. It shouldn't be long now."

Nadine applied a generous amount of salt and pepper to her soup. "Wonderful!" She slanted a curious gaze in Conneca's direction. "Was Alexis auctioned off separately?"

"She didn't come," Conneca was almost ashamed to admit. She wasn't sure if Alexis's absence was good or bad. Apparently she and Maurice did not always travel in the same circles. At least professionally speaking.

Nadine seemed to smile with approval. "I suppose that explains why the brother seemed in no hurry to go anywhere," she said, stirring the soup. "He didn't have a certain someone looking over his shoulder."

Conneca was not quite sure how to respond. She didn't believe for one minute that Maurice Templeton wasn't perfectly capable of taking care of himself. Even in the company of his ex-wife and writing partner.

"Or maybe he did," suggested Nadine with a narrow eye. "I could imagine a beautiful sister patiently waiting in Maurice's room for him to find his way back to."

The thought irked Conneca for some reason. "He's here *alone*," she said tersely. Or at least that is what she had been clearly led to believe.

But then men had a way about them of telling women what they wanted to hear—even if it wasn't what they really wanted to hear.

Nadine put a mischievous smile on her face. "Then I assume he's available?"

"I wouldn't know," Conneca was quick to respond.

Is he truly available? she wondered. Surely a man with Maurice's looks and success would not have to go long without female companionship. That is, unless he was still somehow pining for his ex-wife.

And saving himself for her.

And what difference did any of it really make? Conneca asked herself, feeling hot under the collar and trying not to let it show. Considering that she lived in the Pacific Northwest and Maurice the Rocky Mountains, there was no real reason to expect that they could ever have anything serious between them. She had never had a long distance relationship before and certainly could not imagine trying to carry on a romance with someone who she only saw once or twice a month, if that often. Thanks, but she would pass. She wasn't interested in a here-today, gone-tomorrow type of romance.

"We'll probably find out soon enough if the man's currently spoken for," declared Nadine. "Men that gorgeous and talented don't come around to these parts every day—at least, not that I've seen and recognized. Maybe the forces of nature are at work here, girl?"

"Right," Conneca laughed, hiding an unsettled feeling in the pit of her stomach. "And I think they're telling me that my services are needed elsewhere. So if you're done with me, Ms. Matchmaker, then I'm out of here."

"I get the message loud and clear." Nadine tasted the soup and nodded with satisfaction. "Doesn't mean I won't stop trying, though," she warned. "You know me—never one to let opportunity knock without answering. Too bad I already have a man. Otherwise, you and I might have come to blows over that one."

Conneca frowned playfully. "Hey, you can have him, if you decide to dump your man," she said. "I think I've got my hands full at the moment, without running around, chasing after Mr. Templeton . . . and all the baggage he's carrying."

"So scoot then, girlfriend," Nadine said, trying more soup. "Get back to work—all by your lonesome! We can take it from here."

Conneca smiled at her well-meaning, if at times annoying, friend. "Yes, ma'am," she said, saluting. "Just be sure you leave some of that tasty soup for the guests."

She left the kitchen and began to work the front desk. But Conneca's thoughts were still very much on the topic of Maurice Templeton.

And the matter of his availability.

CHAPTER 7

Maurice went into town that afternoon in hopes of increasing his wardrobe by several pairs of slacks, shirts, underwear, another jogging suit, and even a business or entertainment suit. He had brought only two sets of clothing on the trip to Oak Cliffs, including the jogging suit he had worn on the plane. The tux for the auction had been rented. There had been no reason to anticipate that he would stay longer than one day. *But that was then and this is now.*

As it was, Maurice was not entirely sure how long he would be in Oak Cliffs. He had booked the room for a month just to be on the safe side. However, he seriously doubted that he would hang around that long. How could he possibly justify such a lengthy trip away from Denver, where he belonged? Or try and explain this to Alexis, whose patience might run thin were his boyish infatuation with Conneca to interfere with their writing collaboration?

Maurice could think of one good reason. *Conneca Sheridan.* But was the sister reason enough to be irrational when he was normally so rational? *I can't answer that right now,* he thought, parking his rented BMW outside a shopping strip.

Without further debating his comings and goings, Maurice entered a men's clothing store. The clerk, a short, well-dressed man in his mid-fifties with a receding crimson hairline, approached him.

"May I help you with anything in particular, sir?" he asked.

Maurice looked over and around him. There was seemingly something for everyone, though the store was not very large. He didn't imagine that there were a whole lot of choices in Oak Cliffs for the best in menswear.

"Perhaps you can," Maurice told him. "What I need is a whole new wardrobe."

A broad smile lit up the man's entire face as if Christmas had come early. "I'd say you came to just the right place!"

Forty-five minutes later Maurice emerged with three big bags, looking as if he were doing his own Christmas shopping three months early. He put the bags in the trunk of his car, feeling as if he were ready for whatever—or whoever—came his way.

Before heading back to the inn, Maurice took a short tour of the town. It was far removed from the Mile High City. Folks seemed to be able to walk about with their guard down and little reason to believe they were flirting with danger. Even with the local casino, he imagined that crime was a relatively rare occurrence in this out-of-the-way, friendly, coastal resort.

Small-town life and living had always intrigued Maurice, especially when working on a new novel where diverse and out-of-the-way locations helped heighten the drama, suspense, and romance. Nor could he go wrong if there was a nice looking sister in town who could prove inspirational to the twists and turns in the plot.

Someone like Conneca Sheridan.

In bed Conneca began reading Alexis Maurice's first book, which she had borrowed from Nadine. It was called *The Cliff's Edge*. On the inside jacket it read: "America's most promising new contemporary fiction-writing team since Judith Michael." Below that read: "The Denzel and Halle of romantic suspense novels." Yet another eye-grabber comment declared: "First-rate fiction by a terrific African-American duet of the ages!"

Were they really that in tune with one another on the pages? Conneca asked herself enviously, though the obvious answer was right under her nose. The high-quality writings spoke for themselves.

She wondered how anyone could possibly compete with this larger-than-life romantic image the two portrayed. Wouldn't this aura always come between Maurice and any woman he chose to be with? Or one who chose to be with him? Had the handsome brother's success inadvertently sabotaged any real chance at happiness beyond the bestseller list?

Or reading between the lines?

Conneca read the first five chapters, finding herself fully engrossed. Then her lids grew heavy and she fell asleep still holding Maurice Templeton's creation.

*   *   *

Maurice walked into the lobby after what turned out to be a restless sleep. He had a lot on his mind. The novel had to be written and rewritten. The ending had to plausibly put all the pieces together, like a perfectly aligned puzzle. He felt the pressure of trying to live up to the excellence of writing that the readers had come to expect. He didn't want to disappoint them, Alexis, or himself.

Then there was Conneca. Each time Maurice saw her, he longed to be with her, as if his very life's essence depended on it. He wanted to play with her lustrous, long hair, to touch her full mouth again with his own, to see every inch of her magnificent, shapely body, and to hold Conneca in his arms and never let her go. And last, but definitely not least, thought Maurice ardently, he wanted to make sweet, sensual, and slow love to Conneca Sheridan. The way love should be made between a man and woman. A way he could barely remember, but desired with all his heart. His pulse quickened at the mere thought of he and Conneca in the same bed together.

Maurice wondered if his conflicting fanciful desires and real-life obligations could coexist.

His thoughts returned to Conneca Sheridan. What made the sister tick? How did she end up running what seemed to be a first-class inn? He wondered about the past men in her life.

Were there any suitors at the moment? Maurice contemplated.

The lobby was quiet after midnight. At the desk he saw Lee Azikewe. Maurice remembered from last night that his nametag also read: "Assistant Manager." But he knew that Azikewe was far more than that to Conneca. He had overheard the two of them talking about meeting rich celebrities. Conneca had scoffed at the notion but Azikewe, in a fatherly way, had encouraged such a pursuit as wise and acceptable. Even honorable.

Maurice wondered if this meant that Conneca was presently involved with neither a rich nor celebrated man, if anyone. Or did she simply have a general disdain for male celebrities who happened to be financially secure and wrote books for a living? He intended to find that out. And more.

Maurice headed toward the desk in his new burnt-orange chino sports shirt, black denim jeans, and dark English tan mocs. Lee Azikewe was reading the newspaper to pass the time and deathly late-night silence away.

When he saw Maurice, Lee flashed him a huge smile. "Good evening, Mr. Templeton." "How may I help you?"

"One of those nights where sleep is hard to come by," Maurice muttered. "Thought a stroll might be just what the doctor ordered. Can you use a little company?"

Lee seemed pleased he'd asked. "Would love some," he said. "You're welcome to come down and talk whenever you like. I'm usually here every other night till the wee hours of the morning."

Maurice smiled. "I'll make a note of that." He spied various plaques on the back wall denoting excellence in hospitality and accommodations. He could not argue the point. Conneca's inn certainly beat many of the better-known, larger establishments he had stayed at where even celebrity authors could become lost in the shuffle of faces or were otherwise brought down to earth by cold, impersonal rooms and hosts. He said, impressed, "It appears as if the Sheridan Seaside Inn has been the recipient of many awards over the years."

Lee glanced at the wall, his expression one of pride. "Chalk it up to superb service, hard work, and maybe a little bit of luck."

"I take it Conneca is not the original owner?" deduced Maurice.

Lee confirmed this with shake of the head. "That would be her parents, John and Carmela Sheridan. They turned what had been a run-down farm some years ago into the Sheridan Seaside Inn."

So Sheridan was her given name, rather than married, divorced, or widowed name, ruminated Maurice. He was piqued more than he cared to admit. "Then Conneca and her siblings were groomed to take over when the time was right?" Maurice wondered if she had any sisters as fine as she.

"Conneca was an only child," Lee informed him. "And she wasn't exactly groomed to run the place. But it was always in her blood, and when things worked out as they did, she ended up where she started."

"What *things*?" Maurice gave him an unblinking gaze, fully aware he was asking for more details than he had a right to know.

Lee hesitated. "Maybe you should ask her," he said tersely.

"Maybe I will," Maurice responded, his interest in Conneca Sheridan only deepening, like engrossing himself in a top-of-the-line mystery novel. Only this—no, she—was far more intriguing. "So Conneca's never been married?"

Lee stared. "Close once or twice, but no cigar." He batted his lashes with regret. "And you, Mr. Templeton, if I may ask—what is *your* status?"

Maurice recognized that in his own way Lee was trying to weed out the good from the bad pursuers of Conneca. Or at least the married ones.

"I'm not married," he said simply, leaving out the fact that he was divorced, since Conneca already knew that. "But there's always hope, isn't there?"

Lee grinned understandingly. "Yes, for all of us." He folded the paper. "I understand you're a writer, Mr. Templeton?"

"Some would say that," Maurice replied, resting his arm on the counter. "I prefer to think of myself as a novelist, pure and simple. I tend to separate *real* writers from authors of fiction."

Lee smiled. "And modest, too."

"Just being honest," Maurice said steadfastly. "It's far easier to create a book-length story than to write, for example, an essay on the origin of life. But I must admit, the former can be far more profitable."

"I'll have to take your word on that," Lee told him. "I'm afraid I have no such skills."

"Probably a good thing," suggested Maurice. "Competition in this business can be hell at times."

Lee gave a knowing chuckle. "And in this one also."

"I'm sure." Maurice yawned, feeling tired all of a sudden. "Well, I think I'll give sleep another try. Nice talking to you, Lee."

"You too, Mr. Templeton."

"Please, call me Maurice," he insisted in his attempt to build bridges.

Maurice wanted his stay there to be as informal as possible. He didn't want to be treated differently than others. Especially not by someone so close to Conneca, whom he knew she respected and relied on his good judgment.

Lee smiled respectfully. "Good night, Maurice."

"Good night." Maurice was sure he'd made a good impression on the assistant manager, which could go a long ways in getting closer to the inn's proprietor.

CHAPTER 8

Conneca caught Lee just as he was going off duty in the morning, re-placed by a front desk staffer. He looked tired but alert. Just the op-posite of her, she imagined. They were in the recently remodeled office where Conneca was going over the previous day's receipts.

"How were things last night?" Conneca asked routinely, sitting at her mahogany desk, while admiring the sea breeze paneling and cherry hardwood floor.

"Slow." Lee handed her a bag containing more receipts. "Except that I had a visitor . . . Maurice Templeton."

"Oh?"

Lee had caught Conneca's attention and he knew as much. "Said he couldn't sleep." Lee stretched. "Seems like a really nice young brother."

Conneca had a feeling there was more to the conversation than Maurice's niceness, but she refused to appear overanxious, even if she was dying to know what they had talked about. Or whom.

After a moment or two, Lee satisfied her curiosity by saying, "He wanted to know about you."

"What about me?" She lifted her chin with an air of indifference.

"Basically everything—your past, present, maybe even your future." Lee twisted his mouth sideways. "I told him to get the juicy details from you."

Conneca sucked in a breath. "Thank you, Lee, for that."

"No problem," he said with a dismissive wave of his arm. "I'm not going to make it too easy for anyone who sets his sights on you, girl—you know that."

Conneca felt steam shoot from her ears. What the hell type of game was Maurice playing? *Why are you going behind my back to learn about me?* She didn't know if he was merely prying into her background for personal reasons, or trying to dig up information for that damned book of his. Either way, it made her uncomfortable and not too happy.

"I think he really does like you, Conneca." Lee ran short fingers through his hair. "And he's *not* married!"

"I'm not at all surprised," she spat sarcastically. "At the rate Mr. Templeton's going, one more marriage may be one too many!"

Lee cocked a brow. "What? You got something against successful, charming, handsome, divorced authors?"

Conneca shot him a hard look. "Only those who stick their noses where they don't belong!"

A few minutes later Conneca was banging on Maurice's door. She was wearing a cherry-brown pantsuit and low-heeled sandals, unsure of what she wanted to say. *I'll think of something,* she snorted to herself. Perhaps she would ask him to leave on the grounds of overstepping his bounds as a guest. Or maybe she would tell him that her personal life was not to be used in his books or for his personal amusement.

She knocked twice more, but there was still no answer. Obviously he was out. Probably romancing some sister helpless to his charms, she speculated.

I'll try again later, Conneca told herself angrily, *after I cool off.* Better yet, she would leave a curt note for Maurice at the front desk, telling him that any further intrusions upon her personal life with any of the staff would not be tolerated. Whatever his reasons were.

"Looking for me?" the deep voice said, an amused catch to it. Maurice was grinning as he stood there in an obviously new two-toned red and silver running suit and the familiar black Nikes. Sweat poured down his face but he looked energetic.

"I think we need to talk," Conneca uttered sharply, trying to overlook his strong presence and its effect on her even now.

"I gathered that much," he said hesitantly. "Is there something wrong?"

"Yes, and it's you!" she exclaimed. "How dare you ask Lee about me behind my back! What's up with that?"

Maurice didn't deny it. "He told you, did he?"

Her eyes locked on his. "Did you think he wouldn't? Lee is very loyal to me and this inn."

"I've already come to that conclusion," Maurice said calmly, wiping his brow with a towel.

"You had no right to go prying into my life." Conneca slapped her hands on her hips. "Guests at this inn are here *only* for the accommodations—not the owner's life history. Do I make myself clear, Mr. Templeton?"

"Perfectly," he answered tonelessly. "But I don't know why the hell you're getting so bent out of shape, Conneca. I didn't ask Lee anything inappropriate—just some ordinary stuff I could probably find out on the Internet. Is it so wrong for a brother to want to get to know you better? Or is it your style to push any man away that gets too close?"

"You *bastard!*" Conneca felt her temperature rise.

"I've been called worse." Maurice drew closer and sighed. "Look, Conneca, you've blown this way out of proportion. I couldn't sleep last night, so I went to the lobby to stretch my legs. Lee happened to be at the desk and we talked. You just happened to come up. It was no big deal."

Only *she* had made it one, Conneca thought, suddenly feeling as if she had overreacted in a major and embarrassing way. What had made her feel so self-conscious all of a sudden? So defensive? *Am I really trying to push you away for fear you're getting too close? Or do I fear getting too close to you?* Perhaps her real fear was that at the end of the day he would be too far away to still the patter of her rapid heartbeat.

Maurice inched even closer so that there was no room between them. Not even the air itself. Conneca could almost taste the musky, sweaty, enticing scent that clung to him like expensive cologne. A chill went up and down her spine. Maurice tilted his head down and kissed her softly. Conneca felt her knees buckle in the process, and wondered if she might literally fall into his arms. She found herself pressing forward, hardening the kiss, the feel of his mouth flattened against hers intoxicatingly.

It was Maurice who pulled away. "Now that we've kissed and made up," he said, tasting his lips confidently, "I want to invite you to an impromptu reading and book signing I arranged at the bookstore in town. Fortunately, they had enough stock to make it worthwhile. The proceeds go to charity—something I'm sure you would approve of." He paused. "That is, if I am indeed forgiven for letting my inquisitive nature get the better of me?"

Even if her stubbornness wanted to prevail, Conneca knew she could no longer remain angry with Maurice. Nor could she deny that he was affecting her like no other had in some time, if ever. It still remained to be seen if this was a step forward or backward.

"You're forgiven," she told him, holding her breath in doing so.

CHAPTER 9

The Brookline Bookstore opening had been a big hit among the locals since taking over an abandoned warehouse two years ago. Conneca had gone there many times, mainly to browse through or buy travel and historical books over a café latte or cappuccino. She had even attended a book reading on occasion, fascinated by the written word and respectful of those talented enough to be able to bring their books to life through readings.

Conneca sat in the front of three rows of chairs—all occupied, with others standing—while Maurice sat comfortably at a table reading aloud a passage from *Danger At Sea*. Hardcover and paperback Alexis Maurice books were piled high on the table, waiting to be signed and sold to the bookstore's delight.

Was this the life of a famous author? Conneca wondered. Readings, signings, and goodwill appearances, aside from the writing itself. Was there any room left for a normal life? *Or is this about as normal as it got for the Maurice Templetons of the world?*

Conneca pondered briefly if she could ever become involved with a man who may have been too involved with himself. Hadn't she had enough of selfish men to last her a lifetime? *Yes, I'm sure of it,* she thought.

To Conneca it might well be the biggest mistake of her life to plunge into something that would in all likelihood always leave her playing second fiddle. Make that *third* fiddle, she told herself, thinking about Alexis's obviously still-strong presence in Maurice's life.

All such considerations seemed to vanish as Maurice's striking soot-colored eyes rose from the pages and landed directly upon Conneca's, as if she were the only one present. A tiny tremor zipped through her like lightning. He smiled, as if sensing his ability to get to her even with something as innocuous as a glance.

Following a wink, Maurice turned his attention back to the book and, without missing a beat, continued reading confidently to his captive audience. "Josie felt the pounding of her tender heart as night fell and Lucas was nowhere to be found. Fate could not possibly be so cruel as to take him away from her, she thought longingly. Not when she had just professed her love to him, and he to her. But she could not ignore the feeling burning inside like red-hot fire that something was wrong. *Very, very wrong—*"

Maurice closed the book, showed his sparkling white teeth, and received a standing ovation. Conneca noted that he seemed quite humble, under the circumstances, and down to earth. He signed each and every book, seemingly going out of his way to make every fan seem equally important. Finally there was one book left . . . with one fan.

"This one is for you, Conneca," Maurice told her with a straight face. "What would you like me to write in it—anything special?"

Though honored, Conneca told him reluctantly, "I already read that one, Maurice. Maybe you'd be better off signing it for someone else."

"I don't think so," he said sanguinely. "You've earned it, Conneca, if only for agreeing to attend. Even if you've read the book, now you can have your very own autographed copy. Who knows, it could be worth something someday—if only to you. Besides, sometimes a book is much better the second time around."

He raised his face to hers, and Conneca had the distinct feeling Maurice was somehow reading her mind. She froze like ice, literally unable to move.

Before she could protest further, Maurice was inscribing the inside of the book. Afterward he handed it to her. Conneca opened it and read aloud, unable to keep her voice from shaking as her body was. "To a most gorgeous lady, whose generous benevolent contribution to a great cause I'll never forget. Not to mention the lady herself! On the contrary, I can only hope to get to know her better—much better! Remember, every good book is worth reading at least twice! Always, Maurice."

Conneca was speechless. No one had ever autographed a book for her, much less with such heartfelt words. *Is this man real or a figment of my imagination?* Equally, she wondered whether the words really came from his heart or were more a reflection of Maurice's magnificent gift as a write.

"Thank you, Maurice," she said quietly. "I'll always hang onto this."

He laughed. "Well, I think you can set it down every now and then."

Conneca blushed. "You know what I mean."

"Yes, I do, and I appreciate it." Maurice stood and angled his eyes down at hers. "Just be sure to save room on the bookshelf. You never know what else might have to go beside this one."

In spite of his vagueness, Conneca was left to contemplate the possibilities.

"Do you mind if we stop by the supermarket on our way back?" Conneca asked Maurice, sitting next to him in his BMW. "I promised my head chef that I would pick up a few items."

"By all means," he said. "In fact, I need to purchase some things there myself."

Forty minutes later they returned to the Sheridan Seaside Inn with several bags piled high. They took the service entrance to the kitchen, where the groceries were unloaded onto a wooden corner table.

"There you are," Nadine said frantically, lifting a big jar of pickles from a bag. "If you had waited much longer, Conneca, I would have had to do some major substituting!"

"Sorry," Conneca apologized. "Traffic out there was unusually hectic—"

"It's my fault," Maurice interceded from behind Nadine. "I'm afraid the reading and signing ran over a bit."

"What reading and signing?" Nadine's eyes widened as if she had seen a ghost, instead of Maurice.

Only then had Conneca realized that she had failed to even mention the book event to Nadine, telling her merely that she was going out for a while.

"Oops!" Conneca gasped, covering her mouth. "Maurice did an impromptu author reading and signing at the Brookline Bookstore." When Nadine seemed entranced with Maurice, Conneca felt obliged to say, "I suppose you two haven't met—formally." She looked from one to the other. "This is Maurice Templeton . . . and this is Nadine Waverly, your number one fan!"

"Nice to meet you, Nadine," Maurice said, shaking her hand firmly.

"You too," Nadine swallowed unevenly, looking as though she wanted to hide behind her discolored apron. Making a face at Conneca, Nadine sputtered, "R-Remind me to kill you, girl—after I prepare tonight's menu."

Maurice laughed. "I don't think it will be necessary to take things to that extreme. If you have books, I'll be more than happy to sign them, Nadine."

"Oh, would you?" she begged, holding her hands together in supplication.

"Any time."

Conneca gave a nervous chuckle. "Looks like I'm off the hook on this one."

"Barely," Nadine groaned. "Right now, I have other things on my mind, such as feeding some famished folks! So if you two will excuse me and get out of my kitchen . . ."

"You're excused," Conneca told her, winking at Maurice.

"Wouldn't want to keep starving guests waiting, would we?" he added.

In the lobby, Maurice shifted his bag from one arm to the other. "Seems like a cool sister," he told Conneca of Nadine. "And obviously a true fan!"

"She's also a good friend," Conneca said. "I'm not sure I could make it without her around here."

Maurice nodded knowingly. "Yeah. Kind of like how I feel about Alexis and the writing."

Conneca gave an uneasy chuckle. "Maybe we're both too dependent for our own good," she suggested.

"Maybe," Maurice allowed. "But who's to say that the alternative would do either of us much good?"

"Not me," she readily admitted. The notion of replacing Nadine was hard for Conneca to imagine. Obviously the same was true of Alexis as Maurice's collaborator—even if Conneca thought it might be interesting to see how he wrote totally on his own.

"That doesn't mean we each can't make room in our lives for others," emphasized Maurice, a catch in his voice.

Conneca bit her lip as their eyes locked and she felt the vibes between them penetrate right to her very soul. "There's only so much room," she hinted, averting his face.

"There's as much room as *we* are willing to allow," he stressed, as they reached the stairwell.

How much was she willing to allow? Conneca did not know the answer. Only that her world was basically filled and non-expansive. Any adjustments—especially of the romantic kind—would only complicate matters. But weren't they already becoming quickly complicated with each passing moment that she was in Maurice's presence or that he was in her thoughts?

She lifted her chin. "Hadn't you better get that bag to your room?" she asked, trying to change the subject.

He favored her with a crooked smile. "Yeah, I'd better."

Conneca sensed that some unspoken thoughts and feelings remained between them. Perhaps waiting in hiding to explode like a time bomb at any time.

"Will we be seeing you in the dining room this evening, Maurice?" she asked politely. "Or will you be having your meal in your room?"

Maurice pretended to think about it. "I think I will eat downstairs," he said succinctly. "I hate eating alone."

Conneca used to hate it also. Yet she had become so used to it that it almost seemed natural and even desirable at times. Now she felt a renewed hunger that had little to do with food.

Maurice shifted the bag in his arms and said sweetly, "Thanks again for a nice afternoon together."

Conneca felt as though she should be thanking him, but her mouth went dry. Smiling awkwardly, she said, "I guess I'll see you later then."

Just before Maurice began his ascent up the stairs, he responded confidently: "Oh, you can count on it."

CHAPTER 10

The more time he spent at this inn, the more Maurice felt a sense of belonging. *This really is like home away from home,* he told himself in his room. Though he had managed to keep his feelings for Conneca in check, they had nevertheless welled deep within him, aching to come out in full force like a tidal wave. Even then Maurice was fighting what he saw as bailing out on Alexis, at least emotionally if not physically. Yet he had never been convinced that there was *ever* a real emotional bond between them. As husband and wife they seemed constantly at odds on an emotional level, often merely going through the motions.

It was different with Conneca. Everything about the sister and her small world in this little community loomed large for Maurice. Being part of something with an intrafamilial slant to it had been the one thing missing in his life—having been an only child with parents who were loving but distant.

Can I have that sense of belonging here? Maurice asked himself.

And with the lady of the house?

Maurice freshened up and slapped on some Vera Wang cologne, before slipping into a pair of khaki cotton pants, a plum silk Polo shirt, and coal leather shoes. He left the room and headed downstairs for dinner, his stomach growling. Even the prospect of having a good meal at the Sheridan Seaside Inn had taken on a whole new meaning—especially if he could invite Conneca to join him.

Maurice found her playing host in the lounge, smiling and chatting amicably with guests like they were her best friends. Conneca's box braids and Senegalese twists seemed to shimmer with her every move. She wore a tasteful ruby jacket dress and dark pumps, looking for all the world like not just another businesswoman but one who had flair, style, and beauty to match.

When Conneca saw Maurice, she headed his way, as if drawn by a magnet.

"What don't you do around here?" he asked admiringly, shaking his head with a grin.

She laughed. "Well, I don't fly. And I don't turn into a pumpkin at the stroke of midnight. But," she admitted, "I do just about everything else as needed."

Maurice chuckled. "Whew! And I thought writing was hard."

"It is," Conneca said flatly. "Except for those like you whose natural gift for storytelling makes it easy."

"Flattery will get you everywhere, baby." He raised his eyebrows at her flirtatiously.

"We'll see about that," she cooed dulcetly and paused. "Would you like a cocktail before dinner?"

"I would," he responded. "But I'd like it even better if I could talk *you* into having dinner with me."

Conneca hesitated. "Uh, that could be difficult. I have to do the hostess thing here, then there's a shift at the front desk, and—"

"Just say yes," Maurice pleaded anxiously. "Remember, you're the boss around here. Put some of that authority and advantage to good use."

Conneca twisted her lips in thought. "Perhaps I could do a bit of switching around. Can your stomach last for about half an hour?"

"I'll make it last," he promised, already counting down the minutes and indeed seconds till she could give him her undivided attention.

They were seated at Conneca's private table in the dining room. It was by a large bay window that overlooked the bluffs. Though she rarely ate in there, Conneca did invite certain important or special guests to join her for dinner on occasion. While she certainly hadn't planned on dining with Maurice this evening, Conneca gladly accepted his invitation— even if she suspected it could get certain nosy people to talking.

"How's your book coming along?" Conneca inquired with interest, holding a glass of Sauvignon Blanc.

"Not too good, I'm afraid." Maurice pursed his lips contemplatively, sipping his own wine. "Sometimes the hardest and longest part is the ending."

Yes, tell me about it, Conneca thought. She had found it very difficult to end her previous relationships. Could she be headed down that same disastrous path again? *Not if I can help it.* She knew full well that where matters of the heart were concerned, the unexpected sometimes happened.

Conneca jammed her fork into the tossed salad after adding a touch of French dressing. "Maybe it would come easier if Alexis were here to offer tips and moral support?" she suggested.

Maurice turned stone-faced. "Not likely," he spoke softly. "The climax of a story must come from within—without outside guidance. Alexis, while very good at what she does, would not be able to come to my rescue in this instance."

What other instances were there? Conneca wondered. Then she decided to bag the attack of jealousy, realizing it was being misplaced. *Maurice is not mine to fret over.*

Suddenly Conneca felt sorry for the brother. Being a writer clearly had its own drawbacks that she knew nothing about. It also told her that he took his craft seriously and refused to settle for less.

She felt the same way in wanting the best, which had been the source of her problems with men and life in general—neither of which had measured up to her admittedly high standards.

"Perhaps being here is counterproductive to completing your book," Conneca advanced boldly, though she knew she was stepping out on a limb in saying so.

"On the contrary," Maurice said, slicing his filet mignon with precision. "I'd say being here has helped inspire me to move forward after being at a virtual standstill for some time." He eyed her carefully and put the meat in his mouth, savoring its taste for a moment. "I think I owe that all to you."

Conneca felt the heat steal over her cheeks. "I'm not sure I want that kind of pressure on my shoulders, thank you," she told him, an edge to her voice. "Particularly given your admitted lack of productivity."

Maurice gave a brief chortle. "I didn't say I hadn't been productive. Quite the opposite. My problem has been putting the pieces together to my complete satisfaction." He paused. "The worst thing any writer can do is try and cheat the readers. Believe me, they would know it."

"Are all writers this conscientious about their work?" Conneca tasted the wine, licking her lips afterward.

"Most of the ones I know are." He tilted his head with a nod. "That doesn't mean we always see eye to eye with the critics and booksellers on the value and quality of our writing."

"I see."

The more she came to know him, the more Conneca felt she wanted to know about Maurice Templeton, even if it meant opening up about more of her own life in the process. But she still had to be careful, for she didn't want to make the same mistakes again. Not for anything—or anyone—in the world.

Conneca met Maurice's eyes, seemingly the perfect mixture of cold and hot ebony. "Does your writing leave much time for a social life?" she asked, her voice betraying the personal nature of the question.

"It hasn't always," he fully admitted, holding her gaze. "For a time after Alexis, I was a social butterfly, understandably so. I needed time to get my head together." He put the wineglass to his lips thoughtfully. "I've had my fair share of women friends, but no one quite earth-shattering enough to make me forget I'm a writer."

Well, I'm certainly not earth shattering, Conneca thought glumly. *Looks like you can hang on to your social butterflying for a while longer.*

A look of reflection crossed Maurice's face. "Now that I'm getting older, I've come to realize that my priorities are all wrong. Or at least they are beginning to shift in the right direction now that I don't have to constantly worry about trying to make a comfortable living."

Conneca knew nothing about the business of writing, royalties, and such. But she imagined that with several bestselling books and strong popularity, as evidenced by the turnout for his book reading and signing, Maurice was obviously financially secure. But for her, money still did not grow on trees, though she knew that many others were far lass fortunate than she. Of course, Conneca considered, Maurice did have to share his earnings with Alexis. Even with that, she suspected, there was still likely plenty to go around.

Conneca had a feeling that money itself was not all that important to Maurice. Commendable, she thought. But exactly what and who was important to him she still had yet to figure out. And she wasn't sure she should even try.

"I don't imagine you can have an active social life yourself while running an inn?" Maurice contended, his tone making it clear that his interest was more than merely casual.

"Not much of one," Conneca acknowledged sadly. "There's the occasional date—often as a favor to a friend—or a luncheon engagement to drum up business. But mainly, this is a full-time occupation."

Maurice studied her with a single finger pressed to his lips. "What about before this?"

She batted her lashes at him. "What about it?"

"Well, was there someone special in your life?"

Conneca sighed, unsure just how comfortable she felt telling Maurice the intimate details of her life. Not that there was that much to tell. Certainly not enough to make a book-length tale of torrid romance and intrigue.

Maurice favored her with an amused grin. "Not asking for name, rank, and serial number, Conneca," he laughed. "Just trying for a little quid pro quo here."

Conneca nibbled on lettuce. "There was someone special," she responded in deliberation. "Actually two people."

A frown formed on Maurice's face. "What happened?" His voice deepened with curiosity.

"What didn't happen?" She rolled her eyes, the pain still as real as if it were only yesterday that Conneca had been humiliated and disillusioned—twice. "One was married; the other decided he liked my roommate better. Both were first-class jerks, to put it mildly."

"So you came back here to seek refuge from some bad choices in men?"

"I needed a new start," Conneca explained. "This seemed like as good a place as any to put the past behind me."

Maurice raised a brow. "And have you?"

Conneca shuddered. "Completely," she said emphatically. "The inn has kept me too busy to dwell on negative thoughts . . . and negative people."

"And obviously also too busy to dwell on positive thoughts and positive people," deduced Maurice, over the rim of his glass.

"What's that supposed to mean?" Conneca shot her eyes at him in a defensive move.

"A *real* man, baby," he replied bluntly. "Don't give up on us yet. There are a *few* good ones out there, you know."

"I know," she stated matter-of-factly. "But not in Oak Cliffs. Most of the men here are either married, engaged, too old, too young, or—"

Conneca checked herself and Maurice inquired: "Or what?"

"Or too preoccupied with their damned professions to be interested in a serious commitment with anyone." She sighed and fixed her eyes on his face before saying courageously. "Much like you."

Maurice winced, as if he had been pinched, but otherwise remained speechless. Conneca tried to read his mind, but realized she could not detect what lay within, as if it were buried deep within a cocoon.

Had she touched a raw nerve? *Or am I missing something else in the equation?* Conneca asked herself in wonder.

CHAPTER 11

S*erious commitment.*

Maurice pondered the words that weighed heavily on him like a coat of armor as he and Conneca left the dining room. Indeed, in spite of the preoccupation with his writings, he had committed himself to the pursuit of happiness—at all costs. He couldn't deny that he had become thoroughly captivated by something outside his work or collaboration.

Conneca Sheridan had become his true preoccupation of late. *But what did that mean exactly?* he asked himself. How far was he willing to take this . . . or her? Would Conneca put him in the same dark light as the two men who had betrayed her love, should it come to that?

Am I really any different from them in my faults, desires, and self-serving motives? Maurice wondered. Or would he only end up hurting her like they had, and like Alexis had hurt him?

He had managed to divert the dinner conversation to something more neutral and less weighty. Conneca seemed to accept it without suspecting his discomfort that seemed to go hand in hand with some overpowering needs she had managed to tap into, perhaps unknowingly.

They walked in silence to Conneca's office, each trapped in their own thoughts. There, a hysterical black woman in her early forties confronted the two. She was obviously an employee, thought Maurice, judging by the taupe uniform dress that clung to her large body. She had burgundy-colored micro braids and a dime-sized mole on her right cheek.

"What is it, Harriet?" Conneca asked calmly, as if she were always prepared for anything her staff threw at her.

"We have a problem with a leak in the sink in Room 123," she responded frantically. "It's really bad!"

"So have Edgar fix it." Conneca glanced at Maurice. "Edgar is our handy- all-purpose man," she explained.

"He called in sick at the last moment." Harriet's puffy face broke into a dozen creases.

"Oh no," Conneca moaned. "Just what we need—a plumber coming in who charges top dollar for a problem that could probably be done in five minutes."

"Sounds like *more* than a five-minute problem," Maurice observed speculatively.

Conneca rounded on him. "How would you know?"

"It just so happens that my old man was a plumber and he taught me a few tricks of the trade. Not to mention I've seen a few leaks in my time that were more like floods." Maurice cast his eyes down at her appealingly. "I'd be happy to take a look at the sink."

Conneca backpedaled hesitantly. "I wouldn't want to take you away from your work anymore than I already have."

"Don't worry about it," he barked tersely. "And it's me who took *you* away from *your* duties, remember? Save the plumber for a real emergency. Let me take care of this for you—free of charge."

Conneca considered it, as if reluctant to incur his debt and any payment that might be due later.

Sensing this reluctance, Maurice said, "I'll tell you what. If I can fix the problem just pay me whatever you would have paid Edgar." He paused. "Better yet, donate the money to your local literacy campaign."

Maurice suspected that was an offer she couldn't refuse. Could she?

It took a moment or two before Conneca said with the voice of desperation: "Show him the room, Harriet. And hurry!"

They detoured to the closet where Edgar kept his tools. Equipped with latex gloves, a pipe wrench, some washers, and determination, Maurice followed Harriet into the room. It had apparently just been vacated by guests, given the unmade bed, empty beer cans, and other trash in an overflowing basket.

A bucket underneath the sink was overflowing from the steady leak that showed no signs of abatement. Towels were spread across the floor to soak up the water.

Maurice immediately shut off the water valve under the sink and emptied the bucket into the tub. He then used the pipe wrench to loosen the pipe, suspecting that someone had probably put something they shouldn't have down the drain and conveniently checked out, rather than doing the right thing by admitting it.

Pulling the pipe off, Maurice immediately found the problem. Someone had actually jammed a pair of red lace thong panties in there—for what reason and under what circumstances he didn't even want to imagine.

Maurice looked up at Harriet, who was visibly embarrassed. "Your guess is as good as mine," he said awkwardly, holding them up.

Harriet stared at the soaked material and rolled her eyes. "Must have had some wild party in here . . ."

"A little bit too damned wild, I'm afraid." Maurice put the panties in the bucket, made sure the coast was clear of any further obstructions, and reattached the pipe. "Good as new," he said, feeling content that he had solved the case of the leaking sink . . . and in the process, maybe earning a few points with the inn's owner.

"Sorry to have to drag you in here for something that should never have happened," Harriet moaned.

Maurice grimaced. "I'd like to give the culprit a piece of my mind."

"You'd have to wait in line," she growled, taking over where he left off in starting to clean the sink. Harriet flashed Maurice a toothy grin. "You know, you're a real lifesaver! Wherever Conneca found you, she'd better keep you around."

Maurice blushed and thought, *I wouldn't be opposed to that one bit,* but said, "We'll have to see about that."

Minutes later Maurice found Conneca in her office. She looked all business, sitting at the oversized desk. He waited until she raised her head before he spoke.

"You wouldn't believe what the problem was for your water show in Room 123."

Conneca hoisted a brow. "Nothing really surprises me these days."

"This just might." He related the tale of the red thong panties and then watched as color filled her high cheeks.

When she recovered, Conneca flashed him an expressionless look but refused to comment further on the panties. "If you ever decide to give up writing," she groaned, "we can use a man of your skills around here."

"Harriet mentioned something to that effect also," Maurice chuckled, and suddenly found himself imagining applying his skills more appropriately to Conneca's sexy body. "Be careful what you ask for," he warned teasingly. "You just might get it!"

"Oh, really?" Conneca flushed brilliantly.

"I've always been good with my hands," he told her boastfully.

Maurice saw a look of awe and anticipation on Conneca's face at the prospect of his hands on her. It matched his own excitement and left him in a frenzied state of wanton desire, with urges that were barely controllable. *Damn, brother, be cool, or you'll lose it altogether,* he chastised himself.

"I assume that most authors are good with their hands," Conneca remarked lightheartedly. "Otherwise you wouldn't be very successful churning out page after page, would you, Mr. Novelist?"

Maurice laughed, humored by her humor and craftiness at getting out of a tight spot. Maybe he could pick up some pointers.

"Can't argue with you there, Ms. Sheridan," Maurice conceded, thankful that he could turn his mind elsewhere instead of on the woman before him and her unique ability to bring him to new heights of yearning. He decided it might be best to vacate the scene before making a complete fool of out himself. "Speaking of hands and writing, I'd better get back to my novel while I'm feeling suddenly inspired to churn out some pages like fresh butter."

Conneca watched him from the vantage point of her desk, as if grateful to have it between them in keeping her own desires in check. She shuffled some papers, almost for effect. "And I'd better get back to the business of running an inn." She showed her teeth, straight and pearly white as could be. "Thanks for the dinner companionship and the sink, Maurice. Good luck with your novel."

Maurice believed she truly meant that last remark. He would need every bit of that luck, and then some, if he were to get this book done on time and to his satisfaction. Almost as much as he needed her and she needed him, whether Conneca knew it or not.

"Now if I can just apply a bit of writing savvy with that luck, then this novel is sure to be a bona fide winner!" He licked his lips, studied hers ravenously, and said, following a long pause, "Good evening then, Conneca Sheridan."

On that note Maurice walked away. But in spirit he hadn't moved an inch, not wanting to let her out of his sight or mind.

CHAPTER 12

The Oak Cliffs Business Association held its monthly meeting at the Sheridan Seaside Inn. Conneca sat in the conference room beside her fellow proprietors while the president of the association, Gail Jenkins, spoke. Gail, along with her twin sister, Freda Mackintosh, owned the Hats, Hats, and More Hats Boutique, which specialized in hats from the West Indies and Northern Africa. The fifty-six-year-old African American widow had recently been elected to her second term in office, unopposed. Conneca thought it was a thankless job to try to get business owners, each with self-serving agendas and often in competition with one another, to see eye to eye. Most had found common ground in making charitable contributions of their time or money as a way of generating business and publicity. Such was the case in sponsoring the celebrity auction last week.

"The auction was a smashing success!" declared Gail in a boisterous voice that somehow seemed fitting for a person of her considerable girth. "We raised over $50,000!"

This was enough to cause cheers and applause to erupt throughout the room like an aftershock. It had exceeded everyone's expectations, topping last year's total by almost fifty percent.

"Now comes the tough part," Gail frowned, her medium-brown spiral weave shimmering. "Deciding which organizations will be the beneficiaries of our donations toward battling illiteracy."

Conneca ran through a list in her mind of some of her personal choices. But she knew that whatever organization they donated the money to, it would be put to good use.

Meanwhile her thoughts drifted to Maurice Templeton. He had been an unexpected source of delight to come from the auction. His presence at the inn had unraveled her normally controlled life and emotions. The attraction was mutual, she knew, but for the most part they had managed to keep things at arm's length since the kiss on the beach.

Then a second kiss outside Maurice's room had once again caught Conneca off-guard, rendering her virtually immobile and wishing for more, while dreading it at the same time for fear of being hurt.

Would anything come out of this? she asked herself. *Should anything come out of it?* Or were these flirtations between them and the rapid beating of her heart in Maurice Templeton's presence merely momentary lapses between two people from different worlds with perhaps two different agendas?

I only wish I knew the answer. Conneca felt slightly disoriented in her daydream.

"Conneca Sheridan has not only generously provided space for our meeting," Gail was saying, "but she personally outbid my sister, Freda, for the chance to have dinner with that gorgeous Mile-High-City brother and author, Maurice Templeton! Bad for Freda," she whined, "but *very good* for charity! Nice to know some of us can afford to pay top dollar for a talented, good-looking man. Obviously business must be booming here at the Sheridan Seaside Inn!"

Conneca's cheeks burned as all eyes focused on her, as though she were magnetized. She certainly had not meant to take away Freda's opportunity to wine and dine Maurice. She wasn't even aware Freda had her eye on him. Quite the contrary, Conneca had wanted nothing to do with the author at the time. But the forces of destiny seemed determined to draw them together as if they had little choice in the matter.

"Come on now, girl," Gail egged Conneca on, "give us the scoop on what it was like to go out on a date with the *better* half of the fabulous writing team of Alexis Maurice."

Being naturally shy, Conneca's first instinct was to run and hide like she did when she was a little girl and the spotlight was put on her. But as the host of this meeting, she had to confront her fears head on. Even if they seemed pronounced where it concerned Maurice Templeton.

Conneca stood, wearing a champagne Belldini suit with a white tulip top, and light gray leather slingbacks. Taking a deep breath, she regained her composure and walked to the front of the room. When she got to the podium, Conneca looked off to the side and saw Maurice standing near the door, causing her heart to lurch.

He gave her a look of amusement, and said, "Now be nice, Conneca. Wouldn't want these good folks to think that authors are everything bad they're cracked up to be."

Laughter floated through the air like snowflakes.

How long had he been standing there? Conneca wondered. How had she missed seeing him come in? *Did he somehow stage this* whole *thing?* Conneca realized that was a foolish thought. Obviously Maurice had wandered into the meeting, which was technically open to anyone who chose to attend, probably by chance. But that didn't still her nerves or the buckling of her knees.

Once she found her voice, Conneca said evenly, without looking at the man in question, "Mr. Templeton was a perfect gentleman. He gave me the scoop on what it's like to be both handsome *and* literate—not to mention a highly skilled author." She risked a furtive peek in his direction and saw the satisfaction spread across Maurice's face like a streak of sunlight, grateful that she had not tarnished his image in the slightest.

You owe me big time! Conneca thought with an inner smile. *And I just might demand payment.*

She regarded Gail's twin, who looked exactly like her sister, save for her mahogany auburn weave. Freda Mackintosh, who sat in the front row, had what appeared to be a scowl on her face. Smiling graciously at her, Conneca said, "Even with that, if I had known you were interested in Maurice, Freda honey, I would have gladly stepped aside. In truth, he wasn't my first choice to bid on."

Or second. Or third, Conneca thought. Feeling the power of his stare, she angled her eyes and saw an embellished aggrieved look on Maurice's face. She assumed it was playful.

Returning her gaze to Freda, Conneca told her in trying to make amends, "Fortunately, Mr. Templeton is a guest at the inn now. I'm sure he would be only too happy to invite you to dinner and share some of his secrets of writing success with you. Isn't that right, Maurice?"

When Conneca turned her head to look at him, Maurice was gone.

Conneca felt a little embarrassed. She had sought to right a wrong in the spirit of fun and Maurice had pulled a disappearing act on her. Did he always run away when things got a bit tense? She wondered if this unpredictability was part of his nature. Or was he simply being rude out of annoyance at her?

The meeting carried on as though Maurice had never been there, making a spectacle out of himself and annoying Conneca in the process. Even Freda seemed unaffected by the turn of events. They moved on to deciding where to donate the money. A half hour later the meeting was adjourned.

Conneca found Maurice in the lounge afterward, nursing a drink. His mind seemed elsewhere. Her first instinct was to simply ignore him and what had happened at the meeting, knowing it was not really that big of a deal—except maybe to Freda. But somehow it seemed too easy to let him off the hook.

"Do you have a minute?" Conneca asked curtly, practically waking him up.

Maurice turned to her with cold eyes. "That depends . . ."

"On what, I hesitate to ask?" She raised a brow. "If it's to explain why you showed up at the meeting and vanished before you could break Freda's heart—"

"On who *your* first choice was at the auction," he responded caustically.

Conneca snapped her head back. "You're kidding, right?" She tried to chuckle but only air came out.

Maurice's mouth was a hard line. "Does it look like it?"

Conneca gulped. Was the man actually jealous that he hadn't been her first choice? *This is crazy,* she told herself in disbelief. She wondered how he would react if he knew that she had never intended to bid for him at all. *Do I even want to know?*

Her eyes narrowed. "I didn't exactly have a first choice," she said truthfully. "I never knew in advance who all the celebrities were. I simply planned to bid on anyone who seemed the slightest bit interesting."

Maurice made like a wounded puppy. "So you ended up choosing me?"

"Yes," Conneca said tremulously. *Or more like the auctioneer chose you,* she thought, but doubted that his fragile ego could take knowing that not every woman fell all over him at the mere sight of.

"So, I'm just the *slightest* bit interesting?"

Conneca had to smile. "You were at the time."

"And now?" He held her gaze, obviously more than a little curious.

Conneca felt her insides tumble. She found the familiar sensations borne by his close proximity, enchanting character, and even ego tripping, beginning to act up again. She was determined to fight this hold he had over her, even if it killed her.

"And now I'm not sure," she stammered foolishly.

"I see." He tasted his drink and looked dour.

"You are an interesting person, Maurice," Conneca admitted in an about face as much to herself as him. "Satisfied?"

A half grin formed on Maurice's lips. "Well, that's progress anyway." He gave an exaggerated sigh. "Was there something else you came to say?"

Conneca found that he was capable of totally disrupting her thoughts, throwing them completely out of whack—and her, as a consequence. She sat on the stool beside him.

"Yes," she managed with a sigh. *Tell him what's on your mind, girl.* "Do you always walk out in the middle of something that you started?"

Maurice looked at her with an odd expression. "No, I definitely wouldn't walk out in the middle of *everything* I started . . ."

His eyes darted across her face, and then down Conneca's body as if to capture every curve, nook, and cranny. Conneca felt her temperature rise. Even when she willed herself to feel otherwise, the effect this man had on her was deepening with each passing moment.

"Why did you even bother to speak at the meeting," she asked him hurriedly, "if you were going to walk out without so much as a word?"

"I couldn't very well say a word while you were talking, now could I? That wouldn't be very polite." Maurice flashed her a steady look. "As for why I spoke at all, it was merely to help you out."

Conneca blinked. "Excuse me. What made you think I needed your help?"

"Didn't you?"

"No!" She pressed her palm against her knee. "At least not in that way."

"Then in what way?" he pressed with renewed interest.

She told Maurice about Freda Mackintosh, and the dinner Conneca had brashly offered her with him.

Maurice laughed. "Let me see if I have this straight. You want me to have dinner with Freda, simply because you're on some sort of guilt trip because she failed to give a high enough bid when the opportunity presented itself?"

"Yes, more or less." Conneca bit her lower lip.

"Is it more or *less?*" he challenged her.

"*More,*" responded Conneca snappishly. "Always better to have friends than enemies in this town," she added, deliberately intending for it to have a dual meaning which she hoped he could relate to. "It doesn't have to take up much of your time, Maurice. You can have dinner here at the restaurant, at my expense. Who knows—you might even find Freda a ton of fun, no pun intended." She thought shamelessly of Freda's extra-large frame.

"Right," he quipped, suppressing a snicker. "Can hardly wait."

"Does that mean you'll do it?" Conneca restrained her optimism.

"Anything for a fan." Maurice finished off his drink. "And I would much rather be *your* friend than enemy any day of the week."

Remarkably Conneca felt exactly the same way. Though somehow she did not see them as merely friends in the true sense of the word. Did he? But then, she couldn't imagine Maurice as a real enemy. Either way, Conneca knew that Freda was hardly a threat to whatever the future held for them. She just wasn't sure exactly what that was.

CHAPTER 13

Freda Mackintosh was ecstatic when Maurice invited her to dinner at the Sheridan Seaside Inn restaurant. Maurice had been less than overwhelmed at the prospect, but kept his word to Conneca. Now he was glad he had. In spite of her size, Freda reminded him of his grandmother when Maurice was a boy—sprightly, charming, and thoroughly entertaining.

Her brown-reddish weave in an updo, Freda cast bold gray eyes with flecks of gold admiringly across the table at Maurice. She was wearing a traditional African skirt suit, black with red embroidery. Maurice gave her a gentle smile. In spite of making many appearances before fans, he never really tired of the adulation, no matter how foolish he felt being the object of adoration by mostly female strangers. It came with the territory, he believed, and kept him grounded somewhat through the direct interaction. Admittedly, Maurice did not often dine with a fan, especially in the absence of his writing partner.

That didn't include Conneca, with whom Maurice was only too happy to spend time alone as they sorted out their differences and, more importantly, common ground. He hadn't decided yet if she was truly a fan of Alexis Maurice or just him.

"When I heard that you were going to be at the celebrity auction," Freda was saying animatedly, "I told Gail that I wouldn't miss the opportunity for the world to have you sign *all* of my Alexis Maurice books." She frowned. "Thought I may have missed my chance when sista Conneca walked away with the grand prize."

Maurice blushed while pondering the grand prize he had found in Conneca. Perhaps it was even more valuable—though that remained to be seen. "All you had to do was ask," he said sincerely. "I would have been only too happy to sign your books."

"So I'm asking, sugar!" Freda reached in her bag on the floor and removed every book Alexis Maurice had published. She even had a pen ready.

Maurice was delightfully amused. "It would be my pleasure, Freda," he told her, taking the pen. He opened one book. "Is there anything in particular you'd like me to say?" He knew that readers loved to have the autograph personalized.

She thought about it. "How about 'To Freda—a very devoted and life-long fan in Oak Cliffs, Oregon'?"

"No problem." He signed it and proceeded to leave a slight variation of the autographed message in the other books, laying it on a bit thick in the last book, thinking she had earned every word.

"Thank you so much," gushed Freda. "My grandchildren will be tickled to death about this. Collecting signed books has been a longtime hobby of mine—next to hats. But this marks the first time that I didn't have to wait in line for my turn with the author."

Maurice tasted his Pinot Grigio wine humbly. "Well, if you ever come to any of our future signings, Freda, just go straight to the head of the table as one of our *special* fans."

She batted her lashes gratefully. "Are you serious?"

He laughed. "Of course."

Freda looked as if she could burst with excitement. "Do you mind if I give you a hug?"

Maurice chuckled again. "I'd love it." He stood and went to her, leaned down as she lifted, whereby Freda gave him a bear hug. In spite of practically having the life squeezed out of him, Maurice knew it was worth it in making her day—and probably the next twenty years.

It was after pulling away from Freda that Maurice caught sight of Conneca, at about the same time that his nostrils picked up the wonderful fragrance she was wearing—All About Eve, he believed.

"And how are we doing?" Conneca asked, a big smile on her face.

"Terrific!" Maurice beamed, thinking, *But it would still be much better if it was you I was wining, dining, and hugging close to my body.* He felt a burning need to be with her right there on the spot. Glancing at his dinner date, hoping to make Conneca just a trifle jealous that they appeared to be enjoying each other's company maybe a little too much for her comfort, Maurice declared, "Freda is definitely one of Alexis's and my most dedicated fans. In fact, I plan to make it a point to mail her an autographed copy of Alexis Maurice's next novel, hot off the press."

Freda cocked a brow, the unexpected news clearly pleasing her. She favored Maurice a wide grin and cooed: "Oh, thank you, Maurice. I can hardly wait!"

"How sweet and thoughtful of you, Mr. Templeton," Conneca said, pasting something resembling a crooked line on her lips. "I'll bet Nadine would love an autographed book by mail as well—assuming you won't still be around here by the time it's published." She sneered at Maurice, neglecting to ask for a book herself.

Maurice was tickled by her jealous reaction. And turned on even more.

"I'm sure that can be arranged," he said congenially.

"Thanks for letting me borrow him," Freda told Conneca gushingly. "Sure beats playing gin rummy, girl."

Conneca stiffened. "He's not mine to lend," she made clear, "but you're welcome anyhow." She glanced at Maurice brazenly, and then handed them each a menu. "The waitress will be here shortly to take your orders."

"Maybe you could cut that 'shortly' in half," Maurice joked. "You've got two hungry campers here."

"We'll see what we can do, sir!" Conneca tossed him a wicked look, forced herself to smile at Freda, and walked off. Maurice couldn't help but admire the view from behind—not too big, not to small, but a backside that was just right!

"I think the sister likes you," Freda remarked, observing Conneca's hasty departure.

"Really?" Maurice welcomed a second opinion, watching as Conneca disappeared into the kitchen.

"Women tend to know these things," Freda said over the top of her wineglass.

Men do too, Maurice thought wisely. It worked both ways. He liked Conneca too, perhaps more than he had liked anyone in a very long time. Now the question was: what the hell were they going to do about it? A lascivious thought or two crossed his mind on the subject. He wondered if he and Conneca saw eye to eye on the art and soul of seduction . . . and what followed.

Lifting his drink, Maurice proffered a toast to Freda. "Here's to a woman's intuition."

She smiled understandingly. "And to a man's."

Maurice spent the rest of the evening in his room, working on the novel. In spite of his best intentions, he found himself unable to get across what he wanted to in the final chapters. It had been this way ever since settling into the Sheridan Seaside Inn. And he knew damned well why. *She was at fault.*

Maurice simply could not get his mind off Conneca Sheridan. It was as if she had quite literally taken over his thought processes. No novel, no matter how powerful, could possibly compete with the beautiful inn owner for his attention, let alone another woman.

A brief image of Alexis flashed guiltily into Maurice's head. Even during the best of times together she had not made his blood boil like Conneca had. And this was without him and the sexy sister even being intimate. Maurice could only imagine the heights they both would climb to if they ever were. The mere notion sent waves of pleasure coursing through him.

Maurice went on typing on the notebook, almost on automatic. But his thoughts were clearly elsewhere.

He mused about the afternoon at the meeting of local business owners. He'd happened upon it strictly by coincidence after finding himself unable to concentrate on writing. A walk had seemed like a good idea at the time, to clear his head and get the creative juices flowing once again.

Maurice had arrived at the meeting just as Conneca was being summoned to speak. The sight of her walking to the front of the room, looking ravishing in tailored business attire, moved him to no end. Even more intriguing was that it was their date that had prompted Conneca to come forward.

Then he found himself in a position normally foreign to Maurice. He had actually gotten jealous over the prospect that there was someone else who had been Conneca's first choice to be with. He knew it sounded crazy, considering they had not known each other then, and barely did now.

What right did he have to be jealous over someone who may have turned out to be a child, female, or an old man? Especially considering that he himself had no claim on Conneca, just as she had none on him.

Maurice wondered if his feelings had somehow moved beyond mere desire for the lady to something far more profound, more heartfelt. Could he really expect Conneca to somehow belong only to him when she might only see him as little more than a good-looking, successful brother who happened to be an author—to flirt with, even kiss, but not to become actively involved with? *Am I asking for far more than I can possibly give her in return?* he pondered.

Looking at the small screen, Maurice saw that he had actually typed Conneca's name in several places inadvertently. Indeed, he had reworked the plot to involve a mysterious woman in a coastal community that was reminiscent of Oak Cliffs.

Unnerved somewhat, Maurice had to seriously ask himself if he had he gone too far in his thoughts for Conneca Sheridan. Or maybe not far enough? He feared that his perspective on the book had become blurred by his desires for the lovely and most interesting sister. Was the climax he was trying to build toward in the story out of touch with the basic framework of the novel?

Maurice grimaced, and then deleted everything he had spent the last three days working on.

So much for being inspired, he thought, cursing to himself.

CHAPTER 14

"We're short-handed in the maid department," Lee informed Conneca when she came into the office that morning. "Harriet has the flu and Winifred's taking her daughter to the dentist. Something about falling and cracking a tooth."

"Great!" Conneca made a face. At the same time she knew that they were loyal, good employees entitled to be sick or have time off. "I'll do double duty," she told Lee. Meaning she would help at the front desk and clean rooms in the afternoon. All part of the job of inn owner and self-employer.

"We'll all have to pull a little extra weight around here," Lee grumbled, wrinkling his brow. "Especially since new arrivals will be coming in all day." He gave Conneca the benefit of a fatherly smile, as Lee seemed to play back his own words in his mind. "Certainly can't complain about that, now can we, as all paying guests are more than welcome!"

"No, we can't," Conneca agreed wholeheartedly. "But please, Lee, don't *ever* talk about 'a little extra weight' around here. That's something we women can certainly do without!"

Lee laughed and looked embarrassed. "My apologies." His eyes scanned her in her beryl blue jewel neck sheath from top to bottom. "If there's anything extra there, I certainly can't see it. I'd say you have absolutely nothing to worry about, my dear girl."

Conneca fluttered her lashes, amused by her friend's quick fix. "Thanks for saying that, Lee. That's much more what a woman wants to hear."

He smiled and bowed respectfully.

Conneca found herself wondering if her body would measure up to Maurice's scrutiny. She had gone overboard to try and stay in good shape. *I especially like my legs,* she thought. But she never knew if the rest of her was quite enough for herself, much less a man whose image of the ideal body might be of a far more toned and big-chested woman, with a flat stomach and thinner than she would ever be.

Just how did she stack up to the women in Maurice Templeton's life? Conneca contemplated, moving to her desk. How many others had there been besides Alexis? Probably more than a few. The thought was somehow depressing to Conneca. She could never realistically ever hope to compete with Maurice's gorgeous cowriter in the looks category.

Conneca's thoughts were interrupted when Lee said to her, seemingly in tune with her thinking, "So how are things going with Mr. Templeton, er, Maurice?"

"Going . . . ?" She played dumb.

"Is he putting the moves on you?" Lee asked, trying his best to sound hip. Instead he seemed uncomfortably out of his element.

Conneca bit her lip. "We're just friends at the moment," she said evasively. *At the moment?* Were they even that? They almost seemed to be going around in circles—meandering between being casual acquaintances and jealous would-be lovers, she thought. Were they resigned to end up as something in between? Undefined. Wholly unsatisfying.

Did she want anything more? Did he?

"I see," Lee said thoughtfully. "Well, keep me posted. If it turns out that there are some real possibilities here, I want you to know I'll back you up in whatever choices you make. I promised your father I'd be there for you and I will—including someday walking you down the aisle."

Without warning, Conneca stood, walked over to his desk, and gave him a great big hug, startling Lee. Right now, he was the closest thing she had to a father. She wanted him to know that.

"If anything special should ever emerge with Maurice or anyone else," she told him, "I promise you'll be the first to know, Lee." Or maybe the second, Conneca thought. After all, if she and Maurice Templeton actually became an item, it would definitely to be news to her first, all things considered.

It was nearly one in the afternoon when Conneca, dressed in the housekeeper's uniform, knocked on Maurice's door. There was no "Do Not Disturb" sign on the knob, so she assumed it was safe to clean his room. Nevertheless, feeling somewhat ill at ease entering his room, Conneca knocked again to be on the safe side. Only this time she knocked louder, while shouting: "Maid service!"

She half expected a sleepy-eyed Maurice clad only in a maxi robe to appear at the door, apologetic for having slept the morning away after a heavy-duty night of working on his—their—novel. Only there was no such response, for which Conneca was thankful. The last thing she needed was to try and explain to him that she was only there to clean his room. She could well imagine the brother finding a way to turn that into something much more intimate than she had ever intended or might possibly be able to stop.

Conneca unlocked the door, pushed it open a tad, and stuck her head inside. "Anyone home?"

There was no answer.

Sucking in a deep breath, Conneca decided it was safe to enter. She went in and immediately her nostrils picked up the pleasant smell of Maurice's Givenchy cologne. For an instant she imagined actually smelling the man himself up close in person, causing her breasts to heave in desire.

A quick survey of the suite told Conneca that Maurice was either the neatest man she had ever met, or he had hardly used his room at all. She opted for the former since she knew for a fact that he had been slaving away at his computer for much of his time there.

Hadn't he? That was why he had extended his stay, she had been led to believe. Wasn't it?

She went back outside to grab some sheets and towels from the cart.

In Maurice's bedroom, a mirror image of hers in many ways, Conneca removed the sheets and pillowcases, though the bed looked as if it hadn't been used. She wondered if Maurice had pulled an all-nighter on his novel. Would his cowriter approve of the final chapters, even if she apparently no longer approved of the man behind the words?

Will I like the new book and how it all ends? Conneca asked herself curiously. While no book critic, per se, she felt she had a keen eye for plot structure and characterization—and most of all, what merited a satisfying conclusion. She recalled reading many books in which she saw serious flaws—beginning, middle, *and* end—often discussing them out loud, as if to the editor. *Or author.*

Of course, she had never met an author in person—until now. And she wouldn't dream of being critical of Maurice's work—at least not while he was a paying guest. *So maybe what Maurice Templeton means to me goes beyond that,* she conceded. How much more, she couldn't be sure. Conneca chose not to even speculate at this point.

After making the bed and putting the used sheets in the cart bag, Conneca grabbed her bathroom cleaning items, gloves, and a dust brush. She dusted first, finding to her delight that the regular maid had done an excellent job keeping this room virtually dust free.

Conneca saw that Maurice had turned the spare bedroom into a makeshift office. His notebook computer, lid up, sat on the table beside a printer. She pictured Maurice sitting there just pounding those keys away en route to another bestseller. A stack of brochures on Oak Cliffs, including one of the Sheridan Seaside Inn, sat next to the notebook. Beyond it was what appeared to be handwritten notes and a couple of pens. Maurice must have sketched an outline or synopsis, she assumed, which he used as the basis for the book.

Conneca found herself inadvertently drawn to his notes. It was as if she wanted to get inside the head of a writer—this writer, in particular— and see how he went about formulating his ideas and converting them into a romantic suspense work of fiction. At the same time, she knew it was a clear invasion of privacy and surely didn't fall under her job description. If what Conneca had heard about authors was true, most guarded their plots like they were top-secret government projects. Yet here was perhaps the heart and soul of Maurice's novel begging her to take a peek.

Against her better judgment, Conneca eased her way over to the table. Her intent was to take a sweeping glance at the notes, then complete her cleaning—all before Maurice got back. *What harm could there be in that?* she convinced herself. She lifted the entire batch. The handwriting was difficult to read—certainly not the brother's strongest point—but she could make out enough.

Conneca's eyes widened with shock as she read further. The notes were about *her*. Or at least someone closely resembling her named Erica Kinkaid. Maurice wrote about a mysterious, beautiful African-American inn owner on the Northwest central coast, who escaped a dark past before meeting the debonair hero, Aaron Sinclair.

Is Maurice using me and my inn behind my back to create or complete his story? Conneca suddenly became unsettled. Was that his true purpose in staying in Oak Cliffs at the Sheridan Seaside Inn? *Had he planned to keep this his little secret until the book came out?*

Conneca found herself wondering if the Aaron Sinclair referred to in the notes, who undoubtedly wooed the mysterious heroine and captured her heart at the end, was, in fact, Maurice Templeton himself in disguise.

Rather than being flattered at the prospect of serving as a role model for Erica Kinkaid, Conneca felt somehow betrayed. She did not want to be some damned fantasy woman for perhaps thousands of male readers. Or even female ones for that matter. Especially since this was something she could not possibly live up to in her *real* world.

A sound from behind her startled Conneca, causing her to drop the notes. Swiveling around, she came face to face with Maurice, who had a dark, angry look in his eyes.

CHAPTER 15

His countenance was stern as Maurice looked down at the notes spread out like a deck of cards.

"What the *hell* do you think you're doing?" he voiced with clear displeasure.

Conneca felt the raw anger in him, and instinctively took a step backward. She found herself miffed as well, albeit for different though related reasons. Yet it was she who had come upon his private notes about her under less than honorable circumstances. Did that make her more in the wrong than he? She didn't know, but at the back of Conneca's mind was the simple standard that she had always abided by: *guests always came first*. No matter what.

Clearing her throat, Conneca said sheepishly, "Some of the housekeeping crew didn't come in today. I, uh, was just filling in . . . and, uh, cleaning your room."

"It sure as hell doesn't look like you're cleaning anything to me!" Maurice barked. Again he glanced suspiciously over her shoulder at the fallen papers.

"That's because you didn't leave much to clean," she snapped back, not intending to. Conneca lifted the dust cloth she still had in her hand and took an errant swipe at the table where the notes had been resting. "I was just dusting this table. I needed to move your notes to get to it." She gulped. "I'm sorry I scattered them across the floor. But you startled me."

Conneca knelt down to begin picking the papers up, her mind still very much on what she had read in them, but trying hard to keep the disappointment to herself.

Maurice bent down too. He grabbed her wrist, lifting Conneca upright. "Allow me," he said uneasily with a forced smile. "After all, I'm to blame for what happened here."

Conneca stood silently, shaking a bit, as he gathered up the notes. Maurice hastily put the papers haphazardly back on the table as if they were now somehow invisible. Looking over Conneca, he said with an edge to his tone: "I suppose you couldn't help but read what I'd written?"

Conneca knew she was in an impossible position. To acknowledge having read the notes would suggest it had been her intention all along to go behind his back in his room. But to ignore what she had read would be an equal injustice. She opted for saying nothing at the moment.

"If you don't mind," she said in a hollow voice, "I'll do your bathroom now."

"I do mind!" Maurice set his jaw. "I decided this was the ideal setting for the hero to wind up at. I think my—our—fans would enjoy the almost haunting environment of a quaint inn on the rugged and beautiful Oregon coastline." He paused contemplatively. "And, uh, Conneca . . . you seemed to be the perfect composite for a character that the hero would meet to resolve his troubles."

"I am not a character in a damned novel!" Conneca gritted her teeth.

Maurice twisted his lips, seemingly resigned to the knowledge that his ploy had been uncovered. "You have every right to be pissed, Conneca," he said lamely. "But I would never have used you or this inn without first getting your approval."

"And when were you planning to get this approval, Maurice?" She glared at him defiantly. "After the book was already in bookstores? Or the hands of readers?"

He gave her a deadpan look. "Of course not," he insisted. "I was prepared to allow you to read the book once it was completed—before I left."

Conneca wondered if that meant he was planning to leave soon. The thought somehow left her feeling empty and alone. Not that she hadn't expected his stay to be a short one. After all, wasn't that the case with most guests? Why should he be any different?

But he is different, Conneca told herself. *And I'm different as a result.*

She cast her gaze at Maurice, still feeling annoyed. "And what if I don't like your portrayal of me?" she demanded.

"Then I will rewrite it," he spoke insistently, "eliminating your likeness and surroundings altogether if need be."

Conneca began to feel her own anger abate. Maurice seemed to always know how to come up with the right words to say. She wondered if this was because he was a writer, used to working effectively with words. Or was it more his adeptness at getting himself out of seemingly impossible jams?

"So when are you leaving?" she asked cautiously.

Maurice scratched the top of his head in consideration. "That all depends . . ."

Conneca's right brow arched. "On what?"

He stepped toward her. "On how long it takes me to finish what I started."

Conneca felt the weight of Maurice's unyielding gaze, holding her in its intensity like a radiant light. Her legs threatened to give and she could feel her heartbeat quicken with every breath.

"I—I think I'd better clean your bathroom now," she stammered.

"That can wait," Maurice murmured huskily. He put his hands on her shoulders, drawing Conneca up against him. "This can't . . . not for another second."

He crushed his mouth onto hers. Conneca responded instantly, unable to resist him or her own unbridled craving for Maurice Templeton. The dust cloth slipped from her hand that was suddenly paralyzed, as if she had been stricken with a viral infection that was rapidly spreading to every part of her body, inch by inch.

They tasted each other, opening their mouths urgently, the passion of the kiss intoxicating. Using their tongues and lips, Maurice and Conneca probed inside one another's mouths with scrutiny and desire.

Conneca shuddered as Maurice grabbed hold of her buttocks, gently caressing them through her uniform. Her arousal was almost unbearable as her nipples brushed against his rock solid chest. She could also feel Maurice's own overwhelming need as his full erection quavered between them, and his body trembled at her every touch.

It became clear to Conneca that this was something that had to happen, needed to happen. *I want Maurice Templeton badly*, she told herself breathlessly, knowing he felt the same about her. And like actors in a movie or characters in a novel, they had to play it out to the end. And hope the outcome was a positive one.

For an instant Conneca became woozy. Their mouths remained in perpetual motion. She felt as if she were floating on air, waiting to land in a world where dreams really came true. All Conneca's regrets with men and fears of *this* man seemed to vanish into thin air and she knew that she would give herself to him, body and soul.

Suddenly the spell was broken and the magic erased in the blink of an eye when the phone rang.

Both Conneca and Maurice reacted, as if the clouds had deliberately chosen to rain on their parade.

"Damn!" Maurice muttered, breaking away from Conneca's iron grip. He grimaced and looked indecisive.

In her mind, Conneca cried, *Let it ring!* But she didn't really expect or even want him to. It could be an important call, she knew. Perhaps it was a wake-up call to let her know that she was out of her league. Or, worse, playing with fire that could leave Conneca horribly scarred for life.

"I'd better get that," Maurice moaned reluctantly. "Don't leave," he added, as if an omen of what was to follow.

Conneca sighed and straightened her clothing, feeling a little embarrassed at what had happened . . . and what might have. She watched Maurice grab his cell phone off the table.

"Yeah?" he grumbled. Then his tone became much more tolerant, even yielding. "I'm doing fine, Alex." He breathed out of his nose. "I planned to call you. But things have been hectic."

Maurice glanced Conneca's way remorsefully and then turned his back to her, as if she were suddenly intruding on his space and their intimate conversation.

Conneca felt a spate of jealousy course through her veins like an addict's morphine. One simple phone call by Alexis had been enough to send Maurice running to her, in effect. As though they were still married and he was hers for the taking.

Whatever the nature of their relationship, Conneca had a feeling that it had remained intimate on some level—even if they were no longer romantically involved. Wasn't this the case with most ex-spouses and lovers? Perhaps it was especially true where it concerned writers—who happened to be former husband and wife—working so closely together. Much like coal miners who came to depend on each other so much as to be essentially joined at the hip.

Conneca considered that the writing team of Alexis Maurice was so intrinsically bound together professionally, it might prevent them from having other meaningful relationships apart. Could any other woman possibly measure up to Alexis in Maurice's eyes, in and out of the bedroom? *Can I ever be satisfied being in second place with a man who is obviously still hung up on another woman?*

Conneca wondered if the connection she felt with Maurice had been doomed from the start. Had she gone more with her physical needs in being attracted to the author than her common sense?

I don't need this, she told herself in defiance of her own inner feelings. *And I certainly don't need Maurice Templeton!*

She listened for only a moment longer as Maurice conversed jovially with Alexis about their latest novel. Clearly, Conneca knew, she was no longer wanted on this day. And she doubted there would ever be another day for them to get the magic back.

Walking up behind Maurice, she intruded upon his conversation by whispering: "I'll send someone else to do your bathroom."

Maurice looked at her and tried to say something, but they both knew there was nothing more to say.

Conneca moved away from him and out of the room as quickly as she could. It was only in the hallway that she took a ragged breath and cried. She didn't know if the tears were of regret for what might have been. Or what could never be.

CHAPTER 16

For one of the few times in his life, Maurice felt totally out of touch with his feelings and his loyalties. He smacked his tongue against the roof of his mouth while listening to Alexis yap on the phone, but thought about Conneca. She had just departed hastily like a woman scorned. It had taken every ounce of his willpower to keep from going after her. And that willpower continued to wane with each passing second that he was away from Conneca Sheridan.

Maurice found himself wondering if the damage he'd read in Conneca's eyes—the type he had seen before when women felt betrayed or hopeless—was too much to overcome. *Have I blown it?* he wondered with trepidation.

"I've looked over the first draft of the final chapters you e-mailed me," Alexis said, with a *but* in her tone of voice. "And I have to be honest with you, Maurice, and say that it's not up to the standards *we've* set for our novels."

"Yeah, I know," he sputtered with frustration into the mouthpiece. "I'm trying to work it out."

"Why on earth did you decide to create this new character, Erica Kinkaid?" she questioned suspiciously.

"It seemed like a good idea." Maurice now began to question his own judgment. "Erica can help spice up things a bit."

"She doesn't really fit in," Alexis snapped in blunt resistance. "The readers would recognize that just as surely as I did, Maurice."

Would they? His hand holding the phone felt moist. Or was it just

Alexis's uneasiness with Erica—almost as if she somehow felt threatened by the fictitious woman?

Had he gone too far in trying to give his main character in the novel a love interest that seemed to enter his life out of nowhere? Or had he not gone far enough in establishing a more three-dimensional heroine in Erica Kinkaid?

Either way, Maurice was sure that the answer was somewhere within the Sheridan Seaside Inn. Or, more specifically, with its owner.

"I'll make it credible," Maurice asserted over the phone. "The readers will be completely satisfied when all is said and done. Count on it!"

Alexis gave an unenthusiastic sigh. "Oh, I am," she declared. "You always manage to find a way to come through with shining colors, Maurice, honey. That's what makes you such a good writer—make that great! I'm sure you'll keep that in mind as you put the finishing touches to this book, prior to my smoothing out any leftover wrinkles."

"I'll keep it in mind," he muttered, taking the hint. *If you don't do the right thing, I will, as the more objective, less emotional one in the partnership.*

The hell you will, Maurice thought in response to his imagined words from Alexis.

There was a long silence on the line before Alexis said in a casual way that really wasn't so casual, "So when are you coming home?"

"Soon," Maurice replied tersely without being definitive. "I think I should stay out here until I wrap the novel up."

"Are you sure?" she asked doubtfully. "I think you'd be far more comfortable at home, where you belong."

Maurice wrinkled his brow in misery. He was beginning to wonder just where the hell it was he truly did belong. Certainly not with his ex-wife. Not anymore. "Just bear with me, Alex," he told her noncommittally. "Everything will work out for the best."

"That sounds so ominous," Alexis whined with a nervous laugh. "Are you sure everything's all right?"

Maurice made a noise that sounded more like a grumble. "Of course," he spoke unevenly. "Why wouldn't it be?"

"You tell me, baby." Her voice rang with uncertainty.

"I just need to get this damned book finished, you know what I'm saying?" Maurice heard the discontent in his own voice. He slid the phone across his face and thought wistfully of Conneca. "Look, I'd better let you go now, Alexis. I'll call you in a couple of days and let you know how I'm progressing."

"You'd better!" she gave what sounded like a warning. "I can only keep the wolves at the publishing house at bay for so long."

"Good-bye, Alex," he told her and hung up.

Maurice stood there for a moment, trying to remember what it was like to be married to Alexis. From the beginning they had been at each other's throats to one degree or another. Things seemed to take a turn for the worse the moment the friendship ended and the romance began. The commitment to making it work was there, but never quite in sync with the other aspects of their lives. It was Alexis who decided to turn her attention elsewhere. He was left to try and pick up the pieces of a crumbling romance and, in the process, rediscover who he was beyond the press clippings. It was still an ongoing process.

Maurice found himself turning to thoughts of love. With Alexis, it had always been missing in the true sense of the word. Neither seemed to have much love to give beyond that of loving friendship—at least to each other.

He had never approached the subject of love well. In spite of being together for a long time, his parents had never taught him what it meant to love by way of example. Hence, he had never been able to express himself adequately in that respect.

Maurice wondered if that somehow meant he was incapable of feeling true love for someone. Or that he could never accept the love of another. *Am I looking to repeat history in going after Conneca?* Or was it time to right the wrongs of the past and begin taking concrete steps toward the future?

What a mess he seemed to be making of his life, Maurice frowned in frustration and confusion. Either that, or for the first time in longer than he cared to remember, he knew exactly what he wanted.

And the woman he wanted.

Maurice couldn't deny his overpowering attraction to Conneca Sheridan, as well as hers to him. He could feel it just as surely as if they were slugging out passion in a boxing ring.

The kiss that Alexis had interrupted had ignited embers in Maurice that were inextinguishable. He *had* to have the sister with the sexy Senegalese twists, enchanting cappuccino eyes, and the truly wondrous smile, along with a willowy, taut body that seemed made for his own in every way.

But would *Conneca* have *him*, now that they had apparently missed the boat when the time had seemed so perfect? Would she be able to overcome his creating Erica Kinkaid in her lovely and complex image—right down to Conneca's inn and some of the staff—for his book without consulting her in advance?

Maurice tried not to think of the possible implications. Only what felt like his—*their*—destiny. He imagined it shouldn't be too difficult to find the lady. The problem was what to do when he crossed that bridge.

CHAPTER 17

Conneca had sent Tamara Kelly, one of the three housekeepers on duty, to finish Maurice's room. She had spent a few minutes at the front desk, before developing one of those migraine headaches that ran in her family and retiring to her suite. The headaches always seemed to come when Conneca was under a lot of stress—mentally or physically. She had little doubt that Maurice Templeton was the source of her stress on this occasion.

Whatever she may have expected from him—or herself—Conneca realized now it had been nothing more than a romantic fantasy. Maurice was a successful author with his own obligations and she was an inn owner with hers. They were in two totally different worlds—indeed, galaxies—as far as she was concerned. She could see no realistic room for a merger, or a meeting of the minds, much less bodies.

That she had considered an intimate relationship with Maurice Templeton at all had surprised Conneca. Especially given her less-than-successful track record. It was a mistake she couldn't afford to make again. *And I won't*, she promised herself. Least of all with a man whom Conneca could not trust to always be there for her as she would be for him.

She made herself some herbal tea, which seemed to work far better than the common over-the-counter pain relievers for her migraines. The effects were almost immediate, if not overwhelming.

Conneca washed her face and changed into a turquoise cotton night-shirt, intending to take a short nap before heading back downstairs where they were still short-staffed. Before she could lie down, there was a knock at the door. She almost feared answering it, wondering what else could possibly go wrong today. But she knew there was no choice. It could be an emergency.

After putting on a grass-green terry cloth robe, Conneca treaded gingerly to the door.

"Who is it?"

"Maurice," the voice said stiffly and without preface.

A twinge of excitement invaded Conneca like an alien being, but left just as quickly, replaced by vexation.

"What do you want, Maurice?" she asked curtly.

"I need to talk to you, Conneca." His deepened inflection spoke of a sense of urgency. "Open the door . . ."

"I'm not feeling well right now," she told him. "We can talk another time."

"Now!" Maurice commanded. His tone softened, as he added, "Please, Conneca. Give me just a few minutes, then I'll leave if you want me to."

Conneca wanted nothing more then to quit while she was ahead with this man, wary of whatever he felt the need to say or do. Yet the cravings of her flesh told her that it would not go away by simply staying away from him. She had to come face to face with whatever it was that was drawing them together like a powerful unyielding force.

Reluctantly, she unlocked the door and opened it.

Maurice stood there like an African warrior in an olive plaid shirt and dark tan cotton twill pants. There was an intense look in his stare. "May I come in?"

Conneca parted from his path, self-consciously tugging her robe a bit tighter. After she shut the door, she faced him, cognizant of the raw energy in the room emanating from them like radiation.

"If you've come to complain about not having your bathroom cleaned—" Her voice broke.

"I don't give a damn about the bathroom," he bristled, running a hand across the top of his bald head.

"Well, what, then?" Conneca asked, clutching her robe at the neck, though she knew full well what was on his mind. The same thing that had been on hers since their last kiss. That didn't change the reality of the situation any, she thought.

He approached her tentatively. She stepped back involuntarily.

"I'm sorry about the phone call at the most inopportune time, Conneca." Several irregular lines creased Maurice's brow.

"No need to apologize," Conneca pretended. *Men have this thing about apologizing, as if that will really make everything all right.* "Alexis is, after all, your coauthor. She has every right to call you whenever she likes."

Do I really believe that? Conneca asked herself. Since when did being a writing collaborator give Alexis the same rights as a wife, which she no longer was?

"She wanted to know how I was coming on the book," Maurice muttered defensively, putting his hands in his pockets.

"And, of course, you told her it wasn't going very well," Conneca said sarcastically, recalling what she'd overheard. What else had they talked about? Her mind conjured up the most inappropriate things.

"I didn't want you to leave," he said with feeling.

"I didn't want to leave," Conneca admitted to herself as much as to him. "But it was obvious you two needed to talk, and I needed to get some work done. Then I developed a migraine headache."

She closed her eyes for a moment and realized that the herbal tea had worked its magic once again, as the pain had all but disappeared. Opening her eyes and seeing Maurice looking on with concern, Conneca wondered if he had been the cure for her headache.

Maurice approached her again. This time she allowed him to without stepping back. He put his hands on her shoulders and began caressing them. Conneca shut her eyes once more and felt the soothing power of his touch.

"I get migraines too sometimes," Maurice said, empathizing. "Mine tend to come after I've tried to do too much at once." He continued to press his long, gentle fingers into Conneca's soft flesh, massaging like a masseuse. "Usually stimulating the body works wonders in relieving the pressure of the headache. Feel better?"

More than she could tell him. More than she wanted to tell herself. "Much better," Conneca admitted.

"Good." The massage continued for a minute or two longer, and Conneca actually began to believe that there were definite mystical powers at work—with Maurice being the key. *Don't stop,* she told him in her mind, enjoying his skills as much as the simple feel of his hands on her.

When Conneca opened her eyes, Maurice was playing with her individual braids like they belonged to a doll.

"Your hair is beautiful," he said pleasingly. "But then so are you . . ."

You're beautiful too, Conneca thought, but said, "If you're trying to get back on my good side, I think it's working."

Conneca took great pride in maintaining her appearance and hair, knowing they expressed not only who she was as an African-American woman, but as a smart, sexy businesswoman intent upon succeeding.

Maurice chuckled. "That's nice to know," he said. "However, I meant every word of it—with no ulterior motives, per se. You are one fine sister in every respect of the word, Conneca. Every woman should be so blessed."

Yes, blessed to have your wonderful hands on their bodies, Conneca mused dreamily.

Working his way behind her, Maurice seemed to have read Conneca's mind in resuming his masterful massage of her shoulder muscles, relaxing them. Conneca felt lost in his touch that was sending powerful jolts to every part of her body, though Maurice continued to concentrate only on her neck, shoulders, and upper back.

Conneca shuddered when his fingers suddenly found their way inside her robe and gown. There, they touched the bare skin of her shoulders and chest. Immediately Conneca felt aroused and sensually awakened. Maurice placed his warm, supple hands over her breasts, cupping them like small melons. Her nipples rippled with sensation when he gently ran his fingers across them.

Whatever the future held, Conneca could only think of the moment and the deep hunger this man had brought forth in her. She wanted and *needed* Maurice like she had never wanted and needed a man before. Just as she knew unmistakably that his yearning for her superseded everything else in his life at the moment, including his writing and ex-wife.

That was all that mattered, Conneca convinced herself. What happened thereafter would happen. Just as what was about to happen would as surely as the sun rising. The world spinning. The day turning to night. And the night into morning.

Conneca turned around and into Maurice's waiting lips. He devoured her like a man possessed. "Damn, baby, you're driving me crazy," he said breathlessly. "I want to make love to you."

Her knees buckled, palms sweaty, Conneca whispered to him in a raspy voice, "I want the same thing, Maurice. I need you—"

Maurice seemed to hesitate for a second or two, as if weighing the consequences of his actions—their actions—before giving way to unbridled desire. He easily scooped Conneca up into his virile arms and headed to the bedroom. She clung to him, tasting his lips, and soaking in the distinct masculinity of his scent.

At the foot of the bed, Maurice put Conneca down. He slid her robe and nightgown off her soft shoulders, watching the garments float to the floor like feathers. Conneca kicked them aside, sliding her bare feet from emerald furry slippers so that he saw all of her. Her uneasiness in exposing herself to Maurice had been replaced by a bold courage in presenting everything he wanted unabashedly.

Maurice feasted on Conneca's tender body like one would a five-course meal, taking in the tautness of her caramel skin over five foot, seven inches of woman. Conneca's breasts were not large, but firm and high, her nipples dark and protruding ever so slightly. Her narrow waist expanded into curved hips and narrowed again into long, lean legs. Even her feet, small with straight toes and polished nails in glistening berry, satisfied his gaze.

What self-consciousness Conneca felt in his blunt appraisal was neutralized by the sheer delight she detected in Maurice's gleaming eyes.

She too wanted to know that same satisfaction in his body. She began removing his shirt even as he planted kisses on her upper body, breasts, and stomach, causing her temperature to rise with each contact.

Conneca was taken with the firmness of Maurice's chest and the flatness of his stomach. His skin, the color of toffee, shimmered with manliness. She wanted to see all of him and touch more of him. But right now Maurice had other plans.

"I want to give you everything you desire this evening, baby." He swallowed deeply. "To make sure you are pleasured to your complete satisfaction."

With that, and before she could utter a sound, Conneca was lifted once again and gently laid atop the bed. Maurice lay beside her and moved in for a slow, sensual kiss. Conneca's mouth tingled at the feel of his tongue inside it, as they explored each other with greater detail than the previous kisses. She found herself lost in the man she was with, not knowing quite what to expect, yet expecting everything.

Maurice slid a hand inside her thighs and placed a finger into the dark triangle of knotted curls between them. Then he went inside her, barely at first, as if intimidated by what lay within, before moving in deeply. Conneca could feel him probing her, bent on conquering this new territory, which she welcomed. When Maurice ran his thumb back and forth across that most sensitive of spots, it caused Conneca to inhale sharply as a spasm of euphoria rolled through her lower extremities.

"That feels so-o-o-o good," she murmured unabashedly, through their clinched lips.

"You feel good, baby," Maurice told her salaciously.

Conneca reveled in his remarkable hands and fingers at work, sensing that he was enjoying this at least as much as she was. The room seemed to be spinning, and it was getting warmer by the millisecond.

Maurice broke away from Conneca's mouth, causing her to open her eyes and gaze into the fire of his flaming leer. Wordlessly, he brought his mouth down to her breasts, nibbling on them as a prelude to taking in her nipples, one by one, treating them as tantalizing appetizers. This sent shock waves throughout Conneca, and she bit down on her lip to try and control the uncontrollable gratification he brought. She watched with trembling satisfaction as he moved his mouth down her body with kisses, burning her skin with longing along the way.

When Maurice put his tongue between her legs, landing on her pliant womanhood, Conneca tensed with a shudder. She had not experienced this level of intimacy with other men, and felt a trifle embarrassed. But even that could not compete with the delicious sensations engulfing her like never before. This seemed to spur him on even more, as Maurice orally gratified her like the master that he was, searching for each and every inch of her secrets and scents.

Conneca cried out uncontrollably as a torrent of orgasmic joy rippled inside her like an internal cyclone, quickly working its way across her entire body and into the very depths of her soul. She needed all of Maurice and the feel of him inside her, and clutched his head desperately to that effect. He heeded the call as if reading her mind and body with the quavering intensity of his own powerful needs.

Removing his shoes, trousers, and underwear in a single motion, Maurice slipped a condom from his pocket and covered himself with it. Conneca sighed in anticipation, opening herself to him. He wasted little time in sandwiching himself between her splayed legs and, while gazing into Conneca's pleading eyes, easily went inside her. He drove himself well into her moist and waiting body with a mutual, unstoppable sense of urgency.

Maurice let out a sharp moan even as he slammed against Conneca, and she against him, in a frenetic convergence as one. Their legs locked high and low, Conneca lifted her hips invitingly, feeling the sizzle of his manhood lodged deep within her. She clawed at Maurice's back, slathered in perspiration, and gnawed at his lips and tongue. She wanted everything he would give her and freely gave back everything he wanted of her.

"Oh, Maurice," Conneca heard herself whisper in ecstasy.

"I'm right here, baby," he responded huskily, and promptly rolled over, pulling her on top of him.

Conneca seized the moment, squeezing her thighs around his slender waist and getting a reaction. She then put her breasts in his face and began to slowly move up and down on him, before Maurice took hold of her buttocks and quickened the pace, driving Conneca wild with excitement.

Both grunted and groaned as the moment of abandon swept over them like a vaporizing cloud. Intensity heightened, and the journey to the top of the mountain followed. Conneca hung on for dear life while Maurice clung to her like a coat of armor, as if he never wanted to let her get away.

It all seemed to end far too soon, but Conneca knew its effect would last well beyond the lovemaking itself. Maurice had given her something she thought she might have lost forever—the ability to experience the great pleasures and mysteries of a man.

This man.

But she was also a realist, and fully aware that neither had made any promises beforehand that they might not be able to keep afterward.

CHAPTER 18

"**A**re you sure we can't stay like this for the rest of the day, baby—maybe even for the rest of our lives?" Maurice held Conneca close to his body, still very much caught up in the afterglow of their lovemaking.

Conneca gave him a reluctant look and kissed his lips. "As much as I'd like to, I have work to do. And so do you."

Maurice frowned, knowing that what she said was all too true. This wasn't a damned fairy tale, he thought, even if it felt like one.

Their fairy tale.

But reality stepped in like waking from a dream. What had just happened between them didn't change very much at all in the scheme of things, Maurice mused. Conneca was still a Northwest innkeeper, practically married to her business. And he was a Rocky Mountain author, more or less married to his writings in conjunction with his ex-wife.

But even that couldn't detract from the chemistry Maurice felt he shared with Conneca, and damn near perfected in an hour's time. To him that alone justified continuing to pursue this until it either reached another level of extreme satisfaction or blew up in their faces. The latter was something he was not yet ready to contemplate, if ever.

"When can I see you again?" Maurice asked, wrapping her long braids around his finger.

Conneca stared. "If you mean like this . . . I can't honestly say," she hedged. "Why don't we just see what happens, Maurice. That way neither of us gets hurt. OK?"

A dark shade of brown shadowed Maurice's face. He realized that she was building a wall to protect herself from being hurt by another man. By him. Could he blame her? Conneca Sheridan was obviously not a sister looking for a casual relationship, he thought. Right now, he honestly didn't know if he could possibly offer anything more.

But another side of Maurice wanted to offer Conneca much more. He truly cared for her and didn't want to see this thing end prematurely, if at all. Furthermore, he sensed that Conneca had never responded to a man the way she had to him.

So where the hell do I go from here? Maurice contemplated, even as he felt Conneca literally slipping from his arms. As if the same question was very much on her mind, she gave him a quick noncommittal peck on the mouth, crawled away from him, and out of the bed.

"I'm going to go take a shower," Conneca said without extending an invitation to Maurice. "I guess I'll see you later?"

"Yeah, sure, later, Conneca," Maurice muttered tonelessly, and sat halfway up. He drank in the nude sight of her firm and toned body that was perfect in every way, complemented by her abundant and brilliant hair. She looked slightly uncomfortable while covering herself up with the robe. Maurice thought she was still hiding behind her conservative self, keeping the real woman trapped inside as if waiting to be brought out in her full splendor. If not by him, then by someone else sooner or later. It was a thought that left Maurice weak with envy and despair.

Conneca had found it painful to cut short Maurice's visit. She hadn't wanted him to see how unsteady she was at the thought of being together only one magical, unforgettable time. But she also knew that men caught up in the throes of passion often spoke less from the heart than their physical urges and release. She was certain that Maurice was attracted to her as much as she was to him.

Yet there was no talk of commitment or love and this bothered Conneca deeply. The implication of *"When can I see you again?"* spoke only of sex, and temporary sex at that, she had little doubt. For his days in Oak Cliffs were numbered, she knew, just as hers there seemed destined to go on forever—possibly alone. Though she warmed at the prospect of even a short-lived affair with Maurice Templeton, Conneca was reluctant to go in that direction.

I don't want a few romps in the hay—even with a man who brought me more sexual satisfaction on one occasion than I've ever experienced before, she thought while standing in the shower, where the steady stream of hot water masked her tears.

Wouldn't that be better for her than broken promises? Conneca had already had enough to last a lifetime. Or would it be worse, since it would be absent of any real and meaningful intimacy?

After the shower, Conneca made herself presentable again and went back to work, where she could turn her attention to matters other than Maurice Templeton.

Lee was at the front desk when she got there. He gave her a worried look. "What are you doing out of bed, girl? Thought that migraine was killing you?"

Conneca flashed him a self-conscious smile. "I'm feeling much better now, Lee." At least in some ways. She surrendered momentarily to the memories of being with Maurice.

Lee tilted his head with misgiving. "You sure about that? Things are kind of slow right now. I can handle any emergencies."

"I'm fine." The last thing Conneca needed right now was to lie in her room longing for Maurice, yet fearing the consequences of having him and think about what had just taken place there. "That's the funny thing about migraine headaches," she said lightly, "they come and go without warning." Just like men, she told herself sadly.

Lee regarded her peculiarly.

"What?" Conneca asked, puzzled by his look. Had she tipped her hand somehow? Had she given away her intimate secret through her words? Her body language?

"Nothing, really . . ." he hedged suspiciously.

"Tell me, Lee." Conneca could tell that there was something going on in that head of his. She found herself really piqued now, and a bit nervous for some reason.

Lee scratched his scalp as if he had dandruff. "Well, if you insist," he said mysteriously. "Maurice was just down here. He actually complained about feeling his own migraine coming on. Said something about a woman can be so unpredictable that it can give a brother a headache."

Conneca thrust her lips out. "Oh, really?"

"You wouldn't know anything about that," Lee asked, a brow half-cocked, "would you, Conneca?"

"Not a thing," she lied, not ready to make her relationship with Maurice—if one could call it that—public knowledge.

Unpredictable! That caused Conneca to smile inside and frown on the outside. She wondered why men always saw women as the unpredictable ones whenever men didn't get their way. And why did men see their own selfish behavior as somehow normal and acceptable?

She wondered what Maurice had expected from her. That she would just give herself to him whenever he wanted, only to have him pull the rug out from under her when he decided it was time to pack up and leave? It didn't work that way—not with her anyway.

Damn you, Maurice, for making me feel the way I do about you, she thought, knowing it would be so much easier if she didn't care one way or the other. But she did care, maybe more than she should.

That plain truth annoyed Conneca, and continued to for the rest of the day, though she tried not to show it to her guests, giving them her brightest smile, as always.

CHAPTER 19

The following morning, Conneca did her normal run on the beach. It was an overcast day and the tide was high. She half expected to find Maurice exercising his legs, remembering his powerful quadriceps from the previous day. But he was a no-show, which suited her just fine. She wasn't really ready to deal with him yet.

Maybe I never will be, Conneca mused, though she suspected it was inevitable that she would have to sooner or later.

"Want some company?" Conneca heard a chipper voice say.

It was Nadine, barely keeping pace with her in a gray Portland Trailblazers jersey and bright purple Adidas running pants. A white sweatband held her damp hair back.

"Would love some." Conneca lifted a brow at her head chef and best friend in shock while slowing down. "Since when did *you* start running, girl?"

"Since Larry decided I could stand to lose a few pounds," Nadine moaned.

Conneca's mouth was agape. Larry Anderson was Nadine's live-in lover.

"You're kidding?" Conneca surveyed her friend's almost rail-thin frame. "If you lost any more weight, you would probably disappear."

Nadine gave a little chuckle. "I'm not *that* skinny."

"No—*I'm* not that skinny!" Conneca returned, and quickly realized that no woman was ever completely satisfied with her weight and looks. But that didn't mean a woman had to kill herself for a man. "Trust me," she told Nadine, "you do not need to lose any weight."

Nadine sneered. "So maybe I'm doing this for some body sculpting and better self-esteem."

"I can't argue against a well-toned body." Conneca considered her own firmness and fitness. "But you have more self-esteem than anyone I know." *Present company included,* she thought.

"Maybe you don't know me as well as you think," Nadine groaned. "Good men are hard to find these days. I don't want to lose Larry."

Conneca slowed down almost to a crawl, a frown coating her perspiring face. "You won't lose him," she said, "not if he really cares about you."

"Oh, please!" Nadine rolled her eyes and sucked in a deep breath. "Men say they care, but if you start to slip in the looks department, including developing flabby thighs, they suddenly find they don't want or need you." She pinched her small thigh for effect. "At least not in the same way they did before. Believe me, I know. Just ask my ex why he left me for the *other woman.*"

Conneca had never realized Nadine felt that way, having been under the impression that she and her ex no-good, bastard husband had split up because of financial pressures and changing values. She could never imagine any man in his right mind leaving Nadine because of her looks and weight. Not when some women would kill to look like Nadine and have her body.

But what did Conneca know about men? Hadn't she also been subject to a man's whims on more than one occasion and been left to suffer the consequences?

She suddenly stopped running, prompting Nadine to do the same exhaustedly, and hugged her friend. "You don't need Larry, girl," Conneca said flatly. "Don't ever lose weight to try and please someone else. It never works, believe me."

Nadine pulled back. "And how would you know?" She studied Conneca in her form-fitting, Rocawear running suit. "Obviously *you've* never had a weight problem."

"Maybe not," Conneca conceded honestly. "But I haven't exactly been successful with men either in the ways that count most." Like love, faithfulness, and trust, she thought understatedly. How many of *those* qualities did Maurice have—or not? "I think maybe it's because we try too hard."

Nadine sighed. "You're right, of course, girlfriend. I suppose whatever happens will happen. Not much any of us can do about that, is there?"

"Not a thing," Conneca agreed thoughtfully. *We can't control our own destiny,* she mused bleakly. *Others always seem to control it for us.*

They started walking.

"That doesn't mean we can't become running buddies," Conneca expressed cheerfully. "It's still a great way to torture yourself."

Nadine let out a hearty laugh. "Tell me about it. My limbs are still sore from my first run a week ago. Heaven knows how they'll feel if I keep this up on a regular basis."

Conneca smiled knowingly. "Girl, you'll be running a marathon in no time flat," she quipped.

"Yeah, right." Nadine favored her curiously. "So what's happening with the author?"

"Happening?" Once again Conneca played ignorant.

"Am I your best friend or not, Conneca?" Nadine's voice rang with mild annoyance. "It's been obvious ever since he's taken up residence at the inn that the brother's had his eye on you—with the hope of having a lot more, if you know what I mean. And don't tell me you haven't noticed?"

"I have noticed," Conneca admitted, gazing down at the golden sand ahead, still unmarred by footprints. Just how long had others noticed? Should she care?

Nadine put her hand to her mouth aghast, as if having entered Conneca's head. "Oooh, girl, don't tell me you've become *involved* with him?"

Conneca felt her face fill with color. "So I won't tell you," she uttered dryly.

"Get outta here . . . you have!" Nadine declared like they were schoolgirls again.

"I wouldn't exactly call it involved," Conneca voiced, kicking at the sand.

"But you've slept with him?" Nadine confronted her. "Excuse me— had *sex* with him?"

"Nadine!" Conneca blushed shyly. She had never been comfortable with certain types of girl talk, particularly when it came to sex. It was no easier now. Especially when talking about Maurice Templeton. But she acknowledged to her nosy friend that they'd been intimate once.

"So how was he? And I mean *details*, girlfriend!" Nadine demanded inquisitively. "Was he anything like the ultra sexy hero Maurice and Alexis created in *Danger At Sea?*"

"*Better*," Conneca laughed, feeling a little more at ease. "*Much* better!" And he was real, she thought. Not like a character in his book. Just as she was, unlike the woman Maurice had created in the novel, which not even Conneca could hope to measure up to—likeness or not.

Nadine batted her eyelids. "You go, girl," she said enviously. "Any plans to get hot and bothered with him again?"

Conneca had pondered that very question since yesterday. "I'm not sure," she had to admit. "He's trying to finish his novel, and I'm busy with the inn—"

"And what does Mr. Templeton have to say about that?"

Conneca curled a lip. "It's what he hasn't said," she muttered.

Nadine gave her an intuitive look. "Don't tell me you've fallen in love with him?"

It was something Conneca had not spent a whole lot of time thinking about. She didn't need to. The way her body and mind had reacted to Maurice—even before they made love—she knew deep down that it could only be love. The very notion suddenly gave Conneca a chill.

"You have!" Nadine decided, eyes wide in disbelief.

"I'm not really sure what I feel," Conneca said dishonestly. "But I do know that he won't be here forever. And I probably will be. So that doesn't leave much room for optimism. Does it?"

They stopped again and faced the wavy sea and its endless beauty.

Nadine grimaced. "I hate to say this, Conneca, but I'm going to anyway: it probably doesn't leave room for a future, not realistically. Not if you're looking for something permanent." She squinted at the sun peeking out from behind thick gray clouds. "I'm a big fan of Alexis Maurice books, don't get me wrong, and I think that you and Maurice would make a terrific couple—"

Conneca held her breath while waiting for the proverbial "but" to come.

"But let's be honest here," Nadine said expectedly, a despondency to her voice. "You've known the brother for what, less than a week now? That's hardly enough time to fall in love . . . for either of you." She moved her mouth from side to side. "Maybe Maurice is different, but I've always had the impression or read that most *single* writers—and probably half the married ones—are players, right down to the core. They go from one woman to the next. Most never settle down, or settle for one female, so long as they have an adoring public of pretty, sexy young *thangs* and writer groupies to feed their egos."

"Maurice is not like that," Conneca defended him. She realized she really didn't know very much about his personal life. Only the limited part he chose to reveal. For all she knew, he was seeing someone in Denver, if not Alexis. She had heard of men who couldn't get over their ex-wives, even to the point of remaining romantically involved. Could this be Maurice? No, Conneca told herself, virtually certain Maurice Templeton was not a player—whatever else he may be.

"Just be careful, honey," Nadine warned, putting an arm around her. "Don't want to see you get over your head for a brother who may not be all that he seems—or maybe he is, depending on how you look at it."

"I'll remember that," Conneca responded sourly. "But wasn't it you who told me that men that gorgeous and talented don't come around every day?"

"Yes, and I meant it." Nadine fixed her with a knowing look. "Trouble is, those type of men tend to not stick around very long either."

This was something Conneca had already resigned herself to. Whatever her feelings for the man, she had known from the beginning that Maurice's stay there was only temporary. As soon as he finished his novel, or perhaps even before he was done, he would leave and return to his world, his family, friends, and associates . . . including his ex-wife. What Conneca and Maurice had shared would perhaps be a delightful memory, but just a memory nonetheless. There was no reason to believe otherwise and, therefore, no hope for a future between her and Maurice Templeton.

CHAPTER 20

Maurice spent the better part of two days working on the novel. For the first time in months it all seemed to be coming together. Much like he and Conneca had come together so magically in her room. He wondered if there were some symmetry there. Had her powerful effect on his libido also stimulated his mind? Could he ignore what had happened between them? Had she?

They had managed to avoid each other like mortal enemies ever since Maurice was given the boot from Conneca's bed. He had his reasons and she undoubtedly had hers. He pondered whether or not Conneca felt as empty and still yearning for more as he did. He could only hope.

Maurice had filled much of that emptiness within the pages of a romantic suspense novel. Not too surprisingly, it had begun to flow well as he began to better understand his hero's new lady love and incorporate her into the plot as an important addition. She was as intriguingly beautiful as the woman he had used to create her from. And every bit as complicated.

Readers would no doubt come to know Erica Kinkaid just as Maurice was getting to know Conneca Sheridan. They would fall in love with the fictional woman, just as he believed he had fallen in love with the real-life innkeeper. At least it felt like love. He hadn't had much experience in that department. And it scared Maurice, mainly because he had already been down that path and come up short. Definitely insofar as feeling love and being loved in the way he believed it should be when a man and woman truly gave themselves to each other in spirit, mind, and body.

Could he overlook past misjudgments and experience real love for maybe the first time? Would the lady who was beginning to capture his heart return such love in full force? Maurice wondered if it were possible that when all was said and done he and Conneca could overcome their separate lives and past failures romantically and make it work between them.

Maybe we could, Maurice told himself optimistically. He was aware that there were still major hurdles to jump over. Not the least of which was trying to get him and Conneca back on the same page again—in the real world, much like in his novel.

There was one thing Maurice knew for certain: what he felt for Conneca Sheridan was far different from what he felt for Alexis, even during their best days. But was it enough to uproot his life for this fine sister from Oak Cliffs? Or ask her to do the same for him? He felt powerless to change the events that had shaped his life and times, but he wanted to try.

Whatever his feelings for Conneca, Maurice believed he had to somehow keep them in check for at least the time being, for both their sakes. Hurting Conneca would serve no benefit, other than make him out to be another asshole just like all the assholes before him. Had the damage already been irrevocably done? Had he unwittingly fit the mold established by the men in Conneca's past?

Maurice spent another couple of hours carving out chapters like one would a honey-basted turkey. He was in that groove where he didn't want to stop. Where each word seemed more powerful than the one before it, with the one after being that much more effective. It was the stuff bestsellers were made of. *Alexis Maurice bestsellers.* He could feel it, as surely as Maurice had felt the babylike softness of Conneca's body, and its rapid reaction to his touch.

Or the raw energy coming from their all-consuming intimacy.

The mere thought left Maurice aching to be with Conneca again while fighting the impulses, as though they were his foe.

Conneca was recruited to help out in the kitchen, as a full house was expected at the restaurant that evening. Nadine's staff, as proficient as they were, sometimes could not handle an overflow of impatient diners. And Conneca's budget was such that she wasn't in a position to hire new help right now.

"The bread's in the oven," Nadine yelled. "Now we have to prepare the salad, pasta, and desserts—not necessarily in that order."

Conneca took a deep breath. "OK. So what do you want me to tackle?"

"Anna's on the pies and cakes," Nadine voiced. "And Gina makes a kick-ass pasta when she puts her mind to it. So I guess that leaves you with the salad."

Nadine wore a stained apron and a hairnet, and looked every bit the part of a head chef. Right down to the perpetual frown creasing her forehead, as if they were headed toward a disaster.

"Salad it is." Conneca smiled, confident that everything would work out just fine. She put on an apron, washed her hands, then went over to the refrigerator and removed five large heads of lettuce. After washing them, she put them on paper towels to drain, then gathered the other ingredients, including tomatoes, cheese, cucumbers, green peppers, and carrots. She had never considered cooking one of her strong points, but had learned a lot from Nadine.

Conneca longed to someday be able to cook a multicourse meal for a family. *Her own family.* She wasn't sure at this rate if it would ever happen, with her biological clock continuing to tick as if running on empty and sheer willpower. But you couldn't be penalized for dreaming, she thought.

Even if the dream involved Maurice Templeton, who had given no indication he ever wanted a second wife, much less a family. Conneca had always loved children, but was determined to bring none into the world if they could not be born into a loving home with a mother and father united in matrimony, chemistry, and commitment to each other and their offspring. She had seen too many children who were illegitimate, abandoned, abused, neglected, and unloved. She didn't intend for that to ever happen to her children.

Conneca sliced and diced the vegetables and prepared the salad, feeling almost like she belonged in the kitchen.

Almost.

Grabbing a piece of leftover lettuce and putting it into her mouth, Nadine said while chewing, "Looks scrumptious. If you don't watch it, Conneca, you're going to find yourself in competition for *my* job—even if you look totally silly with that apron on backward!"

Conneca smiled at the flattery and chuckled at the apron. "I don't think so. I'll never be in your league as a chef, Nadine. I'm much more cut out to run an inn than cook for people who can probably tell the difference between a pro and an amateur. The botched job with the apron proves that."

Nadine laughed. "You might have a point there, Conneca. Just as I seriously doubt that I could ever have the patience to deal with whining, bossy, unruly guests—not to mention keeping an everything-is-fine smile on my management face for all to see . . . except for those of us who know the boss all too well."

Conneca giggled. "You're really in your element today, Nadine." She grabbed a leftover piece of cheese and popped it into her mouth. "I guess that's why we make a perfect match—we know each other too well."

"Maybe not perfect," Nadine chirped, "but definitely in tune with one another in the ways that count most."

"Speaking of in tune," Conneca said, eyeing her friend curiously, "how are things with you and Larry?"

Nadine twinkled. "Great as can be! Thanks for asking."

"What about the weight thing?" Conneca inquired for lack of a more politically correct way to put it.

Nadine swung her arm dismissively. "Larry says he was only trying to get my attention, and never meant for me to take it seriously."

Conneca frowned. "Men should know that *all* women take their weight *very* seriously!"

"I think he does now—if he knows what's good for him!" Nadine chortled and rested her hand on the table. "Girl, we're going to go lose a little money in the casino on Friday night. Larry asked if you wanted to come along. He wondered if you could bring Maurice?"

Conneca flashed her a look of provocation. "You told Larry about Maurice?"

"Now don't get all bent out of shape," Nadine implored defensively. "I only told him that Maurice was a writer you were spending some time with. It's no big deal."

"It is to me," Conneca complained. "Things have sort of cooled off between me and Maurice right now. I'd just as soon not give anyone the impression that we're an 'item', thank you. For all I know, he's probably leaving this week."

And if not, she thought, the week after. Or the one after that. It was only a matter of time before Maurice Templeton vanished from her life forever like a snake in the grass—whether she liked it or not. And Conneca still hadn't made up her mind if that might not be for the best, all the way around.

"I'm sorry." Nadine's brow furrowed in earnest. "So forget about Maurice Templeton and all that money he must have stashed away. Great writer that the brother is—and no slouch in the looks department either—there're plenty of other cool fish in the sea. Some are even local, if you look hard enough."

"Thanks," Conneca said, tossing the salad and feeling a sense of relief, "but I think I'll give men a rest for the time being. They're way too much trouble for what you get." She was seriously beginning to believe that fit Maurice to a tee. *I'm better off on my own,* she decided.

"Who am I to argue with that?" Nadine said. "Before Larry, I felt the same way, and I'm still not letting my guard down."

"That's probably a good thing." Conneca hoped that this one was a keeper for Nadine. There was nothing in the book that said they both had to be perennially stuck with losers.

"You're still welcome to come with us to the casino, Conneca," Nadine indicated. "We could both use a little fun in our too-often-boring lives."

Conneca could not disagree with her. She just wasn't sure she could have much fun throwing away hard-earned cash, as was usually the case in the rare times Conneca played the slot machines. Also, there was that "two's a couple, three's a crowd" thing that dampened her enthusiasm. *I'm not good at being the third wheel . . . and I don't want Nadine's pity for poor little Conneca with all the bad luck in men.*

At this point, it seemed like a bad idea to Conneca to invite Maurice along as her date. Whatever else, she knew they were past the stage of just being friends, and probably lovers as well. No reason for either of them to give off the wrong or misunderstood signals to each other.

"Thanks but no thanks," she told Nadine. "I'll be busy that night anyway. We usually have a lot of people checking in for the weekend." As if Nadine didn't already know that, but Conneca saw it as a legitimate excuse anyway.

"Well, if you change your mind," Nadine said disappointedly, "we'll be at the Shoreline Hotel and Casino." She headed toward the refrigerator, where she removed four whole chickens, bringing them over to the counter. "These babies are going to feed some hungry guests tonight," she said enthusiastically.

"What's today's chicken special?" Conneca asked, her own taste buds ripe and ready.

Nadine's mouth curved downward. "I honestly don't know," she said. "I've been going back and forth between the chicken Kiev and the lemon chicken, along with sun-dried tomatoes."

Conneca wet her lips. "Sounds to me like you can't go wrong with either."

"Why not try something totally different?" The voice carried across the kitchen like a cloud of dust.

All heads turned in the direction of the stove. Conneca's eyes rested squarely on the handsome face of Maurice Templeton.

CHAPTER 21

Maurice stood with his hand propped against the stove, as if holding it up.

"Sorry," he said, walking toward Conneca and Nadine, "didn't mean to intrude."

"What are *you* doing here?" Conneca's voice was hoarse.

Maurice fixed her with amusement. "I'm staying here, remember?"

"You know what I mean." Conneca was not amused. "This kitchen is off-limits to guests." She knew she sounded overly curt, under the circumstances. But it was important that he not get the impression that he was practically one of the staff or like family.

Maurice's face took on a distorted expression, as if stung by Conneca's words. "Just thought I could be of some help—to Nadine." He faced the head chef. "Couldn't help but overhear your dilemma."

Conneca bristled. "I think we can manage just fine without your assistance."

Nadine watched Maurice curiously. "Since he's here, Conneca, we might as well hear the man out."

"That's better." Maurice smiled at one of his diehard fans, and glanced approvingly at Conneca. "Actually, I was thinking that you could give your diners a new chicken dish that I *guarantee* will have them coming back for more."

"I'm listening," Nadine said, casting Conneca a skeptical eye, and vice versa.

Maurice smiled. "In Denver, there's a wonderful little restaurant called The City's Finest African Cuisine," he explained. "They make a chicken cacciatore like you wouldn't believe. The Tanzanian owner happens to be a very good friend of mine. He also passed on to me the closely guarded secret of his famous recipe. I'd be happy to pass it on to you. I'm sure Mwamba would be flattered to see his recipe used from coast to coast."

"Thanks but no thanks," Conneca spoke for them stubbornly, even if admittedly tempted by his tasty-sounding offer.

Nadine thought otherwise, regarding Maurice. "As a matter of fact, I've always wanted to add a chicken cacciatore dish to the menu. Tanzanian, huh?" She risked a furtive peek at Conneca. "I say we give it a try. The worst that can happen is we feed the food to the cats that seem to love hanging out behind the inn."

Conneca wanted to object, certain Maurice was mainly concerned with using this chicken cacciatore maneuver to get to her. But she was afraid she was outnumbered. And that was exactly what he was counting on, she suspected.

And it was working. Conneca sighed and said to Nadine, "You're the head chef. If that's what you want, who am I to protest? It's *your* neck on the line."

Maurice laughed. "No, I'd say it's those poor chickens' necks that will be on the line."

Conneca sneered. Even then she could feel the heat that he generated rippling though her, causing her to become moist under the armpits. And a bit hot under the collar.

An hour later, under Maurice's guidance, Nadine had prepared Oak Cliff's Chicken Cacciatore Deluxe. Along with chicken, the dish included sliced bacon, mushrooms, onions, carrots, vinegar, brown sugar, cornstarch, and red wine.

"So what do you think?" Nadine asked Conneca, who had been selected as the official guinea pig. Maurice also watched her with interest.

Conneca sank her teeth into a piece of the chicken cacciatore. It was mouthwateringly delicious, she knew the moment she bit down and tasted the tender white meat. There was little doubt in her mind that the guests would devour it, just as Maurice had knowingly predicted.

She turned to him, blushing. "It's wonderful!"

Maurice beamed. "Glad you think so. I'll be sure to pass the word on to Mwamba."

Nadine widened her eyes. "Now that it's a go, I'd better apply the recipe to the rest of the chicken. The dinner hour is rapidly approaching."

She gave Conneca a maybe-the-brother-is-worth-holding-onto look and then scampered off gratefully, leaving Conneca and Maurice alone.

"So what *other* tricks do you have up your sleeve, Mr. Templeton?" Conneca dared to ask, aware that he had hardly taken his eyes off her since entering the kitchen.

Maurice grinned easily, running a hand over his smooth head. "No tricks, baby," he said. "But maybe a treat or two."

Conneca read deep into his words just as he had wanted her to. The effect left her slightly dazed.

"No wonder you can't finish your novel," she suggested, batting her eyes as a way to regain control. "You're too busy taking on *other* projects." *Like me,* Conneca told herself.

Maurice pretended to type. "In fact, I've made some real progress on the book in the last two days," he exclaimed proudly. "All the pieces are beginning to come together nicely, just like bricks on a house."

Conneca was shocked but excited. "Really?"

"I'm not quite at the finish yet," he warned. "But the climax is definitely in sight . . . and well worth the process."

"I'm happy for you, Maurice." Conneca smiled. Until she met him, she hadn't realized just how draining and difficult it could be to write a novel from beginning to end. She wondered if his coauthor would approve of what he had written. "When do I get to read it?" Conneca asked, feeling as if she suddenly had a vested interest in doing so.

Maurice swayed. "Soon as it's done, you'll at least get to read the last few chapters, which essentially tell the tale." He locked eyes with hers. "I think you'll like it."

What if she didn't? Conneca asked herself. Would he actually rewrite it and omit all references to Erica Kinkaid?

Conneca had an uneasy feeling. *Do I want to shoulder the responsibility of preventing the man from reaching his full potential in the book?*

"I'll look forward to reading whatever part you want to show me, Maurice," she said quietly.

He smiled, then stepped up to her and said in an almost conspiratorial whisper, "I've missed you."

"I've missed you too," Conneca admitted, her heart beginning to beat a bit faster.

Maurice's eyes glazed over. "What would you like to do about it? I'm open to suggestions . . . "

Conneca could feel the invigorating warmth of his breath upon her face. It was all she could do not to fall in his arms at that moment. Were they not in the center of the kitchen and within eyesight of others, she just might have. *Lucky me,* Conneca thought wisely, sucking in a steadying breath.

"Nothing at the moment," she uttered. "Sorry. I have work to do."

Maurice licked his lips. "What about later?"

Conneca glanced at some of the kitchen staff, who were going about their work as if she and Maurice were part of the woodwork. Her pulse was erratic, but her mind was as clear as the sky on a cloudless day. His novel was just about complete, meaning Maurice's stay at the inn was about to end. And, she suspected, his use for her.

"I don't think so," Conneca said without meeting his gaze.

"I won't hurt you, Conneca," he said, his voice wavering.

"Won't you?" she asked dubiously.

Maurice paused, avoiding her eyes. "Not intentionally," he spoke lowly.

Conneca believed him. Yet she knew that "unintentionally" could be just as damaging. Maybe even more damaging. Was she prepared for that? Was he?

"Do you gamble?" she asked abruptly.

Maurice ran his hand along his jaw line, intrigued. "When the prize is worth the risk," he intoned.

Conneca read his thoughts. "I mean casino gambling."

A flicker of disappointment crossed Maurice's face. "From time to time. I've been known to play a mean game of blackjack back in the hood. Why?"

"Nadine invited me—us—to go with her and her male friend to a casino on Friday night." She sighed, already having second thoughts. "If you're too busy, I'll—"

"Count me in," Maurice cut her off. "I'd love to go." He hit her with a sly smile. "Maybe we can bring each other some good luck and walk away with the grand prize."

Conneca felt a shiver as she wondered just what that grand prize might be.

CHAPTER 22

The Shoreline Hotel and Casino was packed with tourists and gamblers. Owned and operated by a Native American tribe, the hotel/casino had been a big boost to the local economy. A portion of the profits had been designated to go to charitable organizations. Conneca had once been opposed to such Vegas-style operations forever tarnishing their small-town atmosphere. But she, like others, had benefited from the new attraction that brought people in from around the country and distinguished Oak Cliffs from other Northwest coastal resort towns.

"Feels like deja vu," Maurice laughed as they made their way through the throngs of people in the casino. "I could swear that we've been to this place before, together."

Conneca flashed him a soft smile. "Perhaps in another lifetime," she quipped.

Indeed, it had seemed like eons ago that they met in this hotel, when she had forked over five thousand dollars for the privilege of Maurice Templeton's company. It had been well worth the charitable contribution, thought Conneca. At least in certain respects.

They both noticed a big banner overhead advertising a blackjack tournament taking place that evening.

"Do you play?" Maurice asked, looking dashing in a silver V-neck sweater, dark indigo jeans, and bone-colored moccasins. He wore a half-ball gold earring in his left ear, while a two-toned gold neck chain sparkled against his chest.

Conneca caught him checking her out. She wore a coral funnel-neck sweater, sage lined skirt, and black suede boots. A silver snake chain hung around her neck, and she wore matching earrings. "Played a little in college," she told him. "But I'm certainly not good enough to enter a tournament." She remembered him saying that he was a good blackjack player. "I suppose you think you could win this tournament?"

Maurice favored her with a cute, confident grin. "Let's just say that if I hadn't become a writer, I might well have made a living as a card shark." He laughed. "Something tells me I made the right career choice."

"Something tells me the same thing," Conneca agreed, thinking about his latest book. She wondered whether she would recognize herself in it. Would she want to?

"So where are your friends?" Maurice used his height to scan the casino over the crowd.

"Good question," Conneca replied. "Maybe they went out for something to eat?" Or were otherwise predisposed? she thought mischievously.

They walked into the lounge and saw Nadine and Larry seated at a table. The two were nursing drinks and keeping a close eye on the Keno computerized boards. Nadine spotted Conneca and Maurice approaching and waved them over.

"You decided to come after all—with Maurice," Nadine gushed, standing and pushing up her glasses. She glanced at Maurice before giving Conneca a hug.

"You know me—always full of surprises," Conneca said awkwardly, realizing that Maurice now probably deduced that she had not wanted to bring him, but had a change of heart.

"I talked her into it." Maurice winked at Conneca, who felt her face flush.

Larry stood. He was white with a deep tan and in his late thirties. A shade under six feet, he had a medium build, thick raven hair with a sprinkle of gray, and blue-gray eyes. He was dressed in a black sportshirt beneath an ivory blazer and tobacco-colored pleated trousers. Conneca thought he wasn't bad-looking, though not her type.

"So you must be this famous author I've been hearing about?" Larry looked at Maurice.

"Probably not half as famous as my writing partner," Maurice joked.

Larry seemed confused for a moment.

Nadine cringed. "Remember, I told you he was part of my favorite novelist collaboration, Alexis Maurice. Alexis is his, uh, cowriter."

Larry rubbed his aquiline nose with embarrassment. "Oh, yeah, right, I get it now."

"Maurice Templeton." Maurice extended a hand.

"Larry Anderson."

The two men shook hands like old army buddies, while the women looked on.

Conneca hoped this had not been a mistake. At the time, it seemed like a good idea to invite Maurice here as a way to retrain her thoughts in a different direction. *Let's just hope this gathering doesn't blow up in my face.*

They sat around the table.

"We thought we'd warm up for a while with some Chenin Blanc and Keno," Larry said.

"Sounds like a good idea to me." Maurice turned to Conneca. "How about you?"

She nodded in agreement.

Maurice signaled a waiter. Conneca couldn't help but think that the two of them almost seemed like the perfect and loving couple. The man was even ordering drinks for her. What would be next? Perhaps roses and a candlelight dinner? She refused to get her hopes up for fear of a crash landing.

"Haven't had the chance to read any of your novels, Maurice," Larry admitted without compunction. "Nadine tells me they're romances?"

"Actually romantic suspense." Maurice sat up straight.

Larry twisted his lips. "I always thought women wrote that kind of stuff?"

Nadine looked as if she wanted to hide. Conneca's eyes twinkled in amusement, realizing that most men and some women did stereotype romance authors that way.

"They probably do, by and large," Maurice suggested smoothly. "But more and more men are trying their hand at it. I've always had a knack for creating romantic adventures in my real life, so it seemed only natural that I find a way to put it into fiction, along with my partner." He glanced at Conneca, who fashioned an awkward smile on her face in return.

Larry tasted his wine. "I've never been much of a writer. I leave that to my secretary."

"And what line of work are you in, man?" Maurice looked sideways at Nadine and directly at Larry.

"I have a PR firm," he said loftily. He got out one of his cards and passed it to Maurice. "If you should ever need someone to promote your books, give me a call. I'm sure we could do wonders in increasing your popularity that much more."

Maurice glanced at the card and stuffed it into his jeans pocket. "I'll keep that in mind." He favored Conneca with a look of pure amusement.

"Where have you been hiding this man, Conneca?" Larry turned toward her. She could tell by the red glint in his eyes that he had probably already had one too many. Nadine had said that he loved his martinis and wine, maybe a bit too much.

"I haven't been hiding him anywhere," Conneca responded tartly. "We're just friends."

Regardless of her feelings for Maurice, Conneca did not want anyone—including him—to think that she was somehow hoarding him as her mate-in-residence.

"In fact, we met at this very place," Maurice pointed out, seemingly willing to go along with Conneca's interpretation of their relationship. "In the hotel."

Larry gaped. "Is that right?"

"Yeah."

"Inside the hotel, huh?" Larry said suggestively.

Conneca felt color steal into her cheeks before Nadine elbowed her man hard in the ribs, causing him to wince. "I told you about the celebrity auction here last week, Larry."

"Oh, yeah, right." He looked embarrassed.

"Conneca saved me from the clutches of an old dragon lady," Maurice chuckled, winking at her in jest. "I'm forever indebted to her, even though we're '*just* friends.' "

Conneca detected the sarcasm in his tone. Or was it disappointment?

"I feel the same way about Nadine," Larry claimed, looking at her. "I owe her a debt of gratitude for entering my life when she did and making me feel whole again. And I feel a hell of a lot more for her than friendliness, if you know what I mean."

Nadine smiled at him sweetly. "It works both ways, baby." She kissed his waiting lips lingeringly.

Conneca glanced at Maurice, who suddenly seemed ill-at-ease, as if a nerve had been struck. She wondered if he could ever be so committed to a woman. Or was there no room in his life for anything—or anyone—permanent, aside from his books?

The waiter brought the wine, and Maurice paid for it despite Larry's insistence at picking up the tab.

"So how do you manage to decide who writes what?" Larry fixed Maurice's face, interested. "Or does your writing partner decide for you?"

Maurice looked mildly amused. "We decide everything together," he offered firmly. "If it were any other way, it wouldn't work."

Conneca realized then that part of the success of Alexis Maurice was the common perception that they were *both* fully involved in the plotting and development of the books. Maurice had shown an unselfishness and loyalty in perpetuating this persona, though he was the one who actually created the characters and wrote the novels.

Alexis must truly be a special person in his life, Conneca thought. Even now. Was that why he had married her? Had Maurice substituted passion for the close-knit nature of their professional relationship? Conneca wondered if this was why the marriage had failed—because there was no real intimate connection there.

Maybe Maurice's standards for involvement were too high, she considered. As such, Conneca had to ask herself if any relationship with Maurice was doomed to failure right from the start. Meaning she could be fighting a lost cause to think otherwise.

More numbers flashed across the electronic board.

"Damn," Larry grumbled, glancing at his Keno slip. "Missed the boat again."

Nadine frowned, indicating the same thing. "I think it's time we give the slot machines a try," she pouted, touching her nose.

That was about the limit of her own gambling, Conneca thought. Even then, she never played anything other than the nickel and dime machines. In her mind, it was always better to lose a little than a lot. Not to mention the fact that she could think of maybe a million other ways she would rather spend her hard-earned money apart from the long odds at the casino.

"You play poker, Maurice?" Larry asked, holding his drink.

Maurice gave a nervous little laugh, sipping wine. "Not if I don't have to."

"The poker machines can be a challenge, but they can't take the place of a *real* game."

"What did you have in mind?" Maurice flashed Conneca a look of reluctance.

She knew then that he had been roped into accepting Larry's thinly veiled challenge. But would it prove to be a big mistake? Had Maurice gotten into something over his head?

And will I then be blamed for having dragged him here in the first place? Conneca asked herself nervously.

CHAPTER 23

The private poker game was held in a back room of the casino. Apparently it was a regular feature for those with the right connections and money.

Maurice had not been overly enthusiastic to participate, but went along for the ride, primarily as a means of stretching his time with Conneca for as long as possible. He had missed being with her greatly, and thought they had come to a dead-end street before the invitation came to go to the casino. He had no idea where things were headed with them. Only that he simply was not prepared to lose her.

But for the moment Maurice simply wanted to avoid losing the shirt off his back.

There were five players in all. Most looked to be seasoned pros to Maurice. Whereas he didn't consider poker to be his strong suit in card games, preferring bid whist. He did have his ace in the hole, so to speak, though. Conneca had painstakingly agreed to stand by his side, just as Nadine was clinging to Larry like a tick.

Maurice hoped Conneca's presence would be just the thing to give him a winning hand.

The stakes were relatively high—ten thousand dollars per man in a winner-take-all game. Not having that type of cash on him, Maurice had gone to a local branch of his bank to get the funds from his account. Though money was no longer an object to him, he still didn't like throwing cold hard cash away if he could help it.

"Things are looking better all the time," Larry cackled, after the dealer, a slender Asian man in his fifties, had given him three new cards. Nadine looked confused, as she hovered restlessly above him.

"Just two," yelled a big Native American with a long, shiny, ink-black ponytail. The elderly, well-dressed British gentleman beside him needed four cards.

When Maurice's turn came around, he elected to have only a single card replaced.

Conneca batted her curly lashes with alarm. In barely a whisper, she asked Maurice doubtfully, "Are you sure you know what you're doing?"

Maurice felt a tingle as her warm breath tickled his cheek. Conneca wore just a touch of makeup, all she needed to bring out the beauty of her face, he thought. The rest all came from within.

"I'm sure, baby," he said simply, the term "baby" more endearing than routine to him.

Maurice had begun with four queens. His last card, still face down, would likely make or break him.

Larry was the fourth man to reveal his hand. Optimistically, he laid out four jacks and a deuce. Grinning broadly at what at this juncture was the winning hand, he challenged Maurice, "Let's see if you can top five jacks, *Mr.* Author."

Maurice surveyed the tense faces in the room, ending with Conneca's. He read the look of sorrow in her eyes, as if she were to blame for him losing ten Gs.

"It won't be easy, Larry," Maurice drawled. "But isn't that the whole point—to do things in life the hard way?" He spread out his four queens, and placed a two of diamonds on top of them. It gave him what amounted to five queens and the winning hand.

But there was only *one* queen in the room that Maurice truly wanted, more than he could convey in mere words, thoughts, or actions. He gave Conneca a big victory smile, and then regarded the somber faces around the table.

Larry was the most devastated. "Looks like I misread you, Maurice."

"Most people do," he grinned matter-of-factly, "whereas others simply *read* me." Collecting his winnings, Maurice said, "Sorry, gentlemen. Maybe next time." He stood, quitting while he was ahead and having no desire for a rematch anytime in the foreseeable future. "Thanks for letting me in on this one."

He took Conneca's hand and led her out of the room that was suddenly as quiet as a morgue. Or maybe like a bank, after all the accounts and vault had been emptied.

"How did you manage that?" Conneca asked once they were far enough away that the losers wouldn't overhear.

"I wish I could say it was the luck of the Irish," Maurice said, his mouth stretched in a contented grin. "But since I'm not Irish, I guess it must have been *your* company that got me over the hump, Ms. Lady Luck!"

Conneca blushed. She was not quite sure what to say. She doubted very much that her presence had anything to do with his apparent mastery at poker. The man seemed quite adept at everything he put his mind to, she thought. Including making her fall for him. Or wasn't that the plan from the start?

She flashed Maurice a look of uncertainty. "You didn't cheat back there, did you?"

He gave her a low laugh. "You mean some sleight of hand like a magician?"

"Whatever." Conneca's eyes rested squarely on his.

"Never cheated in a card game in my life!" Maurice held his stomach tight. "If you can't win fair and square, what's the point of winning at all? That would only make the earnings tainted. And the earner someone lower than a snake's belly."

Instinctively Conneca knew that he would not need to resort to cheating. Maurice Templeton was too damned confident and talented for that. It appeared as if he simply had a knack for always being on the winning side. She wasn't sure if that was good or bad.

They made their way back into the general casino.

"Shall we try our hand at the slot machines?" Maurice posed. "I'm feeling pretty hot."

"I think I'd rather go now," Conneca voiced, having had her fill of gambling and tenseness for one evening.

"That's cool." He angled his eyes at her. "Think they'll survive without us?"

Conneca realized he was referring to Nadine and Larry. "I have a feeling they will be just fine," she told him, knowing they would be pissed that Larry ended up on the losing end of ten thousand dollars.

Out in the parking lot Maurice removed crisp hundred dollar bills he had stuffed in his pocket from his winnings. "There should be fifty thousand here, including the ten grand I put up." He squeezed it into Conneca's purse.

"What are you doing?" Her lids fluttered at him.

"It's yours to do with as you wish."

Conneca stopped on a dime. "I can't take your money, Maurice," she insisted. "You won it, fair and square."

"Only to go along with the program." He ran a hand along his jaw line.

"What program is that?"

Maurice sighed. "The fitting-in program," he explained huskily. "I didn't want to come off as a holier-than-thou brother, so I went along with the card game—for you."

Conneca rolled her eyes in disbelief. "So you're *blaming* me for choosing to play a game that you won?"

He smiled. "Something like that. I wanted to make a good impression on them—and you."

Conneca recoiled. "You didn't need to impress Nadine and Larry," she said solemnly. "And you certainly don't need to impress me, Maurice." She wondered how she could possibly be more impressed than she already was. *But he doesn't have to know that.*

"I'll try to remember that." Maurice relaxed his facial muscles.

"Good." Conneca reached into her purse. "Now that we've got that settled, you can take your money back." Her pride wouldn't let her accept it.

"No." Maurice held her hand in place firmly. "I have more money than I know what to do with, Conneca. Donate it to your favorite charity. Hell, do whatever you want with it!"

"*Fifty thousand dollars!*" Conneca stared at him in disbelief. There was generosity and there was *generosity*. "Let's be real here." It made the amount she bid for him seem like pocket change.

Maurice shrugged it off. "This is as real as it gets, baby," he uttered smoothly. "No big deal. It was never mine to begin with, at least forty thousand of it. Let's just call it an act of benevolence from Larry and the other big spenders that I corralled into one jackpot with a little extra from me for good measure."

Conneca thought of arguing her case on behalf of *his* money, but had a feeling it would be pointless. "Okay, you win," she gave in, though appreciative nonetheless.

"No, *we* win," Maurice insisted, sensing her discomfort. "If it makes you feel better, you can donate the money anonymously. That way neither of us has to take the credit."

"How philanthropic of you." She sneered at him and began to walk toward the car, leaving him behind.

Maurice laughed as he caught up to her. "Don't sound so excited and grateful."

"Thank you very much, Maurice," Conneca said hoarsely, "for your kind donation to charity. I'll see to it that the money is put to good use with the needy."

Conneca realized that whatever Maurice's motives, the more-than-generous sum could certainly help the less fortunate and poor schools in Oak Cliffs. But at what price? She wondered if he would expect a return on his investment. Would she happily pay out dividends? Or take the money and run? *I'll just be grateful that this will help those who need it, and try not to make a federal issue out of some imaginary implications.*

Maurice beamed. "Now that's more like it."

Conneca curled her lip with second thoughts. "Don't press your luck, mister!"

"Why not?" he questioned wryly. "It seems to be working pretty well at the moment."

Conneca thought of another comeback, but sensed she was no match for him.

"Maybe we'll get to do this again sometime?" Maurice suggested opportunistically, matching her stride for stride.

Conneca tried to imagine when that would be. Surely he was close to leaving their small town. Wasn't he?

"The next time," she warned askance, "if there is one, you may not be as fortunate."

"Yeah, but on the other hand," he spoke cleverly, "perhaps lady luck and I go hand in hand."

It was only then that Conneca realized that Maurice had actually taken hold of her hand. And just maybe even her heart again.

CHAPTER 24

"Can I come in?" Maurice peered into Conneca's rich café latte eyes, his own betraying the animal need he had for her.

Conneca felt the intensity of his gaze, for she needed him just as much. "Are you sure you really want to?" she asked doubtfully.

"More than anything in the world," he said in a voice from well within his throat.

Conneca stepped into her suite, Maurice close on her heels. The door had barely closed when they fell into each other's arms like two lost souls who had found one another. The moment their lips touched, Conneca felt as though she would melt into a pool of ecstasy. She pressed her opened mouth eagerly onto Maurice's, wanting to taste him and feel the gentleness of his tongue.

They seemed to be swaying, as if the earth itself was moving around them. Their mouths remained locked in a deep kiss, each reluctant to pull away from the other for even a moment. Conneca stood on her toes but felt as though she were dancing on air. They swirled a time or two and moved even closer, as if to prevent anything or anyone from coming between them.

"Hadn't we better go into the bedroom?" Conneca gasped. Even then she dreaded releasing the man she clung to as if they were somehow glued together.

Something resembling a groan rose from Maurice. "Not sure I can make it that far, baby. I want you right here and now!"

With that, Maurice once again made Conneca's mouth his personal quest, devouring her lips as if only their soft, dark pink moisture could quench his initial thirst. In turn, Conneca gathered in every inch of Maurice's lips, covering them with hers, searching them for the mysteries and magic they held.

His hands, strong and sure, moved across her breasts, scalding them with his fiery touch, as if burning through her sweater. Conneca jerked when Maurice's fingertips grazed her nipples. The sensations tore across her chest and down her spine. A soft moan left her, blending in with the sounds of the ocean waves that crept through the walls like classical music.

"Ohhh, Maurice," Conneca cooed. "I'm so hot."

He pulled her closer. "Me too, baby."

Conneca felt the rock hardness of Maurice's body, slightly tense as it measured up against hers. His erection throbbing to be freed, brushed against the crevice that separated her legs, causing a bolt of delight to careen through Conneca's lower extremities. She wanted to feel him whole and firm inside her. Nothing else seemed to matter, but satisfying the urge that only he could fill.

Wordlessly Maurice heard her cry for him, his heightened breathing speaking in volumes for his own passionate desire. He pulled the sweater over Conneca's head and undid her bra, tossing both aside like yesterday's burdens. Her breasts, taut to the chill, stood in wait for his gentle caresses and desirous mouth. He took in one nipple, giving it singular attention and teasing with his tongue. It reacted in expanding outward and thrilling Conneca inward to no end. When he did the same to the other nipple, she bit her lip from the pure pulsating pleasure.

Maurice lifted and began to move his hands over and around her long braids and Senegalese twist rolls, seemingly captivated with her hair in a way that only men could appreciate. "I want all of you, Conneca," he murmured anxiously, "your body, mind, and soul."

"You already have all of me," Conneca sighed, knowing it to be true, even if reservations remained over the long term.

Maurice needed no more reassurance to continue what he started. He crushed Conneca's mouth against his once again, wrapping his arms around her back and literally lifting her against him. Conneca shuddered at his strength and felt the powerful yearning she had instilled within him, giving her a keen sense of satisfaction. He tasted her neck, ears, and chin, seemingly determined not to miss one speck of what was hers—and now his.

In turn, Conneca went after his chiseled face, nose, and neck, down to the opening of his V-neck sweater where a rigid chest waited for her kisses and fingers to explore. Maurice groaned at her touch, compelling

Conneca to want to touch him more and in more places. They began to grapple with one another's clothing, eager to drink in the sight of each other's exquisite nakedness, until the wish had become a stark reality.

Conneca felt no abashment at exposing herself fully and unconditionally to Maurice this time around. Or, for that matter, combing his firmly magnificent body with her sight. It all seemed as innate as life itself.

"I doubt that you could be more perfect," Maurice intoned, surveying her with appreciation.

Conneca wet her lips at Maurice's wholeness; then at the exciting part of him that sprung from his body like a coil. "Neither could you, baby," she uttered *sotto voce.*

Like the setting of the sun, they sank slowly down onto the Oriental rug. Side by side, Conneca and Maurice discovered one another. Each feasted upon the other like it was their last supper, captivation giving way to primordial, unbridled desire.

Maurice moved his mouth across Conneca's upper body and down to her lower self. Each kiss tapped into nerve endings, thrilling her with warmth and excitement. When he spread her legs, she readied herself for his ravenous approach. Burying his face into the soft curls that formed a triangle to her womanhood, Maurice made Conneca quaver violently, yielding to her own needs and anticipation.

Maurice reacted to her body's vibrations by moving deeper into Conneca's realm of discovery with his lips and tongue. He continued to pleasure her like no other. This man's incredible and full mouth was driving her mad with utter delight. She cradled his smooth bald head in her hands.

Conneca felt as if she would explode with tantalizing and sweeping satisfaction. Biting her lip, she tried to push Maurice away before it was too late, not wanting to experience something so heavenly without him. But he would not deny his need to lavish her with untold enjoyment. He held her thighs tightly and proceeded to bring her to orgasm. She moaned with desire while releasing her sweet nectar.

Unable to hold back, Conneca let herself go in complete abandon, her body trembling ecstatically. Her arched back flattened to the rug sinuously while she watched Maurice skillfully tend to her in grand and erotic fashion.

Suddenly Conneca could stand it no more. The spasms that riddled her body like bullets needed to be satiated as only Maurice could. *I have to feel you inside me,* she thought intensely, hearing her cries of rapture.

"Make love to me, baby—please," she beseeched.

Maurice answered her plea, lifting up, his breathing ragged, lips wet with wanting. "No power on earth could stop me," he uttered surely, and grabbed a condom from the wallet in his pants.

Above Conneca, Maurice gazed hungrily into her equally voracious eyes. Their cravings spoke for them. He guided himself between her legs spread wide, knees bent, and drove into her. She wrapped her arms around his neck, her legs across his firm buttocks, and held on tightly for the ride, as she absorbed his powerful and fluid strokes.

Breathing erratically, Maurice gently nibbled at Conneca's taut nipples with his teeth, causing a powerful reaction, and massaged the curves of her body with long, tender, trembling fingers. Conneca felt his release coming even as her own had already begun to paralyze her with its surge of undulating fulfillment. She cupped his face and sought out the dark heat of his lips.

Together they climbed the mountain, soaring to its highest peak and claiming victory in slow motion, before coming back down to the valley floor. It was a long while before either moved, content in remaining clenched as one. Slowly the air returned to their lungs and the equilibrium to their sense of the world around them.

"Tell me I've died and gone to heaven." Maurice lay on his back and his head turned to meet her face.

Conneca fluttered her lashes languorously. "If you have," she declared, "then I've gone with you."

He kissed her soft shoulder. "Yeah, I'd definitely have to agree that you're one hell of an angel, Conneca," he laughed.

She cuddled against his broad muscular chest. His heartbeat was in sync with hers. She wondered if that meant they were on the same wavelength. Or was it just for the moment?

"Where do you want this to go, Maurice?" Her eyes rose to find his.

Maurice sighed unsteadily. "I don't know," he admitted weakly.

Conneca frowned. "That's not good enough."

He stiffened. "I never made you any promises, Conneca." His gaze averted hers. "I couldn't . . ."

"Why not?" she asked bluntly. *Am I asking too much in wanting to know if there's any future here?*

"It's complicated," Maurice said without prelude.

"Come on, Maurice. You're going to have to do better than that," Conneca stated with annoyance. "Everyone's life is complicated." She paused and found his eyes. "Is it me?" She needed to know.

Maurice took a breath. "No, it's not you," he responded evenly.

"Then what?" Conneca lifted on an elbow, her hair draped across one breast. "I have a right to know." *Or maybe not,* she mused.

Maurice's brow creased along two lines, as though he were suddenly carrying a heavy load. "We come from different worlds, Conneca," he muttered depressingly. "The hustle bustle life in Denver is not the same as in the laid-back Pacific Northwest and Oak Cliffs." He seemed to search for other evasive reasons. "I have my writing, you have your inn. The two don't seem to be entirely compatible."

"Does *everything* have to be perfect for two people to be in a relationship?" Conneca questioned him, dispirited. "Or are you confusing the characters in your novels with *real* life? Or maybe this is about past mistakes and fear of moving forward?"

Maurice pursed his lips. "Maybe I'm just trying not to hurt you by saying only what you want to hear."

Conneca sat up, furious. "I'm not a damned child, Maurice," she sputtered. "I won't crumble into a thousand pieces on the basis of what you say to me. I just want to know where I stand in your life—where we stand—even if it means being hurt."

Conneca had never intended to put him on the spot. Yet she had done just that. She wondered if it would cost them whatever they had. Or save her from further misery down the line?

It's all on him now, Conneca thought, for better or worse, knowing she wanted and deserved something solid in a relationship at the end of the day. She didn't want to settle for anything less.

Maurice put the weight of his eyes upon Conneca and then turned away, as if to analyze his feelings on his own. When he did favor her again, he said with a catch to his voice: "I wish I could tell you in black and white where we stand, Conneca . . . but I can't. All I can say is that I care for you a great deal, more than I have for anyone in some time. I'm sure that's not exactly what you had in mind. But it's all I can offer you for the time being."

Time being. What the hell does that mean? Conneca wondered confused. *What are you trying to say?*

She glared at him. "So you mean you care for me 'a great deal' this night only?" she questioned facetiously. "Or the next night you feel like taking me to bed? Or maybe till you finish your book and are ready to head back to Denver? Is that what this all about, Maurice—we're supposed to last for as long as you're around, but not afterward—?"

Maurice grimaced, sitting up. "No, baby, that's not what I meant."

Conneca got to her feet, suddenly feeling as though she had made a big mistake in sleeping with him again. "I think you'd better leave." She started to gather up her clothes, holding them to her naked body to shield it from his lascivious gaze.

"Let's talk about this, Conneca," Maurice said, standing but showing no such inclination to cover his nudity.

She shot him a cold look. "You know what, Maurice, I really don't feel like talking now. Just go—and close the door on your way out. I'm going to bed."

Conneca walked away, aware that he was watching her backside but not caring. Let him take one last good look, she thought. *I'd rather end things on my own terms than his.*

Even then Conneca expected Maurice to come after her, to perhaps try and make amends, tell her anything that might give her hope that he really did want her as more than a temporary fix to his libido—and hers. But there was no such attempt. Instead, Conneca listened from the bedroom as Maurice got dressed and walked out the door.

Conneca sank to the floor, putting her hands to her face, and cried. If there were any doubts before, she knew now that what she felt for Maurice was far more than the quenching of her physical needs. Or even the appeasement of her mental cravings and stimulation. She had fallen in love with Maurice Templeton, plain and simple. It was not the love of lust, but rather of the spirit and heart. Of man and woman. Of two people who belonged together. At least she wanted to believe that.

Yet it was obvious to Conneca that Maurice was not bound by such affections and commitment to her. His attachment, she suspected, was more physical in nature—as it seemed was the case with most men. Maybe he could never love. Or maybe he wanted to but was afraid of it, like a child being afraid of the bogeyman.

Conneca had resigned herself to the fact that Maurice never had any intention of this—whatever this was—lasting. He would leave Oak Cliffs—and her—as soon as he had completed his mission. Whatever they had would be romanticized and fictionalized in his novel, as if it were never real beyond the pages of a book. And there was nothing she could do about it other than accept the inevitable.

But how can I? she thought miserably, wiping tears away. *Not when I want so much more—and need it.*

From Maurice Templeton and no other.

Can I possibly go on with my life without him in it in a significant way? Conneca could only wonder. She had no answers, only more questions about the man she'd just made love to.

CHAPTER 25

"**Y**ou must be in love!" Lee exclaimed, a tender smile crossing his lips. Conneca looked at him like he was crazy, but said nothing. Was it really that obvious? She was trying hard to ignore what she knew was true.

"I saw the same look in your mother's eyes," Lee told her affectionately, standing on the other side of the front desk where Conneca waited for arriving guests. "She and your father felt the same way about each other till the very end."

Conneca detected a maudlin tone in his voice. She knew he dearly missed them almost as much as she did. She was also aware that Lee had put most of his energies into helping her run the inn since his own beloved wife passed away, having nothing better to do with his time or someone to do it with. For that she was more grateful than she could ever say.

"Well?" Lee widened his eyes. "Am I wrong?"

Conneca clamped her hands onto the counter's edge dreamily. "You're not wrong," she spoke with mixed feelings. "I'm afraid you know me all too well, Lee."

But that fear was not half as great as not having such love returned. Conneca had not thought she could love a man again, much less open her heart and soul to him. Now she had done both and could live to regret it, if she weren't already.

"Mr. Templeton, I presume?" Lee leaned forward in earnest.

Conneca nodded wistfully. "I wish I could say that we were slated to live happily ever after," she muttered. "But it seems that fairy tales are just that."

Lee inclined his head woefully. "Maurice doesn't feel the same about you?"

Does he? Conneca had to ask herself. *I doubt it, if I'm reading him correctly.* It seemed like most men didn't know the meaning of true love . . . or commitment. She wondered if her appeal to Maurice was strictly limited to great sex and a good-luck charm in the casinos.

"I honestly can't tell you how he feels, Lee," Conneca admitted sorrowfully. "Other than that he apparently, for his own reasons, doesn't want a serious commitment again." Did that speak for itself? Was it simply a case of once bitten, twice shy with him, or was there more to it?

"Perhaps you should ask him!" Lee narrowed his eyes at her paternally. "If the brother is half the man I suspect he is, he shares your feelings wholeheartedly and may only need to have it drawn out of him, slowly but surely."

"But just how am I supposed to do that?" Conneca chewed on her lower lip. She felt like she was still in high school, when Lee could always be counted on for advice with boys, whether she wanted it or not. This time she felt that any such advice would be more than welcome.

"By telling him exactly how you feel and asking Maurice—no, demanding—that he do the same! My guess is that Maurice doesn't want to lose you any more than you want to lose him." Lee put a hand on the counter and forced a smile. "Nothing too elaborate really."

Conneca wished she could be so certain. She had laid it all on the line before with men whom she had been far less attracted to and affected by. Only to be humiliated or told, in effect, that they wanted to take everything without giving anything but empty words and false promises. She was not sure she could stand to have Maurice reject her love. *I have my dignity*, she thought, even if he had her heart.

Perhaps it would be better to leave well enough alone, Conneca deliberated. If it was simply not meant to be between her and Maurice, then no amount of pouring out her affections would make one damned bit of difference. Would it?

The front door swung open and in walked a tall, gorgeous, honey oak–complexioned woman in her early thirties who looked both lost and as if she had suddenly found herself. Or at least found the place where she wanted to be. She wore a black-on-black button-front shirtjacket with a pullover shell and A-line maxi skirt, contoured to her streamlined figure, and coal high-heeled leather pumps that made her look even taller. Her naturally dark brown hair with light brown highlights was stylishly cut around a taut, heart-shaped face to just above her shoulders, and there was not a strand out of place. She tossed a glance about the place, almost with disdain, before approaching the desk with a model's strut.

"Looks like royalty has come to Oak Cliffs," Conneca gulped, suddenly feeling more than a little inferior in her aubergine double-breasted pantsuit with a moss-green ruffled top.

Lee appeared almost in a trance, gazing admiringly at the fine and elegant-looking sister. "If only I were twenty years younger," he chuckled, "and six or seven inches taller, maybe I'd have a fighting chance."

Conneca smiled enviously. "Something tells me that she already has some brother at her beck and call."

Conneca shuffled her feet, watching the woman come forward, as if at her directly. There was an air of familiarity to her, the closer she came. Had they met before?

"Good afternoon," Conneca said sweetly to her. "Will you be checking in?"

The woman gave her the once-over with dazzling gray-brown eyes, and then dismissed Conneca as if she had more important things on her mind. "I'm looking for someone I believe is staying here."

"The name?" Conneca continued to study her face without making it too obvious.

Without hesitation, the woman responded in a dainty voice, "Maurice Templeton."

Conneca flashed Lee a look of surprise, and received one, as this request registered in both their minds. She gathered herself as best as possible on shaky knees.

"Yes. Mr. Templeton is one of our guests." Conneca felt her throat go dry and she swallowed unevenly. She now knew where she recognized the woman from. It was on the back of an Alexis Maurice novel, right alongside Maurice's image.

The woman sighed with satisfaction. "Well, that's good. My name is Alexis Templeton."

"Yes, I thought you looked familiar," Conneca said, trying to sound chipper, though her heart was beating like a drum. Something told her that Alexis's presence spelled danger—at least for Conneca.

"Oh, really." Alexis favored Conneca with an intrigued look.

"You're, uh," Conneca stuttered, "collaborating with Maurice on some romantic suspense novels."

Alexis fixed her sharply. The casualness with which Conneca had referred to him as Maurice had not gone unnoticed.

"I'm more than merely his writing 'collaborator'," she spoke curtly, adding as if it were unknown but carried weight: "Maurice and I were once married."

As perhaps was intended, Conneca found herself focusing more on the word *married*.

CHAPTER 26

You're one damned fool, man, Maurice told himself as he stood on the beach, tossing shells back into the ocean where they belonged. He often retreated to being by himself as a boy when troubled by something. But this was not a boy's problem. It was a man's.

He had desired Conneca Sheridan too much to want to stay away from her, having jumped at the chance to make love to her again. And she had responded to him as no other woman ever had. They belonged together, at least on some level. Of that he was certain.

What was far less certain to Maurice was just how far they could or should go.

He wondered why the hell he hadn't come clean with Conneca when he had the chance, and now felt disappointed in himself. *Why didn't I simply tell her that I was just as scared about being hurt as she was? That I wasn't sure I even knew what love was anymore?* Alexis had made sure of that. The last thing Maurice wanted was to try and build a future with another woman, only to find out that they too had deluded themselves into believing there was more to their feelings than there really was.

He couldn't go through that again and neither should Conneca. Hadn't they both been through enough heartache for one lifetime? Maybe it was better if they drifted apart now rather than later. Even if she grew to hate him because of it. She might come to understand in the long run.

Conneca was a successful businessperson in her own right just as he was, Maurice reflected. Weren't they simply asking for trouble if they tried to merge the two, aside from everything else?

Make that the three. Maurice realized that Alexis came with the package whether he—or Conneca—liked it or not. She was his coauthor contractually and to their fans. Changing that would not be smart business. He had worked too hard with Alexis to want to see their professional collaboration end as their marriage had.

Maurice wondered if he could effectively hold onto Alexis Maurice even if his heart belonged elsewhere. He knew that women, even when there was no direct competition, could be at each other's throats, making it damned difficult for a man to keep the peace. His fervent wish in the ideal world was that Conneca and Alexis would be as accepting of each other as he was of both women, albeit with two entirely different agendas. But he feared that there would only be animosity between them with him caught squarely in the middle—so that they all lost out at the end of the day.

Maurice flung another shell into the blue water. Was he truly only interested in sparing Conneca the hard facts about his life and the hazards they faced in trying to make this work? *Or am I really only trying to convince myself?* he mused.

Maurice climbed the sand dune, his thoughts and emotions still spinning like a vortex, and made his way back to the inn. He deliberately avoided the front entrance, suspecting that Conneca might be working the front desk. At this point, it seemed best all the way around if he stepped back a bit from her—them—to put his life into perspective. Only then could he hope to come to grips with his feelings and the emotional knots he felt inside where it concerned Conneca Sheridan.

Maurice came in the side door, which led to the pool and lounge. Once upstairs, he saw that the doorknob tag to clean his room had been removed, meaning the housekeeper had come. The thought of a hot shower with fresh towels was invigorating to him.

Maurice never noticed that someone was in the room, until he heard a familiar voice say: "I was wondering if you'd ever bother showing up, baby."

He fixed his eyes on the couch and his pulse checked itself. There sat Alexis all cozy, with her long legs crossed, and a smile lighting her face at his obvious surprise.

"What are you doing here?" were the first words to form in Maurice's head and spit out of his mouth.

"Hello to you as well," she said, batting her curled lashes, as if insulted. "I was bored and decided I could use a break from Denver. And since you described Oak Cliffs in such glowing terms, I wanted to see it for myself. I also wanted to talk to you about the book, face to face. And since you seemed in no hurry to come home, well, here I am."

Maurice was glued to the spot where he stood. And speechless. *If I say what I really feel I might regret it,* he thought.

"Well, don't look so happy to see me, Maurice," Alexis moaned exaggeratedly, rising to her feet.

Maurice took a deep breath and made his lips curve at the corners into a placating smile. He met her halfway, and they embraced warmly, if not affectionately. He could smell her strong perfume—Eden, her favorite.

"Of course, I'm glad to see you, Alex," he said tonelessly. "I just wasn't expecting you to fly halfway across the country without consulting me first, that's all."

Alexis withdrew and gazed peevishly into his eyes. "If I had, you would have told me it wasn't necessary," she pointed out flatly. "And I didn't want to take no for an answer."

Do you ever? Maurice thought. Only when it suited her purposes. That had helped spell doom to their marriage, but it had proven to be an asset when dealing with hard-nosed publishers and editors over the years.

Alexis painted a thin smile on her lips, revealing perfect, small white teeth. As usual, she was impeccably dressed, and still to Maurice a fine-looking woman, in spite of everything else.

"All the same—" he started to say.

Alexis cut him off, pointing out, "Besides, remember, it was *my* idea that you come here in the first place, hon. I didn't expect you to practically want to camp out in this quaint little out-of-the-way coastal town."

"I'm spending most of my time working on the novel," Maurice said in a surly voice. He saw no reason to go into his personal business in Oak Cliffs, especially since she no longer had a right to know what he was doing and with whom.

"I know," Alexis said, as if never in doubt. "Some things never change."

"Meaning?"

She poked a finger at his chest playfully. "Don't sound so defensive, Maurice. I was only teasing you. Why, if you weren't so dedicated to the books, where would either of us be today?"

Maurice was tempted to say still married. But he knew it would be a lie. Their breakup had less to do with the writing than simply being mismatched from the start, romantically speaking. And when Alexis decided to stray, they both knew whatever had existed between them intimately was over.

"Believe me," she assured, "I'm every bit as dedicated. That's why I'm here. I wanted to discuss in person my editing on the material you e-mailed me. This is, after all, another Alexis Maurice book and it takes *two* to make it work."

Maurice found it hard to argue the point, and she damned well knew it. While he created the characters, storyline, and subplots, Alexis's expertise in trimming the excesses and filling in the blanks had proven to be every bit as important. She was as much responsible for the success of

Alexis Maurice romantic suspense novels as he was. And for that he could never imagine going it alone. That is, till now.

Clearing his throat, Maurice said in an apologetic undertone, "I didn't mean to shut you out, Alex—if that's how it seemed."

"Don't be silly. I know that." Alexis ran a silky smooth hand down his cheek and smiled sweetly. "It's all right, Maurice. No harm done."

Maurice got a whiff of her perfume again, which he never particularly cared for, and took a step backward. "So how was the flight?"

"Too long," she whined dramatically. "But worth the trip!"

"Housekeeping let you in, I take it?" he asked curiously, considering that they were no longer man and wife.

Alexis curved her full lips crookedly. "Actually I managed to borrow a key from the woman at the front desk," she said boastfully. "Conneca something or another. I think she recognized me from one of the books."

Maurice got a sinking feeling in the pit of his stomach. *Oh damn.* He could only imagine what must have gone on in Conneca's head when she realized that his ex-wife had shown up out of the blue. Would she believe that he had no advance knowledge of Alexis's arrival? Did he need to explain to her that it was strictly business with Alexis these days? Or was that a moot point, considering that he wasn't sure if there was much left to say to Conneca regarding their future. Or even their present, if there was one.

Maurice made himself grin resignedly. "Welcome to Oak Cliffs, Alex."

Maurice and I were once married.

The words replayed over and over in Conneca's mind, as though stuck in an irregular groove. Indeed, for a moment she had felt as if her legs would go right out from under her, though she was not quite sure why. The fact that Maurice was once married to Alexis came as no surprise.

But Alexis's appearance in Oak Cliffs had. Maurice's ex had shown up as if uninvited and unexpected. Or had Maurice requested that she come? If so, was it to work on their novel? Or to reenact scenes from when they were married?

Conneca considered that Alexis could be the real reason Maurice was holding back from giving his all to a relationship with her. Was it fear of history repeating itself? Or of letting go of the past once and for all?

This is ridiculous! Conneca sat on the sofa in her suite, listening to a Sarah Vaughan CD. It was supposed to cheer her up but seemingly had the opposite effect with its melancholy tone. *I have no business being jealous over Maurice's ex-wife, beautiful as she is, who also just happens to be his current writing partner.* It was not like Conneca to be angry as though she had caught her lover with his hand in the cookie jar.

But even rational thinking could not still her feelings that Maurice was slipping away from her grasp—if she had ever had him at all—with Conneca being helpless to prevent it. Had he been up front with her about the true nature of his relationship with Alexis? *Do I have reason to feel suspicious?*

Might Maurice have deliberately left out a small detail or two about his personal life? *Maybe—if he wanted to seduce me,* Conneca thought, while knowing he had not entirely broken away from the woman he was once married to.

And seduce her he had. Though deep down inside it was debatable to Conneca just who had seduced whom. But that didn't help. A good cry seemed to. She found herself unable to just pretend that what happened between her and Maurice hadn't, and simply go about her business as usual. That included work. Lee had taken over at the front desk, himself at a loss for words to ease Conneca's misgivings. There were no such words in existence, she knew.

For she had been down this path before, where she had given far more than Conneca had received. Only this time was the most devastating yet. Not only had she given herself to Maurice in every way she could imagine, but had fallen hopelessly in love with him to depths as with no other.

Now Conneca had to wonder if this emotional investment had been all for naught. Would she once again be left feeling empty, betrayed, and humiliated by a man? When Maurice had told her he didn't know where they stood, was he really saying he knew *exactly* where they stood in terms of what he wanted from Conneca but wasn't willing to give in return? When all was said and done, was Maurice really no better than the other men she had tried to forget?

Conneca decided that whatever the case, Maurice would likely be heading back to his world now that Alexis had come in search of him. And that would probably be best all the way around.

The sooner Maurice Templeton put some distance between them, the sooner Conneca could get on with her life. Difficult as it would be. She knew there really was no other choice.

CHAPTER 27

"That *bastard*!" Nadine cursed from the kitchen that evening. "How could he?"

Conneca glanced solemnly at the plate Nadine was preparing with marinated beef strips, baked potato, and fresh steamed vegetables for a diner. She had told Nadine about Alexis's ceremonious arrival and watched her friend jump to conclusions. Both seemed to put aside for the moment the fact that Alexis's presence could be perfectly innocent or business-related, under the circumstances.

Except for the fact that Maurice had never bothered to warn Conneca of her arrival, as if it were a secret among secrets. Or perhaps because he didn't respect her enough to do so. This left Conneca more than a little suspicious of his underlying motives in romancing her, using her as research for a novel, then hedging on where they went from there, as if Maurice had known from the start it was a dead-end street.

Alexis Templeton's abrupt appearance seemed to solidify that notion.

"Quite easily, I'm afraid," Conneca responded to Nadine resentfully. "Maurice saw something, or someone, he wanted—me—pursued successfully, and didn't give a damn if I got hurt in the process."

Conneca wasn't sure she really believed this, but it sounded good at the moment, if only to make herself feel better.

Nadine stopped what she was doing and looked up with narrow eyes. "I almost hate to say this, Conneca, but I told you that man was not to be trusted! And that maybe you shouldn't expect too much to come out of your relationship—if you could call it that." She growled. "Why couldn't he have proved me wrong?"

Conneca seemed to shrink in shame at the prospect that she could have been so wrong herself about Maurice Templeton. Why hadn't she stuck to her guns about not getting involved with men? *This man.* Why had she allowed herself to succumb to his charms and her own pent-up needs, along with the promise of so much more?

Conneca tried to put on a brave face. "It probably wouldn't have worked out anyway between us," she contended. "Aside from everything else, Maurice lives in Denver and I live in Oak Cliffs. There seems little ground for bridging the gap."

"Especially when he has his ex-wife to fall back on when the going gets tough." Nadine made a face. "If you ask me, those two deserve each other—in misery!"

Conneca wondered if there might be some truth to the deserving part, if not the misery. Ever since first seeing Alexis and Maurice on the back of their book, Conneca had always believed they looked like a handsome couple who were madly in love. Now she wondered if they still could be, in spite of no longer being bound by a piece of paper. It wouldn't be the first time a divorced couple found themselves drawn back together.

"I think I'll start looking for a new favorite author," Nadine grumbled. "If you want to know the truth, the quality of their writing was never really the same after the first novel. Obviously Alexis Maurice was basically just a one-hit wonder."

Conneca appreciated her support, knowing Nadine was venting her frustration in the wrong direction out of friendship and loyalty. But Conneca didn't want anyone else to have to suffer because of her involvement, or lack of, with Maurice. Least of all one of his biggest fans. "This has nothing to do with his—their—books," she insisted.

"Doesn't it?" Nadine added a pumpernickel roll with a pat of butter to the plate. "How can you respect one's creation, if not the man himself?"

A point well-taken. Yet Conneca refused to let this ruin her. She had come too far to be pushed back into the abyss of doom and gloom by Maurice Templeton or anyone else. What was meant to be would be, and there was nothing she could do to change it.

"Well, I respect *your* creation, girl," Conneca said on a light note, favoring the superb and mouthwatering dish Nadine had put together. "And I'm sure the guest will as well, assuming he or she ever gets to eat it."

Nadine got the message and handed her the plate, as Conneca was playing waitress this evening.

"You're right, Conneca, I suppose one can only rearrange this plate so many times," Nadine said wryly. "It's time we both got back to work and saved our bitching for another time . . . and maybe another, more dependable brother."

Conneca gave a weak, "no comment" smile, before heading into the dining room.

She handed the diner, a frail-looking, elderly gentleman with only a few strands of snow-white hair left, his food. "Hope you enjoy your meal, sir," she voiced enthusiastically. "I'm sorry it took so long."

"You needn't be. The appetizers kept me busy." He crinkled his eyes at her and put his nose to the plate. "Smells delicious. I'd say that's a good sign."

Conneca smiled with relief, knowing that they had another happy customer. She took out her pad and went to look for the next hungry mouth to feed. Out of the corner of her eye, she spied a waving hand connected to a long, thin arm. Turning in that direction, Conneca saw that the hand and arm belonged to Alexis Templeton, who stopped waving once she realized she had gotten her attention. Seated next to Alexis, almost expressionless, was Maurice.

Maurice wished he could bury his head in the sand outside the inn. When Alexis had complained about being hungry, he had tried to steer her to one of the local eateries. Instead, she had pulled him into the inn restaurant, as though determined to aggravate the situation more than it already was.

Even then Maurice felt he might be able to avoid Conneca, at least until he could try and explain things to her. Instead, there she was, approaching them, order pad in hand, looking at him as if he were a perfect stranger. Or invisible, as far as she was concerned.

Could he blame her? Maurice squirmed uncomfortably. What must she be thinking in seeing him and his ex-wife together—even if they were cowriters in a perfectly platonic environment? *You're way off base, baby,* he thought instinctively. But that didn't change the fact any that it didn't look good to the naked eye—Conneca's eye. Maurice found himself still struggling with how best to mend fences and come to terms with his own heart, which ached more and more whenever he was near Conneca.

"I was beginning to think we'd have to wait here *all day,*" Alexis complained to the waitress.

Conneca pursed her lips. "Sorry but we're a bit shorthanded today."

"Yes, I can see that." Alexis flashed her a look of recognition. "Weren't you the one who checked me in earlier today?"

Conneca nodded without ever looking at Maurice.

"Doing double duty?"

"I do whatever needs to be done," Conneca answered laconically.

Maurice knew he had to say something. But what? He didn't want to come off sounding like a damned jackass. Or carry on a private conversation in a public setting.

"This is Conneca Sheridan," he told Alexis proudly. "She's not only the desk clerk and waitress, she also happens to be the *owner* of the Sheridan Seaside Inn."

Alexis practically turned ashen. "Oh. Well, how interesting." She glared at Maurice, as though curious as to how he knew so many details about the woman.

"Conneca was the one who won the bid for me during the celebrity auction," Maurice said without apologizing.

"Is that right?" Alexis swung her eyes from person to person, settling on Conneca, who looked stone-faced. "Then I suppose I should be thanking you?"

"Thanking me?" Conneca looked confused.

"Yes. You see it was *my* idea that Maurice come here for the auction." Alexis swept a gaze across the dining room and back squarely on Conneca. "Looks like you've taken good care of him."

Conneca managed a forced but polite smile. "We try and take good care of *all* of our guests."

Maurice read through her calm façade. She was seething. Hurt. Confused. Disillusioned. And understandably so. He had beaten around the damned bush as to what he wanted, giving the impression that what he didn't want was her. It couldn't be further from the truth. Conneca needed someone who could be there for her, in and out of bed—someone who would treat her right. And that was him. He needed her, in more ways than she could possibly imagine.

Have I sabotaged any chance we have for continuing any semblance of a relationship? Maurice asked himself. If so, he blamed it on a number of fears, warranted or unwarranted. Cold feet at jumping back into the fire. Reluctance to risk ruining a good thing. Uncertainty about maintaining an accord between his past in Alexis and a possible future with Conneca.

Maurice wrestled with these thoughts as he sat in the presence of the two women. The tension was so thick he almost expected fireworks to erupt. But it didn't happen.

"If you're ready," Conneca said with pursed lips, "I can take your order now."

Maurice realized she was speaking to him. Alexis had apparently already ordered.

"What would you suggest?" he asked in a dispassionate voice, closing the menu, which he had barely looked at.

Conneca shot him an indecipherable look. "You're a writer," she hurled. "I'm sure you can use your imagination to conjure up something."

Alexis seemed to take this all in with amusement.

Or was it mystification . . . or possibly indignation? Maurice wondered, wishing he could dig himself out of a hole that seemed to be getting deeper with each second.

He settled on the marinated beef strips special.

"What on earth was that all about?" Alexis regarded Maurice wide-eyed.

"What?" He looked away nonchalantly.

"It was plainly obvious that the waitress—desk clerk, innkeeper, or whatever she is—had something on her mind." Alexis wet her lips with Cabernet Sauvignon. "If she had been any chillier, I'm afraid you would be frozen solid by now!"

Maurice gave a chuckle that sounded more like a grunt. "Conneca . . . Ms. Sheridan has been stressed out trying to do everyone's job around here," he said with more than a grain of truth. "It's not surprising the guests sometimes bear the brunt of it. I doubt she meant anything by it."

Alexis flitted her lashes, piqued. "And how would you know about the stress she's under?"

Maurice sighed, realizing Alexis was watching his every move like a hawk. They had not sought to control each other's social calendar since the divorce. But neither had gone out of their way to divulge much about their personal lives either. It seemed to work best that way—keeping their business relationship separate from their private lives. He saw no reason to change that.

Besides, Maurice doubted he could make Alexis understand what Conneca had come to mean to him, when he didn't fully understand himself.

Grabbing a bread stick, Maurice broke off a piece with his teeth. "It's been obvious," he said carefully while he chewed. "This place isn't exactly the Taj Mahal. It only takes spending a few days of snooping around to get a good idea of who's carrying most of the weight here, figuratively speaking."

Alexis drank more wine. "Is there something about her that I'm missing?"

Maurice sipped his own wine. "It depends on what you're looking for."

Alexis batted her eyes snidely. "Nothing I haven't already had, baby."

Maurice curled a lip. "Then I think we understand each other," he said curtly. "Since I'm not prepared to go down that path again either. One mistake was enough."

Alexis seemed to shrink back in her chair.

Maurice felt a certain amount of satisfaction in that moment, as well as optimism where Conneca was concerned.

Their food was served by another waitress.

CHAPTER 28

Conneca had dinner in her quarters, not particularly in the mood to eat with the kitchen staff, much less the dining room guests, as she liked to do from time to time. She thought back to seeing Maurice and Alexis in the restaurant. It was all Conneca could do not to run out of there at that very moment. She had never been jealous over other women before, but rather had chosen not to be in competition with those who were often as powerless as she was in controlling their own fate with men. Such was true as well where it concerned Maurice Templeton.

With Alexis she felt a mixture of envy and admiration, even as Conneca tried to fight it off as if threatened by her. Alexis was even more beautiful in person than on her book jackets, Conneca thought. She was also talented and, though an ex-spouse, Alexis apparently had her claws dug into Maurice so deep that Conneca doubted anyone could wrest him away even if a person wanted to. Least of all her.

Conneca tried her best to eat something, even if her stomach was not into it. She wasn't so desperate that she needed to try and come between Maurice and Alexis and any agreement they had as to the precise nature and terms of their relationship. Which Conneca still had not quite figured out for certain, other than that it was a special bond that even divorce could not break.

So why should I try to? Conneca asked herself. When it was obvious that Maurice could not handle more than one sister in his life at a time. Or did not care to. That left her as the odd one out.

Clearly Alexis took credit for successfully running their writing empire, Conneca considered. Even while Maurice was the one who created and skillfully told the stories. Yet he seemed perfectly content to allow Alexis that role, as if it were her right. Was that the major basis of their relationship? Role-playing? An imbalance of power? Did it amount to a give-and-take scenario where each had their own strengths and weaknesses, creating harmony when they pooled their talents?

Whatever way she looked at it, Conneca could only come to the conclusion that she and Maurice had been a mistake. He had played on her vulnerabilities and attraction to him, using her for physical comfort. He seemingly wanted the best of both worlds. One in Denver and another wherever the spirit moved him—in this case, Oak Cliffs. He chose to make a life in only one world, the one that he could control without losing any of it.

The knock on the door was so soft that at first Conneca thought it might be the wind brushing against the window like a tree branch. The second and third knocks came louder and heavier, as if more decisive in their intent.

Conneca stood up from the dining room table where she had been nibbling on chicken casserole, part of yesterday's leftovers from the kitchen. She had slipped into jeans and an oversized shirt, flipping her hair to one side so it hung across her shoulder. Padding across the floor barefoot, she went to the door.

"Yes?"

There was a pause. "It's Maurice."

Conneca's heart did a little leap and check. But she would not grow giddy at the sound of his voice. Not now. Not ever again. How could she? *I don't need this emotional roller coaster*, she told herself. *And I certainly don't need Maurice Templeton.*

"Go away, Maurice," Conneca said tartly. "I don't think we have anything more to say."

"I have something to say," he insisted. "All you have to do is listen."

Listen to what? More lies and head games? Indecisiveness? She'd had enough rearrangement of the truth. Distortion of the facts. Playing on her emotions and her body's impulses, thank you.

"I'm really not in the mood." Conneca took a ragged breath. "Just leave me alone!"

She saw the doorknob twisting furiously. But the door was locked.

"Seems like we've been down this road before, Conneca," Maurice groaned. "You have every right to be hurt, confused, angry—and even mistrustful. Just give me a chance to explain things and then I'll be out of your hair. Assuming that's what you want."

As much as Conneca wanted to resist succumbing to his charm, she also had a burning need to put some type of closure to whatever it was that had drawn her to this man who somehow seemed larger than life in so many ways. *Maybe this is something I have to do in the scheme of things.* Maybe.

She unlocked the door. Maurice stood there, looking bedraggled and unsure. Whatever else, Conneca knew she could never trust him again. She believed her trust had been abused and taken advantage of.

"You have five minutes to say your piece," she warned unsteadily. "Then I want you to leave. Understand?"

"Perfectly." Maurice marched past Conneca like a soldier, and waited for her to catch up to him.

When she did, Conneca found herself unable to meet Maurice's gaze head on. She did center on his face, as she asked bluntly, "So where is Alexis? Or did you drug her so you could slip up to my room?"

Conneca recalled Alexis demanding a key to Maurice's room, as though she had every right to. She had acquiesced to Alexis, assuming it was also his wish. Conneca could only imagine how the two former lovebirds might have made up for lost time.

Maurice brought his brows together and his nostrils grew. "You've got this all wrong, Conneca."

"Got *what* all wrong?" she questioned furiously. "The fact that you couldn't quite make up your mind about what you wanted out of our relationship? Or that you neglected to mention during our lovemaking that Alexis was coming and would be staying in your room? Strictly as professionals, I'm sure." Conneca made a hissing sound. "Am I missing anything?"

Maurice gritted his teeth. "Yeah, you are," he said flatly. "For starters, Alexis is *not* staying in my room. She checked into her own room an hour ago. I wouldn't have had it any other way. There is absolutely *nothing* going on between us romantically. There hasn't been for a long time . . . and that's not going to change." He sighed. "As for drugging Alex, the long flight from Denver and two-hour drive to the coast accomplished the trick nicely. Last I knew, she was on her way to bed for the night— alone."

Conneca felt utterly foolish. She had clearly drawn the wrong conclusions as to any possible intimacy between the two, even if she had every reason to be suspicious under the circumstances. Admittedly, this made her feel better about where she and Maurice had gone and could still possibly go.

But it did not erase the nagging doubts Conneca had about Maurice's ability to make a commitment to her or anyone else at this stage of his life. Or if he even had a desire to.

Conneca wasn't sure where it left them. Or if she even wanted to pursue a relationship. Suddenly it seemed as if playing second fiddle to Maurice's writing career was more than she could or should handle. But she owed him at least an opportunity to say whatever else was on his mind.

Conneca said, her voice softening, "I'm sorry if I came across as a jealous, insecure woman. But with Alexis's unexpected arrival and *our* unsettled status . . ."

Maurice bit his lower lip. "She didn't tell me she was coming," he said regrettably. "But that's Alex for you—always expect the unexpected! The last thing I wanted was to hurt you, Conneca. You've got to believe that, baby."

"I'm not sure what to believe anymore, Maurice." She glanced at him askance. "You don't seem to know what you want, or who you want. Maybe it just isn't me."

He ran a hand haphazardly over his bald head and frowned. "Dammit, I never made any promises to you, Conneca! This isn't a novel where everything is cut and dried, black and white, open and shut—"

"I'm not asking for a storybook ending." Conneca heard the snap in her voice. "And, obviously, you are incapable of such, once you get beyond the pages of your books. Maybe that's your problem, Maurice—it's too easy for you to go from woman to woman without stopping long enough to make it work with any of them."

Maurice stared at her and Conneca could see that she had struck a nerve. While not unsympathetic to a degree, she felt he deserved it as far as she was concerned. *The truth hurts*, she thought. *I'm the one who's been wronged here, not him.* She had been prepared to give Maurice that part of her which belonged to no other man. At the very least, Conneca expected honesty and straight talk in return. Not a man who proved as unreliable as some of the characters in the Alexis Maurice novels.

Maurice shot Conneca a cold stare. "I have *never* gone from woman to woman," he insisted. "Not in the way you might think. Alexis was the one who caused our marriage to end, not me. I wanted nothing more in the world than to make it work. But she turned her attention and body elsewhere. That told us both that we meant more to each other as writing partners than husband and wife. Since then, there hasn't been anyone to speak of that captured my attention in a meaningful way. That is, until you."

Again Conneca felt as if she had misjudged Maurice in some ways, but clearly not others. He wanted her, yes, but only on his terms. This was not good enough for her. And maybe he wasn't either. Sweet talk and a hot body could only go so far, she thought.

"Whatever we have, Maurice," Conneca told him lamentably, "it doesn't seem to be working. I think we both know that."

He rubbed his nose. "So what are you saying?"

She made herself look into his eyes. "I'm saying that I don't think I can compete with the demands of your life as a writer and collaborator. I'm just a small-town innkeeper, looking for a simple but committed relationship. Certainly not one as complicated and unreliable as what I would get from you."

Maurice shook his head disappointedly. "I never thought of you as one who would throw in the towel without a fight for what you want."

Conneca gave a dismissive shrug. "Maybe you don't know me as well as you think you do," she uttered painfully.

"Maybe I don't," Maurice huffed.

"I am *not* Alexis," Conneca tossed at him, "and I never will be."

"Never asked you to be," he said bluntly. "I'm anything but a fool, Conneca. History has taught me what *not* to look for in a lady."

"But you've obviously found something with Alexis that was—is—working for you." Conneca fluttered her lashes. "Even if you can't, or won't, admit it."

"What Alexis and I have is complicated," Maurice threw out, smoothing his jawline with his hand.

"Isn't that true of most relationships?" Conneca asked, perhaps unfairly. "Some couples thrive on complications."

Whatever else, Conneca no longer believed that there was any further physical intimacy between Maurice and Alexis. They'd had their thing and it was over and done with, she decided, at least on Maurice's part. But the emotional and creative bond they shared still left Conneca a little shaken and less than certain that anyone could ever come between it.

Maurice turned to her. "Alex has been there for me from the very beginning—when brutal rejection letters threatened to break my spirit and destroy my self-confidence. She coaxed me back to writing time and time again, and used her own writing and language skills to bring the books up to publishable standards." He sighed. "I'd be lost without her."

Conneca batted her eyes petulantly. "Heaven forbid, Maurice, for you to ever lose your way," she said cynically. "And far be it for me to stand in the way as you try and oscillate between two women. Not to mention, no doubt, countless adoring fans."

Maurice sucked in a deep breath. "You're being unreasonable."

Conneca threw her arms up in the air. "So now I'm the bad guy here? Give me a break!"

"There are no bad guys, Conneca," he said tersely. "Just stubborn ones!"

"Ditto," she shot back. "I think you'd better leave now, Maurice. I wouldn't want to keep you and your cowriter from honing your next bestseller."

Maurice put a hand to her cheek and Conneca fought tooth and nail to ignore its most soothing effects that coursed through her entire body and very being like her blood itself.

"Try as you will to pretend you simply don't give a damn, baby," he said, his fingers touching her tight lips, "it won't work. Not entirely. What-ever we had together, I think we both know was real. Our lovemaking was everything lovemaking should be. You made me feel things I never knew I could. You made me want someone the way I've never wanted anyone before or likely will again."

Conneca allowed him to move his hand the length of her face, filling it with color and heat. Whatever hold Maurice may have still had on her, she knew she had to resist it. Or she would forever leave herself open to him and the further pain he could cause her.

"No matter what you may think of me at this moment," Maurice ut-tered thoughtfully, "I never planned for things to happen between us as they did. But forces brought us together in spite of ourselves. It was all as natural as the softness of your skin."

Conneca stepped away from his touch, difficult as it was. She wouldn't allow him to seduce her again—or vice versa—and then watch as Maurice Templeton disappeared from her life, perhaps forever.

"What we had was nice," she conceded. "But it's over, Maurice. I think it's best for both of us if we end things here and now. That way we can de-part as friends, without further disagreements and disappointment threat-ening even that."

Maurice gazed at her with sad eyes. "If that's what you really want . . ."

Conneca held back tears that wanted to come out in buckets, not wanting him to see how much it hurt to come to this decision. But deep down, she felt certain that she was sparing herself greater anguish later. It was better if she ended it rather than have him do it whenever the de-mands of his life or his own indecision dictated such.

Conneca looked up at Maurice and, before she lost her nerve, said convincingly, "Yes, it's what I want."

Maurice started to say something, but his mouth remained a hard line. He walked silently to the door, turned to her, and said out of the corner of his mouth, "I'm sorry, about everything . . ."

So am I, Conneca told herself, watching tearfully as he left the room. *I'm sorry that I allowed myself to be charmed by you.* Sorry that she had made the mistake of falling in love with a man Conneca could never have in whole. Sorry that Maurice had seemed more committed to his writing than the most important things in life. Sorry that they both had been weakened by bad relationships that ultimately came between them. Sorry that the man she had given her heart to had never found the words or desire to say he loved her.

Yes, Conneca was sorry about a lot of things too. And even sorrier that most were outside of her control. Except for perhaps the feeling that, all other things aside, she and Maurice were truly meant for each other. Even if he would never know that.

CHAPTER 29

Conneca had just left the inn for her morning jog, when she heard the recognizable voice behind her call out: "Ms. Sheridan?"

Approaching her in a light blue warm-up suit and white sneakers was Alexis Templeton.

Conneca immediately tensed. It was as if she expected Alexis to want to engage in open combat for muscling in on her territory. She hoped it would not come down to that. After all, it was Alexis who had won the war, in effect, if not having lost a battle or two along the way.

"Good morning, Alexis," Conneca uttered in a strained but friendly voice. In fact, it was not the best morning. It was cool, damp, and cloudy, with the ocean lacking its usual luster as a result. And Conneca was not at her best, wearing no makeup, and her hair tied up haphazardly. Whereas Alexis looked like she'd just stepped off of an *Essence* magazine cover.

Alexis proffered a polite nod. "I was told you're a runner."

"Not of marathon caliber," Conneca admitted. "But I try to run as often as I can."

"Same here." Alexis flipped her head back, her fashionably styled hair remaining remarkably in place. "Actually, I ran in the Boston Marathon once," she bragged.

Conneca was suitably impressed. "The most I've ever competed in was a 10k race," she said, as if it were an embarrassment by comparison. "But I can do better."

Alexis looked at her with misgivings. "Mind if I run with you?"

Conneca glanced over her shoulder expecting to find Maurice within sight. He was nowhere to be found. She wasn't sure if that was good or bad. *Why does she want to run with me?* Conneca wondered suspiciously. *Do I really want to know?*

To Alexis, she responded respectfully, "I think it should be the other way around."

Alexis chuckled. "How about we run together?"

Conneca breathed more easily. "Sounds like a plan."

The two women began to move lightly along the black rocks that led to the water. The waves were in an antsy mood this morning, bouncing upon the shore as if its sworn enemy.

"I suppose I can understand Maurice's attraction to this resort community," Alexis commented, her eyes darting down the coast. "It does have its own little charm."

"We like it," Conneca said proudly. She gazed out at the farthest reaches of the ocean. "Not as easy to lose oneself here."

Alexis made an amused sound. "You mean like in Denver?"

"I mean any big city where so much goes on that you become caught up in it, whether you like it or not."

Alexis lifted an arched brow. "I take it you're speaking from experience?"

Conneca looked at her. "Sort of. I spent some time in San Francisco and Los Angeles, and have visited other cities with sizable populations before drifting back to Oak Cliffs."

"Then you grew up here?" Alexis's voice rose an octave in surprise.

Conneca smiled. "Yes, it's home sweet home."

"I grew up in Denver," Alexis noted. "Not exactly country living, but it does allow a person space to find what she or he is looking for."

"Is that where you met Maurice?" It only stood to reason, Conneca told herself, though wondering why she was suddenly curious about the particulars.

"As a matter of fact it is." Alexis turned her head. "At the Metropolitan State College of Denver. We were both English majors. I knew right away that Maurice had what it took to be a successful writer. Since I was an equally eager and confident collaborator, I knew we could make a dynamic duo." She seemed to relish the thought. "We had considered a pseudonym that had nothing to do with our real names. But that would be taking away a part of our identity. Hence, Alexis Maurice was born."

They reached the golden sand, not yet spoiled by footprints or debris, and began to pick up speed.

Conneca couldn't help but wonder if the name was Alexis's idea. Was it a means to bind Maurice to her? Or her to him? Either way, it seemed to have backfired for one or both insofar as their marriage was concerned.

"Do you think you'll ever try writing books separately?" Conneca inquired bravely.

"What on earth for?" Alexis snorted, rolling her eyes. "We're a team, and a very good one at that. There's no reason to mess up a good thing!"

Conneca sighed. "I didn't mean give up your collaboration altogether," she said, feeling foolish, "but writing independently as well. I would think that would be a natural growing experience for a fiction writer, but maybe not . . ." As if she knew from experience.

At the same time, Conneca wondered if Alexis was even capable of writing on her own, outside of editing and suggesting ideas for what were mostly Maurice's creations, from what Conneca understood.

Alexis's brow creased. "Who knows? Perhaps someday Maurice and I can see if we have the same gifts apart that we bring to readers together."

Yeah, right. When hell freezes over, Conneca thought. Not in this lifetime! Alexis knew a good thing, or man, when she had it—at least as a writing partner—and was not about to rock the boat any time soon by attempting to go solo. Could she blame her?

Conneca knew as well as anyone how difficult, if not impossible, it was to find compatibility with another in any sense of the word. She'd learned to treasure it when the connection was there. Even if only temporarily. As was the case with Maurice.

Yet there was more to symmetry than artistic success and adoration by the reading public.

Had Alexis ever truly been in love with Maurice? Or vice versa? Might their marriage have worked had professional success not come early for them? Or had it been doomed to failure from the very start?

Maybe you should be minding your own business, girl, Conneca told herself. Especially now that Maurice was no longer her business to be bothered with.

"And what about you, Ms. Sheridan?" Alexis intruded upon her thoughts. "Is running a small coastal inn making you happy?"

Enough of the formalities, Conneca decided, as if it put Alexis on a higher platform of civility and ceremony. "It's Conneca," she said sanguinely. "As for the inn, I wouldn't exactly say it's making me all that happy. It's all I have going for me at the moment, though, not that I'm complaining." She decided she might as well be brutally honest.

Alexis fixed her abruptly. "But is it all you want?"

Conneca flushed, as if Alexis somehow knew that she wanted perhaps the one thing—or person—she could never have wholeheartedly. At least not without stiff competition in one respect or another.

"I want a family someday," she said wistfully, "along with the white picket fence and maybe even a dog. But I'm not holding my breath."

Alexis chuckled thoughtfully. "Sounds like you've had your fair share

of disappointments when it comes to men—or brothers, to be more specific?"

"More than my fair share." Conneca bristled at the thought. *Brothas,* or
black men, had certainly proven to be a problem where she was concerned. Especially the latest disappointment, which had been by far the
most devastating. And the hardest to overcome.

"Haven't we all, girl?" Alexis looked straight ahead.

"You mean Maurice?" Conneca asked coolly on a breath.

"Yes, and others as well." She glanced cautiously at Conneca. "It's no
secret that Maurice and I are divorced. We both made mistakes along the
way. I may have made the biggest mistake in looking elsewhere for what
was lacking in my marriage. And I paid the price, big time . . . "

Conneca couldn't help but think that the price was still being paid—
by both Alexis and Maurice. Not to mention at least one other who entered the picture inadvertently.

"Do you still love him?" Conneca asked ingenuously, somehow feeling
some sort of bond with the one woman Maurice once chose to make it official with.

Alexis raised her eyes, as though caught off guard by the question.
"Not romantic love, if that's what you mean," she made clear. "There will
always be a special kind of love between me and Maurice. The kind that
comes from shared experiences, good or bad, that took you from one
point to another in life. But that's about it."

This came almost as a relief to Conneca, almost as if it validated her
own brief relationship with Maurice. She would have hated to think that
it had come at the expense of another who cared for him just as much.
Particularly one who had so much history with Maurice Templeton.

Alexis bit her lip pensively. "If we had to do it over again we probably
never would have mixed business with a personal agenda. I think that
somehow along the way we may have gotten the two confused and re-
versed, leaving something important missing in the equation. Am I making any sense to you?" she asked, doubt ringing through her voice like a
siren.

"Yes, you are," Conneca told her sympathetically. "I too have been
down that road before with disastrous results." She considered that it was
the business of charity and literacy that brought her and Maurice together. Only to have things come to a head once it became personalized.

"Sometimes I think that brothers and *sistas* are simply better off as
friends—with no romantic strings attached," quipped Alexis.

Conneca laughed. "You may be right about that." *Things would certainly have worked out better in my life had I lived it according to those rules,* she
told herself.

The two women, seemingly given a boost of support and energy from
each other, put on the burners, leaving tracks in their wake.

A few minutes later, Alexis sucked in a deep breath and asked Conneca, "So what made you choose Maurice in particular to spend your money on at the celebrity auction? Not that I can blame you for that. From what I understood when booking him for that event, there were any number of prominent and eligible celebrities in attendance."

Conneca couldn't help but wonder if Alexis had meant for Maurice to be bid on by *only* married or elderly women. Or women who were not young, single, unattached, and looking for a husband. Or maybe even unattractive and, thereby, less threatening women. Had at least a part of Alexis wanted Maurice to remain single and uninvolved seriously, or at least meet someone much closer to home, so as not to disrupt the professional harmony and image they had established?

Conneca wiped her brow, feeling warmer with each step. She rejected her own feelings of competition where there really were none, and said to Alexis with embarrassment, "To be perfectly honest, my winning the bid on Maurice was the result of a complete and stupid misunderstanding."

Befuddlement crossed over Alexis's face. "Misunderstanding?"

"I was simply scratching my face," Conneca explained, "when the auctioneer mistook that for the next bid to the tune of five thousand dollars!" Even now Conneca found herself reliving the moment and wishing she were anywhere but center stage for Maurice and everyone else on hand.

Alexis guffawed. "You've got to be joking, girl?"

"I wish," Conneca groaned, breathing out of her mouth. Even if part of her was glad it had come to pass given the intimacy she and Maurice shared. "Of course, what was I to do? There were no other bidders to let me off the hook. And the cause of promoting literacy was important enough to me to see it through. End of story."

"And an outlandish one at that." Alexis licked her lips into a broad smile. "I suppose you never told that to Maurice?"

"Not a chance!" Conneca chuckled to herself. "Didn't think his ego could take it."

Alexis laughed. "You're probably right about that. Maurice's *super ego* might just have imploded."

Conneca considered the possibility that they were both giving Maurice less credit than he deserved. Could be that his ego was not so fragile after all, that he needed *all* women to fall at his feet or he would fall to pieces?

Conneca seriously wondered was if any woman could come to mean as much to Maurice as his writings. Or maybe the fictional women he created, as if he molded them into his way of thinking—the perfect woman without the complexities, character flaws, and physical shortcomings of real women.

"Whether unintentional or not," Alexis commented, a catch to her voice, "it appears that you left quite an impression on Maurice, Conneca."

"Oh?" Conneca feigned innocence, batting her eyes.

She wasn't sure just how much Maurice had told Alexis about them. Or, for that matter, how much she should divulge to Alexis. Even if Conneca's own intimate relationship with Maurice had ended.

"He followed you to your inn, didn't he?" Alexis cocked a brow at her.

"He needed a room," Conneca said lamely.

"And he needed inspiration," Alexis pointed out. "Something that had been lacking for a while. That was partly why I wanted him to do the auction, an event which we often attend together across the country, to give him some distance and a chance to regroup." She sighed. "It obviously worked. Maurice has written more in the last week or so than he had in the previous six months."

Conneca wrinkled her nose. "Not sure I can take credit for that, Alexis." Nor did she particularly want to. Being responsible for someone's success or failure other than her own was not a load Conneca was prepared to shoulder.

Not even if that someone were Maurice Templeton.

They turned around and began heading back in a slow jog.

"You deserve at least some of the credit," Alexis insisted knowledgeably. "Maurice used you and your inn to develop a new and fascinating character as part of the plot's strength and resolution."

"Did he?" Conneca regarded her dumbfounded. The alternative was to tell Alexis that she had already taken a sneak peek at Maurice's notes, and found out what he was up to in studying her life.

Or at least that was part of his rationale. The other, she knew, was far more personal.

"You mean he didn't tell you?" Alexis fluttered her lashes, disbelieving.

"Why would he?" Conneca gave her a straight face. "I thought that most writers kept the inspiration for their story lines all to themselves?"

"You have a lot to learn about writers, Conneca," Alexis laughed. "And just how much of themselves they're willing to give to strangers."

I'm learning all the time. Conneca pondered the limits of precisely what Maurice was willing to give to a perfect-stranger-turned-lover.

CHAPTER 30

Maurice had watched from the tower room window as Conneca and Alexis trotted down to the beach.

Together.

Damn, he thought uncomfortably. *This is bad news.*

He felt as if he were being ganged up on by the two women who meant the most to him, even if in completely different ways. Had he bitten off more than he could chew? Would their note-swapping leave him out in the cold or in more hot water?

Somehow Maurice couldn't bear the thought of losing Alexis's organizational and editing skills and her longtime camaraderie, even when all else failed.

But he was even more concerned about losing Conneca's considerable talents at making him feel like a real man—full of pep, desire, excitement, fantasies, optimism, and love.

Maurice thought back to Conneca's painful words to him last night: *Best for both of us that we end things here and now.*

Had she truly meant it? Had he pushed her away with his own wavering about what he wanted from her and was prepared to give in return?

Maurice felt like he was walking on pins and needles for the mess he'd made of things with Conneca. *Do I just sit back and allow what we had to abruptly end as if it had never begun?* Or was it really in both of their best interests to simply walk away?

He wondered if his writing would ever be the same again if his heart belonged somewhere else. Somewhere beyond his reach . . .

Maurice faced the reality that what he was feeling for Conneca went way beyond lust—though that too was something that filled his thoughts every time he was near her. For perhaps the first time in his life, he understood what it meant to truly love a woman and want to spend each and every day by her side, pampering and pleasing her in every way possible. He could only imagine what it would have been like to have met Conneca Sheridan years earlier, giving them that much more time to have cultivated what they had. What it would have been like to share in each other's metamorphoses through life.

Maurice felt he'd made a big mistake to have married Alexis for all the wrong reasons. But it would be an even graver one to turn his back on the potential he felt still existed between him and Conneca for a wonderful life together. Something that he now saw with more clarity than ever before.

As he listened to the CD player churn out the soulful, emotive sounds of Norah Jones, Maurice was well aware that he would have to make some tough decisions that would affect the rest of his life, as well as the lives of two others to one degree or another. That is, if it wasn't already too late.

He went back to working on the novel. The hero, Aaron Sinclair, had survived every imaginable disaster, including failing at love, and come out smelling like a rose. With the new heroine that had come into his life, Erica Kinkaid, Aaron was willing to throw caution to the wind for a chance at true love and lasting happiness.

Could Maurice possibly emulate his hero in his own life? Or were happy endings only in fiction and fairy tales?

"How's it going?" Alexis asked over his shoulder, fresh from her jog.

"It's just about a done deal," Maurice told her zealously. "I only have to get Aaron out of one more jam. Then there's nothing but light at the end of the tunnel."

"Does that light include living happily after with his new lady love?"

"That remains to be seen." Maurice kept typing but his thoughts were anywhere but the page before him. "What do you think?" He almost dreaded to ask, aware that she had been against adding a new character so late in the story. In fact, he had added some passages about Erica earlier in the book to help set the stage for her important role in Aaron's transformation, perilous adventure, and romance.

"I think it will probably work after all," Alexis shocked him by saying. Maurice looked up. "You do?"

Alexis rested her hands on his shoulders. "Why not? Today's romantic suspense fans tend to like unusual twists and turns that propel the hero out of danger and into the arms of a mysterious, beautiful woman."

Maurice was not quite sure how to respond. He wondered if Conneca

had told Alexis about using her life as the basis for Erica Kinkaid's character. Or had Alex figured it out herself? What else had they talked
about? He found himself more than a little curious.

"Glad we see eye to eye on this, Alex," Maurice told her sheepishly.

Alexis chuckled. "We usually do in the final analysis, baby. That's why
we make such a terrific team—at least where it pertains to writing and
selling books!"

They did at that, Maurice concurred. Too bad the same couldn't be
said for their marriage. Or maybe it wasn't such a bad thing after all, he
thought. For it opened the door to a new romance for him, with even
greater potential for long-term dividends.

"I just happened to run into your inn proprietress, Conneca Sheridan,"
Alexis tossed out nonchalantly. "*Run* being the operative word."

The word *your* caught Maurice's attention, as he had certainly never
referred to Conneca as such. Even if he felt that way deep down inside.
Trouble was, he wasn't quite sure what feelings she had left for him at
this stage, if any.

"Oh?" Maurice touched the side of his head.

"An interesting lady," she said, "in her own way."

"Most people are," he responded generically.

"But most people are not captivating enough to be personally added
to a book's plot at a time when the key characters were supposedly long
introduced," Alexis offered.

Maurice froze.

Alexis leaned to face him, and grinned. "Don't look so shocked,
Maurice. One doesn't have to be a genius to know that Erica Kinkaid is
clearly Conneca Sheridan in disguise."

There was no sense in denying it, Maurice realized. *I may as well come
clean and take my lumps.*

"It seemed like a good idea," he said equably, "to develop an interesting character like Conneca Sheridan who owned her own rustic little inn
where Aaron could hide out—"

"And be swept off his feet," Alexis finished with amusement. "Or
sweep the damsel off hers."

Maurice's jaw clenched. "But only after he—they—have resolved some
tough issues."

"Which, of course, they will—as always."

Maurice glanced at the notebook screen while thinking of the paral-
lels to his real life. Was Alexis thinking the same thoughts?

"From what I've read thus far," she told him, "I really think you need
to work on Erica's character a bit, hon. She needs to be *less* polished and
independent-minded to be believable."

He eyed Alexis. "You mean more down to earth?"

She nodded. "It's fiction, but you don't want her to be too artificial or unreal—you know what I'm saying?"

Maurice wondered if she were referring to the character or Conneca. He settled upon the character, as there was nothing he could see about Conneca that was artificial or unreal. The sister was everything good and right, from where he sat.

Nonetheless, Maurice realized that Alexis was right to an extent. His objectivity had been compromised somewhat in seeing Erica Kinkaid clearly. That was where Alex always seemed to come in handy. Her insight and grounded nature helped keep him on the straight and narrow in writing.

And their books continually on the bestseller lists.

What more could he ask for as a writer?

Not too damned much, Maurice conceded. But there was certainly more he could ask for as a man. One very lovely, sexy lady came to mind.

"I'll work on it," he promised Alexis, studying the newly created words on the screen.

Alexis moved to the side of the table. "You like her, don't you?"

Maurice faced his ex-wife. He briefly thought of evading the question, but saw no reason to. After all, their romantic relationship had been over for some time now. And neither of them were foolish enough to think it could ever get back on track.

"Yeah, I do," he said.

She gave a hint of a smile. "Figured as much. Especially after I saw how lovely Conneca was. I take it the feelings are mutual—even if she did a good job to suggest otherwise?"

Maurice was thoughtful. "I'm not so sure," he had to confess. "We've run into a rough stretch at the moment." That was putting it mildly. "It's that men-from-Jupiter, women-from-Pluto type thing."

"Well, I think I know a little bit about that," Alexis said contemplatively.

Maurice crinkled his eyes at her. "Yeah, I'm sure you do."

"But that's over and done with, as far as you and I go," she uttered steadfastly. "Both of us may be a little wiser since."

"Yes, a little," he agreed.

Alexis frowned. "I know it hasn't always been easy being around each other as ex-husband and wife," she said. "Heaven knows that sometimes the tension has been thick enough to slice with a sword. But I'm not your adversary, Maurice, and I never will be. I really do want you to be happy, and not just as part of the hottest African-American novel writing tandem around. Even if that happiness is with a woman in Oak Cliffs."

"I want the same for you, Alex," Maurice told her, moved by the sincerity in her words. "You deserve someone who will make you happy."

"I know, hon." She kissed the top of his head. "My advice to you is don't let Conneca get away, if she's what you truly want."

"Easier said than done," he muttered, knowing Conneca had rebuffed his efforts to close the gap.

Alexis folded her arms like a parent disappointed in her child. "And since when has difficult ever stopped you, Maurice Templeton?"

Maurice asked himself the same question. Only he wasn't so sure if the difficulty was more with him or Conneca. Or, for that matter, if there was room in either of their lives for compromise.

CHAPTER 31

That evening, Conneca did her usual helping out in all areas of the inn, determined to keep it running as smoothly as possible. Besides, keeping busy was just what she needed to avoid thinking about Maurice. And Alexis.

Though they were no longer married in the technical sense, Conneca wondered if Maurice and Alexis weren't still meant for each other in many respects. Perhaps the collaboration was their way of holding onto each other. Or keeping others from invading the inner world they had created for themselves through fiction.

Conneca did not want to spend her time musing about what might have been or harboring thoughts about what could be. She didn't want a man at the expense of her own principles and the life she'd conscientiously created. Nor did she want a relationship filled with uncertainties and too many bridges to cross. She'd been down that road one time too many. All she got out of it was a lot of pain and despair.

It was with these thoughts that Conneca made a decision that seemed wise. If not, she was prepared to live with the consequences, hard as they might be.

"I think I'll ask Maurice to leave the inn," she told Nadine in the office. "Assuming he wasn't prepared to anytime soon."

They had been working on the food budget for the next month, avoiding any mention of Maurice as if the scum of the earth. Or like the man was the devil in camouflage. Conneca rejected these notions, but still felt just as strongly about her position.

Nadine tilted her head. "It's probably best all the way around," she agreed. "Even if he's not sleeping with Alexis, there's still something about Maurice that makes me believe he'll never be totally reliable and trustworthy. You deserve better than that."

Conneca was inclined to agree. What worried her was that she was not sure there would ever be anyone better for her than Maurice Templeton. *The man is definitely a very tough act to follow,* she thought.

"Besides, it's not as if you're so hard up that you need the money he paid for the room in advance," Nadine said. "Business is not *that* bad."

"It's not about business," Conneca pointed out, fully prepared to refund Maurice the difference on his prepayment. "It's about what's right," she said bluntly. "And more importantly, what isn't!"

Conneca told herself that the sooner Maurice was far away, the sooner she could still the erratic pattering of her heart and regain control of her unstable equilibrium, which she blamed him for.

"Maybe Maurice and Alexis weren't really meant for each other either," Nadine suggested. "I mean, some brothers are simply too into themselves to want to relinquish enough of that to a woman to make a relationship work. Maurice may fall into that category. In which case, I reiterate that you're better off without him."

Am I really? Doubts rang in Conneca's head like alarm bells. Would her life truly be better had she never laid eyes on Maurice Templeton? Or would she have simply missed out on a brief romance that, in spite of everything else, Conneca would cherish for the rest of her life?

"Don't look now," hissed Nadine, "but I think we have company. Or should I say *you* do?"

Maurice's solid frame stood tall in the doorway.

"Lee told me where to find you," he said, his voice lowered conspiratorially.

"I'll have to be sure to talk to him about that," Conneca responded offhandedly, though she knew that Lee meant well.

Nadine made a coughing sound. "Are you going to be all right?" she asked Conneca doubtfully.

"I'll be fine." She gave Maurice a hard glance.

"Then I suppose I'd better get back to the kitchen before all hell breaks loose." Nadine looked at Maurice with narrowed eyes, and then left the office.

"Appears as if I've lost a big fan," Maurice moaned humbly.

"She's only looking out for my best interests." Conneca sat stiffly.

"And I commend her for that. In fact, from what I've seen around here, everyone looks out for each other."

Just who are you looking out for? Conneca wondered. *Other than yourself. And maybe Alexis. Along with your writing interests.* She doubted it was her.

"I'm really busy, Maurice," Conneca said tersely. "If there was something you came to say . . ."

"There is." Maurice walked up to her desk and looked Conneca squarely in the eye, then said straightforwardly: "I'm in love with you, Conneca."

The words stunned Conneca; she never saw them coming. She was thankful she was sitting down, otherwise the shock might surely have bowled her over. It took Conneca a moment or two to calm herself before she could speak.

"I want you to l-leave the inn," she stammered, as if his words had gone in one ear and out the other.

Maurice furrowed his brow and took a sharp breath. "Did you hear what I just said? *I love you*, Conneca Sheridan!"

"I heard," she murmured with difficulty.

The words were like sweet music to Conneca's ears, and matched her own thoughts toward Maurice. But she was not convinced she was hearing what really came from his heart and soul. Was he making a last-ditch effort to salvage whatever existed between them by telling her what she so desperately wanted to hear? *Or does he truly love me in every sense of the word?*

"Well?" Maurice said flatly.

Conneca turned away from his gaze. "Don't do this, Maurice—"

"Do what?" His voice sounded totally perplexed.

She faced him. "Don't say what you don't mean."

"I never do," he insisted. "My problem has been *not* saying what I really felt. Now I am."

Conneca desperately wanted to believe him. But, even if she did, there were still major hurdles that stood between them like a concrete wall. She doubted that love alone could conquer the serious differences their lives entailed. She feared she didn't have the courage or wherewithal to try and make what, at times, seemed like insurmountable obstacles diminish into something workable.

"I'm afraid it's too late, Maurice," Conneca said so softly that she wasn't sure if he'd heard. Raising her voice she said, "Even if it is love you feel for me, this just isn't meant to be. We live in two completely different worlds and are seemingly better off on our own."

Maurice sighed. "We live in *one* world, Conneca," he countered brusquely. "What we do in it is entirely up to us! This is our chance to take a leap of faith, in each other. Give us that opportunity."

Conneca steadied her hands against her lap. "I can't play second fiddle to your writing career," she said shakily. "Or live life in the fast lane. I've been there, done that and vowed to never do it again."

"I don't want you to play second fiddle to anything or anyone," Maurice argued. "You'll take center stage in my life, as I hope to in yours. I realize now that it's you I belong with, baby, regardless of where we've come from and where we're going. And I know deep down inside you feel the same way."

Conneca could hardly argue the point, conceding that it was true. But was that enough for either of them?

Looking at his face, Conneca offered weakly, "Doesn't really matter what I feel, Maurice. I'd rather not go down that path again where I can't be sure of the outcome. It would be too devastating to me if we failed." Her voice faltered. "It won't work between us, I'm sorry—"

"We can make it work, Conneca." Maurice leaned over her. She could smell the Obsession cologne he wore, making him all the more irresistible. And her decision that much harder.

"Maybe in your novel we could," she told him soberly. "But not in real life, where the complications and divisions can't be so easily overcome."

Maurice pursed his lips. "Just tell me you don't love me, Conneca, and I'll walk away."

Oh yes, I do love you, darling, with all my heart, Conneca told herself. She'd known that for some time now. Like she had loved no other. Yet fear that she might live to regret those powerful words if she ever said them aloud kept Conneca's emotions in check.

"I don't love you, Maurice," she told him, forcing herself to meet head-on the hard gaze he laid upon her like a whip. "What we had was fun and enjoyable, but it was never meant to last. I think we both know that now. Let's just leave it at that."

Maurice's nostrils ballooned but he remained speechless, as if at a loss for words. "Looks like a *complete* role reversal here," he muttered. "Interesting. If this is to get back at me for putting you through more than I should have, you've succeeded, Conneca. I'm man enough to admit when I've been a damned fool. Are you woman enough to admit it?"

Conneca clamped her teeth onto her lower lip. "I'm not a damned fool," she shot back austerely. "Forgive me for having the courage to tell the great author Maurice Templeton precisely how I feel. I'm sorry if it's too much for your ego to handle." She turned away from him, lest she lose her resolve altogether. "I think it's best if you and Alexis leave the inn as soon as you can make arrangements to stay elsewhere. Or return to Denver."

Maurice drew in a ragged breath. "Are you sure about this?" he challenged her angrily. "Because once I walk out that door there will be no turning back—for us."

She had never been so unsure, Conneca knew in her heart and soul. Yet she truly believed it was the right thing to do. He and Alexis were a team, professionally if not personally. Trying to turn it into a threesome seemed like a perfect recipe for failure all the way around, even if Maurice could not see it. Perhaps Alexis couldn't see it either.

In her way of thinking, Conneca feared that a relationship with Maurice at this point in their lives might only bring about resentment and hostilities that could carry on well into the future. She could even imagine the quality of Alexis Maurice writings suffering, were Maurice to devote too much of his time elsewhere. Such as with her.

Conneca wanted no part of what she could not control. *This I can control.*

After sucking in a deep breath, Conneca gave Maurice the benefit of her watery eyes, and said in a deceptively calm voice, "I'm very sure this is what I want."

Maurice's face darkened with fury. "Then so be it! Alexis and I will be checking out first thing in the morning—if that's all right with you?"

Her inflection brittle, Conneca managed to say, "First thing in the morning will be fine."

She felt the sting of his look for a long moment before Maurice stormed out of the office.

Tears flowed out of Conneca's eyes in buckets and her heart filled with sadness. Never before had she felt so alone. So empty. So disillusioned with regrets and second thoughts.

Part of Conneca wanted to run after Maurice, say she had made a mistake, accept his love, and declare her own undying love. But that part must stay hidden forever.

This is the way it has to be for my sense of well-being and stability, Conneca thought.

What other choice did she truly have?

CHAPTER 32

Maurice stayed up all night finishing the novel. It was the only thing he could do to keep from going completely insane. He was sure he had done the job in intermixing the characters and plot superbly. Aaron and Erica had passed the test and would live to see another day.

But what about me? Maurice mused. *How are my days going to be spent without Conneca Sheridan in my life?*

He had shared what he felt inside with her like Maurice had never done before with a woman. He had given Conneca his heart and willingly expressed his love for. It had not been nearly as hard to do as he had imagined, because Maurice knew it was Conneca that he belonged with. He probably understood it from the moment his eyes first made contact with her beautiful face, but just needed time for it to register in his brain and body.

Only Maurice hadn't counted on Conneca breaking his heart by dismissing his love as if insignificant. Not even allowing him the chance to prove it to her. He was certain that she felt the same love for him, but Conneca was too afraid to admit it even to herself. As if to do so would shatter the wall she'd built around herself to keep from being hurt.

Maurice suspected that his own success as a writer might have also proven to be his albatross as a man, as far as Conneca was concerned. The notion of building a life with him and all that came with the package, including his collaboration with Alexis, may have been more than Conneca believed she could handle.

And who the hell am I to say any differently? Maurice asked himself. Maybe she could see the future better than he could? Then again, just maybe Conneca was too blinded by the past to be able to see that far ahead. Maybe she was too unwilling to take a chance on happiness. To take a chance on him.

What could he do now that he had come to terms with his own emotions? Maurice contemplated this very notion while looking at the blank computer screen. He could not force Conneca to see things his way or make himself fall out of love with her.

The thought of never making love to Conneca Sheridan again, receiving and giving her love and devotion, seeing her smile, and even the tantalizing smell of the woman was excruciating to Maurice.

Worse would be to torture himself for not handling things in a different way from the start. If he had been in touch with his feelings then as Maurice was now, it might have worked out between him and Conneca.

But would've, could've, should've would not change a damned thing, Maurice reflected painfully. He couldn't go back and right his wrongs. Or make Conneca see things his way. She had made her decision and he would have to live with it like a man and move on. He would not remain where he was not wanted. Or pine for a woman who—if she was to be believed—did not want him in her life. He had too much self-respect for that.

Even with this realization, Maurice felt depressed and lonely like never before. He knew now that all the success in the world meant absolutely nothing, if there was no one to share it with on an intimate level. Someone he could spend the rest of his days with, treasuring each other.

And there was not a soul Maurice could imagine who fit the bill more than Conneca Sheridan. If only she were willing.

Maurice knocked hard on the door.

He heard some shuffling inside, then a voice yell hoarsely: "Just a minute!"

When the door opened, Alexis stood there, sleepy-eyed, bundled in an ankle-length crimson cashmere robe. Maurice walked past her, resisting the desire to yawn. He faced his co-writer and ex-wife.

"What time is it?" she whined drowsily.

"Seven a.m.," Maurice said matter-of-factly. He made sure she saw the diskette in his hand.

Alexis favored him, mouth open. "Have you been up *all* night?"

He nodded, exhausted. "It's done."

"Wonderful!" She broke into a laugh, hugging him. "I'm sure you did a great job putting the final pieces together like the director of a movie on the silver screen. And, with any luck, that's precisely where this one will end up. I'll read and start editing it while you go get some sleep."

"You can do that when we get back to Denver," Maurice stated tightly. "Pack your bags. I've booked us a flight out this morning."

Alexis cocked a brow. "Why so early?"

"Why not?" He pointed his eyes at her, not really in the mood to talk about it. "I only stayed here to wrap up the novel. Now that I'm through, I can see no reason to stay."

"I can think of *one* reason," Alexis said tentatively. "Conneca Sheridan . . ."

Maurice reacted, but was unable to speak. Indeed, Conneca was more than reason enough to stay. As well as leave.

Alexis ran fingers through her tousled hair. "So what happened between you two, Maurice?"

He twisted his lips thoughtfully. "That's just it," he grumbled, "absolutely nothing is happening between us."

"And why is that?" she questioned.

Maurice swallowed. "We've decided it's best that we go our separate ways. End of story."

"I see," Alexis said, not content to leave well enough alone. "Would you like me to talk to Conneca? We seemed to hit it off, after a rocky start."

If he thought it would make any difference Maurice might have said hell yes. As it was, he didn't believe that Alexis's excellent negotiating skills were enough in this instance. Conneca's mind seemed to be set in stone, and he had to accept that for what it was worth.

"Thanks," Maurice replied lowly. "But there's nothing left to talk about."

Alexis seemed to think otherwise, but wisely did not argue the point. "If you say so," she said calmly. "I can be ready in thirty minutes."

And not a minute too soon, Maurice thought. He was afraid if he delayed his departure from this town any longer, he might not have the will to leave behind the woman he was more than willing to devote his life and love to.

CHAPTER 33

Lee was at the front desk when Maurice and Alexis came down to check out. This suited Maurice just fine since he couldn't bear to see Conneca there, knowing it was killing him to be leaving her inn for good. Not to mention the lady herself. It was best that they had said their good-byes, in effect, last night.

"I'll wait outside," Alexis suggested, having paid for her room.

"I won't be long." Maurice watched her walk away, wishing with all his heart that she was going back to Denver alone. And that he was staying to rediscover the magic that he and Conneca shared.

"Hope you had a pleasant stay, Mr. Templeton." Lee spoke stiffly, as if they were suddenly strangers again.

Maurice noticed. He wasn't surprised that he was being given the cold shoulder by much of the staff. They must have felt he had taken advantage of their boss and was now abandoning her. If they only knew the truth. But why should he tell them anything Conneca preferred not to?

"It could have been better, Lee," he was willing to admit, adding, "But the visit did have its moments."

"Yes, I'm sure of that." Lee lifted Maurice's room key. "If I may say, Conneca is a very good catch for the *right* man. I was honestly hoping that might have been you, brother."

It crushed Maurice that it wasn't to be him. Damn her, he thought. And damn himself for waiting too long to make his move. "Some things don't work out the way we plan," he muttered.

"Seems that way." Lee looked at the computer screen. "Did you have any charges to your room since last night?"

"None." Maurice looked around. The place that had seemed so warm suddenly felt frigid to him, like being at the North Pole.

Lee gave him a narrow eye. "I'll need your credit card to make the adjustments since there's still more than two weeks left on your prepaid reservation. Should be no problem filling the room."

"Keep the charges as is," Maurice said laconically. "Who knows, maybe I'll return in time to use what's left of my reservation."

If only that were true, he thought, doubting it to be the case. Maurice had a strong sense that this was the last he would ever see of the Sheridan Seaside Inn.

Lee handed him a receipt. "Good luck with your writing, Maurice." He set his jaw. "I'll be sure and tell Conneca you said good-bye, assuming that was somehow lost in the shuffle."

"Don't bother," Maurice voiced tonelessly. "I think it's better if it goes without saying." He reached into a side pocket of his bag and removed a small envelope, sliding it across the counter. "But you can do me a favor. Give this to Conneca."

Lee studied the envelope as though a foreign object. "What is it?"

"A going-away present," Maurice said simply.

Lee gave a slow nod. "No problem. I'll make certain she gets it."

Maurice afforded him a respectful gaze. "Take good care of her, Lee."

Lee seemed moved by the words. "I'll do my best." He suddenly reached out to shake Maurice's hand. "You would probably do better in that capacity," he said frankly.

"Not so sure about that," Maurice grumbled sadly. "I certainly haven't made a very good impression on Conneca. And doubt that I ever will, at least so that it means something."

Maurice sensed that Lee would, in fact, always be there for her in a fatherly way. But he also realized that it couldn't begin to compensate for Conneca being taken care of by a man who could love her romantically and intimately. He would never get the chance to prove to Conneca that *he* could be that man.

Grabbing his bag, Maurice headed for the exit. At the last moment he took one last look at the place he had called home approaching two weeks. Though it had seemed like months. Even years. He would surely miss it.

But not half as much as he would miss Conneca Sheridan.

Maurice walked out the door without looking back.

"He left this for you," Lee told Conneca when she came down that morning.

"Who?"

"Mr. Templeton . . . Maurice." A frown wrinkled Lee's face. "He and his lady partner checked out this morning."

"Oh," Conneca said with nonchalance. Inside a deep pain of regret flowed through her veins like a toxic substance, though she knew Maurice was only following her demands. It would have happened sooner or later anyway, she realized, and would not have been any easier to stomach. Maurice and Alexis were going back to the world to which they belonged, and their successful writing career.

Whereas she was returning to the life Conneca had been basically happy with until Maurice had shown up. Like it or not, he had entered her life in ways she could never have dreamed little more than a week ago. And things would never be quite the same again. *I'll just have to live with that*, she thought glumly.

Conneca examined the five-by-seven yellow envelope. By the feel of it, she could tell that it held a diskette.

It was Maurice's book, Conneca was certain. Or at least part of it. He had finished the ending after all. And he must have kept the character patterned after her, she suspected, even if their relationship had ended on a sour note. It made her feel a little guilty, but still certain she had made the right choice in letting Maurice go.

Conneca looked at Lee curiously. "Did Maurice leave a message . . . or anything?"

Lee offered her a look of regret. "No message, I'm afraid."

That's no surprise, Conneca thought. After all, what was left to say that hadn't already been said?

Lee raised his brows. "Wait . . . come to think of it, Maurice did tell me to take good care of you. I promised I would, till someone more capable came along."

Conneca felt warm all over. Part of it was the notion of someone— maybe Maurice in another lifetime—taking the reins in caring for her emotional and physical needs, if not financial ones. The other part was for dear Lee always being her Rock of Gibraltar, in sunshine and stormy weather. Not to mention frustration, hurt, and lost love.

She smiled gratefully at him. "Thank you, Lee."

He put a hand on hers. "Things will work themselves out, Conneca," he promised. "They usually do."

"I'm not so sure that will be the case this time," she told him sullenly. "Some things are simply not meant to work themselves out."

"You're a strong woman, Conneca." Lee fixed her. "You'll get over this, over him . . . and move on."

Will I?

Can I ever get over Maurice Templeton? Conneca asked herself. Or would he leave an indelible mark on her that would curse all other men who entered her life?

"As usual, Lee, you know just the right things to say." Conneca squeezed his hand, while cradling the envelope to her chest. "I'll put this away and be right back."

"Take your time," Lee told her. "Althea's manning the front desk, and things seem to be slow this morning."

Conneca curled her nose. "I'm not sure I like the part of that statement about things being slow. The last thing we need is an empty inn."

"It won't be for long," Lee promised. "This evening we have a busload of folks coming in from Seattle. The place is sure to be lively and full!"

"Excellent!" Conneca beamed. That was just what she wanted to hear. Now she could look forward to focusing her attention on running an inn and making the guests want to come back.

At the moment, Conneca found she was overwhelmingly excited at the thought of reading the manuscript on diskette Maurice had left her. She wondered what changes, if any, had come about in the character of Erica Kinkaid? And what about Aaron Sinclair?

Will I like the story? Conneca mused. Or regret having ever met the writing team of Alexis Maurice?

CHAPTER 34

The United flight to Denver was encountering turbulence, but it was nothing to be alarmed about, the pilot assured everyone over the intercom. Seated in first class, Maurice looked out the window and saw nothing but clouds. Yet through the clouds he could see Conneca's face. It was cheerful, beautiful, and melancholy all at once. He wondered what he had done to her self-esteem and psyche by entering her life so abruptly and leaving it the same way—albeit the latter was her choice and not his.

Could he ever forgive himself for proving to be far less skilled in romancing a woman than writing romantic suspense novels? When all was said and done, would Conneca come to see him as being no better than the previous men who had betrayed her trust, abused her affections, and were unable to express themselves adequately and in a timely fashion?

I'd hate for Conneca to lump us all in one pool of despicable and forgettable men, Maurice grumbled to himself. *I'm a hell of a lot better than that, even if I never got to show it.*

"Do you see anything out there?" Alexis asked, slightly alarmed.

Maurice glanced at her sitting beside him, realizing that Alexis had a fear of flying in spite of taking more than her fair share of flights. "Nothing to be concerned about," he promised.

"Well, that's a relief." She batted her eyelashes. "I'd hate to think that after all the flights we've taken, this one would turn out to be our last."

"If that were the case," Maurice said logically, noting their current elevation, "believe me, we'd never know what hit us."

Or remember what they'd found, he thought maudlinly. And lost.

"But we would let a lot of people down." Alexis frowned while sipping on a cocktail. "We have a number of social and professional engagements awaiting us when we get back. There are book signings, radio interviews, photo sessions, banquets—not to mention getting *A Woman To Die For* sent off to the publisher at long last."

A life every writer dreamed of, Maurice thought wryly. Only it was not all it was cracked up to be. Not by a long shot. He recalled an old adage that writing was the world's loneliest profession. He would attest to that, as he had never felt more lonely and alone than he did right now.

He had spent years trying to understand Alexis, to no avail. Now Maurice found himself even more perplexed about Conneca. Why hadn't he been able to get through to her when the opportunity presented itself? What had she expected of him? He really didn't know if there was anything that would have made a difference.

Maurice put the glass of white wine to his lips. "Don't worry about us letting anyone down," he muttered to Alexis. "We always manage to meet our social and professional obligations, don't we?"

Alexis curved the corners of her lips upward. "I suppose that's why we work so well together, baby. We do what we need to in order to keep everyone happy."

Everyone, that is, but each other, Maurice thought. He wondered if they would ever be able to put their own happiness ahead of everyone else's for once. He had tried to and failed miserably. Was that to be the story of his damned life—one bad choice in a woman after another? Or would he someday come up with the answer that would make his life truly worthwhile and satisfying?

Maurice turned toward the window and realized he was moving farther and farther away from Conneca and the world she lived in. He would give anything if she were the one sitting next to him now and they were flying off to paradise somewhere.

But, he knew sadly, it was not to be.

The pages flowed like running water. Maurice had left Conneca the entire novel on disk, and it had mesmerized her. His gift for words and creativity shone like polished brass. The characters were at once three-dimensional, complex, charming, and quite convincing. The handsome African-American protagonist, Aaron Sinclair, managed to be both original and a hero for the ages. Like Don Juan, he masterfully weaved his way through a series of adventures, dangers, and women, before Erica Kinkaid entered his life and turned it upside down.

Erica was not only beautiful and feminine, with a butterscotch skin tone that had the other women drooling with envy, but she was smart, sexy, sensual, strong-willed, calculating, and every bit as resilient as Aaron.

The two understood their differences and fought through them, while reveling in their similarities. They truly belonged together, Conneca thought, stealing each other's hearts and affections while claiming true and undivided love.

Conneca trembled as she read through their courtship, and realized that Erica was remarkably a composite of her own life—dramatized and exaggerated, but still essentially her. Maurice had given her the gift of immortality and captured all her emotions, strengths, and weaknesses in the character. Even the inn had been well-represented and filled with such passion and intrigue that Conneca was on the edge of her seat from page to page, as if she had been transported to this fictional world.

In the end, Aaron and Erica survived those who sought to harm them, as well as the inner conflicts that had tested their resolve and love.

Conneca felt a shiver, as she scrolled down past the last paragraph of the book and saw that Maurice had left her a personal message. It read:

> *Conneca . . . Hope this unedited but basically solid story meets with your approval. I owe you more than I can possibly repay in giving me the inspiration and motivation to complete the book. Sorry if I disappointed you in the end. I never meant for things to heat up between us, and then chill out as they did. I certainly had no preconception that I would fall in love with you and maybe have that love returned on some level, even if you spoke to the contrary. But then, life isn't always as predictable as it is in a novel or as fulfilling at the end of the day and night. Hope you eventually find a man who meets your expectations in all respects. A man who earns your love, trust, and admiration. Obviously, I fell short of this, much to my chagrin. Best of luck in your life . . . Maurice.*

Tears flowed from Conneca's eyes almost uncontrollably as she read the words again. No matter what she may have tried to tell herself, she was very much in love with Maurice Templeton and doubted she would ever feel the same way about a man again. But that was little consolation for the pain Conneca felt. She had sacrificed that love out of fear that it would not lead to a happy conclusion, leaving her with even more heartache and regret.

Conneca had had her fill of men who thrived on empty promises, sweet words, and good looks. She simply didn't want to be caught up in the undertow of powerful love and unwavering devotion only to be devastated again.

Surely Maurice must have understood that, she thought. Neither of them could realistically be expected to give up the lives they'd made for the other. It wouldn't be fair to either of them. Anything less would fall far short of the happiness Conneca sought this time around in a relationship where they were equals and equally considerate of one another's feelings and situations. She would be better off going it alone than having only a part-time, divided romance.

If only their circumstances had been different, Conneca thought tearfully. More favorable to her and Maurice making a life together.

But fate had another plan. To Conneca this was the greatest tragedy of all.

CHAPTER 35

Maurice arrived home to his cold and empty apartment overlooking downtown Denver. It was the penthouse of a luxury high-rise, and offered him everything a person could want in a place—including more rooms than he could use, bamboo flooring, African and Italian furnishings, and top-of-the-line appliances, lighting, and electronics. He had used some of his portion of their royalties to invest in the property, figuring it to be a security blanket.

Now Maurice wondered if he hadn't made a mistake, as he looked out the arched windows in the living room. He seemed to see everything in view, but felt only emptiness. No longer did this seem like home. It was missing the warmth and tenderness of a woman's presence.

One woman in particular.

Maurice tried to imagine Conneca being there to bring life to the place, as only she could. He knew that it was merely a pipe dream. Their time together was over, whether or not he wished otherwise. Instead, it would be him alone occupying the space within these walls.

Maurice had hoped to have a family once upon a time. It had not worked out with Alexis. In the back of his mind he had believed that it could still happen, were he ever to settle down with the love of his life. Now, fearing the window of opportunity may have been shut for good, Maurice resigned himself to having to settle for these he visited during charity work around the city and elsewhere as his extended if not real family.

The door buzzed, seemingly echoing throughout the apartment.

Maurice walked across the room and down a long hall towards the vestibule. He was expecting Alexis. They were to go out for dinner to celebrate the completion of *A Woman To Die For*. His heart wasn't in it, but since he had nowhere else to go, he only wanted to try and get back some semblance of normalcy in his life. This seemed the best way to circumvent what was forever etched in his mind: Conneca Sheridan.

He opened the door.

"Hey, hon," Alexis said unenthusiastically, walking in.

"Hello, Alex," Maurice told her, watching as she strode by, dressed to the nines. Beneath her open wool red gabardine coat, she had on a mulberry knot-front dress and black high-heeled mules. Ruby earrings and a coal-crimson choker complemented her fine-boned face and full red lips. "Are you ready to go?" he asked rhetorically since the answer was obvious.

Without looking directly at Maurice in his Jos. A. Bank gray plaid suit, Alexis said unevenly, "I think so."

Maurice detected something strange in her disposition. Alexis refused to meet his eyes, as if to do so would break her in two.

"What's going on, Alex?"

Alexis sucked in a deep breath, holding it for a moment or two, as if under water. "Well, I've been thinking," she uttered with a catch in her voice.

"About what?" Maurice raised his brows, the suspense killing him.

Her gaze centered on him. "About *this*—you and me," she said tersely.

"I don't understand," he said, befuddled.

"Don't you see, Maurice—you should be back in Oak Cliffs, celebrating with the woman you're in love with," Alexis said bluntly. "And me . . . well, the truth is, I've met someone too that I see some great potential with. There's no reason why either of us should be held back from getting on with our lives because of the writing. Who says we can't find new loves, while keeping the writing collaboration going strong at the same time?"

Maurice looked at her with surprise. He hadn't realized she had been seeing someone—at least not seriously. Not that it should have been that much of a shock, he thought. Alexis was, after all, still very striking, and was not one to settle for being alone.

Trouble was, Maurice was not nearly as confident as she was that Oak Cliffs was where he belonged. Would Conneca actually welcome him back with open arms? Or would she tell him in no uncertain terms to take his black ass back to Denver . . . and his dreams with it?

Maurice sighed, having second thoughts about everything. "Maybe you're right, Alex," he told her. "Could be that we've both lost sight along the way of what's really important in life."

"I know I have," Alexis said reminiscently. "For far too long. Can't change the past, but I can do something about the here and now. We both can—especially when opportunity is staring us in the face."

Maurice grinned, realizing that Alexis wasn't quite the self-centered, head-in-the-clouds woman he'd long painted her to be. "What about the dinner celebration?" he asked.

"We can save it till the book is published, honey."

Maurice actually began to feel that maybe the future was not so hopeless after all. Or even, he dared believe, the present.

"It's a deal," he said, buoyant as though he had a reason to be.

Alexis hugged Maurice, whispering in his ear, "I messed up, I know. Maybe we can *both* learn from our mistakes the second time around— and do it right from the beginning."

"I really hope so," Maurice choked out the words. He was happy for Alexis and whatever her prospects were romantically and otherwise.

As for himself and second chances, the outcome was still very uncertain. But he was certainly willing to try and make things happen, and let the chips fall where they may.

Thoughts of Conneca and children—*their* children—suddenly filled Maurice's head like a bright light.

All of a sudden the future looked brighter than it ever had before.

Now all he had to do was convince Conneca of that.

Conneca spent a rare day off from the inn at a local elementary school, where she read a Dr. Seuss book to children. Not only was it a great way to contribute to children's literacy, but it also helped mitigate the reality that she would probably wind up childless.

And without a man to share her joys and sorrows with—a man who would also be the father of her children.

Conneca felt thankful that, at least she had her health, and people who loved her almost as if they were family.

She also had the inn which, though hardly bringing in a king's ransom, kept her busy and should be able to support her simple existence for years to come. For that she was grateful, well-aware that so many had far less.

Yet another voice in Conneca's head reminded her that so many others had far *more*. Why couldn't she? As usual, she resigned herself to believe that it just wasn't in the cards or stars.

Conneca was patient as she read aloud for all to hear. The children seemed genuinely taken with her as much as the story, crowding around her like elves. Some even found the courage to touch her long braids that were hanging down to one side. Out of plain curiosity. Or perhaps unadulterated affection. It reminded Conneca of her own youth and the joy she received from others reading the popular Dr. Seuss books.

Earlier Conneca had donated half of the fifty thousand dollars Maurice had given her to the Oak Cliffs School District. The money would go a long way toward purchasing new books, school supplies, and computers. The other half had gone to programs to feed and provide shelter for the homeless. The money was perhaps the one thing Maurice had left behind that truly meant something special to Conneca. She pushed further back in her mind the special memories of the man himself.

By the time she finished reading, even the teacher was applauding Conneca for doing a terrific job, and invited her back whenever she wanted to visit. The children were in full accord.

Conneca, feeling uplifted as well, promised to do just that.

Returning to the inn, Conneca was satisfied that she had spent her time off in helping children to improve their reading skills. Now all she wanted was to take a long hot shower and have some tea. She might even watch some television, which usually was limited to catching the news, old movie classics, and Oregon Public Broadcasting programs.

Conneca went straight to her room, wanting to prove to the staff that she didn't feel the need to be looking over their shoulders twenty-four hours a day like a mother hen. She noted that her door was slightly ajar, as if she had forgotten to close it or someone else had.

Conneca didn't see the housekeeper's cart, but guessed that one of the staff had cleaned the room and thought she had pulled the door shut. Sometimes the wind played havoc on the door's ability to latch properly, she knew.

Nevertheless, Conneca pushed open the door with caution. Oak Cliffs had a relatively low crime rate compared to big cities. However there had been some local burglaries of late, usually by juveniles for kicks or drug users seeking anything of value to help support their habit. She hoped the inn had not been targeted or her specifically.

There was nothing unusual that Conneca spied at first glance. And the room did appear to have been cleaned.

She breathed a sigh of relief. *Don't get paranoid, girl,* she told herself. *Next thing you'll be seeing ghosts and goblins.*

Conneca locked the door behind her just to be on the safe side. Kicking off her loafers, she entered the breakfast nook, and nearly had a heart attack. Sitting at the table, as if invited for toast, eggs, and bacon, was Maurice Templeton!

CHAPTER 36

"**W**hat are you doing here?" was Conneca's immediate vocal reaction, not even allowing herself time to think.

"I came to see you." Maurice's voice was remarkably calm under the circumstances. "Sorry if I scared you half to death. I had hoped the message I left you at the front desk might tip your hand that you had a visitor."

"What message?" Conneca flashed him a disbelieving glare.

"I left it with Lee." He frowned. "Evidently you didn't get it?"

Admittedly she hadn't gone to the front desk or her office before coming up. That didn't alter the fact that he was in her suite. She had assumed he had gone back to Denver, which was obviously a false assumption. Wasn't it?

Conneca's gaze was still hard as she tried to gather her equilibrium. "Who let you in?" *I'll fire her for sure*, she thought.

"I borrowed one of the housekeeper's keys," Maurice confessed. He stood tall in a heather gray Polo shirt, charcoal linen pants, and merlot Oxfords.

Why? Conneca wondered haughtily. She didn't appreciate this shock one bit. Especially from a man she thought she had seen for the last time.

It had been a week since he and Alexis had checked out of the inn. Had they remained in Oak Cliffs all this time? Or had Maurice returned alone?

Again the question was why, Conneca mused uneasily. Was he here somehow expecting her to simply melt into his arms? Forgetting all else that led to their breakup?

Conneca sneered, fighting the powerful effect Maurice still had on her and probably always would. "Please leave the way you came in, Maurice," she said firmly. "I don't think we have anything more to say."

Maurice stepped closer, tentatively. "Yes, we do." He sighed, moving even closer to Conneca so that she could feel his warm breath. "I do . . . "

Before she could protest, he kissed her on the mouth. Conneca wanted to pull away, but the potency of the kiss, of the man, left her virtually helpless to resist. This, in spite of her reservations about him. Them. Which conflicted with the other emotions she knew were there in full force.

It was Maurice who stopped the kiss. Looking deeply in Conneca's eyes, he said straightforwardly, "I'm in love with you, Conneca Sheridan, and I know you love me too."

Conneca caught her breath. Without denying it, she stammered, "We've already been over all this, Maurice. I—"

"Not quite," he interposed. "We never discussed the part about I want nothing more than to spend the rest of my life with you, Conneca. All I'm asking is that you give us a chance at the true happiness that seems to have eluded us both to this point in our lives. I promise you won't regret it."

Conneca was speechless. He was telling her precisely what she needed to hear from a man—this man. And she had heard him with all her heart. Yet there was still hesitancy on her part.

"Where's Alexis?" she asked, aware that they checked out together. *Is she lurking around the corner, waiting to make her grand entrance?* Conneca couldn't help but wonder.

"In Denver," Maurice replied equably, "which is where I was till a few hours ago. Alex was the one who talked me into my senses about us. I realized then that if you weren't worth fighting for, I didn't know what or who the hell was."

"What about your collaboration?" Conneca looked into his face with concern. Had he sacrificed their successful novels in the process of coming after her? This was something Conneca could not accept, only to haunt them both later.

Maurice licked his lips. "Neither of us sees any reason why we can't still continue to work together on a professional level," he said confidently. "Alexis didn't want to end it, and I didn't either. But neither of us could pretend any longer that our social lives weren't in major need of repair, even if it was at the expense of the writing. She had her answer in a man who used to play ball for the Denver Nuggets, but now makes a good living as a financial planner. I found mine in a quiet little inn in the Pacific Northwest, owned and operated by a gorgeous, one-of-a-kind lady."

Maurice held Conneca's hands. She took in his handsome features up close and personal, his eyes beaded on hers like beams of dark light, and immediately felt lightheaded. Her heart suddenly seemed to be pounding at warp speed.

"Tell me that you want what I do," Maurice said huskily, "and make me the happiest brother and novelist on the planet!"

Oh, I do want the same things you do with all my heart, Conneca told herself. Starting with the man himself. And for the first time she began to believe such a future was actually possible.

But there was still no talk of marriage, which concerned Conneca. Had he intended for them to spend the rest of their lives together in cohabitation? Unwed? Which probably meant childless as well. *I'm not sure that's good enough,* she thought, wanting even more from him.

"So what about the fact that I live here and you live in Denver?" Conneca's eyelids fluttered questioningly. She wasn't interested in a long-distance relationship, no matter how much they loved each other. The thought of only seeing Maurice once a month or every other month would be unbearable. Just as giving up the inn would be at this time with so much to do and so many people depending on her.

"A temporary setback," Maurice said without prelude. "I don't see why I can't move to Oak Cliffs. The Internet and the post office make it pretty simple to send files and manuscripts, no matter where you live in the country, without missing a beat. In fact, I see myself as being even more effective as a writer living here—considering that I would be happier than I've ever been in my life."

Maurice put his hands to Conneca's face and she quivered from their blistering touch. She too had never known such happiness. The mere notion thrilled her from head to toe. But she still wondered if he had a long-term plan in mind. Or was he content to take things slowly . . . one day at a time?

Conneca gazed up at Maurice. "What *exactly* do you want out of this relationship?" Her voice shook with each word.

Maurice did not waver. "To wake up each morning with you," he said fluidly. "And go to bed each night with you. To make love to you as often as time will permit. To make a life with you. To help you run this inn in a real *and* equal partnership." He paused, fixing her eyes steadily. "And to have children with you, baby—as many as we can. To love and cherish each other till death do us part and even beyond that . . ."

It was all Conneca could do to keep from screaming with sheer delight. She could feel the surge of adrenaline as her resistance melted away. Maurice had seemingly bent over backward to appease her, presenting nearly everything she could have asked for in a mate, and she loved him dearly for it.

Yet Conneca still had not heard the very words she had dreamed of for as long as she could possibly remember. Though she was certain Maurice was of the same mind as she was, it was not the same as the spoken words.

Her eyes widened at him. "Are you saying . . . ?"

Putting her hands to his chest, Maurice smiled and uttered affectionately: "I'm saying that I want to marry you, Conneca Sheridan, just as soon as possible—if you'll have me, that is?"

With tears coming out of her eyes and her mind swirling as if in a whirlwind, Conneca opened her mouth and murmured gaily, "Yes, Maurice! I'll *definitely* have you. And, yes, yes, yes, I'll marry you!"

"You will?" he asked as if to hear it again.

"Yes!" Conneca shouted the words, knowing in her heart this was right for both of them. "Only I want a great big wedding where everyone we know will be invited to share in our joining as one." She wrapped her arms tightly around his neck and began kissing his lips like a woodpecker. Her mind and body in sync, Conneca declared, unabashed, "I love you, Maurice Templeton!"

Maurice laughed. "I love you too, sweetheart. If it's a big wedding you want, it's a big wedding you'll get. We can even have two receptions. One here and one in Denver." He kissed her softly. "So long as I never have to lose sight of you as my beautiful wife and best friend."

"You won't," Conneca promised, wiping tears away.

They kissed each other again, this time passionately and full of renewed longing and unabridged joy.

"Please don't make me wait until the wedding night to have you again," Maurice pleaded. "I don't think I could bear it."

"Neither could I," Conneca uttered candidly in a raspy tone, trying to catch the breath that he had taken away, and still her overpowering desire for this man. "But could we at least wait until after I've had a shower before we do anything? When you've been working with young children as I have this afternoon, sometimes they're all over you."

Maurice chortled. "Get used to it. If I have my way, before long you'll have your own batch of little angels to drool all over you." He grazed one of her nipples deliberately, watching her react with pleasure. "Forget the shower. I want you just as you are, baby."

Conneca fell into his arms, unable to resist Maurice's remarkable powers of persuasion.

CHAPTER 37

In the shower Conneca hummed delightedly as Maurice ran the soap across her breasts, settling for a long moment on one nipple, then the next. In turn, she placed another bar across his chest, moving it around in a slow circle and watching him tremble with appeasement. She went lower, leaving a trail of lather and heat bumps. His erection throbbed and she teased it with the soap and her gentle fingers.

Conneca leaned back against the wall, closing her eyes as Maurice soap-massaged the wet curls between her thighs. Then he slid the bar into her secret garden and began to lather her there. She braced herself, holding onto his back and the shower wall as best she could.

"Oh, Maurice," Conneca intoned, soaking in the intense feelings he was reawakening in her as if she were Cinderella. Only she knew this was very much the real thing. *Cinderella never had it so good,* she thought lustfully.

Maurice moaned out something resembling Conneca's name while stimulating and being caressed by her. She opened her eyes to read the burning passion in his.

"Baby . . ." he gasped.

"Honey . . ." she cooed.

Both realized that their powerful need for each other would not wait until they made it to the bed.

Maurice brought his mouth to Conneca's and they drank in each other ravenously. He lifted her, careful to keep his footing, and brought their bodies into perfect harmony. Conneca scissored her legs across his buttocks and brought herself down to him, running watery hands across his bald head. Maurice reacted as if he had just entered a warm, friendly cave, never wanting to leave.

They began to make love in slow motion, content to savor the triumph of their togetherness for all time. Each brought into it the yearning and fulfillment that comes with loving each other to no end, with only beginnings. Conneca felt tiny vibrations jerk the lower part of her body, till the rippling effect threatened to overtake her in one all-consuming climax.

Maurice was every bit as absorbed in their lovemaking, urging himself deeper and deeper into Conneca, thrilling in her invitation and complete surrender. Perspiration intertwined with water and poured across and down them like a waterfall.

They slammed against each other like desperate lovers, intent upon achieving victory at all cost. Higher and higher they climbed, till reaching a new peak that left them moaning exuberantly and in the rarified air of sexual ecstasy.

Satisfied that they had achieved their carnal objectives beyond their wildest dreams for the moment, Conneca and Maurice cooled down with a mouthwatering kiss that left them spent and probing for the untapped treasures of each other they had yet to discover.

In bed, they picked up where they left off until there was nothing left to yearn for till another day.

Afterward, a contented Conneca chimed: "By the way, I loved your book, Maurice. Especially the ending." She remembered his heartfelt note, bringing tears once again to her eyes.

"I hoped you would." Maurice's long arms were wrapped around her like an octopus, while Conneca rested her head on his wide strong chest. "You're responsible for making the novel what it is, baby."

Conneca looked at him. "You mean Erica Kinkaid?"

"No, I mean *Conneca Sheridan*," he said flatly. "Without you there would never have been an Erica Kinkaid. And without her, I might never have completed the novel the way it deserved to be."

Conneca batted her lashes while blushing, feeling more than honored. "Am I *really* a woman to die for?" she teased him.

Maurice chuckled. "Actually, I changed the title. I thought it was much more appropriate to name it *A Woman To Live For*. After all, I intend to be around for a very long time—living and loving you *each* and *every* day."

Conneca turned upward to his lips and kissed them voraciously. "And I intend to do the same for a man who is *definitely* worth living for!"

Dear Reader:

May I say that I am thrilled to be able to write contemporary romance novels for Arabesque as a male author. I have long since believed that men were just as capable of writing romantic, sensual, passionate, and electrifying novels that warm the soul and cause the heart to skip a beat or two as women authors are.

Now that I have been given the opportunity to prove that theory, I definitely plan to deliver again and again with new and exciting romances sure to please!

Dark and Dashing is the first of these novels. I hope you'll agree that it has all the qualities you have come to expect from Arabesque romances, and then some.

I hope to meet some of you here and there at book signings, conferences, conventions, or wherever I travel across the country and abroad.

I welcome feedback on *Dark and Dashing* through the Arabesque authors' website; as well as through reviews that can be posted at online booksellers, such as Amazon.com and BN.com.

Stay tuned for my next moving and ultra passionate romance novel, *The Loves of His Life*, which will be released in 2006.

Soulfully yours,

Devon Vaughn Archer

ABOUT THE AUTHORS

Wayne Adrian Jordan is a high school teacher who lives on the island of Barbados. He has a BA in English and Linguistics and an MA in Applied Linguistics from the University of the West Indies.

The founder and editor in chief of *Romance in Color*, his passion has always been the promotion of the African American romance.

A member of Romance Writers of America, he belongs to the Outreach Chapter and is currently the chapter's PAN/PAL liaison. *Capture the Sunrise* is his first published work.

Devon Vaughn Archer grew up in Detroit, Michigan, as one of five children. He attended Michigan State University and upon graduation, moved to California. He currently resides in the beautiful Pacific Northwest in Oregon. His hobbies include traveling, jazz music, reading fiction, mystery and romantic movies, dancing, and photography.

Devon will continue to please his fans with the upcoming spicy romance novel, *The Loves of His Life*.

To learn more about this multitalented author, visit the Arabesque authors' website at: *http//:www.arabesqueauthors.com/flowers.htm*